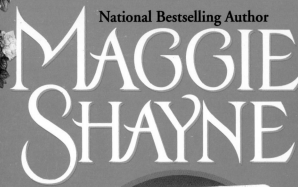

National Bestselling Author

MAGGIE SHAYNE

Love now.
Love forever.

"A hauntingly
beautiful
story of a
love that
endures
through
time itself."
—Kay Hooper

Eternity

J

JOVE

$6.99 U.S.
$8.99 CAN

Don't miss the next spellbinding novel
from Maggie Shayne . . .

INFINITY

ETERNITY

Maggie Shayne

JOVE BOOKS, NEW YORK

This is a work of fiction. Names, characters, places, and incidents are either the product of the author's imagination or are used fictitiously, and any resemblance to actual persons, living or dead, business establishments, events or locales is entirely coincidental.

ETERNITY

A Jove Book / published by arrangement with
the author

PRINTING HISTORY
Jove edition / December 1998

The Penguin Putnam Inc. World Wide Web site address is
http://www.penguinputnam.com

ISBN: 0-515-12407-9

A JOVE BOOK®
Jove Books are published by The Berkley Publishing Group,
a division of Penguin Putnam Inc.,
375 Hudson Street, New York, New York 10014.
JOVE and the "J" design
are trademarks belonging to Penguin Putnam Inc.

PRINTED IN THE UNITED STATES OF AMERICA

10 9 8 7 6 5

This story is dedicated to
Sarah Osborne
Who died in jail on May 10, 1692.

Bridget Bishop
Who was hanged on June 10, 1692.

Sarah Good and her unnamed child
The baby died in jail just before its mother was hanged on
July 19, 1692.

Elizabeth How
Susannah Martin
Rebecca Nurse
Sarah Wildes
All of whom were hanged on July 19, 1692.

Reverend George Burroughs
Martha Carrier
George Jacobs
John Proctor
John Willard
All of whom were hanged on August 19, 1692.

Ann Foster
Who died in jail sometime after September 10, 1692.

Giles Corey
Who was pressed to death on September 19, 1692.

Martha Corey
Mary Esty
Alice Parker
Mary Parker
Ann Pudeator
Wilmot Reed
Margaret Scott
Samuel Wardwell
All of whom were hanged on September 22, 1692.

And to
Sarah Dastin
Who was pardoned when the madness of 1692 came to an end,
but who died in jail all the same, unable to pay her jail fees.

May we never forget.

The Witch Upon the Hill

Her eyes are black, the midnight sea,
Her hair, a sooty cloud
Her voice, the winds of fantasy,
Her heart like fire, and proud

I could not help but watch her
As beneath the moon she danced,
She whirled, she cast, she conjured
She sang a mystic chant

She soared into my soul that night
The starry sky her wings
She whispered secrets in my dreams
And spoke of sacred things

In my mind, she entranced me
Her kiss was magick-laced
Her touch, it left me trembling,
And craving her embrace

The skies obey her every wish,
The elements, her commands
She wields a power o'er me,
My heart lies in her hands

For her I'd cross the universe,
For her I'd swim the sea,
But what could an Enchantress want
with a simple man like me?

She came, and said, "I love you,
And likely, always will."
My heart, I pledge, forevermore
To the Witch upon the hill

—DUNCAN WALLACE

ETERNITY

Part One

1

I always knew I was a Witch.

The definition of the word has since broadened somewhat, and rightly so, I imagine. Today anyone with the determination to learn and practice the Craft of the Wise can call herself—and deservedly—a Witch. But in my time there were no books written to guide a seeker, save the books of the Witches themselves, but the grimoires were kept secret. Back then one was only a Witch if one was born to, or adopted by, another Witch. And even then the young one wasn't told all of the secrets. Some of them I didn't learn until much later.

My mother was a wise woman, a Witch, and from the time I was very young I was taught the ways of drawing on the power of the sun and the moon and the stars and of nature itself. Above all else, I was taught the importance of keeping all that I learned secret. For the penalty meted out to practitioners of the Craft in those days was harsh. Mother never told me just how harsh. I learned that when I was twenty and one, in a lesson so cruel its memory remains burned in my mind, though three full centuries have passed. And yet it was because of that cruelty that I first set eyes upon Duncan Wallace.

The key to my mother's ruin was her kindness. My father

had died only a fortnight before, of a plague her simple folk magick could not fight. Many lives were lost in our small English village that brutal winter of 1689, and perhaps my mother simply could not bear to see one more death after so much grief.

At any rate, it was Matilda, the sister of my dead father, who came pounding on our door that dark wintry night. Looking startled at Aunt Matilda's state—wild hair and wilder eyes and not so much as a cloak about her shoulders—Mother drew her inside and bade her take the rocking chair beside the hearth to warm herself. I offered tea to calm her. But Aunt Matilda seemed crazed and refused to sit down. Instead, she paced in agitated strides, her skirts swishing about her legs, her thin slippers leaving damp footprints on our wood floor.

"No time to sit an' sip tea," she told us. "Not now. 'Tis my youngest, my little Johnny, named for my own dear brother who has gone to his reward. My Johnny has taken ill!" She whirled and grabbed my mother, gripping the front of her dress in white-knuckled fists. "I know you can help him. *I know*, I tell you! An' if you refuse me now, Lily St. James, I vow, I'll—"

"Matilda, calm yourself!" My mother's firm voice quieted the woman, though only for a moment, I feared. "I would never refuse to help Johnny in any way I can. You know that."

"I *don't* know it!" my aunt shrieked. "Not when you let your own husband die of the same ailment! Pray, Lily, why didn't you save him? Why didn't you save my brother?"

My mother's head lowered, and I saw the pain flare anew in her eyes—a pain that sometimes dulled but never died away.

"I tried everything I knew to help Jonathon. But I couldn't save him," she whispered.

"Perhaps because you brought the illness on him from the start."

"Aunt Matilda!" I stepped between the two, forgetting to respect my elders and tugging my aunt's arm until she faced me, rather than my mother. "You know better. My parents shared a love such as few people ever know, and

I'll not stand by and hear you sully its memory."

"Raven, don't," Mother began.

But I rushed on. "No one can bring on such a plague as this, and well you know it!"

"No one but a Witch, you mean, don't you, Raven? *Raven*. She even named you for some dark carrion bird. Are you practicing the black arts as well, girl?" Aunt Matilda gripped my shoulders, shook me. "Are you? *Are you?*"

I could only blink in shock and stagger backward, pulling free of her chilled hands. My aunt *knew*. But how? How could she know the secret that had been only between my mother and me? Even my father had been unaware. . . .

"What makes you say such a thing?" my mother asked gently. "How can you accuse your own sister?"

"Sister-in-law and not by blood," Matilda reminded my mother. "And I know. I've always been suspicious of you and your Pagan ways, Lily. From the time you helped me birth my firstborn and somehow took away the pain. And later, when you nursed me through the influenza that should have killed me. You with your herbs and brews." She waved a hand at the drying herbs that hung upside down in bunches from our walls, and at the jars filled with philters and powders, lining the roughly hewn wooden shelves. "No physician could ease my suffering the way you did." She said it unkindly, made it an accusation.

Slowly my mother nodded, her serene expression never changing. "Herbs and plants are given by God, Matilda. Knowing how to use His gifts can surely be no sin."

"I saw you last full moon."

The words lay there, dropped like blows, as we stared at one another, my mother and I, both remembering our ritual beneath the full moon, when we chanted sacred words 'round a balefire at midnight.

"I know you have . . . powers. And I don't care if they're sinful or not. Not now. I need you to help Johnny. If you didn't conjure this plague, then prove it. Cure him, Lily. If you refuse . . ." Her eyes narrowed, but she didn't finish.

"If I refuse, you'll do what, dear sister? Bear witness against me to the magistrate? See me tried for Witchery?"

Matilda didn't answer. She didn't need to. I saw her answer in her eyes, and my mother saw it as well.

"You've no need of such threats," Mother told her. "All you had to do was ask for my help. I'll try my best for your son, just as I did for Jonathon. But Witchery or no, I may not be strong enough to help him."

"If he dies, I vow, I'll see you hang!" Aunt Matilda lurched toward the plank door, tugging it open on its rawhide hinges. "Gather what you need and come at once. I must make haste back to his bedside."

She left us in a swirl of snow, not bothering to close the door. I went and shut out the weather, then stood for a long moment, my hand on the door. I had a terrible premonition that the events of the past few moments would somehow change our lives forever. I didn't know how, or why, but I felt it to my bones. Drawing a deep breath, I turned to face my mother. I knelt before her, taking her hands in mine, staring up into eyes as black as my own. "Don't go to him," I begged her. "You cannot help him any more than you could help Father. And when he passes, she'll blame you."

"He is my own nephew," she whispered. She tugged her hands away, got to her feet, and began to make ready, taking sprigs of herbs from the dried bunches hanging on the wall, pouring a bit of this powder and a bit of that into her special cauldron. The one with the hand-painted red rose adorning its squat belly. She added steamy water from the larger cast-iron pot that hung in the fireplace to the brew.

"We should leave this village," I pleaded as I worked at her side, measuring, stirring, holding my hands above each concoction to push magickal energy and healing light into it. "We should leave tonight, Mother. Our secret is known, and you've told me how dangerous that can be."

"I can't break my vows," she said. "You know that. When someone needs help, asks me for help, I am bound by oath and by blood to try. And try I will." She looked into my eyes. "You should pack a bag and go to London. Take the horse. Leave tonight. I'll send for you when—"

"I won't leave you to face this alone," I whispered, and I flung myself into her arms, stroking her raven hair, so like my own, though hers was knotted up in back while mine hung loose to my waist. "Don't ask me to, Mother."

Her mouth curved in the first smile I'd seen cross her lips since my father's death. "So strong," she said softly. "And always, so very stubborn. All right, then. Come, let us hasten to Johnny."

We quickly packed our potions and some crystals and candles into a bag, pulled our worn homespun cloaks over our heads and shoulders, and stepped out into the brutal winter's night.

But my cousin was dead before we even arrived at my aunt's house. And we were greeted by a wild-eyed woman who'd once claimed us as kin, and the group of citizens she'd roused from slumber, all bearing torches and shouting, "Arrest them! Arrest the Witches!"

Cruel hands gripped my arms, even as I turned to flee. Accusations rang out in the night, and people stood round watching as my mother and I were surrounded, and then dragged over the frozen mud of the rutted streets. I cried out to my neighbors, begging for help, but none was forthcoming. And my heart turned cold with fear. As cold as the wind-driven snow that wet my face.

'Twas a long walk, the longest walk of my life. The poor shacks of the village fell away behind us as we were pulled and pushed along, and we emerged onto the cobbled streets that ran between the fine homes of the wealthy in the neighboring town. At last we stood before the house of the magistrate himself, trembling in the icy wind while our accusers pounded upon his door.

The man emerged in his nightclothes after a time, looking rumpled and irritated. "What's all this?" he demanded, white whiskers twitching.

"Two Witches!" shouted the man who gripped my mother's arms tightly. "The ones who brought this plague on us all, Honor."

The old man's eyes widened, then narrowed again as he perused us. Beyond him I could see the glow of a fire in a large hearth, and feel its heat on my face. I longed to go warm my hands by that fire. My fingers were already numb from the cold.

"What evidence have you against them?" the magistrate asked.

"The word of this one's own sister," said another, pointing at my mother.

"Matilda is not my sister," my mother said, her voice ever calm, despite the madness around her. I would never forget her face, beautiful and serene. Her eyes, so brave, no hint of fear in them. "She is the sister of my husband."

"Your husband who died of the plague!" the man cried out. "And now your nephew is taken as well."

"Many have been lost to the plague, sir. Surely you wouldn't accuse every bereaved family of Witchery?"

The man glared at my mother. "Matilda St. James bears witness, Honor. She's seen them practicing their dark rites with her own eyes."

" 'Tis a lie!" I shouted. "My aunt is maddened with grief! She knows not what she says!"

"Silence." The magistrate's command sent shivers down my spine. He stepped forward, glancing down at the woven sack my mother still clutched in her hands. "What have you there, woman?"

Mother lifted her chin, meeting his gaze. I could see the thoughts moving behind his eyes, the way he looked at us, judging us, though we were strangers to him.

" 'Tis only some herbs," she said softly, "brewed in a tea."

"She lies," the man said. "Matilda St. James said this woman was bringing a potion to cure her young son. But she feared the Witch would deliberately wait until it was too late to help the lad, and her fear proved true. A Witch's brew lies in that sack, Honor. Nothing less, I vow."

" 'Tis no potion nor brew," my mother told him. " 'Tis simply some medicinal tea, I tell you."

"Are you a physician, wench?" the magistrate demanded.

"You know that I am not."

"Give me the sack."

The hands holding my mother's arms eased their grip, and she gave her sack over. The magistrate opened it, pawing its contents, and I shuddered recalling the stones we'd put inside. Glittering amethyst and deep blue lapis, for healing. And the candles, made by our own hands and carved with magickal symbols to aid in Johnny's recovery. We would have set them around his bed, where they would have burned all night to protect him from the ravages of the plague.

The magistrate saw all of this, and when he looked up again, his eyes had gone cold. So cold I felt even more chilled despite the warmth from the fire at his back. "Put them in the stocks. We try them on the morrow. Perhaps a night in the square will convince them to confess and save us the time." He withdrew, leaving the door wide, and reappeared a moment later with a large key, which he handed over to one of the men. "See to it."

"No!" I cried. "You mustn't do this! We've done nothing wrong. Magistrate, please, I beg of you—"

His door closed on my pleas, and again I was pulled and dragged as I fought my captors. But my struggles were to no avail. And soon I found myself being forced to bend forward, my wrists and my neck pressed awkwardly into the stock's evil embrace. The heavy, wooden top piece was lowered as my own neighbors held me fast, and I heard the chain and the lock snapping tight.

I could not move. Could not see my mother, but I knew she was nearby, for I heard her voice, strained now, but steady. "Tell the magistrate he shall have my confession," she said. "But only if he will let my daughter go free. She knows nothing of this matter. Nothing at all. You must tell him."

The man to whom she spoke only grunted in reply. And then the villagers left us. In the town square, bent and held fast, we waited in silence for the dawn. The freezing wind cut like a razor, and the wet snow continued to slash at us. I shivered and began to cry, my face stinging with cold, my hands numb with it, my feet throbbing and swelling.

And then I heard my mother's gentle voice, chanting softly, "Sacred North wind, do us no harm. Ancient South wind, come, keep us warm." Over and over she repeated the words, and I forced my teeth to stop chattering and joined with her, closing my eyes and calling to the winds for aid. My mother's folk magick could not make iron chains melt away. But she could invoke the elements to do our bidding.

Within minutes the harsh wind gentled, and the snow stopped falling. A warmer breeze came to replace the bitter cold, and my shivering eased. I was still far from comfortable, bent this way, unable to relieve the ache in my back. But I knew my mother must be suffering far more than I, for her body was older than mine. Yet she did not complain. I took strength from that, and vowed to keep my discomfort to myself.

"Hard times await us, my daughter," she told me. "But whatever happens tomorrow, Raven, you must remember what I tell you now. Promise me you will."

"I promise," I whispered. "But, Mother, you mustn't confess anything to them. Not even to save me. I couldn't live if you were to die." The thought terrified me, and I pulled my hands against the rough wood that held them prisoner, though I could not hope to work them free. She was all I had in this world. All I had.

"Perhaps this is my destiny," she said softly. "But 'tis not yours."

"How can you know that?"

"I know," she whispered. "I've known from the day you were born, child. By the birthmark you bear upon your right hip. The crescent." Tears burned my eyes. But my mother went on. "You're a far more powerful Witch than I have ever been, Raven."

"No. 'Tis not true. I can barely cast a decent circle."

She laughed then, softly, and the sound of it touched my heart. That she could laugh at a time like this only made me love and respect her more than I already did, though I'd never have thought it possible.

"I speak not of the form of ritual, but the force, Raven. The power is strong in you. And you will need that strength. When this is over, child, you must leave here. Go to the New World. My sister, Eleanor, is there, in a township called Sanctuary, in the colony of Massachusetts. She is not a Witch, and knows nothing of our ways. She was born of my father's faithlessness and raised by her own mother and not in our household. But she is kind. She will not turn you away."

"Perhaps not," I said. "But *I* will not leave you behind."

"I fear 'tis I who will leave you behind, my darling. 'Tis the night of the dark moon, when our powers ebb low. But even were our lady of the moon shining her full light down upon us, I doubt I could save myself. Do not cry for me, Raven. Dying is part of living, a birth into a new life. You know this."

"Oh, Mother, stop saying such things!" I cried loudly, sobbing and choking on my tears.

When Mother spoke again, I could hear tears in her voice as well. "Raven, listen to me. You must listen."

I tried to quiet myself, to do as she wished, but I vowed she would not die tomorrow. Somehow I would save her.

"When 'tis over," she told me, "you must return to our cottage in the village. But do so by night, and be very careful. You mustn't be seen. Do not wait too long, child, lest they burn the house in their vengeance or award it to Matilda's family in return for her testimony against us. You must go back in secret. Gather only what you will need for your journey. Then go to the hearth. There is a loose stone there. Take what you find hidden beyond that stone."

"But, Mother—"

"And take the horse, if she is still there. You may sell her in some other village. But take care. Should you meet anyone, do not tell them your true name. And as soon as you can, book passage on a ship to the New World. Now promise me you will do these things."

"I'll not let them kill you, Mother."

"There is nothing you can do to prevent it, child. I'll have your promise, though, and I will die in peace because of it. Promise me, Raven."

Sniffling, I muttered, "I promise."

"Good." She sighed, so deeply it seemed as if some great burden had been lifted from her shoulders. "Good," she whispered once more, and then she rested. Slept, perhaps. I could not be sure. I cried in silence from then on, not wishing to trouble my Mother with my tears. But I think she knew.

When dawn came, it brought with it the magistrate, and beside him a woman, looking distraught with red-rimmed eyes. Behind them walked a man who wore the robes of a priest. He had an aged face, thin and harsh, with a hooked nose that made me think of a hawk, or some other hungering bird of prey. He was pale, as if he were ill, or weak. And then they came closer, and I could see only their feet, for I could not tip my head back enough to see more.

"Lily St. James," the Magistrate said, "you and your daughter are charged with the crime of Witchcraft. Will you confess to your crimes?"

My mother's voice was weaker now, and I could hear the pain in it. "I will confess only if you release my daughter. She is guilty of nothing."

"No," the woman said in a shrill voice. "You must execute them now, Hiram. Both of them!"

"But the law—" he began.

"The law! What care do you have for the law when our own child has become ill overnight? What more proof do you need?"

At her words my heart fell. She blamed us for her child's illness, just as my aunt had done. No one could save us now.

I heard footsteps then, and sensed the magistrate had gone closer to my mother. Leaning over her, he said, "Lift this curse, woman. Lift it now, I beg of you."

"I have brought no curse upon you, nor your family, sir," my mother told him. "Were it in my power to help your child, I would gladly do so. As I would have for my own husband and for my nephew. But I cannot."

"Execute them!" his wife shouted. "Michael was fine until you arrested these two! They brought this curse on him, made him ill out of pure vengeance, I tell you, and if they live long enough to kill him, they will! Execute them, husband. 'Tis the only way to save our son!"

The priest stepped forward then, his black robes hanging heavily about his feet and dragging through the wet snow. His steps were slow, as if they cost him a great effort. He went first to my mother, saying nothing, and I could not see what he did. But he came seconds later to me and closed his hand briefly around mine.

A surge of something, a crackling, shocking sensation

jolted my hand and sizzled into my forearm, startling me so that I cried out.

"Do not harm my daughter!" my mother shouted.

The priest took his hand away, and the odd sensation vanished with his touch, leaving me shaken and confused. What had it been?

"I fear you are right," the priest said to the magistrate and his wife. "They must die, or your son surely will. And I fear there is no time for a trial. But God will forgive you that."

Pacing away, his back to us, the magistrate muttered, "Then I have little choice." And the three of them left us alone again. But only for a few brief moments.

"Mother," I whispered. "I'm so afraid."

"You've nothing to fear from them, Raven."

But I *did* fear. I'd never *felt* such fear grip me as I felt then, for within moments the priest had returned, and he brought several others with him. Large, strong men. People filled the streets as my mother and I were taken from the stocks. The people shouted and called us murderers and more. They threw things at us. Refuse and rotten food, even as the men bound our hands behind our backs and tossed us onto a rickety wagon, pulled by a single horse. I crawled close to my mother, where she sat straight and proud in that wagon, and I leaned against her, my head on her shoulder, my arms straining at their bonds, but unable to embrace her.

"Be strong," she told me. "Be brave, Raven. Don't let them see you tremble in fear before them."

"I'm trying," I whispered.

The wagon drew to a stop, and the ride had been all too short. I looked up to see a gallows, one used so often it looked to be a permanent fixture here. I was dragged from the wagon, and my mother behind me. But she didn't fight as I did. She got to her feet and held her head high, and no one needed to force her up the wood steps to the platform, while I kicked and bit and thrashed against the hands of my captors.

She paused on those steps and looked back at me, caught my eyes, and sent a silent message. *Dignity.* She mouthed the word. And I stopped fighting. I tried to emulate her courage, her dignity, as I was marched up the steps to stand beside her, beneath a dangling noose. Someone lowered the rough rope around my neck and pulled it tight, and I struggled to be brave and strong, as she'd so often told me I was. But I knew I was trembling visibly, despite the warmth of the morning sun on my back, and I could not stop my tears.

That priest whose touch had so jolted me stood on the platform as well, old and stern-faced, his eyes all but gleaming beneath their film of ill health as he stared at me . . . as if in anticipation. Beside him stood another man who also wore the robes of clergy. This one was very young, my age, or perhaps a few years my elder. In his eyes there was no eagerness, no joy. Only horror, pure and undisguised. They were brown, his eyes, and they met mine and held them. I stared back at him, and he didn't look away, but held my gaze, searching my eyes while his own registered surprise, confusion. I felt something indescribable pass between us. Something that had no place here, amid this violence and hatred. It was as if we touched, but did so without touching. A feeling of warmth flowed between him and me, one so real it was almost palpable. And I knew he felt it, too, by the slight widening of his eyes.

Then his gaze broke away as he turned to the older man and said, "Nathanial, surely 'tis no way to serve the Lord."

The kiss of Scotland whispered through his voice.

"You are young, Brother Duncan," the older man said. "And this no doubt seems harsh to you."

"What it seems like to me, Father Dearborne, is murder."

" 'Thou shalt not suffer a Witch to live,' " the priest quoted.

" 'Thou shalt not kill,' " the young Scot—Duncan—replied. And he looked at me again. "They've nay been tried."

"They were tried in the square by the magistrate himself."

"It canna be legal."

"His Honor's own child is ill with the plague. Would you have us wait for the wee one to die?"

The young man's gaze roamed my face, though he spoke to the old one. I felt the touch of those eyes as surely as if he caressed me with his gentle hands, instead of just his gaze.

"I would have us show mercy," he said softly. "We've no proof these women have brought the plague."

"And no proof they haven't. Why take the risk? They are only Witches."

The beautiful man looked at the older one sharply. "They are human creatures just as we are, Nathanial." And he shook his head sadly. "What are their names?"

"Their names are unfit for a man of the cloth to utter. If you so pity them, Duncan, ease your conscience by praying for their souls. For what good it might do."

" 'Tis wrong," Duncan declared urgently. "I'm sorry, Father, but I canna be party to this."

"Then leave, Duncan Wallace!" The priest thrust out a gnarled finger, pointing to the steps.

Duncan hurried toward them, but he paused as he passed close to me. Then turned to face me, as if drawn by some unseen force. His hand rose, hesitated, then touched my hair, smoothing it away from my forehead. His thumb rubbed softly o'er my cheek, absorbing the moisture there. "Could I help you, mistress, believe me I would."

"Should you try they would only kill you, as well." My voice trembled as I spoke. "I beg you . . . Duncan . . ." His eyes shot to mine when I spoke his name, and I think he caught his breath. "Don't surrender your life in vain."

He looked at me so intently it was as if he searched my very soul, and I thought I glimpsed a shimmer of tears in his eyes.

"I willna forget you . . ." he whispered, then shook his head, blinked, and continued, ". . . in my prayers."

"If there be memory in death, Duncan Wallace," I said, speaking plainly, even boldly, for what had I to lose now? "I shall remember you always."

He drew his fingertips across my cheek, and suddenly leaned close and pressed his lips to my forehead. Then he moved on, his black robes rustling as he hurried down the steps.

"Do you wish to confess your sins and beg the Lord's forgiveness?" the old priest asked my mother.

I saw her lift her chin. " 'Tis you who ought to be begging your God's forgiveness, sir. Not I."

The priest glared at her, then turned to me. "And you?"

"I have done nothing wrong," I said loudly. "My soul is far less stained than the soul of one who would hang an innocent and claim to do it in the name of God." Then I looked down at the crowd below us. "And far less stained than the souls of those who would turn out to watch murder being done!"

The crowd of spectators went silent, and I saw Duncan stop in his tracks there on the ground below us. He turned slowly, looking up and straight into my eyes. "Nay," he said, his voice firm. " 'Tis wrong, an' I willna allow it!" Then suddenly he lunged forward, toward the steps again. But the guard at the bottom caught him in burly arms and flung him to the ground. A crowd closed around him as he tried to get up, and he was blocked from my view. I prayed they would not harm him.

"Be damned, then," the old priest said, and he turned away.

The hangman came to place a hood over my mother's head, but she flinched away from it. "Look upon my face as you kill me, if you have the courage."

Snarling, the man tossed the hood to the floor and never offered one to me. He took his spot by the lever that would end our lives. And I looked below again to see Duncan there, struggling while three large men held him fast. I had no idea what he thought he could do to prevent our deaths, but 'twas obvious he'd tried. Was still trying.

" 'Tis wrong! Dinna do this thing, Nathanial!" he shouted over and over, but his words fell on deaf ears.

"Take heart," my mother whispered. "You will see him again. And know this, my darling. I love you."

I turned to meet her loving eyes. And then the floor fell away from beneath my feet, and I plunged through it. I heard Duncan's anguished cry. Then the rope reached its end, and there was a sudden painful snap in my neck that made my head explode and my vision turn red. And then no more. Only darkness.

Duncan didn't even know her name.

He didn't even *know her name*.

And yet he felt as if he'd lost a treasured friend . . . more than that, even. 'Twas as if a part of his own soul had just been brutally murdered in the town square.

Her surname, St. James, he'd heard that much muttered in the streets. More than that he didn't know. Might never know.

"I tried," he whispered. "God knows I tried."

He'd been moved, beyond all reason, all logic, when he'd heard her strong, deep voice and the courage it held as it rang out over the spectators, shaming them as they should well be shamed. And he'd known then that he had to try. Though he had no idea now what he could have done, even had they let him pass. Even had he reached her again. Perhaps he'd been a bit mad.

Perhaps she truly was a Witch and had cast some spell, some enchantment, o'er his heart there on the gallows. He didn't know. He only knew that something had possessed him—some sudden, violent, *desperate* need to save her.

And that he'd failed.

She swung slowly from the end of a rope beside her mother, her life snuffed out far too soon. And he realized, by the cold dampness seeping through his robes and chilling his legs, that he knelt now, before the gallows. He seemed to have fallen right where he'd been standing when the trapdoor had jerked away from beneath the beautiful girl. And he remained there still, kneeling in the snow.

He got to his feet, but his legs felt weak and his chest hollow. Staggering forward, he snatched a blade from a local man's belt as he passed the fellow. Ignoring the man's outcry, he moved beneath the gallows, to gather the young woman's body into his arms. He held her tight to him as he sawed at the rope until it gave way. Her weight fell upon him, head resting on his shoulder like a lover's. Satin soft hair, snow damp and fragrant, brushed against his cheek. He closed his arms round her body and turned his face full into that hair to inhale it and to feel it and to commit it to memory—as well as to hide the inexplicable tears that welled up in his eyes. So warm, her face on his skin. So much as if she were only sleeping.

"What might you have been to me?" he asked her, his voice a strangled whisper. "What might we have been to each other?"

But he spoke to death, and death did not answer.

"Though it makes no sense, lass, my heart is broken. I didna know you at all, an' yet it feels so very much as if I did. As if I always have." He rocked her in his arms, and a sob choked him. "Can you hear me? Are you out there, somewhere, listenin', lass? I'll give you a proper burial, I vow it. An' your dear mother, too."

He held her close, enveloped in a sadness he could not explain and a new certainty about the path he'd walk in this life. And he owed her thanks for that, if nothing else, he realized.

A heavy hand fell upon his shoulder. "What sort of spectacle do you wish to make of yourself, boy?"

Duncan turned to see the murderer himself, Nathanial Dearborne, his own trusted mentor. "Do you ken what you've done this day?" he asked the man.

Nathanial's eyes narrowed, and he signaled to someone with a flick of his wrist. Immediately three men rushed forward to tear the beauty from Duncan's arms, even as he cried out in protest. They bore her away, dumping her body on the back of a rickety wagon where her mother already lay. The man in the driver's seat snapped the reins, and the wagon trundled away.

"Where are they takin' her?" Duncan demanded, addressing Dearborne but keeping his gaze riveted to that wagon—to *her*—until it rounded a curve and disappeared from sight.

"To the pit beyond the town. Best to get their kind as far from decent folk as possible, lad. You'll understand one day. This was . . . for the best."

" 'Twas murder," Duncan spat out, "an' sin of the most vile sort!" He glared at the man now that the wagon was gone from his sight. "I canna continue under the tutelage of a man who would condone it. My studies end here, today, Nathanial. I want no part of your priesthood, for you've shown it to be one of purest evil."

Nathanial's cloudy blue eyes narrowed, but not in anger, and he didn't shout "Blasphemy!" as Duncan had expected.

He simply said, "I'd hold my tongue, were I in your place, Duncan. You have no idea what sorts of forces you are dealing with."

"I willna hold my tongue. I *canna*."

Nathanial shook his head slowly. "You know the teachings of the Church. The elimination of Witches is our duty as Christians, Duncan. 'Tis imperative we wipe them from existence, rid the world of the scourge of Witchery."

Duncan searched the old man's face. He'd been close to him once, thought of him almost as fondly as he did his own father. No more. "An' what will you do next, Nathanial, when you've murdered them all? What will your next mission be? To rid the world of anyone else whose beliefs differ from your own?"

Nathanial smiled. "The Crusades attempted that and failed. I simply seek to do my duty, Duncan. And 'twill be a service to all Christians if I succeed."

"Nay," Duncan said. "Not all." And he turned from the man, feeling nothing now but loathing for him. A man he'd once thought to be closer to God than anyone he'd known. But Duncan realized now that Nathanial was nothing. Less than nothing. A killer who seemed to enjoy his work.

"Where are you going?" Nathanial demanded. "Don't turn your back on me, boy! Answer my question!"

With a glance over his shoulder and an awareness of the people looking on, listening in, Duncan replied. "I'm goin' to gather my things, Nathanial. An' then I'm goin' to see those two women get a proper burial. After that, I only know I'll be goin' as far away from you an' your kind as I can. You are no man of God, but a hypocrite an' a killer, an' I canna abide bein' in the same village with you."

Then he continued on his way without another word, hearing the gasps and whispers of the townspeople as he passed.

It surprised him when a hand fell upon his shoulder. Stopping in his tracks, he didn't turn around. For he knew that gnarled old hand well.

"Duncan, wait," Nathanial said. "Perhaps I was too harsh. 'Tis obvious this morning's work has distressed you. But there is truly no need to take such drastic measures. Surely you don't mean to leave here—"

"Aye, Nathanial, that I do."

"You cannot!"

Frowning, Duncan turned. Nathanial composed himself, tempered his voice. "Duncan, you've been like a son to me. Believe me, boy, were this action not necessary, I'd never have—"

"But you did. 'Tis done, Nathanial, an' there's no undoin' it now."

Lowering his head, Nathanial drew a breath. "I am ill, Duncan. Surely you know that."

"Aye, I know it. I've seen you growin' weaker by degrees, an' wished to God I could do somethin' about it, Nathanial. But I canna help you. An' being ill, even facin' death itself doesna give you the right to go about hanging innocents."

"I . . . I had no choice."

"An' I have no choice now," Duncan said. He turned away, having nothing more to say to the old man he'd once loved. But as he walked on, he heard Nathanial continue.

" 'Tis because of the girl, isn't it? This is *her* doing."

Duncan kept walking.

"Damn her," Nathanial cried. "Damn her, she'll pay. I'll *make sure* she pays!"

"She's beyond your reach now, Nathanial."

"Oh, don't be so sure of that, my boy," Nathanial muttered.

Duncan turned then, only to see the old man walking away. He didn't know what Nathanial could have possibly meant by his words. But it didn't matter. The lass was gone now. Dead, and Nathanial was as responsible as if he'd pulled the lever himself. Duncan would never forgive the man.

He went to his stark room in the back of the church, to gather his meager possessions into a sack. He would never return here again; he'd meant what he'd said. This place had been his home for two years as he studied for the priesthood at Nathanial's feet. But that was over now. What he had seen today—and what he'd *felt*—had changed him forever. He sensed it deep inside, though he had no idea how this change would manifest. He only knew he had to leave.

He only knew the strange beauty had touched him, touched his heart, and his soul, and his life, and that he would feel that touch for a long, long time to come.

Slinging his sack over his shoulder, he walked out again into the streets. People whispered and pointed as he passed. He didn't care. He would have liked a horse. It was a long walk to the place where they'd taken the girl and her mother. But he sensed it would be only the beginning of an even more distant journey. That the steps he took now were the first steps on the way to his destiny.

The darkness that descended on me when I reached the end of that rope was a temporary one.

I remember so clearly the sudden, desperate gasp I drew, the blinding flash of white light that stiffened my body and made me fling my head backward as I dragged in as much air as my lungs could contain. The rapidly fading pain in my neck and my head. And the shock I felt as I realized . . . I was still alive.

I was . . . alive!

I blinked my eyes open and looked around me, and then my stomach lurched. 'Twas daylight, morning. Still early, I guessed. I lay upon the ground with the bodies of the dead strewn around me. The bodies of hanged criminals, and those taken by the disease plaguing the area. This was the pit they'd dug for this purpose. Every so often men would come here with shovels to cover over the dead, and ready the place for another layer of victims of the plague and the gallows. But I was not dead.

I was not dead.

I sat up slow, gagging at the stench of rotting flesh, and looked around me, frantically searching for my mother. I'd had no idea her magick was strong enough to save us from the gallows, but it must have been, for I was alive, and she—

She . . . no. Oh, no.

I found her, and my heart shattered. She lay still, her neck broken, her eyes open but no longer beautiful or shining like onyx. They were already dulled by the filmy glaze of death.

"Mother! No, Mother, no!" I gathered her into my arms, sobbing, near hysteria as I held her close, and rocked her against me. "You can't be gone! You can't leave me this way. Why, Mother?" But she did not answer, and so I screamed my question again, to the earth and the sky and the corpses all around me. "Why am I still alive? Why do I live, and not my precious Mother? Why?" But I knew I would get no reply.

Not from the dead. Not from my mother. Her spirit no longer lived in this body. She was gone. Gone, and I was alone.

Eventually I sat back and looked down at her poor body, an empty shell, yes, but even so 'twould not remain here in this vile place. Not while my heart still beat on.

Gently I lifted her in my arms. I was taller, larger than she. But even then it shouldn't have been so easy to carry her. I thought perhaps 'twas my grief making me strong.

I made my way out of the pit and took my mother's body into the forest nearby. And there, I scooped away the snow, and scraped out a grave for her with no more than my two hands and a flat stone for a tool. My nails were split, my fingers bleeding and throbbing with cold when I finished, but I was beyond noticing the pain. I buried my beloved mother there, and then I lay upon her grave and cried.

When at last he reached the gruesome place of the dead, Duncan shuddered at the sight of the bodies strewn there. He pressed a handkerchief to his face, and even then the stench was sickening. And disease, too, hung on the very air here. One could smell it, almost feel it. Yet he searched for the dark beauty among the dead.

"Where are you?" he whispered as his gaze scanned the carrion. That she should be here in this filth even for a short time brought a fury more powerful than any he'd felt before surging through his veins. What was it about her that caused such reactions in him? Why did he care so deeply for a girl he didn't even know?

"Duncan!" a voice called, and he turned. "Come away from there afore you take ill!"

At the rim of the pit a young man Duncan had called friend since they were lads together in Scotland sat astride his horse. Samuel MacPhearson leaned on the pommel, looking down at him.

"I'll nay go until I find them," he said.

"Well, you willna find them, my friend, for they be elsewhere. I searched myself only an hour ago. Arrived here faster by horse, I suppose, than you could by foot."

"Are you certain?" Duncan asked.

"Aye. I wouldna lie to you about this, Duncan. I can see 'tis important to you. Or she is. Did you know the lass?"

"Nay," Duncan said, making his way to the edge. "But it felt as if I did." When he began to climb up, Samuel dismounted and bent to offer a hand. Duncan got his footing at the top and brushed at his soiled clothes. Homespun, and barely fitting. But all he had once he'd discarded the robes he no longer felt able to wear.

"Why were you looking for them, Samuel?" Duncan asked.

"Same reason as you, I'd guess. To bury them proper. I liked what was done no more than you did, Duncan." He looked out over the dead and grimaced. "I didna find them, though."

Duncan's heart twisted. "Where can they be?"

Samuel smiled, but 'twas bitter. "No doubt your friend Dearborne would claim they used black magick to rise up an' walk away. But I suspect there's a far more simple solution. Some relative came for their bodies in secret. It happens, Duncan."

Duncan nodded but met Samuel's eyes. "Nathanial Dearborne is no friend of mine."

"He was here, you know."

Duncan frowned. "Nathanial? Here?"

"Aye, lookin' for those two women himself, I do believe. An' if he got here afore me, Duncan, he must have run his horse ragged the whole way. I meant to ask him why that was, but he beat a hasty retreat when he saw my approach."

The thought of that bastard laying his hands upon the girl set Duncan's teeth on edge. "He didna find them? You're certain of that?"

"Certain as I can be," Samuel said. "He seemed to be still searchin' when I arrived, and he had no bodies o'er his saddle when he galloped away."

"What could he want with them?"

"Nothing good, I'll warrant."

"The bastard."

Samuel's brows rose in twin arches. "Ah, so your great teacher is a bastard, now, is he?"

Duncan sighed, looking at the ground. "You were right about him all along, Samuel, an' I should've listened to you. Aye, he's a bastard, an' a killer, an' I told him as much."

"Indeed," Samuel said, slapping Duncan's shoulder. "Half the town knows of it by now." He tilted his head to one side. "They're sayin' she bewitched you, Duncan. Stole your heart right there on the gallows."

Duncan lifted his head to meet his friend's eyes. "Perhaps she did," he whispered.

"Aye, I can see this has shaken you deeply."

"An' what's shakin' me more is that I willna know where she rests. Even that small comfort has been stolen from me. 'Twas wrong, what was done to her, Samuel."

Samuel nodded. " 'Tis yet another reason I've decided to move on. I'm takin' Kathleen and leavin' this place. An' Duncan, my new bride an' I would be proud to have you come along with us.''

Duncan searched Samuel's face. "Where will you go? Back to Scotland?''

"Across the sea, my friend. To the New World. They say 'tis far different there. Opportunity for every man. The rich an' the poor livin' as equals.''

Taking a deep breath, Duncan thought hard about saying yes. He'd heard talk of this New World, this America, where religious persecution, 'twas said, did not exist. Wild and new and exciting. The idea appealed. But he had matters to attend to. Responsibilities to uphold.

"I'd like nothin' better than to do just that, Samuel. But not now. I must first return to Scotland to face my father with what I've done.''

Samuel shook his head. "Angus will be furious, no doubt. He paid Dearborne an' the Church a goodly sum to take you in for trainin'.''

"And I'll repay every bit,'' Duncan vowed.

"After you've repaid the debt to your father, Duncan . . . what then?''

Duncan shrugged, looking off into the distance, seeking something he couldn't name. "I dinna know. In truth, I just dinna know.''

Samuel slapped his shoulder. "If you decide to join us in America, my friend, just come along. We'll welcome you gladly.''

"Thank you,'' Duncan said. "I might just do that.''

"I hope you will.'' Then Samuel frowned. "In the meantime, Duncan, I hope you'll put this day's doings behind you. You've a haunted look about your eyes that worries me.''

"Haunted,'' Duncan muttered. "Aye, 'tis just the way I feel. I think that bonny lass will be hauntin' me for some time to come, Samuel. An' I doubt—rather seriously doubt—there's any way on God's earth I can put her memory behind me. I'm not even certain I want to.''

•   •   •

Hours passed as I lay weeping atop my mother's grave. And then the day itself waned as well. 'Twas night again before I could even think of leaving her. Even wonder about what I was to do now. And 'twas then I recalled her words to me the night before. I had promised I would do as she asked. I had promised her. I must keep that promise. But first . . .

I dried my tears, tried to reach for the calmness necessary to do what must be done. I searched for that serene place inside me. My breathing deepened. My heartbeat slowed. In silence I pointed my forefinger at the ground and drew an invisible circle round my mother's resting place. And within that circle I sat, closed my eyes, and wished my dear mother goodbye.

For just a moment the wind whispered through the trees overhead in such a way that it seemed my mother's voice spoke to me. *Be strong, Raven. I am with you . . . always. . . .*

"Mother?" Rising, I looked all around me but saw nothing. Only the very thin sliver of the newborn moon appearing in the sky. Like a sign. To start anew. To find a way to go on.

'Twas what my mother would have wanted.

I brushed my fresh tears away and nodded. 'Twas time. But I did not close the circle I'd cast. I left it there, willing it to protect her unmarked grave from harm of any kind. That done, I forced myself to leave her there, so that I could begin doing what she'd asked of me.

I followed her instructions to the letter, sensing she might know, somehow, and be disappointed in me if I did not.

I went to our cabin under cover of darkness, and slipping inside I saw chaos. Our home had been stripped of anything we had of any value. Blankets and clothing, our copper and iron pots. Everything. Even my mother's precious cauldron, which I'd hoped to take with me that I might be reminded of her each time I brewed a magickal potion or used it in ritual. She'd painted a tiny red rose upon its face. It had been her most cherished possession.

But it was gone now.

Something glittered up at me from the floor, and I bent to scoop up a tiny bit of amethyst the looters had somehow missed. Caressing it as if 'twere a diamond, I placed the stone in my pocket.

Our dried herbs had been torn from the walls and trampled beneath booted feet. Not a stick of furniture nor even the braided rugs that had covered the floors remained, and I knew without checking the shed that the horse had been taken as well. They'd left nothing untouched.

I went to the hearth though, tugging at the smooth round stones until I found the very large one that came free at my touch. And then I set it aside and reached into the hole it left. There was a cloth bag there, stuffed full. Frowning, I pulled the bag out and sat down on the floor, untying its drawstring and looking inside. There was a smaller pouch within its folds, a pouch I found to be heavy with coin. And a dark, hooded cloak, lined with fur, all rolled up tight to make it fit in the bag. And there was a book. A beautiful leather-bound grimoire, filled with page upon page of my mother's delicate script.

I opened the cover and saw a necklace, a golden pentacle, with a cradle moon adorning one curve of its circle and the beautiful image of a goddess reclining in the moon's embrace. I lifted the pendant and beneath it, on the page, saw a note just for me.

My dearest Raven,
If you are reading this, you are on your own now. Do not mourn me, child. If my lifetime ended, 'twas only because it had served its purpose, and now I will go on to another. But for you, child, it is only the beginning.

Wear the pentacle, for it holds all the magick I ever possessed. My strength and my wisdom are within it, and they are yours to call upon so long as you wear it. But keep it near your heart, and not out for the world to see. 'Twas never mine to wear. I only held it in trust for you. It marks you as who and what you are.

In this book are all the secrets I've learned. But the one I will tell you now is the most important of all of them. My daughter, my beloved Raven, you are not like me. And the path before you will not be an easy one.

Raven St. James, you are an immortal Witch, a High

Witch, though you've never known such beings existed.

When you suffer and die for the first time, you will know that what I say is true, for within a short while your body will revive itself. And from that moment on you will be stronger than before, and will never grow older.

I know this must shock you. But you are not the only one. There are others like you, though their numbers are few. And not all of them are good and pure of heart, as I know you to be.

The stories of them have been handed down through the generations of my family, and I will tell you all I know, and hope you put the knowledge to good use, to keep you safe. But I fear there is much I do not know, Raven. Things you will have to learn on your own.

There are two kinds of immortal Witches. The dark, and the light. The evil, and the good.

In some previous lifetime, my daughter, you died while attempting to save the life of another Witch. Because of this, you were born into this lifetime with the gift of immortality. But this is only one of two ways that gift can be passed on.

The other way is far more sinister. By taking the life of an immortal Witch, one also takes that Witch's immortality, indeed, all of her power. I can imagine you crooking your delicate brow as you read this, wondering how one can kill someone who is immortal. There is but a single way, child. And that is to take the Witch's heart from her very breast, and to lock it up in a small box where it will go on beating forever. Whoever retains the box, retains the power. Witches created in this way are dangerous to you, Raven, for they are never content with the power they have acquired. They cannot be, for eventually, the captive heart will weaken, its life force drained by the dark one who took it. The Dark Witch begins to weaken, to grow pale and sickly just as any mortal suffering from the ravages of old age might do. And so the Witch must kill again and again, in order to survive.

Always beware of others like you, Raven. For you'll have no way of knowing whether they be dark or light. You will recognize them as Immortals, however. By the

*necklace many of them wear, one such as the one I give
you now, and by the first touch of their hand. I do not
know how or why that is, but I know 'tis true. Be careful,
my love. Let no Dark Witch take your heart.*

*Hidden in the center of this book is a dagger that has
been handed down through the generations of my family
from time immemorial, just as this pendant was, to be held
for the day when a special one was born to us. 'Tis as if
they knew, somehow. It is yours, Raven, meant for you all
along, I am certain. Keep it with you always and learn to
wield it with skill. You will need to defend yourself from
attack by those others. Above all, child, trust no one.*

No one.

*And know that wherever you are and for as long as
forever, my love remains with you. Always with you.*

*Your loving mother,
Lily St. James*

Blinking in shock at all I had read, I let the book fall
open to its center and saw a jewel-encrusted dagger, tucked
inside its sheath and hidden by the clever way my mother
had cut away the centers of some of the pages. I took the
weapon in my hands, turned it slowly, felt its weight, and
tried to imagine myself using such a tool to do harm to
another living being. The thought made me shiver. I did not
believe I could ever do it.

But there was more to try to understand. More, so much
that my mind could barely comprehend the enormity of it.

''Immortal,'' I whispered. And I knew, I already knew,
'twas the truth.

3

The sack over my shoulder, my face concealed within the hood of the dark cloak my mother had left for me, I left the only home I'd ever known for the very last time. There was but a sliver of moonlight to guide me as the moon moved from its darkest void toward its first quarter. The thin slice of its gleaming white crescent was barely enough to light my way. I saw no one as I started down the worn dirt path on foot, more alone than I had ever been. But I should have sensed the presence. I was too wrapped up in sorrow and overwhelmed by grief to use my senses. Even as a mortal, I would have felt the danger, I thought later, for a Witch is more attuned to her senses than most. And since I'd quickened from a state of death, my senses were even sharper than before. They seemed to grow stronger and more acute with each passing hour. But for some reason that night, I tuned them out and focused only on my loss. My sadness. The fact that I'd lost the only person left with whom I'd had a special bond, a connection.

There was, I realized, one other, now. Another to whom I felt a powerful bond. An inexplicable link. A man whose touch made my heart flutter like the madly beating wings of a captive butterfly. A man . . . I must never, ever see again.

Those thoughts, those feelings, clouded my mind, dulled my senses, or at least made me ignore them. And then the cloaked figure stepped from a small copse of trees, into the path in front of me, and a harsh voice whispered, "I knew you'd come back here."

I came to a halt, narrowing my eyes to see his face, but it was hidden just as mine was, by the folds of a dark hood. My dagger was still secured inside the book, tucked deep in the bag that hung on my shoulder. I thought of it now, and wished I'd been wiser in heeding my mother's warnings. And yet part of me still believed this stranger to be no more than a simple mortal. He couldn't know who I was, much less *what* I was. Everyone here believed me to be dead.

"Who are you?" I asked him. "What do you want of me?"

And in a flash a dagger appeared in his pale, gnarled hand—a dagger so like my own that the sight of it took my breath away. "Not so much," he rasped. "Only your heart."

It couldn't be! But 'twas true, I realized as he lifted the blade and came closer and I backed away. Another immortal, one who wished to *kill* me. The horror of it was suddenly real, far more real to me than it had been as I'd read and scarcely believed the words of my mother's letter. I glanced around me desperately, but the snowy, twisting road and a few lightless, silent cottages were all I saw. No one would come to my aid. A breeze blew snow into my eyes and pushed at my hood, driving it down and away from my face, revealing me to him. Though I realized now he'd already known who I was. He had the advantage, then, for I had no clue as to his identity.

I walked backward, my eyes unalterably fixed to the blade, the way it gleamed when it caught a thin beam of moonlight. "I've no quarrel with you," I whispered, fear making my voice taut and low. "Leave me alone, I beg of you!"

His laughter came then, low and frightening. Harsh and raspy, that sound that made gooseflesh rise on my nape. "That's not the way this works, young one. A shame you won't live long enough to learn the rules of this particular game.''

Suddenly he lunged forward, swinging the blade in a deadly arc. I jumped back, gasping as I felt its razor-sharp tip brush past my midsection. I slipped, damp slippers and numbly cold feet unwieldy on the snow-covered road. I nearly fell but caught myself. And he lunged again. I side-stepped this time, yanking the sack from my shoulder and swinging it at him with all my might. It caught him from behind and sent him stumbling forward. He went to his knees, and I turned to run for my very life. But within seconds I knew he was after me. I heard his steps keeping pace, gaining on me. Heard his breaths rasping in and out of his lungs as we ran. It seemed his lungs would burst if he pushed himself any harder. He seemed weak . . . it must have been desperation, then, that drove him on. My own heart pounded in my ears, and my breaths escaped in great puffs of silvery steam.

A tree's limb loomed before me, and I saw it only an instant before I would have run into it. I had to duck low, and as I did, I gripped the branch, pulling it forward with me, and letting it go when it would give no more. It snapped back, slicing the air with a high keen, and spewing snow, and I heard him grunt as it hit him. I thought he went to the ground again, but I could not be sure.

The woods along the roadside were my only hope. I could not fight him, whoever he was, no matter how old or weak he might be. I stood no chance of winning, for I knew nothing of battle. And he'd wielded his blade with the skill of long practice. Ahh, but the woods—they had been my haven all my life. I knew them as well as I knew the cottage where I'd lived. And I took to their protection now, running as fast as I could, never tripping or falling once. I'd bragged to my mother that I could traverse these woods blindfolded. Now I was forced to live up to the claim. I stepped into the deeper snow, shivering as its chill embraced my ankles, soaking through my stockings, and wetting the hem of my skirt. I knew my way, and chose a meandering deer path that bisected the woods at their deepest. And soon I was surrounded by the heady scent of pine and the whispers of those needled boughs brushing one and another with every breath of night wind.

I heard him enter the forest, crashing about like a lame bear. I heard his foul cursing as he hunted for me, and his labored breathing as he grew ever more frustrated. But *he* would not hear *me*. My soft slippers and light steps, though my feet were nearly frozen now, were all but silent. And yet I almost believed the monster could hear the thundering of my pulse and the roar of blood through my veins.

I kept moving, and soon I didn't hear him anymore. Breathless, I made my way to the far side of the small wood, emerging on the road that led to the harbor where the tall ships would be docked. I looked behind me often, but I saw nothing of my attacker. I had eluded him.

This time.

I realized now how very dangerous it was for me to remain in England. Word of my execution would spread quickly, and the tales of my body disappearing would make for wonderful gossip. If there truly were evil immortals out there who sought to take the hearts of their own kind—and I knew beyond doubt now that there were—they would find me all too easily here. I had to leave. Tonight.

So I continued on the road, eight miles to the harbor.

And there, tired from my long walk and shivering with cold, I paused, taken aback by the graceful beauty of those tall ships rocking gently upon the water. Naked masts rose high. The sliver of moonlight reflected back a hundred times from the surface of the briny deep and spilled generously upon the painted hulls. In fact, I thought, I'd never in my life seen anything quite so lovely as those majestic ships floating gracefully upon the water. Like powerful creatures at rest. And it might have been that I could see so much more than I ever had before. Yes, my night vision was getting sharper, but I could also see farther and pick out more details. Like the mermaid with the flowing golden hair, carved into the bow of one ship, and the words *Sea Witch* painted in elegant gold script along either side of her. Lovely.

I was jostled by several people as they passed, and I jumped, startled. There were people here. Many people, and

Mother had warned me often that 'twas not safe for a young girl to come to the docks alone. Even more true now, I thought. If I were recognized . . .

Yet I had little choice. I had to leave England, and this was the place from which to do so. I simply pulled my hood closer, better to hide my face, and moved on. There were taverns where the seamen ate and drank, fought and swore. And women of the most disreputable sort, lounging with heavy lidded eyes and painted faces in doorways, calling out to every drunken man who staggered past. The stench of fish, and of liquor, hung heavy here. So much so that the salty fresh smell of sea air was nearly obliterated by it. I heard bawdy songs, off-key and slurred, coming from one establishment, and I dared not go inside. But 'twas not the drunken seamen I feared as much as recognition. Who knew which of these men had been in the crowd who'd watched as I was hanged only the day before?

Tugging at my hood again, I gathered my courage, and approached a woman in a ragged, revealing dress and smudged face paint. She stood near the entrance to a tavern, leaning tiredly against the building as if she'd been standing far too long. But she straightened at my approach.

"Can you direct me, mistress?" I asked her.

She perused me, top to bottom, and I kept my face lowered, one hand holding the hood in place. She smoothed her coppery curls with one hand. "You in hidin', are you?"

"Of course not." It startled me, how obvious I must be. Would she know? Would she guess? Would she alert someone in authority?

She only shrugged. "Yes, you are," she said, "but 'tis nothin' to me one way or the other. What are you doing here, missy? Lookin' to find yourself a seaman to warm yer bed?"

I felt my face heat, glad she couldn't see. "I only wish to know if there's a ship sailing for the New World tonight," I told her. "I need to book passage."

"Ahh, a runaway then? Is it yer man you be escaping?"

"Is there a ship or not?"

Her drawn-on brows arched high. But she concealed her surprise quickly, giving me a crooked smile. "Yer a spunky one, you are. You sure you want to leave? I could put you to work right here, if you like.''

"I *have* to go to the New World," I whispered. *"To-night."* Several men passed and I fell silent, sensing their gazes on me. They didn't move on right away, and I was careful to keep my back to them. "Please," I said. "If you know of a ship . . .''

"Let's have a look at ye.'' She yanked my hood down suddenly, and I heard a soft gasp from the onlookers even before I jerked it up again. The woman was shaking her head. "Shame yer leavin','' she said. "Yer a pretty one, fetch a goodly price.''

I lowered my head and turned to leave her. She wouldn't help me if I stood here begging her all the night through. I had no time to waste this way.

But then she surprised me. "Hold on, pretty one. There be a ship leavin' at dawn. The *Sea Witch*.''

I stopped, and slowly turned to face her again. "Not until dawn?'' My disappointment must have been clear in my voice.

"Dawn is only a few hours off, girl.''

"Is it?'' I hadn't noticed. Nervously I glanced behind me, in search of the fiend who'd attacked me earlier. And then toward the group of young men who'd seemed so interested in watching us. They still huddled in the shadows not far away. And I still felt eyes on me. When I looked to the woman again, she was frowning, staring at me as if she'd seen something she hadn't before. Perhaps 'twas my fear that finally touched her.

"I can fetch the captain, bring him to you,'' she said. And there was a softness to her voice that hadn't been there at first. Speaking still lower, she added, "Come with me, girl. I can hide you just fine while you talk with Cap'n Murphy.''

I jerked my head up suddenly. "And what makes you think I need to hide?''

She only smiled. "I been there, darlin'. I know the look. Come on, now.'' She took my arm and guided me around to the rear of the tavern, over the cobblestones that were blissfully free of snow, and through a door into a dark and musty room with several blankets strewn haphazardly upon a sleeping pallet, and little else. She lit a lamp and left me there, and 'twas only a short while later she returned with a finely dressed man who reminded me vaguely of my father, rest his soul.

He looked me over, sent an uneasy gaze to the woman, and then said to me in a gruff voice that seemed far too loud in the small chamber, "I understand you wish to book passage to the New World?"

"Yes," I said.

" 'Tis not cheap."

I fished several coins from my bag. "I can pay."

Again he nodded. "I'll need . . . a name. To put in the books."

I knew the woman must have told him I was hiding, or running away. And I had no idea why he would help me on her say-so alone. But the looks they exchanged were familiar ones, and perhaps he trusted her judgment, as unlikely as that seemed. A man like him, a woman like her. Still, he made it clear he was asking for any name I cared to give him, and I gave him the first one that came to mind. "My name is Smith," I said in a soft voice, one quite unused to lying.

"Smith," he said.

I thought he battled a slight smile. He lowered his head, but crinkly lines appeared at the corners of his eyes. My father had lines like those when he smiled.

"It will not do. You'll need to be a bit more creative in the future, dear lady." He looked up again and winked. " 'Tis more convincing that way. For now your name is Mistress Hunsinger. Rebecca Hunsinger, and you are traveling to visit your . . ." He rubbed his bearded chin.

"My aunt," I told him, relieved that at least that much was true.

"Of course." He took the coins I offered, examined them in his broad palm, then eyed the small bag from which I'd taken them. "Is this all the luggage you'll be bringing along?"

I lowered my head. " 'Tis all I have."

He nodded thoughtfully. "Well now, look here. You've

given me more coin than is needed. Perhaps you'll allow me to use the excess on your behalf.''

I tilted my head to one side. ''I don't under—''

''Certainly there's enough here for a simple dress or two, wouldn't you say, Mary?''

The woman nodded. ''I know just where to find what she needs.''

The captain pressed one of my coins into her hand. ''Good. You'll send them along with one of the men, then. Meanwhile, Mistress Hunsinger, I have a feeling you'll feel better aboard the *Sea Witch,* behind the locked door of your cabin, will you not?''

I blinked in shock at these two strangers and their unexpected kindness. ''Why are you helping me?''

The captain shrugged. ''I'm known to be a good judge of character, mistress. But Mary here is even better. Perhaps one day, 'twill be me in need of help from a stranger.''

''I'm grateful,'' I told them both. ''You've no idea how much.''

''Course we do, lass,'' Mary said. ''Go along with Cap'n Murphy now. He'll see you safely to where yer goin'.''

The man offered his arm, and I took it gladly. Eager to put England far, far behind me.

He'd seen her! The woman . . . the girl . . . the Witch . . .

But that was impossible. He'd watched her die, held her lifeless body in his arms, cried for her, even.

And yet, for just an instant he'd sworn . . .

Duncan had come with Samuel and Kathleen Mac-Phearson to the harbor, for they were two of the finest friends he'd ever known, and he'd be no kind of friend to either of them if he didn't see them off and wish them well. He'd long since exchanged his dark robes for plain breeches and a white shirt, and he'd joined them here.

With Kathleen settled in their cabin aboard the *Sea Witch*—Duncan had writhed in bitter irony at the name of the craft—he and Samuel had gone back to the docks for a pint of ale and a long goodbye. They'd been talking with some other men of their acquaintance outside one of the taverns, when he'd glimpsed the small form of the woman.

And though she'd been concealed beneath a dark cloak and hood, something about her had caught his attention and refused to let it go.

As Duncan looked on, the whore to whom she spoke reached out and yanked the girl's hood down. And Duncan gasped aloud as he glimpsed her face. Her beautiful, haunting face. Huge dark eyes, and curling ebony tresses of hair. A face that had burned itself a place in his mind. He wouldn't mistake that face.

She'd tugged the hood up again, almost desperately. He'd only glimpsed her for a moment. And he knew what he thought he'd seen was impossible. And yet 'twas not possible he'd been mistaken.

He couldn't shake the feeling that overwhelmed him. The feeling that this was the same woman he'd seen die on the gallows. Though she couldn't be. She *couldn't be*.

He battled a burning need to see her more closely. To make sure. To know . . .

A spell. She must surely have been a Witch after all, and he was under her spell. Imagining her face on strange young women. Thinking of her eyes each time he closed his own. Catching the scent of her hair on every stray breeze. 'Twas unnatural!

And he was sounding like the fearful townsfolk who clamored to see Witches burned or hanged or pitched into the sea. What he felt may be magnified, exaggerated. But 'twas certainly natural. All too much so.

"Easy, my friend," Samuel said in a low voice, one hand on Duncan's shoulder. "She only looks like the dead girl. 'Tis not her."

"You saw?" Duncan asked.

"A brief glimpse of ebony locks is all I saw, an' all you saw, Duncan. Get hold of yourself."

"Nay, I saw more." He strained his ears to listen as the girl spoke to the whore, and he heard her saying she must go to the New World, heard the whore mention the *Sea Witch*.

" 'Tis only the ale playin' tricks on your mind, Duncan," Samuel said softly.

Closing his eyes, Duncan whispered, "Aye. I suppose you're right."

But he didn't believe the words he spoke. And the woman . . . she'd be aboard that ship. That same ship, with Samuel and Kathleen. And if she were a Witch, they could be in danger. And if she wasn't, then she should be dead. Hell, either way, she should be dead. But he was compelled, obsessed perhaps. Whatever drove him . . . he had to be sure. He had to.

Lowering his head, rubbing his temples, willing his lips not to utter the words hovering on his tongue, he said them anyway. "Samuel, I've changed my mind. I'm comin' with you."

When he dared lift his head, 'twas to see his friend gaping. "Duncan?"

"I'm comin' with you," he said again.

"But . . . but the debt you owe your father . . ."

"I'll send him what I owe as soon as I find employment in the New World. As easy to pay the debt off from there as from Scotland."

Samuel stared and searched Duncan's face, concern etched on his own. And then he glanced over toward the cloaked woman and the whore, but the two were already hurrying away, around to the rear of the building.

"What made you change your mind, Duncan?" His sharp gaze probed Duncan's as he awaited an answer.

Duncan only shrugged. "A feeling," he said. "Just a feeling in my belly that 'tis the right decision. I can explain no more than that." He met Samuel's gaze. "Dinna ask me to."

Samuel nodded, but again stared off in the direction the women had gone. "I dinna *need* to ask, I fear. Duncan, think! You saw the girl die."

"Aye. I'm not likely to forget it, Samuel."

Still Samuel stared at him.

Duncan forced a smile. " 'Twas only a momentary lapse," he said. "An' my decision has naught to do with her. I only feel . . . a need to be away. To go to some shore so distant that I'll forget the blood I saw spilled here. Forget . . . forget *her*.'' But even as he said the words, he knew 'twas impossible. He'd never forget her.

Sighing deeply, Samuel nodded. ''I'll take you at your word, for now. And be glad of it, too.'' He slapped Duncan on the shoulder. '' 'Twill be the adventure of a lifetime, Duncan Wallace. I promise you that!''

''I have no doubt 'twill be all of that and more,'' Duncan said, but he wasn't smiling the way Samuel was. Instead he felt physically weak, and shaky, as if a fever were coming on, and atop that was an icy chill in his heart—indeed, in his very soul.

He was able to purchase space in a cabin for the passage to Boston Harbor in Massachusetts Bay Colony aboard the *Sea Witch*. He had his bag with him, the one containing all his worldly possessions, which amounted to a pathetically small bundle. He'd been planning to go on to Scotland as soon as he saw his friends off. But now his destiny seemed to be taking a sudden and unexpected turn. He was going to the New World, lured there, perhaps, by one of the very sirens he'd heard the seamen talk of. A Witch. A specter. A dead woman crooked her finger, and Duncan Wallace followed. He felt foolish, too foolish to tell Samuel the truth . . . that he still believed he'd seen her.

But not too foolish to make inquiries about her once he boarded the ship. He tried to be subtle. But though a few of the other passengers did indeed say they'd seen a woman such as the one he described aboard the *Sea Witch*, just as many denied it.

The ship weighed anchor at dawn, just as planned. And Duncan stood at the rail and watched England—and with it an entire phase of his life—disappear into the morning mist. Before his eyes it became a part of his past.

Except for her. She was present, in his mind, haunting him, always. In his dreams she came to him. He could not shake her image from his every thought. Duncan haunted the decks, searched every group of faces for her cream-skinned beauty, but never saw her. And finally he asked the captain himself. For if anyone would know, he would. He met the man at the helm, overseeing his navigator and manning the wheel. A stiff breeze mussed his silvery hair, but he faced it as if loving it, even as Duncan posed his question.

Captain Murphy shook his head slowly. "No. Sorry, but I can't say we've anyone aboard like that."

"Are you sure?" Duncan asked. And he knew he must sound desperate, but he'd *seen* her. He hadn't imagined it or hallucinated or dreamed it. He'd *seen* her.

The captain smiled. "I'm not so old I wouldn't notice a beauty such as the one you've described, son. No, I tell you, she's not aboard ship." Then the older man frowned, searching Duncan's face. "You don't look well, young man. You be feeling poorly?"

The man's face was more than speculative, and Duncan couldn't blame him. This ship had departed not far from a town ravaged by the plague of late. If Duncan showed signs of illness, the captain would have no choice but to put him off in a dinghy, for the protection of the passengers and the crew. And the truth was, Duncan wasn't feeling up to snuff, and hadn't been since boarding this vessel. And he was worried. But he was also taking great care not to touch anyone else physically, and he stayed well away from the others as he searched the decks for his mysterious beauty. He had no desire to spread illness, if indeed he were becoming ill.

Samuel, of course, had been far too busy, in the confines of his cabin with his new wife, to notice Duncan's behavior. All for the best.

"I'm fine," he told the captain. "Tired, though. An' a wee bit seasick, I fear."

The captain nodded, smiling. "It will pass, once your stomach gets used to the rocking," he said. "You haven't told me your name, lad."

"My manners are lacking. I am Duncan Wallace."

"I thought I detected a hint of the Scot in your voice."

"Aye, 'tis true."

"Captain Davis Murphy," he said, extending a hand.

Duncan couldn't shake, for fear of making the man ill. So he pretended to lose his footing, and gripped the rail. "If you dinna mind, Captain, I'll be goin' back to my cabin now."

"Of course."

As he left, Duncan felt the man's eyes on him. And he wondered if he'd fooled the captain even for a moment.

The journey was going to be exciting, I knew it from the moment we set sail. I spent much of my time sewing, mending my old clothes while wearing the ones the captain had sent to my cabin. I was grateful that I'd have presentable clothing to wear when I met my aunt Eleanor. But more of my time was spent on the decks of the magnificent vessel, staring out over the endless waters. I did so by night, of course, for I could not risk being recognized. But I loved the night, and always had. There was a magickal quality about wandering the decks alone, with no one else about save a few crewmen doing their jobs.

There was something about the sea that moved me. Such a magnitude of power surging beneath the tall ship. I was mesmerized by its endless rhythm, its mystery. And the wind that made those sails billow never let us down. I heard the captain remark more than once that he'd seldom seen the weather more cooperative. I only smiled to myself, and silently whispered thanks to my mother for all she'd taught me.

But as Captain Murphy approached me one night, I saw a certain grimness in his eyes. And I frowned at him. But he merely smiled in return, easing my mind somewhat.

"How are you enjoying the journey?" he asked me.

"Tremendously! I saw a great fish," I told him. "Big as a house, way off in that direction." And I pointed.

"Then your eyes are better than my lookout's, mistress. He's reported no such sighting."

I lifted my chin a bit. "No, neither did the crewmen I pointed it out to. I fear they didn't believe me."

"Of course they did. 'Twas a whale, dear girl. They've seen them before."

I nodded. A whale. My vision had reached a whole new level now, enabling me to see much farther than the mortals aboard. And my other senses were sharper, too. These things amazed me but troubled me, also, for they only served to remind me how very little I knew of my new nature.

"I have some news which might disturb you," the captain said. And as I tilted my head, he went on. "There's a man aboard ship who's been asking after you."

My heart froze. I swore it stopped beating as I recalled the hooded figure who'd attacked me. And the captain must have seen my reaction in my face, for he paled.

"What man?" I asked. "What did he look like?"

"Young, dark hair and brown eyes. Said his name was Duncan Wallace."

I caught my breath, but the captain was still speaking.

"There's no need for you to fear him. I told him no woman such as he described was aboard. But 'tis of no matter at any rate. I plan to put him off soon."

"Put him off?" I felt my eyes widen. He mustn't.

The captain nodded. "I'll wait until we reach a port, if I can, but if his symptoms continue, it will have to be sooner. I can't risk everyone aboard for the sake of one soul."

"I don't understand," I said, searching the captain's face. "I know you to be a kind man, Captain Murphy. Why would you do such a thing?"

The captain lowered his head. "I believe the man to be ill."

My eyes grew still wider. "No," I whispered. Not him, not the man I thought of nightly, the man who visited me in dreams I knew would never be more than that. "The plague?" I asked, breathlessly, thinking of my father, and little Johnny, and how helpless my mother and I had been to help either of them.

"I can't know that. But 'tis not a risk I can take."

I nodded slowly. Duncan Wallace. He was more than just a man who'd touched my soul. He was a priest, or would soon become one. A man who was associated in some way with the priest who'd murdered my mother. A man who'd tried to save us. Who'd seen us die. Was he following me? And if he was, then to what purpose? Did he know, or suspect that I lived still? Would he execute me again himself if he knew what I was? Was he working with that horrible old man? Or was there some other reason?

I could not trust him, despite his honorable and brave actions that cold dawn. Despite the feelings his touch had brought to life inside me. I could not trust him.

But I could not let him be put off this ship, for he would surely die. He'd tried to save my life, no matter what his intentions toward me now. I owed the man.

"I've had experience with the plague, Captain Murphy," I said quite softly. "I could easily tell by examining the man if it is that or some other illness."

The captain frowned at me. "You could be infected yourself, mistress. Even the ship's physician refuses to go near the man to examine him."

I shook my head firmly. "I won't become infected. I've cared for countless victims. I've never become ill." He still looked reluctant. "Surely you'd not wish to send a man to his death needlessly?" I asked him.

"Of course not. But, mistress, I thought you . . . you feared this Wallace."

I shook my head. "No, I do not fear him." I should, I thought, but somehow, I couldn't manage to convince myself to be afraid of the brown-eyed priest. I cleared my throat. "Nor do I trust him. Captain, if I could look on him without him seeing me . . ."

The captain lowered his head, rubbing his chin whiskers in thought. "There might be a way." Then he nodded. "Yes, I think it might work. Let me work on this now. Wait for me in your cabin. I'll come for you when all is ready."

I nodded my agreement. But I was not at ease as I returned to my cabin and waited there for word from the captain. I paced, nervous and frightened. I was taking a risk, I knew it. But as I thought of Duncan, of his eyes and the feeling, that sense of connection, that had passed between us there on the gallows, I knew I had no choice. Secretly, I'd longed to see him again. To thank him for what he'd tried to do. To feel that force moving between us once more. To touch his face, his hair, the way he'd touched mine. I'd longed . . . but secretly. It had been a fantasy. A dream I'd believed had no chance of coming true. Not ever.

And now it seemed . . . it would.

A tap came at my door, and I closed my eyes and stiffened my spine. "Who's there?"

"Captain Murphy."

I opened the door and faced the man. It had been more than an hour since I'd seen him last, and I wondered what he'd been up to, but I didn't have to wonder long.

"We put a sleeping powder into some food and left it for him. I peered in only moments ago. He's eaten every crumb and is resting quietly."

I nodded, battling a chill of foreboding. "Then I'll look in on him now. Take me to his cabin."

I started forward, but the captain caught my arm. "Are you sure, mistress?"

Solemnly, I nodded. And then I moved beside him into the passage, toward the cabin of Duncan Wallace, and with every step, my heart beat a bit faster.

4

Just when Duncan had decided his illness was little more than a passing case of the sniffles, his fever climbed dangerously high, giving him renewed reason for doubt. He'd taken to his bunk, pulled the covers up to his chin, and drifted in and out of sleep, alternately freezing and sweltering, shivering and sweating. Each time he woke, he felt worse than the time before.

Damnation. He was thirsty. *Terribly* thirsty, and his throat felt so raw it hurt to swallow. Bleary-eyed, he reached for the pitcher beside his bunk, only to find it dry. And the flickering candle beside it was burning low. How long had he been on his back? Hours? A day? He thought he might be approaching delirium.

The knock at his door couldn't have come at a worse time. If anyone aboard saw him in this condition, they wouldn't hesitate to pitch him into the sea. And he couldn't say he would blame them. From his bed he called, "Who's there?" in a voice gone hoarse and thready.

"Steward, sir. The cap'n asked that I bring a meal down to you. Said you were feelin' a mite seasick, he did."

Closing his eyes, Duncan prayed there would be water. Or ale. *Any* liquid would sooth his parched, burning throat. "Leave it by the door," he called, softening his voice slightly because it hurt to speak any louder. "I'll come for it by and by."

"Very well."

He heard nothing more and waited a good while to be sure the man was gone. He still didn't believe he was sick with the plague. Miserable, feverish, aching, yes. But not dying. Not even close. Still, there was no use risking the health of others. When he felt it was safe, Duncan got to his feet, but his head began to spin the second he did so. He gripped the back of a chair, and it tipped over, toppling him to the floor along with it. Damnation. He was sicker than he'd realized. Could he not even walk on his own?

It seemed better not to try. The ship seemed to be rocking a bit more than usual tonight. Perhaps that was the blame. He crawled on all fours to the door, opened it, and glanced quickly up and down the passage. No one was in sight, so he hauled the tray inside. A fresh pitcher of ale stood upon it, and his thirst burned anew.

The food, the very sight of it, followed quickly by its aroma, made his stomach turn over. He dragged the tray to his bunk, managed to right the chair, and set the pitcher and cup upon it. Then he pulled himself to his feet and, leaning weakly against the wall, struggled to open the porthole. He dumped the food into the sea, eager to have it out of sight. Perhaps his stomach would settle down some, then.

That done, he let the tin dishes fall to the floor and sank down onto his bed. It seemed he'd used every ounce of energy, all his strength, just to accomplish this one small task. He was disheartened to realize just how weak he truly was.

He managed to pour himself a bit of the ale, slopping too much of it onto the chair as he did. His hand trembled and his wrist felt barely able to lift the pitcher. Then he drank, *deeply.* Hellfire, he'd never been so thirsty in his life. He struggled to fill the cup again but gave up, deciding he was wasting too much of the precious liquid. This time he grasped the pitcher in both hands and tipped it to his mouth, gulping the cool, frothy brew, letting it numb and sooth his throat, and dull his pain. It warmed him some—eased the aches in his bones and joints.

As a student of the priesthood, Duncan had never imbibed in ale overly much. Even that night at the docks before leaving England, he'd only sipped at a single mug, making it last the entire time he'd spent in the tavern. He'd had wine, of course, in very small doses. It had never disturbed him. But suddenly he began to feel even more light-headed and dizzy than he had before. He glanced at the empty pitcher in his hands and realized he'd drained it. The flickering candlelight made him dizzier still, so he lay back on his bed, fully clothed, and closed his eyes. 'Twould pass. The spinning in his head would pass, if he just lay perfectly still.

How long he lay there, he had no notion. He drifted, dozed, woke again only to find his head still spinning. But when he blinked his eyes open this time, the candle's weak flame cast a dim glow upon a face.

Soft. Beautiful. Opalescent in the candle glow. The face of the woman he'd been dreaming about. The dead beauty. His Witch. His enchantress. Was he still dreaming, then?

She leaned over him, one hand sliding gently over his cheek, clasping his jaw and easing his mouth wider. She lifted the candle and seemed to be looking into his mouth. But he could only stare at her. The candlelight danced in her black eyes like the very flames of passion. Her lashes were as dark and thick as if she were a gypsy girl. And that hair. That magnificent hair, cascading and tumbling over her shoulders. Shamelessly free, and uncovered.

He moved his lips, tried to speak. "You . . . you're alive. . . ."

Her black eyes widened and snapped toward his, seemingly surprised to see him awake and staring back at her. Quickly, with a pinch of her fingers, she doused the candle and set it on the stand. And he heard her moving away, heard her soft, nearly silent steps crossing the floor.

"Please . . ." he whispered, and he reached out a weak hand toward her even though she couldn't possibly see it. He couldn't let her go, let her slip away again. He had to know. . . .

Hinges creaked as the door moved. Her voice, the voice of his fantasies, spoke softly. " 'Tis not the plague, Captain, but merely a fever that will pass him by soon enough. If you keep everyone away, there will be no danger to the others aboard.''

''Are you sure?'' The captain sounded less than certain himself. ''Because unless you are, mistress—''

''I am certain. I would not tell you so if I were not. I owe you a great deal, Captain Murphy. I'd never repay you by lying about a matter so grave.''

The captain might have nodded, because he didn't utter a word. Duncan's head was swimming, and he was trembling with cold again, yet he strained to listen.

''I'll stay with him for a while,'' the enchantress said. ''If you would bring some blankets, and the freshest water to be found, heated in a kettle. Just leave them outside the door.''

''But if 'tis truly safe—''

''I only said 'twas not the plague. Though his illness is not deadly, Captain, 'tis most miserable. Best you spare yourself and anyone else from falling prey to it if you can.''

''All right. I'll bring what you need. Shall I send the physician, as well?''

Duncan frowned when she spoke again, because her words made no sense to him.

''I can care for him far better than your physician can.''

Then he heard the door close and tried in vain to see her in the dark room. Her footsteps brought her nearer, but he might as well have been blind, the room was so devoid of light of any kind.

Her weight sank onto the bed beside him. One of her cool hands stroked his fevered brow, while the other tucked his blanket more closely around him. Her touch was heaven, cooling, calming.

''You're going to be all right, Duncan Wallace. I promise you that.''

He closed his eyes, sighing at the comfort her touch brought to him. ''You . . . you're the Witch,'' he muttered. ''I saw you die.''

''No, Duncan. I'm but a stranger with a gift for healing. And you've never met me before. 'Tis the fever making you see another woman's face instead of mine.''

She was lying. Even in this state, he knew she was. He lifted a hand, touched her hair, felt its silk just as before. He could even smell it, and he knew its scent was the same. "If you're not the woman I saw hanged in the town square," he whispered, "then light the candle and let me see your face."

"The candle has burned out."

He tried to sit up, to grip her shoulders, but she easily pushed him back down. He was too weak to fight her. Too sick. Sick. Damnation, he'd forgotten. "You should go, whoever you are," he told her. "You could take ill, as well."

"I've cared for many sick ones, Duncan, but I've never once become sick myself. You've no need to worry on that."

He frowned, and as she leaned over him, pressing her ear to his chest, he buried both hands in her hair, caressing its softness, committing each curl to memory.

She caught her breath and went very still. But she did not pull away. Was she closing her eyes as he was, then? Relishing the feel of his hands in her hair? The beat of his heart beneath her ear? He imagined she was, even thought he heard her sigh in pleasure, before she stiffened her resolve once again.

"Stop, now, Duncan," she said, but her voice was raspy and soft. "I'm only listening to your lungs, not embracing you."

He ran his fingers gently up and down her nape. "I canna stop thinking about you," he told her. "You've haunted me . . ."

"Don't say these things."

But he had to say them. Who knew when he'd get the chance again? "You mustn't leave me again. You must tell me the truth. How could you have survived the hangman's noose? How . . ."

She lifted her head away, and Duncan's hands fell limply to the bed. "You are burning up with fever and imagining things. I've never even seen a hangman, nor a noose, much less survived such horrors. I vow, your imagination is a fertile one, Duncan."

He sat up slightly, supporting himself on his elbow, so dizzy he could scarcely hold his head up. And when she moved close to him again, as if to ease him back down, he clasped her shoulders and drew her even closer. "Are you certain you willna catch this fever from me?"

"Of course," she whispered, and he heard the fear in her voice. The delicious fear. She wasn't pulling away, and she had to know what he intended.

"Good."

His lips found hers in the darkness as if by second sight. Soft, moist, so tender. He kissed her mouth the way he'd dreamed of doing since he'd watched her die. The way no man of his background should even consider doing. But 'twas as if he moved, and acted, without his mind's consent.

She tasted delicious. Sweet and cool and salty. Her lips were full and responsive, her tongue like satin when he touched it with his own. She shivered, or trembled. A soft sigh escaped her mouth, and he swallowed that sigh. His hands dived into her hair, and he deepened the kiss, parting her willing lips further, exploring her mouth, pulling her so close her breasts crushed to his chest. Her arms had gone around him, he realized, stunned. She was holding him, too, kissing him back. He lay back on his bunk, pulling her with him, until she lay stretched atop his body. He ran his hands down over her back and caressed her buttocks, and ached to be inside her, beyond the barriers of clothing.

She braced her hands against his chest and pulled her lips from his. "No," she whispered. "You . . . you're a priest."

"And how could you know that unless you are the woman I believe you to be?"

He felt her shake her head in denial. "The captain . . . he said . . ."

"He'd not have known it either, pretty one." Duncan closed his eyes, dizzy, and aroused to the point where it made him even more so. "I was only a student of the priesthood, lass. An' I gave it up the day I saw my teacher do murder."

She was silent for a moment. "You gave it up?" A slow breath, he felt it warming his face. "Because of . . . of what you saw?"

"Admit you're the one," he begged her. "I've feared for my sanity, lass. Tell me you're she who was hanged for Witchery in the town square. She who has haunted my mind ever since."

"I am not." But her voice trembled. "And you are quite drunk."

"Aye, I fear 'tis true. They brought me ale and I drank it as if 'twere water. I admit, I am unused to its sting."

"And you're half out of your head with fever."

"An' the other half with wantin' you." He pressed his palms to her back to bring her close, kissed her mouth again. His hands moved down her back, low on her thighs, and he bunched up her skirt to stroke the satin skin underneath. He arched his hips against her.

She pressed against him in return, and he heard her shuddering breaths. But she seemed to steel herself against him, and broke the kiss by turning her head to the side. Quickly she whispered, "When you gave up your studies, did you give up your beliefs as well, Duncan? Is it no longer a sin to fornicate?"

She said it in a clipped and harsh tone, and yet struggled to get enough breath for each sentence. As if she were as hungry for him as he was for her.

"I dinna ken *what* I believe. I've never . . . I've never wanted like this before. Perhaps you *are* a Witch, and I've fallen under your spell. . . ."

She jerked free of him so roughly he knew he'd said the wrong thing. He tried to open his eyes, but it was so dark and he was so disoriented, he couldn't be sure if they were open or closed.

" 'Tis a typical male who would find a way to blame his lust on the object of it. I've put no spell on you, Duncan Wallace. And if I did, 'twould be a spell designed to sharpen your dull brain, not to make you desire me."

"Nay," he whispered, feeling cold and empty as he listened to the sounds of her getting to her feet, righting her dress. "You'd have no need of a spell to make me desire you, my beauty, because I already do."

"You're out of your head with the ale and the fever."

He sensed she'd turned her back to him. "You know not what you say."

"Just tell me 'tis true. That you're alive. That 'tis not all of my imaginin'. 'Twill be enough to sustain me if only I know—"

"I am sorry, Duncan. But I cannot tell you what you wish to hear. If things were different, perhaps—"

"Dammit, woman, there is somethin' between us, an' well you know it. Somethin' alive an' real passed between you an' me on those gallows, an' you felt its power as much as I did, I know it. I saw it in your eyes. You stole my heart, lass . . . an' I dinna even know your name."

"You . . . are mistaken. . . ."

A knock at the door interrupted her, but Duncan thought he'd heard tears in her voice. He feared she was leaving when she answered that knock, but she didn't. She only took what was delivered and came back to him. He could sense the fever soaring high again. He was shivering cold, and damp with sweat, and his mind was wandering, drifting away before he forced it back with an effort. She brought him another blanket, and a cup of something hot and fragrant. She laid cool cloths, across his forehead. And then she told him to sleep. Gently she said the word. Again and again. Until he did.

But not soundly. Not so soundly he didn't know when she spoke again a long while later, after he'd drifted in and out of sleep, perhaps for hours. Her words fell in a songlike cadence, or a chant, perhaps. He opened his eyes and saw her standing above his bed. How long she'd been there, he didn't know. But moonlight spilled through the porthole now. A full moon, or nearly so. And she stood, bathed in that ethereal glow, and he could see her. He could see her with perfect clarity. Her eyes were closed, head tipped back, and she stood with her feet wide apart. Her left arm stretched upward toward the moon, her palm turned up as if to catch the pale moonlight that spilled into it. Her right arm was extended downward, toward him. She turned her palm down and pressed it gently to his forehead. And as she chanted, he felt energy flooding him. Filling him. Warm, potent, zinging energy.

Moon Goddess, Diana, send your healing hands,
Move through me, renew me, and heal this good
*   man.*

She repeated the chant three times as he lay there. And
then she went rigid, eyes flying wide. And Duncan felt a
surge of something white hot and tingling jolt right through
his entire body. 'Twas sudden, and brief, and then 'twas
gone.

He blinked his vision into focus and scanned the room,
trying to understand what had just happened. Then he spotted her. She leaned on the back of the chair, head hanging
down between her arms, her face curtained by her glorious
hair. Breathlessly, she murmured, ''Sweet lady, never has it
been like that. . . .''

Duncan was breathless himself. But as he took stock, he
realized . . . his head was clear. His pain gone. His throat,
no longer sore. His head, no longer spinning. And he turned
again to look at her, to see her and drink in the sight by the
light of the moon—only to see her eyes widen in alarm.

''You're dreaming,'' she told him. ''This has all been no
more than a sweet dream.''

''No, lass, 'tis no dream. An' what you just did—''

She held her palm toward him. ''Sleep now, Duncan.
Sleep.''

A wave of drowsiness suddenly swept over him, and his
eyelids felt so heavy he could barely hold them open.
''Dinna go,'' he whispered. ''I beg of you, dinna go. I dinna
care what that was . . . what *you* are. I only need you to stay
. . . please, angel . . . stay with me.''

''Sleep,'' she whispered. ''Sleep and regain your strength.
You're exhausted. Rest, Duncan. Sleep.''

His eyes fell closed, though he fought to keep them open.
And he felt her lips, warm and soft upon his . . . all too
briefly.

''If I could stay with you, Duncan, I would. Believe me
I would. 'Tis better this way. I wish 'twere not true, but 'tis,
Duncan.''

He heard her leaving, heard the door creak open. Battling
to stay awake, he forced words through his lips before losing

himself to the veil of sleep that he could not resist. "I'll find you again. I swear I will. I'll find you. . . ."

I'd never felt the power surge through me as it did that night. No, nor had I ever before felt the other forces that came to life in my blood then. The ones that burned in me when Duncan pulled me into his arms, when his mouth mated with mine, when he whispered that he hadn't stopped thinking about me.

I'd never felt such things for a man. Not for any man. But I did now. For Duncan. From the moment our eyes had met I'd sensed there was something between us. Something new and powerful. I'd had no idea how powerful.

And yet, I could not trust him, could not tell him the truth. Secrecy was vital, especially from any man associated with the Church and her Witch-hunters. He'd told me he'd given it up. But wouldn't he tell me that even if he hadn't? Wouldn't that be the perfect way to fool me? To entrap me? Lure me into his trust, into his arms, into his bed, gain my confession and then haul me away? And what if I foolishly told him the only way I could be killed, what then?

No. I was weak where Duncan Wallace was concerned. My mother had trusted my own aunt Matilda, and now she was dead because of it. She'd written the words, emphasized them: *Trust no one. No one.*

I'd become hard that day they killed my precious mother. Harder than I had ever been before. But my hardness melted when Duncan's lips touched mine. My wisdom faded away like mist in the morning sunlight. He'd tried to protect me once, yes. But hadn't he just now accused me of bewitching him? Of making him want me by using some spell?

I'd heard it myself. Though he'd taken back the words, the sentiment that spawned them likely still lived in his heart. So 'twas best I not see him again. Not ever.

I remained in my cabin for the rest of that journey. The captain brought me my meals, spoke with me for a few minutes each day, and seemed concerned for my well being. He told me how Duncan had been quite crazed since his recovery, insisting a woman had come to him and made him well that night, demanding to know my name and where my cabin was. Most of the crewmen and passengers thought his bout of fever had warped his mind. Even his friends, the couple with whom he was traveling, seemed to fear for his sanity.

It disturbed me to let him go on unsure just what had happened that night in his cabin. To let him go on wondering how much of it had been real and how much a dream. But I had no choice. 'Twould do me no good to be with Duncan Wallace. Nor him, either. For what could come of it, after all? What could come of my falling in love with him? And I would—I knew I would. I'd have to watch him grow old, I'd suffer through losing him. He'd be forced to see me remain young and healthy, while he aged and withered. No. There was no point in following my feelings for him, none at all, for they would only lead to heartache for us both.

But often as I sat alone in my cabin . . . and more often when I sneaked up onto the decks in the wee hours before daylight, I wished it could be different. And when I thought of Duncan, of his kiss, a great heaviness seemed to settle atop my heart. It added its weight to the sadness already there, that which I'd carried with me from the night I'd lost my mother, and so I became quite melancholy. Silent and pale. I was told my eyes seemed haunted more often than not.

I'd mourned my mother for the whole of my journey, gone over the events that cost her life again and again, each time wondering if I could have done something to save her. But I knew this terrible grief, this near despair, was not what she would have wanted for me. She'd have wanted me to find my own life, to go on, somehow. She would hate knowing that I cried each time I thought of her. Her memory, she would say, should bring me warmth and joy, not sorrow. So eventually I vowed to try to make it so. I could not spend my life grieving. Not for her, and not for what might have been between Duncan and me, had our situations been different.

Often, in those long days of my solitary journey, I found myself thinking of the way Duncan had tried so valiantly to help us that day at the gallows. If he had succeeded, and

died in the attempt, what would have been the result? I
wondered if he would have returned to his next lifetime
immortal, as I was. Such a thing seemed beyond belief to
me. Surely not a priest, nor a man studying to become one!
And yet the undeniable proof was in me. I had become
immortal in just such a way.

I was changing daily—almost hourly—and these changes
also occupied my thoughts. How far would they go? I wondered. Each day I grew stronger. My senses continued to
sharpen themselves by gradual degrees. And I found that if
I focused on my new nature, 'twas easier to escape my crippling grief. So many new and strange things were happening
to my body.

I could hear conversations from a goodly distance, and
hear them more clearly than before. I could see as sharply
in the darkness now as I could by daylight, and had been
able to do so since that night in Duncan's cabin, even after
I'd extinguished the candle.

By the time we sailed into the harbor at Boston Town, I
could hear the fish swimming beneath the waves. I could
detect—even distinguish between—the scents of each person aboard. Duncan's above all others, and why that was, I
did not know. I saw the purple line of the New World fully
an hour before the lookout shouted "Land ho!"

Sanctuary was but forty miles from where the ship docked
at Boston Harbor, and I was told 'twas a town on its own
tiny peninsula that curved like a crooked finger into the sea.
I was eager to see it. I waited, of course, until everyone had
left the ship. Long, long after that I crept out of my cabin,
half afraid Duncan would be waiting for me, even then. I
even looked for him, searching the few faces I saw as I
walked softly down the gangplank and along the dock and
into the town. But he wasn't there. I saw him not at all.

And perhaps a very small part of me . . . was disappointed. I told myself how foolish that was, but the truth
was a lot of the feelings I'd been having lately were foolish.
It didn't stop me from having them, all the same. It didn't
stop me from craving a man I could never have.

5

At Boston Town I purchased a horse with most of the coins still remaining in my purse. A fine black mare with fire in her eyes and spirit in her step. The livery man pleaded with me to take a more gentle animal instead, but I was insistent. From the moment my eyes met the animal's, and she gave a sassy shake of her dark, flowing mane, I knew she was the one for me. I called her Ebony, for that was her color.

I'd taken to carrying my dagger strapped round my thigh, held there by the red garter my mother had made for me long ago. All the Witches of her family had worn one, she'd said. 'Twas laughable that I still wore the garter, when my stockings were long since too tattered to wear.

Beyond the dagger, I had only the drawstring sack my mother had given me, all my worldly possessions tucked away inside. Armed with a crudely drawn map, and pitifully few coins, I set out at dawn on the day after the *Sea Witch* had docked, bound for Sanctuary. My new home.

I rode on narrow paths, amid forests of such grandeur I'd never seen their like. The trees towered to the heavens, their trunks incredibly large. I marveled at the natural beauty around me, the forces of nature I could feel thriving in this place. There was great power here. I sensed it the way an animal can sense the approach of a storm.

After riding for an entire day, I estimated my journey to be nearly half complete, and stroked Ebony's neck, praising her in soft words.

The dampness that coated my palm and her gentle nicker told me 'twas time to stop for the night. "All right, girl. Time you had some rest. And me, as well. Though one would not think I should be the one to feel so tired when you've been doing all the work."

The mare snorted as if in agreement, and I glanced at the area around me. Truly, there was little here. Woods that might be the homes of giants towered on either side of me. Ahead, there was only the dim outline of a well-worn dirt track, and even that vanished a short distance away as the sky turned dusky with twilight.

Sliding from the mare's back, I gathered the reins in my hands and went very still, closing my eyes, listening to my instincts to tell me which way to go. 'Twould be far from wise to camp beside the road, lest some ne'er-do-well come upon us in the night. Besides that, Ebony needed water. She'd last drunk at midday.

Softly I scented the breeze, waiting. And my senses did not let me down. I'd suspected as much. I could hear, very faintly, the trickle and splash of a stream off to the left. Moreover, I could smell the water.

I glanced at Ebony and realized I needn't have bothered. She smelled it, too, and looked eagerly off toward the woods in that direction. "Come on, then," I told her, and led her off the trail and into the darkness of the forest.

It took a long while to find that stream. It seemed we walked a mile, though it could not have been that far. But surrounded by the lowering darkness and towering trees, I felt the full extent of my solitude here more than I had since leaving the ship at Boston Harbor. I was alone, in a strange, new land.

And yet, not *quite* as alone as I might have been. Somewhere in this New World was Duncan Wallace. And I wondered if he might be staring in awe at the virgin forests, or gazing up at the same purple sky. I wondered if he thought of me.

Ebony tugged at her reins, and I glanced ahead to see the

stream, wide and bubbling like an excited child. I released her, and she trotted to its banks and bent to drink from its crystalline waters.

Hands on my hips, I inspected the lush grasses here. '' 'Tis a good spot,'' I told the mare. ''Tonight, we'll sleep right here.'' Using the length of worn and fraying rope the liveryman had given me, I picketed Ebony in a spot where she could reach both the sweet grasses and the water. Then I tossed my bag on the ground to use as a pillow. My cloak would be my blanket, the grassy ground, my bed. 'Twould do quite nicely.

A twig snapped in the woods to my back, and I stiffened, turning to look around. I saw nothing, but for the first time I wondered what sorts of beasties might roam these woods. Large ones, if the size of the trees was anything to go by. I'd not expect an animal to harm me unless I provoked it. A Witch is in tune with nature, and its creatures, and I'd come to believe that even wild animals could sense that and know instinctively that I meant them no harm. But these might be new creatures, animals with which I'd had no experience.

A rustling sound came then, and I forced my brain to calm, my senses to open. Slowly I moved toward the center of the place I'd chosen as my camp for the night and stood there, still and silent for a long moment, letting my eyes fall closed and my breathing slow, and lengthen. Opening my mind, I sensed the intense energy of the earth thrumming beneath my feet, and instinctively I crouched down to place my palms flat to the ground, the better to feel it, to absorb it, and fall into harmony with the forces moving here. Then, after a moment, I rose again, gradually unfolding my body until I stood upright. Tipping my head skyward, opening my arms to the heavens, I let the energies of the sky above me flow into me.

When I felt the familiar sense of being in perfect harmony with all around me, I lowered my arms to my sides and opened my eyes, feeling confident again that nothing in nature would harm me here.

And then I saw him, peering at me from within the trees, so much a part of the forest he nearly blended into it. But

once I'd spotted him, my eyes focused, and he became
clearer and clearer to me. A red man, dressed in animal hide
all adorned with beads. His long hair hung in streaks of dark
and light, and his eyes were very dark.

I'd heard talk of these natives of the New World. Indians,
they were called. Or savages. 'Twas said they murdered and
raped at their pleasure, and took the scalps of their white
victims. And a chill of unwelcome fear slithered up my
spine as I held his gaze with mine.

He did not move. Nor did he look particularly savage nor
bent on my murder. In fact, he seemed natural there, in the
woods . . . as if he belonged there. As if he were even more
in tune with his environment than I could ever hope to be.

And then I realized . . . this was his home. It had to be
his home. The sense of that came to me too strongly to
be a mistake. I'd simply walked in without knocking and
decided to spend the night without an invitation.

Licking my lips, rather nervously, I said, "I'm sorry if I
have intruded. I'd like to sleep here tonight. If 'tis all right."

He remained as he'd been before. Perfectly still, unblink-
ing. Just watching me. And it occurred to me that he might
not speak my language. So I spoke to him with my hands,
as best I could manage. I pointed to myself, then folded my
hands beneath my head, closing my eyes to indicate sleeping, and then pointed to the ground. Looking back at him,
I waited.

He nodded, just once, and so slightly I might have mistaken it. I should thank him, I realized. But how did one
make a sign for "thank you"?

Perhaps a gift. Kneeling, I opened my pack, searching my
mind for something to give the man to show my gratitude
and friendship, and finally found the small piece of glittering
amethyst that I'd salvaged from my plundered home. But
when I glanced up again, the man was gone.

I went to the spot where he'd been, but saw nothing, and
the woods were so utterly undisturbed, I might have imagined him.

But I hadn't, had I?

I didn't think so.

Kneeling, I placed the stone on the ground, then returned to the grassy bank where my pack awaited.

I had a single biscuit in my pack, saved from my last dinner aboard the *Sea Witch*. I ate half of it, washed it down with water from the stream, and then lay down upon my pack, beneath my cloak, and slept. And dreamed that another man watched me from the shelter of the woods. A beautiful man whose face, it seemed, would haunt me until I died.

My nose woke before the rest of me. It twitched and sniffed and smelled something that made my stomach rumble. Then warm sunlight brushed my eyelids open, and the first thing I saw was food. Something golden colored and fragrant, resting on a slab of bark very close to my face.

Blinking and wondering vaguely if this were a dream, I sat up, grabbed the bark, and looked more closely. It was fish! Coated in something and cooked . . . still warm, in fact.

"Who in the . . ." I turned my head, scanning the woods around me, but saw no one. But it had to have been the red man I'd seen the night before.

I ate the fish eagerly, closing my eyes at the heavenly taste. And when I finished, and licked every crumb from my fingers, I leaned back, sighed in contentment, and muttered, "Savages, indeed. That man is kinder than many a white man I've known. Don't you agree, Ebony?"

The mare only looked at me. Getting to my feet, I gathered up all my belongings once more, making ready for the second leg of my journey. But before I left that place, I crept into the trees where I'd seen the man the night before and looked for the stone I'd left him.

The amethyst was gone.

Nodding in approval, I mounted the mare, and we meandered out of the woods, to the trail, and began our long trek again.

And again, we traveled all the day through. I hadn't expected it to take so long and, in fact, hoped to arrive at Sanctuary well before dark. I ate my remaining half biscuit, stale and crumbling now, at midday, and thought fondly of my delicious breakfast. But the trail seemed endless. Nightfall came, and still hours went by.

I was quite weary, and terribly hungry, when I finally rode into a small settlement with muddy paths running between a handful of small log structures more roughly built than any I'd ever seen before.

"Hello, mistress," a deep voice called.

I turned in the saddle to see a heavy man with whiskered jowls and curious eyes.

"Elias Stanton is my name," he said. "I be the town elder. What business have you in Sanctuary?"

"*This* is Sanctuary?" I asked, my heart sinking. I should have been glad, I suppose, that my journey was finally at its end. But this place was hardly what I'd expected.

The man's eyes narrowed on me, and I realized my tone might have offended him. "I hadn't realized I had come so far," I amended. "My name is Raven St. James." I saw no reason now to use a false name. My aunt would wonder why, if I did. "I am looking for my aunt, Eleanor Belisle. Do you know her?"

His bushy dark brows drew close. "I know her well," he said, and I sensed a grimness settling about him. "Have you traveled far, then?"

"All the way from England. My ship only arrived at Boston two days past, and I rode from there."

At that his frown changed to one of disapproval. "You traveled alone? Spent a night on the road? Unchaperoned?"

I'm afraid my chin lifted a little, when I likely should have assumed a humble and apologetic posture. "I had little choice, sir."

"Well now, such impropriety will not be tolerated here, mistress. You might learn it now as well as later. Unmarried young ladies do not go about—"

"I am not unmarried," I blurted. And my own words surprised me, for I had loathed liars for as long as I could remember. Yet the man's attitude reminded me so much of the arrogant priest who had murdered my mother that I could not help but wish to take precautions. "My husband died, during our crossing."

"You're a widow-woman, then," he said. His gaze roamed down my body, to my slippers, and up again. And I did not care for the shadow that darkened his eyes. Nor for the way his tongue darted out to moisten his lips. " 'Tis still unwise to travel alone, mistress, but at least not quite as scandalous."

"I am weary, sir. My journey has been very long. Pray, direct me to the home of my aunt before I fall from the saddle."

"Ah, yes, your aunt. I'm sorry my news is not better," he said. "But your aunt has been taken ill. A physician came from Boston, as he does once a month when the roads are passable. He examined her and said there was nothing to be done."

"What ails her?" I asked, my heart in my throat.

"Old age," the man said. "Her heart has worn itself out. She's all of fifty years, you know." He shook his head sadly. "But 'tis good that you came. She needs caring for, being so far from Sanctuary proper. 'Twill be good for her to have you there."

"I'll go at once. If you'll just—"

"Yes, yes. Follow this road, mistress. It runs along the coast, all the way to the very tip of the peninsula. High on the cliffs above the sea is where she and that man of hers, God rest his soul, built their cabin. Though the good Lord only knows why. 'Tis no more than two mile."

"Thank you, sir." I snapped the reins lightly, and the mare, though likely as weary as I, lunged forward. Perhaps she sensed this journey's end was at hand. Or perhaps she simply found the little man as distasteful as I had.

I found the cabin just as the man had said, on the cliffs, with the mighty sea and its waves crashing below. But unlike Elias Stanton, I saw immediately why my aunt had chosen this site. I could envision no place more magnificent. Surely the gods themselves would gladly place their thrones along such majestic cliffs, while far below the rolling power of the sea paid homage.

The log cabin was humble but neat. And there was a crooked shed, which housed a cow and some hens, though the cow looked as if she'd been neglected of late, her ribs showing, her bag swollen. Though 'twas fully dark, no light shone from within the cabin. But of course, I could see quite sharply in darkness by now.

I took Ebony into the shed, relieving her of saddle and bridle, and rubbing her down as best I could with a rag that hung from a peg on the wall. Quickly I gathered hay from the small stack outside, and a pail of water from the well for her, and for the poor cow as well. And then I took up my sack and went to the cabin.

The door creaked as it opened, and I stepped inside to see a frail form hunched in a rocking chair beside a dwindling fire. I moved closer and softly whispered, "Aunt Eleanor?"

The graying head came up, turning slowly toward me in the dim room. The dying fire was the only light, so I stepped closer that she might see me better, and knelt beside her chair. "Aunt Eleanor, I am Raven, the daughter of your half sister."

Her parched lips parted, and her eyes widened slightly. "Lily's girl? You be Lily's little girl?"

"Yes, Aunt Eleanor. Lily's little girl."

"Saints be praised," she whispered, and tears brimmed in her clouded eyes. "Oh, mercy, child, I thought I would never live to see you." She opened her arms, and I embraced her. Her thinness made me wince, but though weak, she squeezed me tight. Sheer joy gave her that strength, joy at seeing me. A welcome I'd neither expected nor hoped for . . . from a woman who was all that remained of my family.

Family.

All at once so much emotion rose up inside me that I could scarcely speak and my eyes burned with tears. She would never know what such a welcome meant to me. Never. But I'd be grateful for it all my life. And I hugged her back just as firmly, though with great care.

"You're not to worry anymore," I told her. "I'm here now, and I'll care for you." I sat away slightly, and kissed her careworn cheek. "You'll be well again soon, Aunt Eleanor. I promise you that."

And, of course, she was.

I pampered my aunt in every way I knew. By day I took long walks in the woods, finding, growing wild in this lush land, many of the herbs and roots that would help her. I never told her of it, of course. My mother had warned me to trust no one, and though I was certain my dear aunt would never intentionally bring harm to me, I was equally certain it was best I never give her the means to do so. I seasoned the meals I prepared for her with the natural remedies for her weakening heart and made teas of the tonics I brewed. Hawthorn berries and devil's claw. Valerian root and chamomile, and wild garlic.

By night I performed quiet rituals over her bed as she slept, calling on all the powers of the Universe to aid in restoring her health. And of course, my magick was effective ... though not as dramatic and shattering as it had been that night in Duncan's cabin aboard the *Sea Witch*. Never once did I feel the surge of power I'd felt when I'd called down the power to heal Duncan. Never once. And I wondered why.

I thought of him often. Mostly when I lay alone in my bed at night, wondering what would become of me. Would I live alone for all eternity? Would I ever stop seeing the longing in his deep brown eyes every time I closed my own?

In between struggling with these unanswerable questions, I milked and cared for the cow and the hens, so that we had fresh milk and eggs aplenty. More than we needed, in fact, so that each day I would ride into town and trade the excess for other goods. Vegetables and game and freshly caught fish. Good for my aunt's health, all of it.

Within a week Aunt Eleanor was strong enough to walk outside in the sunshine for a few minutes each day. Within two weeks she was gaining weight again, and the color had returned to her cheeks. After a month she was vigorous enough to supervise me as I planted a vegetable garden near the house. And at the end of my second month in Sanctuary, she was helping me gather eggs and nagging at me to take her to the Sunday meetings in the settlement.

I did not want to do this. The very idea of another clergyman, like the evil one back in England, glaring down at me with judgment in his eyes made me feel ill. And though this small church was no part of the Church of England, I was reluctant. But there was really no choice. I had to keep my secret, and attending services was necessary if I hoped to do so.

Since my arrival, no one had come to call on my aunt Eleanor, and I was quite happy to have it that way. People asked after her, of course, when I made my excursions into town. And each time I was asked, I would say that Aunt Eleanor was improving, and that we were fine and in no need of assistance. When they remarked that they hadn't seen me at the Sunday meetings since my arrival in Sanctuary, I replied that I dared not leave my aunt alone for that long.

I truly thought I was handling things well, and discreetly.

But when I walked beside my aunt into the meeting hall that first time, I knew that I hadn't. There were gasps and exclamations at the sight of my aunt's rosy cheeks and shining eyes and renewed vigor. And for the second time in my life, my neighbors began looking at me with suspicion in their eyes.

Duncan worked like a mule, pouring himself fully into physical labor. And not just to help his friends, though he told himself that was the reason. He was trying to make himself forget. Forget *her* and the brief flirtation with madness he'd suffered while he'd been ill aboard that ship.

But no matter how hard he worked, she haunted him still. Her eyes, gleaming black and full of mystery and promise. Her lips, full and tasting vaguely of honey as they moved in delicious, erotic response against his own.

It hadn't been real. He told himself that again and again as he worked by Samuel's side, sawing timber, building a cabin, hunting and fishing, and tilling the soil. Cutting firewood, harvesting vegetables.

And though he did the work of three men, Duncan still couldn't escape the memory of her. Neither the real memory, of her swinging from that noose, too beautiful and full of life to be dead, nor the false memory, the fantasy, of holding her body tight to his in a bed, of kissing her and begging her not to go.

He barely slept anymore. Each time he closed his eyes, he saw her there. She came to him in his sleep and loved him to the point of exhaustion. A gentle succubus. A seductive spirit. And though he knew 'twas only a trick of his mind that had created her, it felt just as real. Just as powerful.

He grieved her loss as if she'd been his lover. Ridiculous. But true, for she'd become his lover in his dreams. He was well and truly obsessed, and he knew that was no overstatement when he found himself searching the township of Boston for her. Everywhere he went, he sought her face, her hair. He was always, *always* searching.

And he feared he was cursed to do so for the rest of his life. For two full years had passed since that fateful voyage. And still, he found himself searching. 'Twas as if, though she'd died, part of her had remained alive inside him. Possessing him. He'd become depressed and moody, restless and irritable. And all the hard work in the colonies couldn't cure him.

Samuel and Kathleen had tried to convince him to return to the pulpit. How would they feel if they knew the thoughts that plagued him? The fire that burned in his loins for a dead woman? He couldn't do it. Not now, and perhaps not ever.

He'd earned enough by hiring himself out to help other settlers, and the debt he owed his father was finally paid in full. That goal reached, he felt adrift, directionless. The emptiness he felt threatened to consume him.

And then one day Kathleen returned from the marketplace with news that changed everything.

"I believe, dear Duncan, that I have found permanent and perfect employment for you." Her red hair danced in the breeze as she bent to set her basket of goods on the ground.

Duncan had been assisting Samuel in patching the roof, and looked down at his friend's pretty wife in surprise. "You've done what your husband and all his cronies couldna do, then."

"And it should not surprise you!" she teased, sending Samuel a wink and running a hand over her bulging belly. "There is a town two days' ride north. Sanctuary, 'tis called. Their minister was called away, Duncan, and they're sorely in need of a new one."

Duncan lowered his head then, disappointment washing over him. "I'm no priest, Kathleen. You know that. I canna

be, not after seein' my own confessor, my mentor, commit
murder.''

He didn't tell her the other reasons, nor did he mention
that it was that very same murder that kept him awake
nights. The murder of the most beautiful creature he'd ever
laid his eyes upon.

''You're the closest thing to one, Duncan. Your trainin'
was all but complete when you left England. Besides, they
don't want a priest, just a pastor.''

'' 'Tis true,'' Samuel said. ''I've heard of this place.
Sanctuary is but a small settlement. They've no need of
pomp and circumstance there. Only guidance and a stirrin'
sermon of a Sunday morn. 'Tis not the Church of England
we're discussin', after all.''

''I've already spoken to the man makin' inquiries, Duncan,'' Kathleen continued. ''He's at the Boar's Head, and
he's hopin' you'll come by.''

Duncan heaved a great sigh. ''Samuel, you know my feelin's on this matter. We've discussed it before.''

''Aye, I know them. But what better way to teach people
tolerance and love for their neighbors than from the pulpit?
You could change things, Duncan.''

''Not all men of God are like Nathanial Dearborne,''
Kathleen said softly, sympathy for Duncan in her eyes.
''I've known many fine, honorable men who preached to a
flock. And so have you, Duncan Wallace. You cannot condemn the callin' because of the acts of one vile man.''

Duncan knew she was right. ''You're a wise woman,
Kathleen.''

''And well you know it,'' she said. ''Come, Duncan.
What harm will it do to speak with the man? You've certainly had no better offers. The pay is fair and includes a
cabin for you to live in.'' She patted her round belly again.
''And while I love havin' you here, I fear 'twill soon become crowded in this one.''

''Nonsense!'' Samuel cried. ''I'd been plannin' to put
Duncan to work as a governess, woman. Don't go chasin'
him off now.'' He laughed and nudged Duncan with an
elbow. ''At least talk to the man.''

Duncan shook his head in surrender and glanced down at Kathleen's gleaming eyes.

"His name is Elias Stanton," she said. "And he'll be leavin' town in the morn."

"I fear I'm outnumbered," Duncan said softly. And perhaps they were right, after all. Perhaps he could do some good in one small settlement . . . *if* he were to take the position. He probably would not. But 'twas high time he leave his friends to their new life, their new home, and growing family. Time he struck out on his own.

And perhaps he'd find a way in Sanctuary to exorcize the beautiful ghost from his soul. He'd failed to forget her in all this time and seemed to think of her even more since he'd come here. Again and again, he would close his eyes and see her body swinging from a rope. Feel her in his arms or catch the scent of her hair on a stray breeze.

"Duncan?" Samuel tapped his shoulder.

Duncan started from his morbid thoughts. "All right," he said. "I'll speak with this Stanton."

"Good," Kathleen said with a laugh. "I told him you'd be there directly. Off that roof with you. And wash your hands afore you go. If I had time I'd take a blade to that hair of yours, but I suppose there's naught to be done for it now."

"You'd best run, Duncan, before my wife domesticates you thoroughly."

"You make a good point, my friend." Duncan climbed down the ladder and washed his hands. Perhaps part of the void growing inside him was because he'd left what he'd once considered his life's work behind. In the various congregations scattered about here in the colonies, a preacher wasn't expected to be without sin, as it seemed he was in England. Here he was still considered a man, flaws and all. Which was as it should be. Ministers married and raised families. Desires of the flesh, then, should not necessarily mean he could not serve.

Perhaps he would give it a try. Perhaps he could fill the emptiness in his heart. And perhaps, by doing so, he'd rid himself of the woman who lived eternally inside his soul.

•   •   •

Elias Stanton looked like a man with many grave matters on his mind as he sat before a pint of ale at a slab table, across from Duncan.

He shook Duncan's hand but seemed distracted.

"I hope you didna wait long," Duncan said, apologetic.

"No. If I seem impatient, sir, 'tis only because I have many problems to tend to. However, finding a new man to minister to the township takes precedence over the rest."

"I hope your troubles are not too dire," Duncan said, curious. Elias rubbed his hairy chin, and Duncan thought he had jowls like a mastiff.

"Oh, quite dire indeed," he said. "Our town has a temptress nestled in its midst. A most improper young woman, truth to tell. An' I believe she's come to damn the souls of all the menfolk in Sanctuary."

Duncan tried not to smile, though the man's words amused him. "How shockin'," he said. "But surely the men of Sanctuary have enough moral fiber to resist such temptation?"

Elias shook his head slowly. "I'm in hopes you can help them in that regard," he said. "But 'twill not be easy. The girl is possessed of an unnatural beauty, and there is hellfire in her eyes. She's neither humble nor obedient. Nor devout, for she misses services as often as she attends them." He shook his head in disgust.

"Perhaps the girl is unaware of the effect she has on the men."

Elias took a long sip of ale, then set the glass down heavily. "She's aware. Even enticed *me* to impure thoughts. An' I tell you, not all our men have the moral fortitude and spiritual strength that I have. Some might be moved to do more than dream. They'll fall victim to her wiles, surely. And that will be their downfall. 'Tis why we cannot afford to go long without a minister."

"I see." Duncan wasn't certain he did. Was Elias saying that because he desired a woman, 'twas *her* fault?

"There's something evil about her," the man went on.

Duncan felt a cold chill dance up his spine. Damnation. Such ridiculous discussions were what led to more serious accusations. Accusations like the ones that had caused the death of his phantom lover. And suddenly he thought that perhaps this was why he'd been led to this man, to this position. Perhaps he'd get the opportunity to prevent such an atrocity from happening to another innocent young woman.

Aloud, he said, "We all have a darker side, Elias. We only learn to control it."

Elias frowned. " 'Tis more than a dark side, I fear. Abundance seems to surround this girl. While others in Sanctuary simply get by from one year to the next, she and her aunt grow wealthier by unnatural measures, and in an unbelievably short time. Two years ago the girl rode into our town with little more than the clothes on her back, and one feisty mare. Now she is quite possibly more wealthy than I, the town's foremost elder! Imagine!"

"Aye. Imagine." So the man's pride was suffering, as well. Aye, Duncan thought, he had to take this position. He had to enlighten ignorant fools such as the one sitting across from him. Maybe he had a purpose in this life after all.

And there was something else, something Stanton had said, that had set off bells ringing in his mind. And then it hit him.

Two years ago.

Exactly when Duncan himself had come here. Exactly when the *Sea Witch* had docked at Boston Harbor. And if the ghost he'd seen aboard that ship *had* been real . . .

'Twas ridiculous. He was letting his thoughts run wild again.

But what if 'tis her?

"What is the name of this temptress?" he asked.

Elias sighed deeply and shook his head. "No matter," he said. " 'Tis my responsibility to put a stop to her mischief, and I've taken steps already . . . precautions really. You need only concern yourself with the moral well being of the community. Keeping them strong and steadfast while I make sure she does no harm."

Duncan frowned. "What steps, exactly, are you referrin' to, sir?"

Elias shook his head. "We should be talking about you." And he began asking questions as to Duncan's background, his schooling and experience, and positions on various scriptural debates.

Duncan found it very easy to guess the answers the man most wanted to hear, and those were the ones he gave. He had decided he wanted this position—wanted it badly. Because despite how little sense it made, he had to see for himself that this woman of whom Elias Stanton spoke was not the same one who'd haunted him all this time. And because, even if she were not . . . he had a grim feeling things in Sanctuary were heading rapidly toward disaster. And this time, perhaps, he could do something to prevent it.

If that wouldn't exorcize his demons, he didn't know what would.

"You simply must come to meeting today, Raven. People will think it odd if you don't. The new minister is here!"

Aunt Eleanor fussed with the skirts of the new dress I'd made for her, then stopped herself. "Vanity," she said. "At my age one wouldn't think it a sin that would tempt me."

"Wishing to look one's best when greeting a newcomer is not vanity, Aunt Eleanor," I told her sternly. " 'Tis simply good manners."

'Twas the beginning of my third summer with my aunt, and the cottage looked very different than it had when I had arrived. We'd truly prospered. And my knowledge of natural magick was only a small part of the reason why. At least part of our success was due to simple hard work and smart thinking.

We'd set aside fertile eggs and allowed the hens to hatch them, over and over, until we'd raised well over a hundred chickens. We sold most, and kept many more, enough to keep our business going, and supply half the town with eggs. We'd twice bartered for the services of a neighbor's bull, and our cow had produced twins both times. And, yes, I had used my knowledge of magick to help with that. All four calves had been female, and two would be producing milk and calves of their own very soon. Truly, we were doing exceptionally well.

We'd used our newfound wealth to hire the labor of some

men, and now a small barn stood where the shed had been, and the chickens had a coop. We'd enlarged the hearth and built an oven among the cobblestones. And real glass, purchased in Boston, filled our windows.

"If you knew so much about good manners, child," my dear aunt said, "you would accompany me to church."

She made her eyes soft and pleading, like those of a child wheedling for a sweet. And again I marveled at how youthful and vigorous she had grown under my care.

"Please come with me, Raven."

I closed my eyes in defeat. "Oh, all right. But if he's as fond of shouting and pounding his Bible as the last one was, I shall get up and leave."

"You wouldn't!"

I smiled to let her know I was only teasing, and went to the bedroom we shared to fix my hair and put on one of my own new dresses, of shamelessly fine fabric and cut. I couldn't help but think 'twas a far cry from the rags, tattered stockings, and worn slippers in which I'd arrived.

Reluctantly I tied my hair into a knot at the back of my head, and covered it with the small white cap with its dangling ribbons, as was customary. 'Twas considered sinful for a woman to wear her hair loose, though I failed to see why those silly townsfolk said so. I wore my hair down and flowing all the time, unless I was in town. And I was often tempted to do so publicly as well, to show them what I thought of their conventions. However, I had not forgotten the lessons I'd learned. 'Twas best to keep my strange ways to myself.

I was not a fool.

Though, perhaps I had been behaving as if I were. That Aunt Eleanor's fortune had shifted so completely from the moment of my arrival had not escaped the notice of some. I could feel the eyes on me, hear the speculation in the whispers they shared as I walked among them. Perhaps 'twas time I convince Aunt Eleanor to sell the cabin and move away with me. I would not wait until it was too late a second time.

Sanctuary was becoming unsafe for me. I couldn't quite

smell the danger on the air . . . yet, but I felt it drawing slowly, inexorably nearer.

We had acquired a modest wagon, and I hurriedly went outside to put Ebony into her harness. She hated towing the thing, and I couldn't say that I blamed her. However, the sight of my aunt and I riding double upon my horse's back would likely have caused some of the townsfolk to faint dead way. And Aunt Eleanor might well end up on the ground, at any rate.

My aunt came outside the moment I had the wagon ready, a large basket in her hands filled with food for the meal that would follow services. I helped her into the seat, then climbed in beside her and clicked my tongue at Ebony. She set off at a jaunty gait, and despite the fact that she detested it, she did look fine pulling the wagon, feet stepping high, her long mane dancing with every step.

'Twas a fine day in May, not yet summer, but feeling every bit as if it were. A warm breeze came in from the ocean, carrying that sea scent I so loved along with it, and caressing my face and hair. A few strands fell loose, but I was enjoying the ride far too much to fuss over them. We traveled the worn track they called the Coast Road, along the very edge of the peninsula, and 'twas well and good I trusted Ebony to stay on course, for 'twas more than I could do to stop gazing out at the frothy whitecaps winking at me from that broad blue expanse.

It could be said that I disliked and distrusted the people of Sanctuary. Elias Stanton in particular. But I was utterly enchanted with the place itself. The ground beneath me and the sky above. Sea to my left, and forest to my right. 'Twas like a magick circle unto itself. I felt the earth's power here as I never had before, and perhaps it wasn't all because of the forces moving in and around this wild, new land. Perhaps 'twas another bit of my new self making its presence felt. The ability to feel the places where Mother Earth's power pulsed strongest. I sorely wished I understood more about my own nature. I knew instinctively there was far more to it than what my mother had been able to tell me. And yet how could I learn? How could I know? It plagued me like an unsolved puzzle. Why this gift of immortality? Was there some purpose to it all?

We arrived in town, and Elias Stanton himself hurried to our wagon and reached for my hand to assist me from my seat. I took it, though his touch made gooseflesh rise on my arms. The man's gaze tended to linger on my form in ways that made me uneasy, and in his eyes I often glimpsed lechery, though on the surface, he acted every bit the gentleman. I knew 'twas a lie. I could see the worms in his soul.

"Ladies," he said. "So good to see you both." His hand lingered on mine, grasping briefly when I pulled. Then he cleared his throat, averted his eyes, and released me, turning to assist my aunt. "A fine day, is it not, Mistress Belisle?"

"Fine, indeed, Mister Stanton," she replied. "But 'tis not the weather I wish to discuss, as you might well guess."

"Ah, you're curious about our new pastor, no doubt," he said with a smile.

"Tell me about him," she urged. "Is he young or old? Plump or poor?"

"You will soon see for yourself," Elias responded. And turning, offered her his arm. She took it, and he offered the other to me.

I was loath to accept. But people were watching. And more than ever, I was wary. I sensed something . . . something that made the fine hairs on my nape bristle. But I could not name what that something might be. I took his beefy arm and tried to hide my distaste.

"I vow," Aunt Eleanor said, "nothing so exciting has happened in Sanctuary since . . . why, since my dear niece arrived and restored me to health."

" 'Twas the Lord restored you to health, Aunt Eleanor," I said quickly, and I glanced at Elias from the corner of my eye. "I only took away your loneliness." To Elias, I said, "I do believe it may well have been the loneliness making her feel so poorly all along."

"Indeed," Elias asked, lifting his brows. "And are you a physician, Mistress St. James?"

My blood ran cold, and for a moment 'twas as though I was back in England, shivering outside the magistrate's door while cruel hands held me fast and a demanding voice asked a similar question of my mother.

I blinked away the rush of fear that shot through me, and reminded myself I was no longer in England. That nightmare was behind me. And then I prayed it was true.

Fixing a smile to my lips, I said, "A woman physician? Oh, Mister Stanton, surely you jest. I wouldn't know where to begin!"

His eyes, when they met mine, were filled with dark suspicions and blatant lust. And as we approached the plank steps leading up into the church, he pretended to stumble and leaned toward me, brushing his forearm against my breast. That I knew beyond doubt it was deliberate might have been intuition. Or something more. But regardless, I knew.

Startled, I turned and backed away, only to collide with a solid chest. Two warm hands closed on my shoulders, and suddenly I felt light-headed and breathless. His scent touched me, embraced me, and I knew before I even looked upon him who he was.

"Pardon," a painfully familiar voice with a sweet Scottish lilt said from behind me. "Are you all right, lass?"

I stiffened, closed my eyes, opened them slowly. And then I turned, unable to do otherwise, and looked up into the face of the man . . . the man who, more than two years ago, had seen me die. The man who'd embraced me to the point of madness, made me want him as I'd wanted no other. The man who, by rights, should believe me to be dead. The man who'd told me he'd given up his ministerial studies. Duncan Wallace. Looking just as I'd seen him that first time, on the gallows. Once again dressed in the black robes of a clergyman.

6

"So sorry, Mistress St. James," Elias blustered. He straightened away from me, but I barely felt his unwelcome presence anymore. "A damnable pebble caught in my . . . oh. I see you've met our pastor."

"St. James?" Duncan whispered, wide-eyed and suddenly pale.

If he revealed what he had seen on those English gallows . . . if he let on . . .

He suddenly gripped both my hands in his. His gaze never left my face but kept roaming it as if he couldn't believe what he was seeing. Panic caused my heart to pound. Panic . . . and his touch. His thumbs moved in gentle circles on the backs of my hands, and I thought he might not even be aware of it. I squeezed his fingers to remind him, and stared into his brown eyes, willing him to keep my secret. And then, reluctantly, I tugged my hands from his, though 'twas the last thing I wanted to do.

I remembered this man. Oh, he'd changed. He was no longer a handsome young priest, but a man grown now. And though it had been only two years, I knew that two years in this rugged new land were more than enough to bring about such changes. He was larger, broad across the shoulders and chest, and solid with strength. Even his neck seemed hard and corded with muscle. His hair was longer than before, but the same dark sable, pulled back with a thong. And his face . . .'twas harsher now. He looked weathered, as if he'd been through trying times.

All of this I took in, realizing that to his probing brown eyes, I was exactly the same. I had not changed. I never would. That he remembered me, too, was obvious.

"Do you know one another?" Elias asked, stepping closer, eyeing Duncan, and then me.

"No," I said softly. "We've never met." And I looked into Duncan's brown eyes, silently begging him to say the same.

He licked his lips once, then looked past me to Elias. "Aye, the lass speaks the truth. Had we met, I'd surely recall it," he said, his eyes laden with meaning. "Besides, I only arrived yestereve." And then, smiling, he turned to my aunt, who all but shouldered me aside to take his hand in welcome.

"I am so pleased to meet you, young man," she said. "I am Eleanor Belisle, Raven's aunt."

"Raven," he said softly, glancing my way once more. When his gaze touched my skin, 'twas as if he touched me himself. I could feel the warmth of his eyes. "So that's your name. You can't know how I've wondered . . ." Blinking, he shook his head and turned back to Aunt Eleanor. "I only hope I live up to your expectations, dear lady," he told her.

"Oh, I'm confident you will, Reverend." And taking my arm, my aunt urged me up the steps and into the church, leaving Duncan to greet other worshipers as they filed past. But I could still feel his eyes on me.

When the sermon was ended, I realized I hadn't heard a word. I'd been too caught up in the comforting sound of his voice to pay heed to the words he used. It didn't matter what he said, so long as he said it in those rich, deep tones, with the lilt of Scotland in every word. I couldn't stop staring at him, watching the graceful, powerful strides with which he would pace before the congregation as he spoke, and his magnificent hands gesturing to punctuate each line. His eyes met mine often. Those were the only times I would shake out of my state of blatant admiration of him enough to hear the words he spoke. Double entendres, shot like arrows at my heart as his dark eyes razed me in mingled anger and wonder and . . . something else. Scriptures about lies and deceit. And more, about desires of the flesh. The way they could burn a man, destroy him.

Was he bitter, then? Angry with me for leading him such a merry chase? It didn't matter. If anything, the harshness I saw in his eyes now only served to make him the more beautiful to me. I wanted the man. I knew it with a sudden, urgent pang that left me breathless. But I knew 'twas impossible. For he was a minister. And I was a Witch.

I must put him out of my mind.

I *must*.

I could not.

After the sermon and prayers concluded, the entire population of Sanctuary turned out for the mid-day meal to welcome the new minister. It was held outdoors since there was no building yet large enough to accommodate everyone for the meal.

I sat upon a blanket near a shade tree, putting out the food my aunt had brought along, when I felt his gaze on me again. And looking up, I saw him, Duncan Wallace, staring at me. He did not look away when I met his eyes. Instead, he inclined his head very slightly and then turned to go back inside the church.

He wanted me to come to him. He'd made it quite clear. My throat went dry as I rehearsed in my mind what I would say to him. I'd gone over it before, of course. Many times I'd tried to imagine what explanation I could concoct should I meet anyone who'd seen me hang. But always, I'd been imagining this man in my mind's eye. Secretly hoping, perhaps, that I would see him again one day.

"I left my shawl inside," I told my aunt.

She only looked at me and winked. "Best go and find it, then, Raven. Before someone else does."

I think she had some clue, even then, that I was truly going to speak privately with Duncan. But no hint of disapproval clouded her shining eyes.

I went inside and saw him sitting on a bench near the front of the church. My hands trembling, I went to him, stood before him, looking down, and thus having a view of the door beyond as well, lest someone come in and overhear the words he was going to say. Would he accuse me? Condemn me? I did not know.

Lifting his eyes to mine, he whispered, " 'Tis true, then, after all. You *are* alive."

I swallowed hard. More than anything, I did not wish to lie to him. Not to him. But my mother's words seemed to ring in my ears. *Trust no one. No one!* I could not tell him what I was. Especially not while he wore minister's robes. Though it galled me to deny the truth to him.

"You say such odd things, Pastor. Of course I am alive."

Holding my gaze, he shook his head slowly, wonder in his eyes. "I saw you die, lass."

Feigning shock, I lifted a hand to my breast. "You have mistaken me for someone else, then. I've never died, else how could I be here?"

"Dinna lie to me, Raven. Not to me." He rose suddenly, tall and strong and so close his body was nearly touching mine. "I cut you down myself, held your lifeless corpse in my arms, and dampened your hair with my tears. I . . ." He broke off there, closed his eyes and lowered his head as if he were too overwhelmed to go on.

My throat seemed to swell closed. "You . . . cut me down? You *wept* for me?"

He looked into my eyes, and I felt an incredible yearning build within my soul.

"You've haunted my dreams since that vile day, Raven St. James. And now you stand here before me, as beautiful and alive as you were the first time I looked into your eyes when you stood so bravely upon the gallows."

I felt a stinging in my eyes, a burning in my throat. I could not deny who I was, for he would never believe me. No more than I would have believed him, had he told me he was not that young man I remembered so vividly. The lie, then. The one I'd concocted and honed in my mind over these past two years.

"I would know you anywhere," he told me, and his hands clasped my shoulders, warm and firm. I could feel him wanting me, just by his touch. And I wanted him, too.

"I knew you on the ship," he said. "You came to me then, when I was ill."

He searched my face. I said nothing.

"Admit it to me, dammit! Have you any idea how many times I've doubted my own sanity since that night? Have you?"

"I'm sorry," I whispered. "Gods forgive me, I'm so sorry. Yes, Duncan, I came to you that night. I . . . they wanted to put you off, thought you carried the plague. I couldn't let them." With one trembling hand, I touched his cheek. "No matter the cost, I couldn't let harm come to you."

He nodded slowly, closing his eyes in relief. "I knew 'twas you. Even without the light. I'd know you even if I were blind, Raven."

"And I you, Duncan," I murmured, lowering my head. "I . . . I never forgot how you tried to help us."

"Then you will tell me the truth," he said softly.

I looked into his eyes . . . and I wanted to share this burden, this wonder, this miracle of what I was with him more than I'd ever wanted anything in my life.

And I lied to him.

" 'Twas a trick, and nothing more." I had to avert my eyes in order to force the words out. I could not lie to him while looking into his eyes. "The dress I wore that day had a high neck. Do you remember?"

"Aye, I remember everything. The dress was brown, roughly woven, with small yellow buttons up the front, all the way to your chin. An' your hair smelled of lavender."

I was warm inside. His voice was like a caress upon my very soul. "Beneath the dress I wore a steel collar. No one could see it. It protected my neck from the noose."

His eyes narrowed, probed, and plumbed mine.

"An' where did you get this collar? They said you had spent the night in the stocks."

"A friend . . . he stole into the square and slipped it round my neck."

Frowning at me, Duncan shook his head. "Nay. Even with the collar, the fall could have broken your wee neck."

And his forefinger danced across my neck as he said it, sending shivers down my spine.

"Could have," I said. "But did not."

His eyes were piercing, as if he sought to see inside my mind, to the truth hidden there.

"There was no life in you when I held you in my arms," he whispered. "You were not pretendin' that."

"No," I whispered, half afraid he'd see right through the lie. "I fainted. Perhaps from the fall . . . or the fear . . . I cannot say. But I woke in . . ." I shuddered at the memory. "In a horrible place."

His face softened then. Slowly he lowered his head. "Aye, I know about that," he said softly. Then meeting my gaze, he asked, "An' your mother? Did she wear this trick collar as well?"

I closed my eyes, my pain all too real. "Someone saw my friend and he had to run away, or be caught. There was no time for him to help her as he did me. When I woke among the dead, she was beside me . . . and . . ." Tears choked me and I could not go on.

His hand came to me, stroking my cheek. I wanted to clasp it in my own and press a kiss to his palm. But I only stood still, closing my eyes at the feelings his touch evoked. Weak with relief that I was feeling this man's touch again, as I'd so often dreamed of doing. Weak, too, with the remembered pain of finding my precious mother, dead.

"I went there," he said. "To the place where they took you. But you were not there. Nor was your mother."

I looked at him through my tears. "Why?"

"I couldna save you, lass. I thought . . . at least I might give you a proper burial."

I smiled gently at him, and he brushed a tear from my cheek.

"You're a kind man, Duncan Wallace," I said.

"Nay," he said softly, eyes going harder. "Not so kind, not when I'm lied to."

I swallowed hard. He could be a dangerous man, as well. Dangerous to me. To my life as well as my heart.

"Go on, lass. What happened when you woke?"

"I carried my mother into the forest and buried her there.

She would have been pleased with the spot I chose, I think.''

"She'd have been pleased," he said, "to know you survived.''

"She knew,'' I whispered. And then I sniffed and impatiently dashed the tears from my face. "If you tell them what you know of me, Duncan—''

"I willna tell them.''

I could only blink in surprise.

"I willna betray your secret, Raven. I swear it on all that I am. But you must tell me the truth. All of the truth.''

I couldn't look him in the eye when he asked me that. "I can only tell you that I have never brought harm to another human being. Not in all my life, Duncan. On my mother's soul, I swear 'tis the truth.''

His hand turned my face toward his again. He searched my face for a long moment, his velvet brown eyes as piercing as before. And then he nodded. "I believe you,'' he said. "But there is another question I have, and you must know what it is. I am a man of the cloth, Raven, a man of God, even though I abandoned my studies for the priesthood. And yet . . . and yet you've haunted my soul.'' He closed his eyes slowly. "I have to know the truth. Am I damning myself by lettin' you haunt my thoughts day and night? Am I, Raven? Are you, truly, a—''

The doors burst open then, and Elias Stanton, of all people, marched inside, saw us together, and stopped dead.

"Damning yourself?'' I whispered, and anger swelled in my chest until I thought I'd burst with it. "How *dare* you?''

I took a single step toward the door and stopped when I saw the way Elias was staring from one of us to the other, his cheeks reddening with anger before he hid the emotion. Instead he painted his face with a false smile.

"Wondered where you'd gone, Reverend.'' Then he nodded at me. "Mistress St. James.''

I acknowledged him with the briefest of glances, then turned to Duncan again. "Thank you for helping me find my shawl, Reverend Wallace,'' I said, my tone dripping ice. "Aunt Eleanor says I'd lose my head were it not for my neck keeping it attached.''

"Then I'm glad your neck is intact,'' he said softly, and

there was an apology in his eyes. One I refused to acknowledge. More softly, he whispered, "Very glad."

No. I would not feel this way for him. I would not.

Yet my knees were weak as I strode out of the church. And my heart, a quivering puddle.

'Twas midway through the afternoon when I drove our wagon over the worn path along the shore. My aunt prattled on about the sermon and the food and town gossip and such, but I paid little attention. I could think only of Duncan, the way he'd touched me. The look in his eyes. His promise that he would not betray me. I told myself I was angry with him for implying that my being a Witch could somehow damn his standing with his creator. And yet, I longed for the time when I might see him again. Certainly, my habit of skipping Sunday services was a thing of the past.

We were nearly home when I saw a woman in the road. Small and fair, with golden hair cut scandalously short, she was down on one knee, bending as if to tie the lace of her shoe. I drew the wagon to a halt before I spotted the pendant dangling from her neck, as she had no doubt intended me to see it. A pentacle, very like the one I wore.

As I caught my breath, I noticed the dagger that lay on the road beside her. And this was not only like my own, but identical to it.

The woman was a Witch. An immortal High Witch like me. I'd known 'twas only a matter of time before another one came for me. I'd known I should prepare myself for this day. But I wasn't prepared. Not at all.

When the woman's soft brown eyes met mine, I shivered. Perhaps I would not escape this time. Perhaps this day would be the last one I was to see. I was not willing to die. Not now, when I'd only just found Duncan again.

I was even less willing, however, to risk my aunt's safety. So, holding this strange woman's gaze, I handed the reins to Aunt Eleanor. "Go on to the cabin," I told her. "I'll be along soon."

"But, Raven . . . my goodness, girl, what's the matter? You've gone as pale as a wraith!"

"Nothing. I'm fine. I simply wish to speak with . . . an old acquaintance."

And the woman on the road straightened, gathering her dagger and slipping it into the sheath at her hip as she stepped off the track to allow the wagon to pass. She wore breeches, as a man would wear, and white stockings. Her shirt was white, with laces up the front, and she wore no cap upon her short, golden locks.

"You know this person?" Aunt Eleanor asked in surprise.

"I will tell you all about it . . . later," I promised. "Please, Aunt Eleanor, go on without me."

My aunt rolled her eyes and shook her head to make sure I knew of her displeasure, but after I stepped down, she did as I asked, snapping the reins. Ebony drew her away from me. Away from this strange woman, home to safety.

The Witch took a step forward, and I took an equal step back. And then she smiled, though only very slightly.

"You're right to be afraid, Raven St. James. But not of me."

"No?" I lifted my skirts to pull the dagger from its place at my thigh. "You'll understand if I choose caution over trust." I held the weapon in my hands, though they trembled.

The woman looked at it, then at me. For a very long time she stared at me, as if taking my measure. There was something else in her eyes. "You don't know me at all, do you, Raven?"

Narrowing my eyes on her, I said nothing, and it seemed for a moment a great sadness clouded her face. But she quickly dismissed whatever troubled her, chased it away to some dark corner, and lifted her chin once more. And then she drew her blade from its sheath, and I went rigid with fear.

But she simply tossed it. It landed at my feet, its blade embedded in the rich black earth. I looked down at it, blinking in surprise. Was this a trick?

"I am not one of the Dark Ones, Raven," she said.

"Then . . . then what do you want of me?"

She shrugged. "Would friendship be too much to ask?"

Still, I was hesitant.

Shaking her head, she untied the string that held her breeches, and as I gasped, wide eyed, she tugged them low over her right hip, revealing the crescent mark blazed on the skin there. "Now will you believe I mean you no harm?" she asked, righting the breeches and looking not the least embarrassed.

"That proves nothing. We all have the crescent mark."

"My Lord and Lady, you really are as ignorant as a babe, aren't you?"

I said nothing, only waited for her to clarify.

"The Dark Ones bear the mark on their left flank, Raven. And the moon faces the opposite way. Did you not know even that much?"

Finally I lowered my dagger. "No," I said. "I'm afraid I did not."

"Then I was right to come to you."

I met her eyes, so strangely like the eyes of a doe. Innocent and liquid, while somehow dangerous at the same time. "I don't understand."

She sighed deeply. "I shall begin at the beginning, then. I am Arianna Sinclair, and I am nearly two hundred years old." I gasped in surprise, and maybe disbelief, but she only went on. "Several months ago I heard rumors of a lovely Witch hanged in a village in England, who'd been seen by some sailors alive and well only days later. And I thought to myself, she must truly be young if she took so few precautions to disguise her identity. So I set about the task of finding you, and here I am." She picked up her dagger, wiped its blade clean of dirt, and sheathed it at her side.

I shook my head slowly. "I still do not understand," I told her, no longer backing away in fear, relaxing my defenses. "Why would you want to find me?"

"The hanging ... It was your first death, wasn't it, Raven?"

I nodded.

"Then you've much to learn. You see, young one, if I heard the rumors, if I could so easily track you down, then you must believe others will do the same. I'm here to help you, Raven. To teach you."

I stood before her now, my hands at my sides. She offered her hand, in friendship, I thought, and I took it.

And suddenly found myself twisted backward and held in small arms that had no business being so strong. My own dagger was wrenched from my hand and held to my heart, and I cried out, certain my life was about to end.

Her face close to my ear, she whispered, "First lesson, Raven. Trust no one."

I shuddered at the familiarity of those words, the way they echoed what my mother had told me. And then she released me and gently pressed my weapon back into my hand as my heart thundered against my ribs. I was breathing heavily from fear, pressing one hand to my breast as if to calm my racing heart.

"I would say, Raven, that it is a very good thing I was the first to find you."

"You weren't," I told her. And she crooked a golden brow. "Another one . . . a man, attacked me before I left England."

"And you defeated him?" Her tawny brown eyes were wide now with disbelief.

Ashamed, I lowered my head. "I escaped him. Barely."

"You survived," she told me. "There's no shame in living to fight another day, Raven. Come now, and take me to your home. I'll be needing a place to stay, and I suppose a silly dress so I can pass as one of *them*."

She expected my hospitality? After what she'd just done?

Smiling, she glanced at my dagger. "You can put that away. It will do you little good, anyway, until I've taught you to use it properly."

"I believe I'll hold on to it a bit longer," I responded.

And her smile grew wider as she nodded her approval. "Very good, Raven. You're a fast learner. You always were."

"And how would you know that?" I asked, studying her closely.

She laughed at herself, shrugging. "Oh, don't mind my cryptic comments. I'm a bit of a psychic, you know. I can read people. It's just something I picked up on. Besides, after what you've been through, having to flee for your life, start over, you'd almost have to be a fast learner, wouldn't you?''

She turned and began walking the road toward my home, glancing now and again at the tracks the wagon wheels had left in the dirt.

I had little choice but to follow her.

7

Duncan paced the length of the spartan cabin he'd been given as shelter, turned, and paced back again. The fire snapped and popped loudly, drawing his gaze, and he found himself going still, staring into the flames, remembering.

The trapdoors dropping. The girl falling, the entire weight of her body hurtling toward the ground and then stopping short at the end of that rope. The way she'd jerked at the bottom. The way her head snapped. And then the way it had fallen upon his shoulder when he cut her down, as if her neck were boneless, or made of water.

Steel collar. There *had been no* steel collar.

The flames leaped and danced, and he thought of the fire he'd seen dancing in Raven's onyx eyes. Hellfire? he wondered. Or something else?

If he were truly a man of God, he'd tell what he knew. He closed his eyes and lowered his head. Nay. If he spoke out, she'd be arrested. Harmed. Killed, perhaps. He could not believe that to be God's will, no matter what she was.

Had she done something to him? Put some spell on him? Willed him to feel these things for her? Was such a thing even possible?

Heavy steps sounded outside, and he opened the door before old Elias Stanton could announce his presence. The man's face, whiskered jowls and all, seemed grim. And he said, "We have to talk. There's . . . something you need to be made aware of."

"Come in," Duncan said. And he wondered why he was irritated at the interruption. He ought to be glad to be distracted from thinking about her. To think of her was too confusing. Seeing her again—God, his preoccupation with the woman was bordering on obsession now that he'd seen her. 'Twas all he could do to keep himself from going to her. Right now, tonight.

"I had not intended to trouble you with this, Reverend Wallace, but upon seeing you in the church with Mistress St. James this morning, I felt it necessary."

"This concerns Mistress St. James, then?"

Elias nodded and, clasping his hands behind him, began pacing much as Duncan had been doing only moments ago. "Reverend . . . I fear the woman is trouble," he said. "You recall our conversation at the Boar's Head, do you not?"

Duncan nodded, and instantly knew what Stanton would say next.

"The temptress I spoke of is none other than Mistress St. James herself."

A cold hand seemed to clutch Duncan's heart when Elias's words confirmed what he had already guessed. He lowered his head, hoping to hide the flare of alarm that widened his eyes. *Nay. Not again.*

"I fear, my friend, she may be more than just a temptress. Much more."

"Say what you mean, Elias. I dislike guessing games."

Elias shrugged. "Surely 'tis obvious. The woman could easily be a practitioner of the black arts . . . a Witch."

The hairs on the back of Duncan's neck bristled, and he found himself instinctively defending her, not even giving his words thought before speaking them. "Dinna be ridiculous, Elias. Why would you think such a thing?"

Elias turned slowly, his eyes narrow. "She's unnaturally beautiful, is she not?"

Holding that gaze, Duncan nodded. "Incredibly beautiful," he said. "But why do you say 'tis unnatural?"

"Because of the way she flaunts it before the men of this

congregation. I'll wager not a one has escaped her wiles. All of them lusting after her, I tell you, no matter how God-fearing they be. And that's her plan, Duncan. To lure us all into sin, and damn us before she moves on to the next God-loving congregation.''

Duncan felt his lips pull into a grimace of distaste. The man was a fool. ''Aye, no doubt the ruination of mankind is all the lass lives for.''

He'd meant it as sarcastic and biting. Elias only nodded in enthusiastic agreement, which made Duncan sigh, and try another approach with the thick-skulled man. ''You said before that even you have felt this Witchly allure she exudes,'' he said.

Lowering his head, Elias said, ''Yes. Though it shames me to admit it.''

''An' you dinna believe it could simply be the natural feelin' of attraction any man might feel when he sees a woman of such exceptional beauty?''

''Never,'' Elias denied flatly. '' 'Tis Witchery, I tell you. I be above desires of the flesh. Or was, 'til she worked her devilish wiles on me.''

Nodding, Duncan said, ''I'm glad you've come to me with this, Elias.'' And he was. Glad because in seeing how ridiculous the things Elias believed of Raven were, he could see more clearly how foolish he himself had been, only moments ago. Spells, indeed. He was drawn to the woman and had been since he'd first set eyes on her. And 'twas no more due to Witchery than was the sunrise or the changing phases of the moon. He desired her. And maybe more than that. Maybe . . . *much* more than that.

He searched Elias's face as he concocted his lies. And it occurred to him that he'd rarely lied in his lifetime, had always made an effort at utter honesty. But for her, for Raven, he lied without pause. Without the slightest hesitation.

He thought he'd likely be willing to do far more for her. Die for her, should the need arise.

''I've seen many Witches durin' my time in England,'' Duncan said. ''An' I can tell you beyond any doubt, Raven St. James isna one.''

Elias's face fell, eyes widening. "How can you be so sure?"

Duncan tilted his head. "Have you never *seen* a Witch?"

"No," Elias admitted. "But I was sure I had the day she arrived."

Searching for a plausible lie, then latching on to the first one he thought of, Duncan said, "The eyes of a Witch are two different colors. The left is green, and the right is blue."

"The hell you say!"

"Aye, Elias, 'tis true. And the forefinger of a Witch's hand is longer than the middle one."

Elias's eyes narrowed, and Duncan was certain he'd pushed it too far. Damn, he'd had the man believing him for a moment.

"But a skilled Witch," Elias speculated, "could likely disguise those things. Don't you see, Duncan? Something is not right with the woman! Her crops, her wealth. 'Tis not by natural means she succeeds at everything she sets her pretty hands to. All without a man to aid her!"

"Could it be that she is simply wise an' strong, an' perhaps a hard worker?" Duncan put forth.

"I want you to go out there, Duncan. Mistress Foxgrove claims they've taken in another strange young woman, and I tell you, she's likely another of their coven."

"Their *coven*? Really, Elias, I believe your imagination—"

"Go out there tonight, Duncan. They liked you, the both of them. Pretend to be making a social call. And see what sorts of things they keep about that cabin. See how they behave when they're alone and not in the public eye."

"You want me to spy on them?" Duncan asked, already formulating the firmest refusal he could concoct.

"Yes. And if you won't, Duncan, I'll do it myself. However, I'm loath to get that close to her. I fear she'd bewitch me even further. You're a man of God, Duncan, surely you'd be far safer than I?"

Closing his eyes slowly, shaking his head, Duncan recalled the distaste he'd seen in Raven's eyes when this man had touched her. She wouldn't like him snooping around. And suppose Elias should find something?

He hadn't admitted it, even to himself, at least not con-
sciously, but Duncan knew there must be something to find.
Some truth to Elias's suspicions. Raven *was* magick. Everything about her was mystical and potent. She'd cured him
of whatever illness he'd been suffering aboard the *Sea
Witch*. He didn't doubt these things.

But she *wasn't* evil. No matter what else she was, she
wasn't that.

And even if there were nothing for Elias to find in
Raven's cabin, almost anything could be construed by his
suspicious, fearful mind as evidence. At least if Duncan
went himself, he could return with a favorable report.

"All right, Elias," he said softly. "I shall go. But meanwhile, do one thing for me?"

"Of course, Reverend."

"Tell no one else of your suspicions. Should you be
wrong about Mistress St. James, you could easily destroy
her good name with such gossip. And you wouldna wish to
do that should she be innocent, would you, now?"

He grunted and huffed, saying clearly that he *could not*
believe her innocent, *would not* be proved wrong.

"Please," Duncan urged. " 'Twould only send the town
into panic."

Elias's face softened then. "All right, I shall keep my
suspicions to myself . . . for now. Except for . . ." He narrowed his eyes on Duncan. "Never mind."

"Except for what?" Duncan asked, and he felt a cold
foreboding in his heart. "Have you already spoken these
suspicions, Elias?"

Elias averted his eyes. " 'Tis of no concern to you," he
said. "You'll report back to me upon your return?"

Shaking his fears away, Duncan faced the man. "Aye,
I'll report to you, but on the morrow, Elias. " 'Tis a long
walk, an' I'll no doubt prefer sleep to conversation when I
return."

"Tomorrow then," Elias said, and touching the brim of
his hat, he backed out the door.

He wasn't going to her so he could spy on her, as Elias
wished him to do. He was going to warn her. Duncan was

certain she could have no clue what Elias suspected of her, or she'd have fled this place by now.

For just a moment, as he followed the road that led along the southern edge of the peninsula, overlooking the sea, he paused to wonder at the irony of what he was doing. Raven St. James had been convicted of Witchery and sentenced to death. He'd seen her die with his own eyes, only to find her alive and well, and again suspected of Witchcraft. And yet, he, a man of God, was about to warn her.

Worst of all, it wasn't that he disbelieved the accusations against her. Not that at all. 'Twas that he simply didn't care. *He didn't care.* He remembered all too well the way he'd seen her standing in the moonlight, felt the power surging from her hands into his body that night aboard the ship. It could have been a dream, but he didn't think so. And still, he didn't care.

He only wanted to see her again. To get to know all there was to know of her. To understand the workings of her mind and the mysteries of her soul. To know what she was thinking. And to see to it she remained safe from harm.

Nothing else mattered. And as little sense as that made, he didn't question it. It simply was.

Duncan knew what he would report to Elias, no matter what he found at Raven's cabin tonight. In the morn he intended to assure Elias all was as it should be, thus ending the elder's speculation.

But not, perhaps, ending his lust.

Duncan's flesh heated and he tugged at the too tight collar that suddenly chafed his throat. He wore an ordinary pair of breeches and a white shirt, this night. For some reason, he disliked the thought of going to Raven in the robes of clergy. He sensed the clothing threatened her, somehow, and that wasn't what he wished to do.

He didn't like thinking about the way Elias looked at Raven St. James. He didn't like Elias's insistence that all the men of Sanctuary must be looking at her the same way as he. And he didn't like that he himself was just as drawn to her as the rest. Because he wanted to believe that with him 'twas different.

At last her cabin came into view, and he saw the soft

glow of candles in one of the windows. 'Twas a simple home, graying logs, set high on the cliffs overlooking the Atlantic. Pretty curtains of white, perhaps made by Raven's own delicate hands, hung in the few windows of imported glass. And the door was hand hewn, a single thick board sawed from what must have been a mighty oak tree once. The area around the house was lush with gardens. Herbs grew in tangled patches along with vegetables and flowering plants. All bathed tonight in the light of the moon, so that the place looked wild and untamed and mysterious. The waves crashing against the rocky shore far below were like a chorus, a magickal chorus. This place made him think of the enchanted palace where the sleeping princess of a fairy tale awaited rescue.

Duncan moved closer, lifted his hand to tap on the door, only to pause when the sound of singing reached his ears. Raven's voice, rich and beautiful, drifted over him like warmed honey. He'd heard that voice in his dreams often over the past three years. Heard it ringing out in condemnation of a crowd of bloodthirsty bigots. But he'd never heard it sweetly singing the words of a love song.

> I've longed to taste your kiss, my love.
> To hold you would be sweet bliss, my love.
> My heart shall break, 'ere you wait too long.
> Come to me, come love me, come answer my
>   song.

"Raven," he whispered. His heartbeat quickened, and his stomach muscles clenched as if in response to her words. He steadied himself, or tried to, but he was shaken to the core. And even as he told himself not to, he leaned closer to peer through the window beside the door, where the pretty white curtains stood slightly parted.

Raven St. James reclined in a large metal tub, water and bubbles brimming around her. Her arms moved, long and graceful and shiny-slick with moisture. One hand squeezed a cloth she held high above her as she leaned back in the tub. Water trickled over her neck and shoulders. Bare skin glistened in the candlelight as she tipped her head back, eyes closed as if in some secret ecstasy. And he wondered if she were thinking of him as she continued to sing.

> For two years, in secret, I've yearned, my
> love
> Forever it seems I have burned, my love,
> Your love is forbidden, you can't want
> me, too.
> Come to me, sweet Duncan, and tell me
> you do.

She ran her fingertips slowly along the underside of her chin, tracing a path down over her neck, her chest, and lower, to where he could no longer see.

And then, quite suddenly, she stopped. Slowly she lowered her head and leveled her gaze on the very window he was peering through, and Duncan caught his breath. Her eyes met his—though he was certain she couldn't see him out here in the darkness. Still they met his, and held them. He couldn't look away. Not for the life of him. It seemed to Duncan as if every cell in his body came to vivid life in that moment, stirred by her gaze and aroused to action. He tingled with awareness. As if he were the one caught naked and she the one shamelessly looking on.

And as he remained there, riveted, he heard a voice call the woman's name from another room. Raven's head turned toward its summons. A brief glance toward the window again, and perhaps a very slight smile. So slight he could have easily imagined it. And then she rose from the water like a Pagan goddess of old, and Duncan felt himself burn. Rivulets streamed down her body. She gleamed in the golden light of the dancing candles. Gleamed and shone as she daintily stepped from the tub onto the folded rug beside it. She showed no shyness, no shame as she blotted herself dry with a small cloth. Nor should she, for she was truly magnificent to behold. Sensuality surrounded her like a nimbus, her every movement as graceful as a dance. And he was aroused, tempted as he'd never been before.

'Twas said by those who'd taught him that to bathe fully naked was sinful. To touch one's own body with the delib-

erate caress with which she'd run her hands over hers was
to incite forbidden desires. Even to bathe too often was to
embrace the sin of vanity. He'd never agreed with all of
those teachings, and bathed often himself, feeling 'twas better to be vain than to stink. But for the first time, Duncan
realized that perhaps there was wisdom in those particular
teachings of the Church. For his loins were on fire as he
watched her. She was, in that moment, the very temptress
he'd been warned against.

But unwittingly. She was innocent. She couldn't know he
was watching. And in fact, 'twas he who was to blame for
the fire burning in his soul right now. For he had no business
peering through the woman's windows. And yet, 'twas as if
he'd been drawn there by some power beyond his will. And
then held there by the force of her gaze.

She moved like a seductress, every inch of her body exposed to him as she turned and reached for a robe. And then
she pulled it on, covering her feminine curves and delicate
thighs and full, ripe breasts. And finally she moved out of
the room, toward the sound of her aunt, calling her name
once again.

"Is she as beautiful as you thought she would be?"

Duncan went rigid as the feminine voice came from behind him, and he whirled to face a small, fair woman he'd
never seen before. "I . . . that is, I was only—"

"You're the preacher, aren't you?" she asked.

"Aye. Duncan Wallace, mistress." He fought to regain
his composure.

"Well, Duncan Wallace, if I thought she'd mind your
snooping, I'd gut you right here. Lucky for you I happen to
know she wouldn't mind. Not at all."

He felt his face heating and lowered his head. "I wasna
snoopin', as you put it, mistress. My attention was drawn
by her singin', and—"

"Like a songbird," the woman interrupted. Then she
turned toward the door and pulled it open. "Well, come on
inside. You may as well let her know you're here."

Duncan, uncomfortable at being caught looking at Raven,
and yet sensing somehow the small woman beside him held
no judgment over him, stepped inside.

"Raven," the woman called. "You have a guest."

"Oh?" She stepped from the small bedroom, then went
still as she met Duncan's eyes. "Oh," she whispered.

Was she embarrassed? Did she realize he might have
heard the words of her song? His name floating from her
lips with such longing? At that moment he battled the urge
to sweep her into his arms, even knowing how inappropriate
that would be. They barely knew each other. And yet it felt
very much as if they did.

"I see you've met Arianna," Raven said, as if searching
for something to say.

"She didna tell me her name."

"I got the distinct impression you couldn't care less about
my name, Reverend," Arianna said. "Raven, take the man
out for a moonlight walk. Show him the gardens, introduce
him to Ebony, for heaven's sake."

"I . . . all right. If you want to, Duncan."

He nodded. "Aye, I'd like very much to walk with you,
Raven. We have . . . much to talk about."

Nodding, she took a dark cloak lined with fur from a peg
on the wall, and Duncan impulsively stepped forward, taking it from her hands. Moving behind her, he gently draped
it over her shoulders. His fingers brushed the flesh of her
neck before moving away. God, how he wanted to touch
her.

"Th-thank you."

His hands settled there on her shoulders for a moment.
He didn't want to take them away. But he had to, or she'd
surely know the direction his thoughts were taking.

He opened the door and let her lead him outside. Her hair
was still wet, and as he walked close beside her he could
smell the scent of honeysuckle clinging to her skin.

She didn't show him the gardens, or introduce him to
anyone named "Ebony." Instead, she led him out to the
very edge of the cliffs. The wind gusted there, lifting her
wet hair from her shoulders and snapping it like a whip. She
faced the sea, staring out over the churning water, glancing
down at the sheer drop to the rocks below.

"This is my favorite place," she said. "I love the sea."

It struck him that he'd been thinking the very same thing,

as he'd been walking out here. That he loved the sea.

"There's a small island out there, not far at all from shore. It sits all alone. No one ever seems to go near. I've felt like that . . . alone. Isolated from the rest of the land and surrounded by an element very different from me."

"I've often felt that way myself," he told her. "As if I dinna quite fit in with the rest of mankind. Dinna . . . ken the way their minds work. Canna make sense of them."

She nodded, and was still for a moment. Then, "Why did you come?" She asked the question of him, but she didn't face him.

He stood beside her, staring out over the water just as she did. "I dinna know," he told her. "I was compelled to come, Raven."

She nodded.

"I couldna forget you, after that cold dawn in the square. But I've told you that."

"Yes." She turned to face him. "I believe a bond was formed between us on the gallows, Duncan. Easy enough to understand, really. You were the only man there who seemed to care."

"I did care," he said. And he clasped her shoulders now, stepping closer to her, staring down into those ebon pools. "One look into your eyes, and I cared more than I'd cared for anythin' in my life. Raven, I tried," he whispered. "I swear to you, I tried to stop them."

Her hand came up suddenly, palm flattening to his cheek, cupping it in a way that was somehow soothing. "I know you tried, Duncan. There is no reason for you to feel guilty for what they did. I knew you were no part of any of that. You risked your own life to prevent it, in fact. You don't need to convince me. I was there."

He nodded. And overwhelmed by feeling, by desire, he turned his face against her palm, let his lips touch it, kiss its tender center before rubbing his cheek against it once more. "Aye, you were there. So you know what I do. Raven . . . there is something here. Some powerful emotion between you and me. You must feel it."

She lowered her hand, and then her head. "I feel . . . desire for you, Duncan.'' Then she closed her eyes. ''But 'tis a desire you believe will damn your soul.''

He was stunned at the bluntness of it. He'd never met a woman who spoke so plainly. But he cleared his throat. ''I dinna believe that at all. I spoke . . . without thinkin'. Raven, I burn for you, 'tis true. But I feel for you, too. And what I feel is the purest and most holy sort of carin' I can imagine. It canna be evil. It canna be damning. An' if 'twere . . .'twouldna matter, lass.''

Slowly she lifted her head, met his eyes again. ''And what do you propose we do about this feeling?''

Her black eyes fairly blazed. Duncan drew a breath, battled temptation. ''We resist it, Raven. But only until we can be married.''

''Married?''

The fire in her eyes seemed to cool, and she lowered her chin. He caught it in his hand and lifted it up again, until she faced him. ''The Scriptures say 'tis better a man marry than to burn with lust,'' he said.

''What your Scriptures say means very little to me, Duncan.'' She sniffed and met his eyes. ''My faith has only one rule.''

''Only one?'' He searched her face. ''An' what *is* this rule you live by, Raven?''

'' 'An it harm none, do what thou will.' '' She shrugged. '' 'Tis the only rule I've ever needed, the only one that makes sense to me.''

'' 'Tis a good rule. But it doesna say, 'Thou shalt nay marry.' ''

''Marriage between us . . . is something that can never be.''

''But—''

''I will harm none, Duncan. To marry you . . . I'd harm *you*, you must see that. 'Twould ruin you. I stand convicted of Witchcraft and sentenced to death. And even here, the suspicions about me have begun to stir anew. No, I can be no preacher's wife.''

''Were you my bride, Raven, they would no longer suspect you.''

"Perhaps not," she said softly. "But would you?" She faced him, searching his eyes.

Duncan shook his head. "I will believe whatever you tell me, Raven. If you say you're innocent, I willna doubt it, I swear."

"And what if I can't claim innocence, Duncan? What if I am what they say I am?"

He gripped her shoulders, staring down into her eyes. "Are you?"

She lowered her eyes. "That's just it. I cannot tell you *what* I am. I've seen what trusting others can do, Duncan. Seen it in my mother's eyes just before they murdered her."

"You *can* trust me, lass," he said softly.

"But I can't. And you would want no wife who kept such dark secrets from you, Duncan."

"You're wrong," he said. "Raven, I dinna *care* what you are."

"How can you say that?"

"Because, lass, 'tis the truth."

She shook her head slowly. "Perhaps it is, at the moment. But you *will* care, Duncan. The time will come when you'll demand I tell all, and that is something I can never do." She cupped his face in her hands. "We cannot be together as husband and wife."

"An' I canna go on without you," he whispered.

"Then be with me, Duncan," she urged. "Come to me in the cloak of midnight, and in secret. For that's the only way a love like ours can be. A love for the moment, fleeting and precious. Forbidden, and consigned to darkness."

"'Twill be more," he whispered. "I vow, Raven, I will make it more." And then he pulled her into his arms and kissed her as he'd been dreaming of kissing her. And it didn't matter that she was keeping secrets, or that she hadn't denied the charges against her. All that mattered was this, holding her, alive and warm and real, in his arms, against his body.

And perhaps loving her this way was a sin. If it was, then he'd gladly be damned, because he couldn't resist . . . nor did he want to.

8

He kissed me as I'd never been kissed by another. He kissed me as I'd been kissed only once—by him, on the *Sea Witch* as the fever and the ale mingled in his blood. I'd thought, in some secret part of me, that he wouldn't have touched me had he been sober and well.

But he was sober now. And healthy. And strong.

He swept me away there on the cliffs. His hands in my hair, touching it in some kind of wonder, as if he'd never felt anything so soft. His lips, brushing my neck and caressing my ear as he whispered sweet love words in his soft, Scot's lilt.

I'd told him I desired him. I dared not feel anything more. And yet I was not certain I could resist. He was like the sea, hurling its waves against the rocky shore below us, and slowly, steadily eroding the solid rock away. Bit by bit. As gentle, as softly as water, he wooed me. And the stone I thought was my heart began softening beneath his touch, even now.

"I've dreamed of this," I whispered. "Of you . . . ."

"And I, lass . . . night after endless night."

His hands deftly untied my cloak, and it fell to the ground, shaping itself into a perfect nest. Then his hands touched the robe I wore, trembling, as if he knew there was nothing underneath. And perhaps he did know, for I'd sensed him watching at the window, glimpsed movement there as I'd bathed. One moment certain he had come to me, the next convinced I was only imagining what my mind told me.

Slowly, hesitantly, he parted my robe, and then the sea wind came in to complete his task, pushing it wide so it flew behind me like a cape. Duncan's gaze burned on my body, sliding up and down me as if he were glimpsing Divinity itself.

"You're almost too beautiful to touch," he whispered. Then he met my eyes. "An' far too beautiful not to."

His hands, tender and careful, came to me. Slid slowly from the column of my neck down the front of me, and I held my breath. At last he touched my breasts, palms skimming over them, pausing there as he closed his eyes.

" 'Tis heaven I touch," he murmured.

"No, Duncan, 'tis earth itself." I pressed myself closer. "And I'll not break at your caresses."

At my word he squeezed, gently at first, with more pressure when I closed my eyes and released all my breath at once. And then he pulled me to him for more kisses, and his hands slipped around to the small of my back, and lower to stroke my naked buttocks, and my thighs. I shoved my hands between our bodies to tug at the laces of his shirt and breeches. He'd come to me tonight without the protection of his dark minister's robes. He'd come to me as a man. A man like no other.

And I knew it even more so when I'd undressed him fully and looked upon him. He hadn't been like this before. His chest had broadened, and his shoulders seemed capable of bearing any weight. His belly was tight and hard, hips lean. And he was aroused. Fully so, and the sight of him made my heart tremble. I touched him. Closed my hand around him, and understood, I think, the incredible magickal power of the mating of woman and man. I'd heard of it, of course. But never had it made sense to me. I saw it now, though. How he would fill me, complete me. How the scales of nature would hover for a time in perfect balance while I held him inside of me.

He breathed again only when I took my hand away. And then I lowered myself to the cushion of my cloak, reclining slightly, and opened myself to him. "Come, Duncan. I can wait no longer."

For an endless moment he stared at me lying there wantonly. The sea wind blew harsher, brushing over my nipples with its chilled breath, touching my secret places with icy hands. Goose bumps rose on my flesh, while inside I burned.

I lifted one hand to him, and he knelt. "I have never . . ." he began.

"Nor I," I whispered.

"We've been waiting then. For each other, I think." He looked into my eyes, expecting my agreement, but I said nothing. "Dinna tell me you dinna believe it, Raven, for I know you do. I know you as I know myself . . . somehow. We were meant to be, you and I."

"Perhaps," I whispered, but I could tell him no more. To let myself believe in his romantic notions . . . would only lead to heartbreak.

"I've been told it can be difficult for a woman . . . the first time." He knelt beside me. His fingertips danced over my neck and my shoulders.

"Not for me, Duncan. Not with you."

He kissed me again, so slowly, so deeply. "I'd nay harm you for the world, Raven."

"You won't." My words came in breathless sighs now.

He nodded, bent to nibble my ear, taste my neck. "My best friend . . . he says 'tis easier if the woman is . . . made ready."

I smiled, eager only to be on with it. I wanted him so much I could barely lie still. "How will you make me ready, Duncan? Rub me with sage like a turkey?"

Sitting back slightly, he looked at the nest between my legs, licked his lips. "Like this," he whispered, and then he touched me there. Gently he parted my folds and put his fingers on me, and I drew a gasp as a bolt of pleasure shot through my loins. Slowly he rubbed, exploring, watching my face so intently I thought he was trying to read my thoughts. When he pressed inside me, I cried out in delight, and arched my hips off the ground. How I wanted him.

"You've made me ready, then," I whispered.

"Oh, nay, lass. There is more my friend spoke of."

He bowed over me, and kissed me between my legs like a worshiper kissing the feet of a goddess. He opened me with his fingers, and kissed me again, and I moaned. And then his tongue snaked out, licking me, darting at the tiny nub that seemed to be the core of my desire, and then plunging inside as if he would devour me whole. Tears filled my eyes at the intensity of what he did to me, and I moved against him, pressing closer, losing myself to utter physical sensation as he probed and licked and tasted every part of me. My hands clenched in his hair as the tension in me tightened unbearably. Finally he moved up my body, nipping at my breasts, and then suckling them hard, no longer gentle, but seeming aroused beyond the ability to be so.

He settled atop me. I was so alive with sensation that when I felt him pressing inside me, 'twas as if lightning struck. I pressed my hands to his buttocks, gripping him tight, and I arched hard against him, to take him into me, all the way, all at once. There was a brief stab of pain, but I was so enraptured in pleasure that it felt good to me. Then he began to move, and I moved, too, sensing his needs, knowing his feelings as I knew my own. He fed at my mouth and my throat and my breasts by turns as he plunged himself into me again and again. He drove me nearer and nearer to something I'd never known. And finally the stars seemed to explode around me and I screamed his name, even as he stabbed deeper than before and cried mine.

He held me, slowly relaxing in my arms. Kissed my hair, my face, asked if I were all right, if he had hurt me.

"I am more than all right," I told him, running my hands over the wonderful expanse of his back, his shoulders. So firm and hard to my touch. "I never knew, Duncan. I never understood . . ."

"Understand this, bonny Raven." Framing my face with his hands, his directly above me, staring down with his heart in his eyes, he whispered, "I love you. I love you from the very depths of my soul. I would die for you, Raven St. James, an' never regret it for a moment."

I looked at him, guilt showing in my eyes, I think, when I bit my lip to keep from answering him in kind. The words bubbled up in my throat, but I refused to let them spill out.

"Nay, dinna look that way, my love. I know you dinna return my feelings . . . just yet. But you will, Raven. You will."

Lowering my lids to shield my true feelings from him, I shook my head. "I've given you all I have to give. My body. My virginity. And my promise, Duncan, that there will be no other man for me. Not ever."

"Truly?"

I nodded. "I do not lie."

"But canna quite trust me with the truth."

"I told you I—"

"Nay. 'Tis all right, Raven." He stroked my hair, staring down at me with love pouring from his eyes and spilling over me like the very elixir of the gods. "I am too in love to complain, to demand. I'll lie at your feet like a cur dog, awaitin' whatever crumbs drop from your fingers, and re-velin' should you bestow even a pat on the head. Whatever you give me, I'll relish and cherish and return a thousand-fold, lass. I vow it, until the day I die, I'll love only you." He lifted my hand, pressed his lips to my fingers. "And eventually, you'll see that I'd sooner die than betray you. You'll ken that you can trust me as you can no other. You'll tell me all, my love, and you'll grow to love me, too."

I stared back at him, and wondered how he could miss what seemed to be bursting from my very soul, what must show in my eyes. I already did love him, too.

But if I told him the truth . . .

No, I couldn't. I'd be putting him at risk by trusting him. He'd be stripped of his position, driven from the town or worse, arrested and tried as my accomplice. And yes, there was more. There was that selfish fear, that gnawing certainty inside me that he would stop loving me if he knew the truth.

I'd never tell him. I'd never risk that. What we had— what we shared between us—would have to be enough.

Though I could never say it aloud, I would always, *always* love him.

•   •   •

Elias was waiting when Duncan made his way back to his cabin in town.

Duncan hadn't realized it, of course. He'd been humming to himself, happier than he could remember being, but at the same time battling a sense of dread. He'd sinned. He knew that. He didn't blame Raven for it, didn't even regret it, really. But he did wonder how he could put on his robes tomorrow morn and go about the town folk acting as if he were still their spiritual leader. Their Christian guide. How could he? None of them was likely to have committed the sins he had this night. He'd be pretending, playing a role that was utterly false.

But how *could* it be wrong to love this way? When he felt the emotion bubbling up from some bottomless well within him. It didn't *feel* sinful. It *felt* noble and pure and utterly . . . utterly *right*. It didn't even feel new, but ancient, as if it had been a part of him from the time before time was, if such a thing were possible.

He stopped humming when he reached his door, as doubts crept into his mind once again. But when he stepped inside, a deep voice chased those doubts away.

"Whatever could have taken you so long, Reverend Wallace? You've been gone for *hours*."

Duncan went stiff, searching the darkness and finally spotting Elias in the room's only chair, near the dying fire. "You told me to observe the women," he said. "So I did."

"Surely they're abed by now."

"Of course they are." Duncan walked to a table where a lamp sat and lit it, taking his time, setting the glass chimney in place with great care. Stalling as he sought an explanation in his mind.

"You remained out there, even after the women retired?" Elias asked, running short of patience, Duncan thought.

"Naturally," he replied.

"But why?"

It came to him slowly, and that's the way he spoke, slowly, carefully piecing the words together one by one. "You . . . obviously know naught of Witches, Elias." He paced to the hearth, tossed a pair of logs atop the coals, since Stanton had apparently been too lazy to do so himself.

The flames licked up at the wood, searing the bark black and seeking the meatier wood beneath it. "Their . . . rites . . . are performed by night. Midnight bein' the, ah, the Witchin' Hour."

"Ahhh, the Witching Hour." Elias nodded, and his eyes took on an eager gleam in the lampglow and firelight. "And did they? Did they strip off their garments and dance naked beneath the moon at midnight? Did they kill a calf and drink its blood or mate with a goat possessed by their beastly master? Did they?"

Duncan's stomach clenched. He felt ill. And he knew with unrelenting certainty that Raven would never do such things as those of which Stanton spoke. If she were a Witch, then Stanton's ideas about Witches were pure fancy. There was something spiritual, something holy, about Raven St. James. He'd sensed it from the start.

"They did nothin' of the sort," he said very calmly. "They only slept."

Elias rubbed his chin. "Perhaps they knew you were still lingering about. They can sense such things, can they not?"

Duncan shrugged. "Nay, not in a man of the cloth," he replied. Anything, any lie, to relieve the man of his notions. Elias Stanton was dangerous to Raven. Duncan knew it to his bones.

Elias nodded thoughtfully. "Then perhaps 'twas simply not their night to practice their Pagan rites."

Closing his eyes, Duncan lowered his head. "There was naught in the cabin to indicate . . ."

"You seem so certain, Reverend. Are you sure they didn't bewitch *you*?"

He shook his head rapidly. "I'm utterly sure of that, sir."

"Hmm. Well, the situation bears watching. Just to be safe. Wouldn't you agree?"

Did he have a choice? Nay. He'd already made Elias wary of him. He had to keep the man's trust if he were to have any hope of protecting Raven from him. "I agree completely," he said. "Rest assured, Elias, I will be keepin' a very close eye on the goin's on at that cabin on the cliffs. A very close eye."

"Good." Elias got to his feet. "I'll let you get some rest, then. Good night."

And he hurried out the door.

Had Elias believed a word Duncan had said to him? There was no way to be sure. Raven should leave this place. She should leave at once. And he would warn her of that. Should have done so tonight as he'd intended, but ... well, her touch, her kisses, had chased everything else from his mind. Tomorrow. Aye. He'd warn her of the danger that lived here in Sanctuary for her. He'd warn her on the morrow.

"You have the look of a woman well loved," Arianna said just as she lunged forward and swept her dagger in a deadly arc that could easily have gutted me on the spot. She looked all innocence this morning, with the early sunlight gleaming from her cropped golden hair, and her slight frame and small stature. But she could be a deadly opponent. I'd seen that right away.

And a good friend. I'd come to love her very much in the short while she'd been with us. So much so that I hoped she would never decide to leave. 'Twas as if I'd known her always, though that could not be possible.

"Perhaps there's no need to tell you so ...." She slashed at me again, nearly nicking me this time, but I danced backward just out of reach of the gleaming blade. "But I think it a poor idea."

I thrust, she dodged. "Why?" I asked. "Is he not the most beautiful man you've ever seen, Arianna?"

"With perhaps one exception," she said with a careless shrug. "But he's also a man of the cloth."

"Which means he's in touch with the Almighty, just as we are."

"Which means he believes Witches should be put to death."

I went still, and so did she. Our blades raised, our bodies poised in ready crouches, we paused to catch our breath, and to lock gazes as she awaited my reaction to her words.

"Duncan tried to prevent the hanging that killed my mother," I said. "He's not like the rest."

"Can you be sure?"

I blinked, lowered my head. "I . . . yes, I'm sure."

Arianna shrugged. "I am not," she said. "And I'm equally doubtful of your judgment where he's concerned. I suppose 'tis lucky for you I'm here to watch out for you." She slashed at me again, neatly slicing the fabric that covered my middle this time.

I jumped back. "Be careful, would you? You could have cut me!"

"And what would it matter?" Arianna asked with a grin. "You're immortal. You would heal."

" 'Twould hurt all the same," I replied, scowling, but lifting my own dagger to waist height before thrusting it forward in a quick darting motion, drawing back just as quickly.

"Better *I* hurt you than your preacher man, Raven. I've a feeling you'd recover from the nick of my blade far more quickly than from a broken heart," she said, and jumped sideways to avoid my blade. The act sent her off balance, and I leaped forward, shouldering her hard and sending her to the ground.

"Aha!" I shouted, and leaped on Arianna, straddling her middle, braced up on my knees. One hand gripped Arianna's wrist, immobilizing the dagger she still clutched, while the other held my own blade to my friend's throat. "I have you now!"

Arianna yanked one of her legs out from beneath me, planted a foot on my chest, and shoved hard, all in the space of a heartbeat. As I went sprawling onto my back, Arianna bounced to her feet without using her hands.

"Overconfidence is the quickest path to defeat. Never underestimate the enemy." Then she laughed. "That was good, though. You grow better every day."

"It does not feel as if I do."

"You do." Arianna's smile gentled. "You know I am only concerned for your safety, don't you? If I did not care for you, I'd keep my opinions to myself."

"I know, Arianna. I just happen to disagree."

"You could get yourself hurt. You know that."

She looked so sad, and I wondered if she spoke with the

voice of experience. "I know," I said. "But 'tis worth the risk to have him, even for a little while."

She held out a hand. I took it, and Arianna pulled me to my feet, then spun me around and held me fast, her blade at my throat. "I cannot believe," she said close to my ear, laughter in her voice, "you fell for that one *again*!"

"Raven!"

'Twas Duncan's voice, startled and horrified. He came out of the nearby trees and into view, staring in utter terror at Arianna, her blade, my throat. "Let her go!"

Arianna glanced down into my eyes, her own sparkling with undisguised mirth. Then she looked at Duncan and shrugged. "Oh, all right. If you insist," she said. She released me, and then she threw her blond head back and laughed in a voice that rang with the clarity of bells.

I couldn't help it. I bent my head to hide it, but my shoulders shook as I, too, gave in to quiet laughter.

Poor Duncan only stood there, staring from one of us to the other in confusion. "I dinna ken . . . Raven, are you—"

"I'm fine, Duncan. Arianna and I were only . . . practicing."

He frowned, looking me over from head to toe and frowning even harder. "You're . . . you're wearin' *breeches*!"

"Being a man," Arianna said, "you've likely never tried to fight in skirts, but I can tell you, Duncan, 'tis no easy task."

I sent her a quelling glance and sought a plausible explanation. "We're learning to defend ourselves, Duncan. That is all. We're unmarried women living alone in a small settlement. We simply feel it the wise thing to do."

"The wise thing to do," he countered, "would be to marry."

The mirth fled me and regret replaced it in my heart. "Please stop asking. You know I cannot."

"You will, eventually." He came closer. "So, will you show me the finer points of combat with blades?"

"If I did, then how would I ever overpower you?" I asked.

"The same way you do now, my love, with a simple glance."

I smiled as he came to me, wrapped me in his arms, and hugged me so tenderly I nearly cried.

"How did you find us, Duncan?" Arianna asked him, even now sliding her blade into its sheath. "We thought coming here the height of discretion."

"Discretion is a fine idea," he replied. "For if 'twere someone besides me to see you both in breeches, fighting as if to the death, there would be scandal indeed in the streets of Sanctuary." He lowered his head. "More so than there already is." Then slowly he lifted it, met my eyes again. "Your aunt told me you'd gone walkin' in the woods. Once I got near enough, I simply followed the sounds of battle."

I smiled at that, but the smile he returned was a sad one.

"Something troubles you," I said.

"Indeed. Elias Stanton suspects . . ." He slanted a worried glance toward Arianna, as if about to say something she shouldn't overhear.

"Never fear," she quipped. "I know exactly what that fool suspects. More than likely, he suspects me of the same things."

"Aye, more than likely," Duncan agreed. Then he gripped my hands in his. "You should leave this town, Raven. At once. I dinna believe 'tis safe for you here."

I sighed deeply.

"You knew this day would come, Raven. We've spoken of it," Arianna said.

I nodded but met Duncan's eyes. "I'll not go. I'll not pack up and move away from . . ." I bit my lip.

"From what?" he pressed, squeezing my hands.

Closing my eyes, I whispered, "From you, Duncan. I don't want to leave you."

He smiled, then seemed to catch his lip between his teeth as if to stop its trembling. "You love me, lass. You either dinna ken it yet, or canna admit it to me, but you do. You love me."

"Stop it, please . . ."

"All right. All right." But he pulled me tight, kissed me softly, before he let me go and spoke once more. "I thought . . . I thought to go with you, Raven. If you'd have me."

My brows bent until they touched. "But all you have is here. Your home, your position, your friends in Boston."

"All I have, nay, all I *wish* to have, ever," he whispered, "is here, right here in my arms."

Pressing my lips tight, I averted my eyes. "My aunt Eleanor is not a young woman," I told him. "She'd never leave this place."

"She isna the one in danger here, Raven. You are."

Arianna spoke then, coming closer to the two of us. Though she disapproved of my relationship with Duncan, she seemed to understand it. And she would neither nag nor play the part of my judge. Witches didn't work that way. She'd voiced her opinion. Now she would leave it at that.

"I have to agree with the pastor on this point, Raven," she said, then she glanced at Duncan and lifted her brows. "Imagine that."

I saw Duncan smile at her, a tentative smile, and one Arianna returned, just as hesitantly. They would become friends, in time. I felt certain of that.

"It doesn't matter that you both agree," I said. "Eleanor's husband built that house for the two of them. She clings to her husband's memory by remaining there, and if she leaves . . .'twould be like cutting the roots from some great tree. She would wither and die."

"How can you know that, Raven?" Duncan asked.

"Oh, she can. Believe me, she can." Arianna lowered her head and shook it.

"She took me in when I had nowhere else to go, Duncan," I told him. "And in the time I've been with her, I've come to love her very much. She . . . she is all I have left of my own mother. Can't you see that?"

"Of course I can see it," he said harshly. "What I canna see is you dyin' *because* of it."

Meeting his gaze, I whispered, "She has only a year left in her, Duncan."

"She has . . . ?" He looked at me sharply, then at Arianna, who only lifted her brows and shoulders, and then turned to study a tree as if it held great interest. "How can you be sure of that?"

I lowered my eyes. The truth was, I'd studied the lines

of Aunt Eleanor's palm, and I knew. I'd restored her health, she would enjoy what remained of her time on this plane, but when a person's purpose was done, they moved on, and all the magick in the Universe couldn't change that. "I simply know it."

He nodded. "Another of those things about which you canna tell me?"

"I owe her so much," I said, brushing past his question as if he hadn't spoken it. "I'll not ask her to give up the home she loves, leave the place where her dear husband lies buried, spend the last year of her life miserable. I cannot. 'Tis only a year, Duncan. Perhaps less. Surely Elias Stanton and his suspicions can be put off that long."

Duncan looked frustrated. He turned away from me, pushing a hand through his hair. But when he faced me once more, his jaw was set. "I'll see to it you're protected then. He willna harm you, Raven. I vow it on all that I hold sacred."

"You mustn't do that," I protested. "I won't have it, Duncan. Understand that."

"I love you more than my own soul, Raven, and because of it, I canna do otherwise. *You* understand *that*." He kissed me once more, hard, and walked swiftly away in the direction of town.

I watched him go, then sent Arianna a helpless glance. "What am I to do?"

"Teach me," Arianna said, "the spell that makes a man who looks like that one into your devoted servant."

I only shook my head at her. " 'Tis no spell, and well you know it."

"Perhaps not," she said. "A shame, though. I could have used it once."

I tilted my head. 'Twas the first hint she'd ever given me as to her past. "You . . . loved a man who didn't love you in return?"

"I loved a man," she said with a small, bitter smile, "who'd have been happy to see me dead."

"Then he was a fool."

She shook her head. "No, he was right. In the end I won

his trust, if not his heart. And trusting me is what got him killed.''

She turned and started back toward the house. I hurried after her. ''Arianna?''

''I don't talk about that,'' she said, false gaiety in her voice. ''It is history. I can't imagine what made me bring it up.''

''But—''

''Please,'' she said, and there was a wealth of power in the word. ''Let it be, Raven. And suffice to say that, having seen the way your Duncan looks at you, I am beginning to think I may have been wrong about him.''

I went still and felt my heart swell. ''Thank you for that,'' I whispered. ''But as to this other . . .'' She sent me a quelling look. ''All right,'' I murmured. But I wondered. What kind of man could break a heart as strong as hers?

Duncan didn't come to me by day after that. Only by night. Nearly every night. We'd meet in the forests or on the cliffs above the angry sea. We'd love until we were spent and then lie naked in each other's arms, just resting. Just *being*.

I loved him more each time he smiled at me, each time he whispered my name. I wanted him with me always. And he came to me whenever the sun went down.

Except on my sacred nights, when I would make an excuse. I think he knew I was hiding something, one more secret added to the many I kept from him, but he never pressed. Only hoped endlessly that I would come to trust him enough to tell him my truths. If only he knew that I *did* by now. 'Twas for his own safety that he could not know the truth about me.

Once a month, when the moon was full, Arianna and I slipped away from the cabin very late at night, while Aunt Eleanor lay sleeping. Deep into the woods we'd venture, there to set a small balefire alight, and to cast a magick circle, invoke the elements to aid us in our work, and feel the power of our Goddess growing strong within us. We burned fragrant herbs and special candles we'd made ourselves with loving care and magickal energy. We left offerings of food and wine, or flowers we'd gathered for the occasion as a symbol of our love for the Divine.

I often pondered the nature of my religion and that of Duncan's. I knew, as I'd always known, that his God and mine were the same. Our beliefs about Him differed, as did our ways, but in the end, there was only One. I saw the Divine as every bit as much female as male, and addressed both aspects, by referring to them as my Goddess and my God, my Lord and my Lady. Followers of Duncan's faith no longer recognized the feminine Divine, but still prayed to Mary in times of need.

Prayer was another way in which we were at once the same and different. When in need, we both turned to Divinity for help. Duncan's way was to surrender his will to that of the Almighty, seeing it as a separate entity, and asking for assistance. My way was to connect to that same Source, only to do it believing it was *not* separate from me, just as the Earth and the Air and the very sunlight are not separate from me. I am but a small part of a very large being, and that being is the Universe Herself. When I make magick, I feel *Her* energy flowing through me and then direct that power to bring my will into being. For me, prayer is not a request, but a command, delivered with the very might and power and authority of the Almighty.

But the most important difference between Duncan's faith and mine was that I believed the religions of the world were simply many spokes on a single wheel, all springing from and leading back to the same, singular Source. And his decreed that there was only one way to salvation, and that anyone who chose another path was damned. Guilty of the most vile sin. Deserving of torture and death.

I wondered sometimes if he truly believed that. And if he did, how could he love me and still live with himself?

By the heavens . . . his feelings for me had to be tearing him apart inside. Or were they? I wanted to ask . . . but I couldn't very well begin a theological discussion with him and not reveal more than I wished to.

So I put my questions aside and lived in the moment. I was, for the first time in my life, truly happy. Knowing I'd see him each night made my days pass in a glow of pleasure.

Holding him in my arms until the wee hours of dawn made my nights pass even more beautifully.

I suppose I should have known that it was too good to last.

Should have known. But didn't.

9

To the Most Esteemed Nathanial Dearborne,
Your name is known even here in the Colonies, sir, where tales of your skill and success in exposing the practice of Witchery are passed from one man of God to another in tones of awe and admiration. Such dark practices must be uncovered, wherever they hide, and burned away by the light of righteousness. 'Tis for this reason I post you now. The shadow of the Devil has fallen upon my own beloved settlement of Sanctuary in the colony of Massachusetts Bay. A Witch resides amongst us, of this I am certain. Her wiles and spells have placed the souls of the entire population in dire peril. The Witch's name is Raven St. James, and while I am convinced of her guilt, there remains doubt in the mind of our settlement's pastor. I fear the Rev. Duncan Wallace has lost the ability to see beyond her charms and sorcery, and has perhaps himself fallen victim to her sinful enchantments.

I have heard, Reverend Dearborne, that you have, at times, traveled far in your quest to rid the God-fearing Christian world of the scourge of Witchcraft, and 'tis my fondest hope that you will do so now. I beg of you, sir,

come to Sanctuary. You may well be our town's only hope.
      In God's most holy name, I remain,
      Elias Stanton,
      Sanctuary, Massachusetts Bay Colony

Nathanial Dearborne received the letter three months after it was written to him. Amazing, he thought, how his fame had spread even to the New World. Amazing, and ironic. A High Witch, perhaps one of the oldest dark ones in the world, known far and wide as a Witch-hunter of the highest order.

But what better way to take the power of other Witches than to execute them and take their hearts before they revive?

He smiled to himself as he read the distraught words of this Elias Stanton. He'd found her. At last he'd found the young Witch who'd so thoroughly wronged him.

Raven St. James.

With Duncan, still with Duncan. How? Why? Did it matter? She was a powerful Witch, Nathanial had sensed that from the start. More powerful than most so young. 'Twas the power of her ancestors, the power of a long and unbroken line of natural Witches, all of it appearing collectively in the first High Witch ever to be born to her family. Even she hadn't been aware of the full extent of her powers.

But Nathanial had.

He'd been weakening when he'd come upon the girl in the stocks that snowy morn. Barely functioning, and unsure how much longer he could go on. He'd needed an immortal heart, *any* immortal heart, to revive him, to restore his strength, his vigor. 'Twould give him the power to seek out an older one before he began to decline once more. So he'd touched the accused Witches as they stood imprisoned and bent over in shameful display in the public square. He'd felt nothing when he'd touched the mother.

But a jolt surged through him when his hand brushed over the girl's. And he'd known, young and inexperienced though she was, he would take her heart, just so that he might live to take others.

And then the rest of the knowledge had come to him, whispering through his sharp mind like a breeze before he took his hand away. She had a strong heart in her, Raven St. James did. A powerful heart. He would not gain longevity by taking it, but instead, power. Magickal power. And he wanted it for his own. He wanted her young, tender heart beating endlessly, imprisoned in a tiny wooden box. With the others.

Now, though, there was more driving him than just that. Events had taken an unexpected twist that day at the gallows. A twist that burned in his gut, and one he would not, could not forgive.

Raven had cost him a young man who'd been . . . almost . . . a son to him. She'd turned Duncan Wallace against him, and the hurt he felt was more than he'd allowed himself to feel in centuries. Damn her. *Damn her!*

Nathanial had had a son of his own, once, long, long ago. Before he'd known about immortality, before he'd taken his first heart, and thus stolen the gift for himself. So much time had passed that he remembered very little about that life— the life before. But he remembered the boy, and his love for him.

He hadn't thought it through, this endless life he'd managed to acquire for himself. He hadn't thought it through!

Nathanial's son had grown old. Died, eventually. As had his wife, and his friends and everyone and everything he'd ever known. So much pain swamped him then that he cursed his decision to kill his first Witch; to hold her heart entrapped in a small box, sucking the very life from it to extend his own lifetime.

He'd cursed his immortality. Briefly. He got over that in time.

But he'd never gotten over the loss of his son.

Duncan . . . Duncan had reminded him of the boy in some small way—had, perhaps, come close to filling the void that remained in Nathanial's heart after all these centuries.

Until Raven St. James had turned Duncan against him.

She'd pay. She'd pay with her very heart. If it took him a thousand lifetimes, Nathanial would make sure of that. He'd get her, take her heart, take her special brand of magick and make it his own. He'd repay her for thwarting him, not once, but twice, for he'd attempted to kill her when she'd returned to her former home after the hanging.

But he'd been weak. And she'd defeated him.

Only once before had he been defeated in battle by a woman. Only once. He hadn't been weakened, then, but at his strongest. But she had been a woman possessed of a fury beyond anything he'd ever seen. All because he'd murdered her lover. She'd nearly killed him, *would have*, had he not been clever enough to get away. He'd never face *that one* again if he had his way.

But Raven, he *would* face Raven.

And soon, for it seemed her day of reckoning was at hand. He knew where she was hiding. And as if the fates had decided to take his side for a change, he knew where Duncan was, as well. As if he were meant to go there, to dispose of the bitch once and for all, and to make Duncan come back to England with him. And he would. He would win Duncan back again, he would have Raven's heart. Not because he'd die without it. Not this time. No, this time it was sheer vengeance that drove him. He wanted Raven's heart . . . because she had taken his. She'd taken Duncan.

Duncan stood at the pulpit in the log structure that was his church, going over his notes for this morning's service. His sermons had taken a turn of late. He didn't preach about hellfire and the damnation of sinners anymore. He couldn't. To do so made him squirm inside, knowing that according to the beliefs he was supposed to be preaching, he was damned himself. But more and more he questioned those beliefs. More and more he felt with everything in him that loving Raven St. James could be no sin. No more so than breathing . . . because it came to him just as naturally.

He looked up when the groan of the heavy door announced a visitor, and quickly hid a frown of displeasure when he saw Elias Stanton coming in.

He looked ill, Elias did. Pale, weak somehow. The man came inside and sank onto a wooden bench as if his legs were too tired to carry him any farther.

Duncan set his notes aside and hurried forward. "Elias? Are you ill?"

Shoulders slumped, Elias only shook his head. " 'Tis no

natural illness plaguing me, Duncan. 'Tis far darker than that, I fear.'' As Duncan frowned, Elias lifted his head, revealing the dark circles beneath his eyes. ''But I've not come to you for that. You're no physician. 'Tis my soul needs cleansing, Reverend. I've come to confess. Will you hear me?''

Duncan blinked in surprise. ''Aye, you know I will. But confession is nay part of our dogma here, Elias.''

''Nonetheless . . .'' He lowered his head once more.

Duncan nodded, clasping Elias's shoulder briefly. ''Go on, then. Tell me what troubles you so. I'll help you if I can.''

Tiredly Elias nodded. '' 'Tis the woman.''

And Duncan knew without asking what woman he spoke of, but he asked all the same.

''That St. James wench,'' Elias spat out. ''Who else?''

A tingle of warning whispered through Duncan's limbs. He took the bench in front of Elias, turned sideways to look back at the bowed man, and warned himself to keep quiet. To give nothing away. To simply . . . listen.

''I thought myself strong enough in my faith to resist her, you know. Fool that I was. No man could withstand such an onslaught.''

Swallowing the retort that leaped to his lips, Duncan only nodded. ''What is it she's done to upset you so much?''

Elias brought his head up fast, and his eyes lost some of that tired look when they filled instead with anger. Rage.

''What has she done? Have you not seen it yourself, Reverend? The sidelong glances. The way she parades her beauty so proudly about this town. The devil is in her, I vow it!''

''I've nay seen anythin' of the sort,'' he said, too quickly, he knew.

''She's taken to haunting my dreams,'' Elias went on. ''She comes to me by night, while I sleep. Tempts me to sin of the most vile sort while I'm helpless to resist. I tell you, only a Witch would be capable of such things!''

Duncan closed his eyes slowly. God, he'd been afraid of this. ''Aye, only a Witch,'' he said slowly. ''Or a man lustin' after an innocent. Take care, Elias, not to blame your own failin's on another.''

" 'Tis Witchery, I tell you! And I'm not alone in my opinion, Reverend!"

Duncan felt his eyes narrow on the· man. "Aren't you, now?" And he waited, dreading what he was about to hear.

"I didn't speak of it to you at the time," Elias said slowly. "But I wrote to a man in England about her. A famous Witch-hunter. And now, at last, I have his reply." This as he tugged a folded sheet of vellum from within his coat. "He believes all the signs are there, Duncan. He says she's dangerous and that we ought to exercise extreme caution, that she could destroy us all! Read it for yourself!" He thrust the letter at Duncan.

Duncan recoiled from the sheet as if its very touch could burn him. "Nay, I've no need to read the words of a man like that. How can he judge and condemn a woman from across the sea, Elias? Think on this! He hasna even met her."

"A man with his experience has no need. Besides, he will. He's on his way here. Could arrive within a fortnight. Perhaps sooner. Then we'll see—"

Duncan surged to his feet. "You're bringin' a Witch-hunter here? To Sanctuary? Good God, Elias, do you know what you've done?"

Elias rose very slowly, staring hard at Duncan from head to toe. "I see. I guessed it long ago, but I doubted my own instincts. Now, though, I see it clear. All those nights you spend out there, on the pretense of spying on those women. She's got to you, too. Hasn't she, Reverend? Hasn't she?"

Duncan averted his eyes. "Dinna be a fool."

"Have you fallen even further than I? Has she lifted her skirts for you already? Have you been sampling her tender—"

Duncan lashed out, unable and utterly unwilling to restrain himself. His fist connected with Elias's face, and the man reeled backward, over the bench and onto the floor behind it.

"You dare!" Elias blustered, clutching his nose as blood ran from beneath his hand.

Duncan gripped the front of the man's shirt and lifted him to his feet. "Raven St. James is a fine and decent woman. I'll nay have you sullyin' her name, nor causin' her harm on account of your own rampant lust, Elias Stanton. You're a ruttin' pig of a man, with a mind so bent on the carnal there isna room for reason nor decency left in you anymore."

Elias stepped back and Duncan let him go.

"Leave her alone," he told the bastard. "I'm warnin' you, Elias, *leave her alone.*"

Elias sniffed, rubbed his nose again, and examined the blood on his fingertips. "I'll forgive you, Reverend. Only because I know the power of her spells on a man. She's obviously worked them on you as well. But she'll get what's coming to her. And I've half a mind to set the wheels in motion now, myself, rather than wait for the Witch-hunter's arrival as he advises in his letter. What more evidence do we need, after all?"

"Do you spread any more of this malicious gossip, Elias, I'll kill you myself."

The man's eyes widened, and he took a hasty step away. "You? A man of God, threatening murder?"

"Murder is what you have in mind for Raven. Dinna try to deny it."

Elias narrowed his eyes. "Raven, is it? I knew—"

"You know nothing. She's the innocent here. You're the sinner, Elias. As the leader of this church 'tis my duty to protect the flock from lechers like you."

Lowering his head, Elias shook it slowly. "You make me wonder, Reverend, whether she has enchanted you at all . . . or if perhaps you've been in league with her all along. Mayhap you be a Witch as well."

"Get out!" Duncan lifted a hand that shook with barely contained rage, and pointed toward the door. "Get out of my church. You soil it with your very presence."

Nodding twice, Elias turned and walked away.

Duncan released all his breath at once and sank onto the bench. Damn! Elias was dangerous, and this Witch-hunter, whoever he was, likely even more so. How many of the women in this town might be falsely accused, even executed, now that Elias had started this disaster? How many? Elias Stanton may well have lit a wildfire in Sanctuary that would spread until it consumed the entire settlement.

But it wouldn't consume Raven. Nay, not if it cost Duncan's life to prevent it.

He had to get to Raven, had to speak to her. She must leave this place, now. Right away.

But even now the parishioners were arriving for the service. God, there was no time. Afterward, then. He'd go to her tonight and he would make her understand the danger she faced here. He'd take the lass away from this place if he had to sling her over his shoulder and carry her all the way. Aye, he would!

He closed his eyes slowly and prayed to his God to watch over her in the meantime.

After the Sunday meeting, I lingered. Arianna didn't. She put on a good show, acting prim and pious in her humble, dark skirts, white cap always in place, hair discreetly tucked beneath it. But she hated the Sunday meetings, the townspeople with their false smiles and friendly words when all the while they were whispering their suspicions to one another in private. And as usual, she left as soon as possible. She always did, even if it meant walking all the way back to the cabin. But I was feeling generous today, so I told her to take the wagon. I'd walk home this time, if she couldn't wait to leave.

I was quite the opposite in my feelings about the Sunday meetings. Oh, the make-believe friendship of those backbiting locals riled me every bit as much as it did Arianna. But for me there was reason to stay. For I'd grown to cherish every moment I could spend near Duncan, even those moments when we had to pretend there was nothing between us. For he would shower love on me all the same—in a single glance sent my way and filled with fire, even as he spoke to one crowd of parishioners and I to another. In an accidental touch. In the very way his voice changed when he spoke to me. I knew I was always on his mind, in his thoughts, just as he lingered constantly in mine.

There were, of course, unpleasant experiences awaiting me each time I attended services. For Elias Stanton tended to pay nearly as much mind to me as Duncan did. Only his glances were dirty somehow, leaving me feeling stained when I chanced to meet his lecherous gaze, and even more so when he touched me "accidentally," which happened more and more often.

I was blessed today, though, because Elias did not attend services. Aunt Eleanor, too, had stayed at home, having awoken this morn with a crushing headache that kept her abed. And since Arianna had already gone with our wagon, I was to walk back to the cabin alone. Not that I minded. I was, in fact, looking forward to the walk, for the leaves were turning and beautiful, and Duncan was on my mind.

He'd tried several times to speak with me, and there was a new urgency in his eyes when they caught mine, but each time he'd been swept away by someone else begging a word or asking advice. No matter. He would come to me tonight. In the forest, beneath the stars, we'd make tender love. I'd spend my walk home dreaming of the evening to come.

It did not turn out that way at all.

I'd trekked only halfway, walking slowly along the worn track, singing to myself, bursting with the joy of the changing seasons, the scent of the autumn leaves and the sea at my side. But I was jolted out of my pleasure at the sound of a horse's clopping gait, and the rattling of the wagon it pulled. And when I turned, expecting to see Duncan coming to see me home, I caught my breath. For 'twas Elias Stanton manning the reins. He looked ragged, and there was a vacant look to his eyes that chilled me.

"Good morn, Mistress St. James," he called, drawing the rig to a halt right beside me.

"Good morn," I replied, my voice stiff. "We missed you at the meeting hall this morn." I hadn't missed him at all, but 'twas something to say.

"I had some thinking to do," he said. "Thinking . . . that was best done alone."

Something quivered inside me. Some sense of danger. I kept walking. But he snapped the reins to keep pace.

"I be on my way to call on your aunt," he announced, as if I might care where he were going.

"How thoughtful of you."

"Perhaps you'd care to ride the rest of the way in comfort, rather than taxing yourself by walking?''

I met his eyes, cold and menacing, revealing the lie of his voice, and I gave a quick shake of my head. ''I thank you, sir, but I am enjoying my walk too much to end it so soon.''

''Nonsense,'' he said. ''A woman walking alone is unsafe. Come, ride with me.''

''I walk this way often and never see another soul, Mister Stanton. I assure you, I'm perfectly safe.''

Grunting deep in his throat, he stopped the wagon again, only this time he climbed down. Walking toward the horse, he took its halter in one hand. ''I'll walk with you, then. Lord forbid some harm befall you while I ride safely away, unaware.''

I lowered my head as my stomach clenched tight. ''I prefer to walk alone.'' I blurted it, not softening the words or the tone in any way. There should be no mistake, I thought. I did not wish to walk with this man.

He understood all right, for his face darkened. He released the horse, and turned fully toward me. ''The attentions of a man offend you, do they?''

I did not know what to say. ''You are a married man, Mister Stanton. Surely you should not speak to me in such a way.''

''Married, yes, and pious to a fault, but still subjected to the charms of a sorceress. Just as our preacher seems to be.''

''I know nothing of sorcery! And the Reverend Wallace has never been anything but kind and perfectly polite toward me.''

''That is not what I see in his eyes when they meet your own, lady. No. I see lust. The same lust that rears up in my own heart with each toss of your head.''

''You're being ridiculous!'' I backed away, but he caught my wrists in his cruel hands.

''I know of but one means to rid myself of your allure, Raven. And that is to sate this lust once and for all.''

''Let go of me! Have you gone insane? Let me go!''

''No, mistress. I won't let you go.''

He jerked me closer and mashed his face to mine. His mouth open and wet, his tongue lapping at my lips though

I pressed them tight. I pulled backward, but he clung to me, held me fast to his body so that as I moved he moved as well, until my back was pressed to the trunk of a tree, and his flaccid body held me pinned there. I struggled frantically, but his perverted desire had caused him to have an overpowering strength, and I could not free myself, despite my own enhanced Witchly strength. He groped at the front of my dress, pawed at my breasts.

"Stop fighting, wench! You've brought this on yourself—visiting me in my dreams nightly as you do, tempting me to sin. I no longer rest at night. I cannot eat by day. You're draining the very life from me, woman, and now you'll pay!"

I had to stop him or be raped. The knowledge came clear to me just that quickly. I had no choice in the matter, and since I couldn't reach my dagger, I knew only one way. But it would take all of my focus.

Calm. I willed myself to go utterly calm. Forced my body to relax, and my mind to ignore what he was doing to me. I went inside myself, deep inside, to a place where his grunting and groping did not exist—as if they were happening to someone else and I was but a witness.

Closing my eyes, I whispered, chanted to Mother Earth, attuned to her, felt her strength beneath me and behind me and around me and, finally, surging from within me. I drew her energy up from the ground, centered that power until it thrummed in my veins, and then opened my eyes to find a focus for it.

The limb, above Elias Stanton's head.

With a shout of release, I sent the power shooting forth, and the limb cracked and split. It crashed down, smiting the man and knocking him to his knees, and then flat to the ground, with the limb heavy atop him. He did not move.

I had no wish to stay to see whether he was dead or alive. I ran, leaping into his wagon and snapping the reins hard. His horse reared up and raced forward, and in moments the brute was behind me, and my home, my haven, loomed ahead.

Arianna was waiting when I arrived. She stared at me as

I wheeled the wagon to a stop. Then her face paled, and she ran forward even as I tried to climb down.

"Sweet Mother, what's happened!"

She gathered me gently into her arms, helping me down. And only as she stared aghast did I realize my dress was torn, my hair askew, my face hot and damp.

"This is Elias Stanton's rig," Arianna all but hissed. "He did this, didn't he? Raven?"

Trembling, beyond words, I merely nodded.

"I'll kill him." And even as she said it her dagger appeared in her hand. "Where is he? I'll cut out his liver!"

And finally coherent thought returned. Pushing my hair out of my face, head bowed, I said, "No, Arianna. Wait."

"For what?" Her face had reddened clear to her ears. "Did he rape you, Raven? Did he—"

"No. I'm . . . I'm all right. But Arianna, we mustn't speak of this. Not to anyone."

"And what should we do? Keep quiet and wait for that beast to try again?"

Drawing a deep steadying breath, I shook my head. "We should take the rig back into town. We should say the horse brought it in with no one inside, and that we're concerned about Elias. They'll send men out looking, and they'll find him in the woods, beneath a fallen limb. Alive . . . or, I think he was, when I left him there."

She scowled at me so intently I felt her anger washing over me. "So we cover for him, lie for him?"

"No, Arianna. For *us*. You know what they think of me in this town. No one would accept my word over his. Let them believe it an accident." Again, I glanced down at my dress. "Aunt Eleanor mustn't see me like this."

Lowering her head, Arianna blew a sigh. "Here, take my cloak." And she removed the cloak from her shoulders to cover mine, then gently smoothed my hair. "I'll do as you ask. But I still think he deserves to be drawn and quartered."

"He accused me of bewitching him," I muttered. "Of visiting him in dreams and driving him to . . . to this."

"His own lechery has driven him. Nothing more." She shook her head, eyeing the rig. "I'll bring Duncan."

"He must never know of this, Arianna. Please, don't tell him. He'd kill Elias, I know he would."

"The man *needs* killing."

"Please . . ."

She sighed, lowering her head. "You ask a lot of me, my friend."

"I know." I lifted my head. "Have I told you how grateful I am that you came to me, Arianna? I haven't, have I? But I should. You . . . you're the best friend I've ever had."

She blinked, looking away as if slightly irritated. "I would die for you, you know."

I frowned, confused by the power in that simple statement. "But why?"

She shrugged. "You did for me once."

"Whatever do you mean?"

Meeting my eyes, smiling gently, she said, "Perhaps it's time I told you the truth, Raven. You have this gift, this immortality, because in some previous life you died while trying to save the life of another Witch."

"I understand that, but—"

"That Witch . . . was me."

And before I could say another word, she leaped into Elias Stanton's wagon and snapped the reins.

There had been no love lost between Duncan and the mysterious, mischievous-eyed pixie who seemed to have become Raven's closest friend. They were polite to each other, but cool, and he sensed the smaller woman's disapproval. Understood it, even.

But when he saw Arianna driving Elias Stanton's rig into town that morn, her face expressionless and pale, he immediately felt his stomach tie in knots. He'd been steadily working to free himself of the people who seemed determined to have a word with him—and only now had he succeeded. He'd been about to start out to Raven's cottage on the cliffs.

The pace at which the wagon moved was enough to tell him something was wrong. Terribly wrong. When it stopped in a cloud of dust, Duncan joined the crowd gathering

around Arianna, but her eyes were on him alone, and he
sensed a silent message in them.

"Mister Stanton's horse arrived at our cabin with no
driver," she said, calmly, as slowly as if she'd rehearsed
her words. "We're concerned about his safety." She
climbed down with grace, nimble as a sprite, ignoring all
the shouted questions. "Perhaps some of you might wish to
travel the Coast Road and search for him," she suggested.

Several men immediately shouted agreement and as they
grouped off, and began making their plan, Duncan took Arianna aside. "What has truly happened?" he asked.

She averted her eyes. "Nothing good, Duncan. But I can
say no more. I gave my promise to Raven, and I'll not break
my word to her."

"Is she all right?" He nearly held his breath awaiting her
answer.

"She's unharmed." Finally she met his eyes again, and
he saw the concern there for her friend. "I'd have stayed
with her myself and let that animal Elias rot. But it is you
she needs, Duncan. Go to her."

He nodded quickly. Let the others search for Elias. He
needed to see Raven, to assure himself she was well, and
find out what this was all about. And then he had to take
steps to get her away from here, to somewhere safe.

What the hell had happened out there? God, he knew
she'd been walking alone. But he hadn't seen her leave, and
by the time he realized she'd gone it had been too late to
prevent it. He should have gone after her, right then. Should
have escorted her home, and to hell with what the town
gossips would make of that. Damn Elias to hell if he'd
touched her, frightened her in any way. He'd kill the bastard. He'd kill him with his bare hands.

"Come," he said to Arianna through clenched teeth.
"We'll go together." They were not friends, nay, yet he
still wouldn't like the thought of her alone in this town
should something rile the locals—should something turn
them against her.

"I think I should linger in town. See what the vermin has
to say when they find him. If he's still alive, that is." Her
frown was worried, more now than ever. And Duncan knew

too well that Elias might speak his suspicions about her and Raven if he'd been provoked.

"I think it a bad notion, lass," he said.

She tilted her head, studied him. "Is that worry in your eyes, Duncan? For me?" Her smile was small and brief. "I'm grateful for the thought, but believe me when I tell you I can take care of myself."

He lowered his head. "Stay, then, if you're certain," he told her, speaking lower now. "But keep out of sight, Arianna. You might be judged guilty by association, does anythin' come of this."

She nodded, but when he turned to go, she clutched his arm. He faced her again, and she stared straight into his eyes. "So might you, Duncan. You should be well aware of that. Well aware of the risk involved."

"The only risk I'm concerned about is the risk to Raven," he told her. And meant it. "But I'm aware of it, aye. And willin' to face it. I'll have no regrets, no matter the outcome."

"You truly do love her, don't you?" Arianna whispered.

"Aye, with everythin' in me," he told her. Then he looked at her face, at the force of the emotions in her eyes, and added, "As much as you do, I'll wager."

"You must love her a great deal, then," she said softly.

Nodding, Duncan clasped Arianna's shoulder briefly, a gesture of friendship he thought long overdue. They'd reached an understanding between them, he thought. He and Arianna had one thing in common. They were both utterly devoted to Raven and determined to protect her at any cost. 'Twas a powerful bond they shared, and he thought they'd both finally realized that.

"Take care, lass," he told her. "You an' I have much to talk about when this is over. I'd like you alive an' well for the conversation."

She nodded, reaching out to briefly squeeze his hand in a gesture that told him she understood, and felt as he did. Their eyes met in silent communion, and then he turned and strode away.

10

I felt soiled by Elias Stanton's very touch, could still taste his vile mouth on my lips, and feel his hands . . .

Aunt Eleanor lay asleep, perfectly peaceful and safe. She would not remain so . . . not if I stayed here with her any longer. Stanton, if he lived, would spread his accusations against me, and my aunt would be at risk. Christians did not treat Witches kindly, nor did they show mercy to anyone associated with them. I would have to leave her. And soon, I feared. Duncan had been right. If only I had heeded his warnings.

Without disturbing my aunt, I slipped back outside, a woven washcloth in my fist. I only wanted to cleanse myself of the stain of Elias's hands, rinse my mouth, scrub away the essence of his touch. But I was too frantic to carry water and fill the tub, much less wait for it to warm over the fire. No, I needed to wash *now*. At once. Every moment I waited made my stomach heave.

I hurried to the woods, to a stream there that emptied into the sea, and there I stripped off every stitch and plunged myself into the icy water. I drank in great mouthfuls of it, and spat it out again, over and over. I scrubbed at my arms, at my breasts, at my face. Everywhere he'd touched me. I scoured myself, but to no avail. Even then I didn't feel clean, so I scrubbed some more.

"Raven."

At the sound of my name whispered so hoarsely, I snatched my dagger from the rock at my side and whirled, raising it up, ready to gut the bastard if he came at me again.

But 'twas Duncan standing there on the bank, staring at me with eyes as wounded as dying stars. I parted my lips but could not speak. But I didn't need to speak. He knew me so well, knew at a glance my devastation, my shame, though he did not—could not—know their cause. He came to me, walked into the swirling, icy stream fully clothed, and gently gathered me into his arms.

" 'Tis all right," he whispered, holding me close, turning and carrying me to the shore. "I'm here with you now, my bonny lass, and 'tis all right." His lips touched my hair as he held me like a frightened child in his arms. "What's happened to you, love? What's happened?"

"N-nothing . . ."

He lowered me to the soft, grassy bank, snatching up the cloth to begin rubbing me dry. So gentle, his touch. So careful as he pressed the water from my hair and wiped it away from my body. "You're freezin'," he whispered, and quickly picked up my dress. And then he stiffened, his hands tightened around my dress as he stared at it. I reached out, snatched it away, but 'twas too late. He'd seen the rips and tears down the front.

Slowly he looked at me again, his eyes more thorough this time.

"You're bruised," he whispered.

My hands flew to cover my breasts where I could feel the soreness Elias's cruel hands had left behind. But 'twas too late to hide the marks from Duncan's eyes.

"Stanton did this," he muttered.

I lifted my chin, swallowed hard. "It doesn't matter."

But Duncan's face reddened, his jaw clenched with anger. "Oh, it matters, lass. I'll kill him for this."

"No, please . . ."

He touched his fingers to my lips, silencing me. Then he quickly divested himself of his shirt, and then his coat, dressing me in both with such exquisite care I nearly wept.

"You mustn't take revenge on him, Duncan. 'Twould spell your ruin."

"Aye, an' what do I care about my ruin? Raven, darlin', I care only for you." Pushing my hair back away from my eyes, he stroked my cheek with the backs of his fingers. "Did he . . . ?"

"No." I saw the doubt in Duncan's eyes, held them with mine so he could see that I was being honest with him. "He would have, Duncan, though I fought. But a limb fell from the tree where he . . . where he . . ." I stopped, drew a shuddering breath, began again. "It might have killed him. I hope it did."

"If it didna kill the bastard, I'll do it myself."

"Please, Duncan, I've had all the violence I can bear."

"I'm sorry," he whispered. Then he gently pulled me close, cradling me in his arms, rocking me against his warm chest. I felt utterly surrounded by him, his strength, his love. "I'm so sorry, Raven. I should have been with you, should have protected you—"

"No, Duncan, do not for one moment believe any of this is your fault."

"I love you," he whispered, and he kissed me very softly, his lips on mine instantly erasing the memory of those other, cruel ones.

When he lifted his head away, I touched his face. "And I love you, Duncan Wallace. With all that I am, I love you."

He blinked, searching my face in wonder. "Do you know how long I've waited to hear you say those words?"

I bit my lip, realizing what I'd done. But 'twas too late to take the declaration back now. And it was true, more true, perhaps, than any words I'd ever spoken.

"We have to leave here," he said softly. "Tonight, Raven. There's nay time to wait. I want to take you away, to somewhere safe from fools like Elias and this other bastard who's on his way here even now."

I sat up a bit, frowning. "Who?"

"A Witch-hunter," he said, his voice grim. "I'd no idea until this morn, my love, but Elias wrote to some murderin' cur in England, and the man could arrive at any time. We must make haste."

I felt a shiver of utter dread creep up my spine.

"No, my lass, dinna be afraid," he told me, clasping my hand in his. "No one will ever harm you again, Raven. I vow it on my very life."

And those words made me shiver all the more.

Duncan stayed at my side as I packed a few belongings, and held my hand while I delivered my sad news to sweet Aunt Eleanor.

"You'll come back," she kept saying. And the hope in her eyes was so desperate that I couldn't divest her of it. "You *will* come back once you've taken care of this . . . this . . ."

"Business matter. 'Tis all to do with some property my father owned," I told her. "Very complicated and boring, but I must return to England to clear it up. And yes, of course I will come back."

She blinked back her tears. "I won't worry for your safety, at least. Not with Duncan going along to care for you." She hugged me gently, kissed my face.

"I promise to protect her as if she were my own," Duncan assured her.

I battled my tears, refusing to shed a single one in front of her.

"Don't be any longer than you have to, child. I'll be waiting for your return."

"I know you will, Aunt Eleanor." I squeezed her hands one last time. "I do love you, you know."

"Well, of course you do. Off with you, now. No sense waiting—my, but 'tis already near dark."

I knew it was. Duncan and I had deliberately waited for the night to fall. Like a dark blanket that would enfold and protect us. I finished with my goodbyes, and we stepped out into the night. It had always been our place, the place where we lived, where we loved. Night had been good to Duncan and me.

"I'm worried about Arianna," I whispered.

"Aye, I am, as well. The moment I get you safely away

from Sanctuary, Raven, I'll return, an' I'll find her. I promise you that."

We were walking silently, hand in hand along the Coast Road. My belongings, what few of them I thought I would need, were in my pack, and Duncan carried it slung over his sturdy shoulder.

"Poor Aunt Eleanor," I said softly. "She was heartbroken when we told her that I must leave."

"Aye, no doubt, but she seemed to take the news in stride, all the same," Duncan said.

"Oh, she tried to put on a brave face . . . for my benefit," I told him. "But I saw through it. It broke her heart to say goodbye to me. I know it did, Duncan, for it broke mine, as well." I caught my lip in my teeth and swallowed back a sob. "I'll likely never see that dear woman again. 'Tis almost like losing my mother anew!" The hurt bubbled high in my chest, and tears spilled over.

Duncan pulled me close to his side, his arm strong and protective around my shoulders. "Nay, lass, you shall see her again. I'll see to it. We'll settle someplace safe, Raven, and the moment we do, I'll come back for her. Bring her to us."

I stared up at him in wonder. "You would do that for me?"

"Aye, lass. I'd do anythin' for you, and you ought to know it by now."

"I do know it," I whispered.

"Good." He drew my hand to his lips and kissed it.

'Twas fully dark now, but the light of a full moon made it nearly as bright outside as it might be at midday. We'd hoped to skirt the village unnoticed by waiting until the hour grew late enough. A frightening prospect, indeed. But I felt safe with Duncan at my side. Safe and loved, and yet sad beyond words. Someday I would lose him, just as I'd lost everyone dear to me. It would always be this way, I imagined. Goodbyes. So many goodbyes.

I didn't think I wanted to live to see the day I'd have to say goodbye to him. I didn't think I could bear it.

Running footsteps made my thoughts grind to a halt, and I reached for my dagger, spinning around and lifting it up.

But then in the moonlight I saw Arianna's face, reddened and damp with perspiration. Wide-eyed and breathless, she came toward us. And I knew something was terribly wrong, but even then I couldn't restrain my joy at seeing her.

I flung my arms around her, felt the pounding of her heart and the rapid, deep breaths she drew. Her skin was hot and damp. "I've been worried out of my mind!" I cried. "Thank goodness you're all right."

"Not for long, I fear," she said, hugging me back before straightening away and eyeing first me, then Duncan as she fought to catch her breath.

"Something is wrong, then?" Duncan asked her. And she nodded.

Of course something was wrong, I thought. Ah, but what surprise was that? Nothing had been right today. Not today. Perhaps not ever again.

"Thank the fates I managed to catch up with you." Bending, hands braced on her knees, Arianna dragged in gulps of the bracing sea breeze that wafted up from the cliffs at our side. And slowly her breathing returned to normal.

"What is it, Arianna?" I asked.

"The townspeople. Stanton . . ."

"They found him, then? Alive?" Duncan's voice was grim, and I knew that in spite of his goodness, his generous soul, he truly wished the man dead.

"Yes, alive, and spewing venom. But delirious enough so no one paid much notice at first. But he finally recovered sufficiently to convince them he wasn't suffering delusions. He said you attacked him, Raven. Said you used Witchery to smash him with that limb and then left him to die."

I only stood still and silent, already knowing the answer to my next question. "And they believed him."

"They went out to the cabin in search of you. I raced ahead to warn you, Raven, but you'd already gone."

"Aunt Eleanor?"

She shook her head rapidly. "They've left her alone. I think they will continue to, Raven. You're the newcomer, the stranger here. She is one of their own."

"Thank goodness."

"I have no doubt they're on your heels even now," Arianna rushed on. "I cut through the forest to reach you first. Come, we must hurry."

Nodding, I grasped Duncan's hand all the harder and sent a longing glance down to the sea far below, where jagged rocks peered from beneath the surface only to vanish again with the waves. "What I wouldn't give for a boat. They have to know this road is the only way we can leave Sanctuary."

"Aye, they know it," Duncan said grimly. "But if they try to harm you, Raven, they'll have to go through me to do it."

"Duncan, no. You mustn't do anything to put yourself at risk. I—"

"*Hold!*"

I caught my breath, and whirled to see a mass of villagers streaming toward us and spreading like some oily pool to block our path. And when I spun the other way, I saw more of them. They carried torches. They shouted and accused. The very air around me snapped with the vibrations of their hatred, and their menace.

Trapped. Trapped here on these cliffs with no chance of escape.

"Stand aside," Duncan called, even as he gently moved me behind him. "I know what Elias has told you, but I'm here to bear witness that 'tis nothin' more than a pack of lies spun by a man sick with desire for a woman he can never possess."

" 'Tis as Elias said," one man called to the others in a coarse voice. "She's bewitched even the preacher!"

They closed ranks around us. There was no way out.

" 'Tis untrue!" Duncan shouted back. "I tell you, as a man of God, in the *name* of God, this woman is innocent."

"Blasphemer!" someone cried. "He's in league with her." And they surged forward like one living mass of evil, pressing ever closer on us from all sides. Duncan clung to me, shielded me with his own body, but I was torn from his sheltering arms by cruel hands. Hands that brought back memories I'd hoped never to have to relive.

'Twas as if the veil of time had melted away, and I was back in that poor English village. 'Twas as if I could feel

the icy wind and the snow razing my cheeks, even though
it was merely a crisp autumn night here.

"Get your hands off her!" Duncan roared.

But they held me all the same. And others held him,
though they had a time of doing it.

Where was Arianna? I did not see her. She'd vanished.

The crowd stilled as Elias Stanton himself came forward,
leaning heavily upon a staff and wearing a white cloth tied
about his head. "This wench tried to murder me," he cried.
"Moreover, she's guilty of fornication! With our own minister! A man of God, tempted to sin by a Witch!"

"End this curse! Free the preacher of her spells," someone called.

"Pitch her from the cliffs!"

"Nay!" Duncan tugged at the men who held him. Fought
them, just as he'd fought them before, at the hanging. And
'twas just as useless. "I'll nay stand by and see you do
murder! Nay, dammit!"

"Duncan Wallace," Elias intoned, "do you confess to
the crime of fornication, and to the even darker sin of com-
muning with a Witch?"

"I dinna confess anythin' to you, Elias! For 'twould be
like confessin' to the devil himself!" Duncan shouted. But
he stilled his struggling, standing straight and tall while
lesser men clasped his arms. He faced Elias Stanton
squarely. I'd never seen the like of him as he was that night.
Standing with his back to the sea, the wind whipping his
dark hair into chaos as the waves broke and crashed below,
his eyes flashing.

"What of you, Elias?" he asked softly, and the men
around us went silent at the power in his quiet voice. "Do
you confess?"

"I've nothing to confess to, young man!"

"Nay? What of tryin' to force your attentions upon an
innocent woman and then plottin' her murder to cover your
own sins?"

Elias lowered his head and shook it slowly. "These men
know me, Duncan. They've known me for years, and can
vouch for my character. No, they'll not believe a come-
lately preacher nor a Witch over one of their own." And

lifting his head, he faced Duncan again. "Confess, Duncan. 'Tis the only way to save yourself."

"I'd confess gladly, if my doin' so would save her."

"Alas, her fate is already sealed, my friend. But for you, there remains some dim hope of salvation. Confess, son, beg forgiveness of God on your knees and—"

"Burn in hell, Stanton."

"Duncan, no . . . ." I whispered the words, but it was too late. He'd damned himself already. Because of me.

Elias shook his head sadly and turned toward me. And his eyes were cold there in the darkness, beneath the light of a full moon. Cold and menacing. I had to save Duncan. Somehow, he must not be dragged into the depths of this mess I'd brought upon myself.

"Please, Elias," I whispered. "Duncan is innocent! He knows nothing of me or my ways! 'Twas all me. I bewitched him, just as you said. He doesn't even know what he's doing tonight. Spare him, for the love of God, spare him!"

Stanton looked upon me with utter hatred in his eyes. The men holding me were even now binding my hands behind me, and I saw they were about to do the same to Duncan. I searched the crowd for Arianna, praying to the Great Goddess that they hadn't put their hands on her as well, and sighed in blessed relief when I still didn't see her there. She must have slipped away. Please, I thought, please let her have slipped way.

"Disavow her, Duncan," Elias said softly. "Save yourself."

"Never!"

"Do as he asks, Duncan." I tried to move forward, to get closer to him, but there were too many of them holding me. Even with my strength I had no chance of overpowering them. "Please, trust me. Do as he asks."

Meeting my eyes, he only shook his head. "Not on pain of death, lass," he whispered. "Nay, not if it meant my own soul, would I speak against you."

"Don't listen to him," I pleaded. "He doesn't know what he's saying."

"Perhaps he'll come back to himself," Elias said, "when you lie dead and your spells are finally broken."

Elias looked at the men who held me, gave a nod, and I was lifted. I cried out to Duncan as they carried me to the edge, pleaded with him, prayed he'd understand. "They cannot kill me! Do you hear me, Duncan? They cannot take my life! Save yourself, Duncan, I beg you!"

But already he was tearing free of his captors, lunging forward, struggling to reach me. The men standing at my head and at my feet swung me like a feed sack, and then simply let me go. Out, out into the vast emptiness of space and wind and moonlight I sailed, and Duncan raced toward the edge. I hung in space for only an instant, long enough to see the horror in his eyes, and to know what he would do.

"*No!*" I screamed, and then I plummeted, and Duncan, my beloved Duncan, lunged out, reaching for me as if he could catch me somehow, and haul me back to safety. But he couldn't. He must have known he couldn't. And his reaching only resulted in him falling—he followed the course I took. The wind whistled past my ears, and my body tumbled and spun. I shouted my love for him but couldn't hear my own words for the crash of the sea below, drawing nearer—ever nearer. And then there was an impact, incredible pain. The snap and cracking of my bones as my body hurled itself upon the rocks and into the cold, salty water.

And then the pain blinked out, along with the light of life.

"Raven . . ."

I sucked in a sudden, sharp gasp, so deep it nearly burst my lungs when life returned to me once more. I opened my eyes, blinked the water away, and stared up at Arianna. She sat on the ground near the shore, my head cradled in her lap, the seawater streaming from my hair and soaking her clothes. She held me like a child, stroking my hair, caressing my face. Tears dampened her own lily-white cheeks.

"Raven," she whispered again. "Oh, sweet Raven, I'm sorry. I'm so very sorry."

And it all came back to me.

"Duncan!"

"Hush, now." She soothed, gentled me, but I struggled free of her comforting, struggled free and got to my feet.

"Where is he? Where is Duncan? Tell me!"

Arianna bit her lip as I scanned the shoreline in search of my love. And then I saw him.

His broken body lay upon a jagged cluster of rocks some distance out, waves reaching up at him, tugging him as if they wanted to carry him away in their crystalline arms. I ran into the water, shouting his name, crying uncontrollably. But when I reached him, I knew 'twas no use. Even as I clambered up onto the rocks where he lay and pulled him into my arms, begging him to wake up, to speak to me, I knew. He was as boneless as a rag doll, broken in so many places his poor body barely held its form. His face lay still and pale in the moonlight, blessedly unmarred. The blue of his lips, and his bloodless skin, the coolness of his cheek where I touched it, told a story too horrible to believe. I gathered his head to my breast, bowing over him, weeping as I'd never wept before.

"Oh, Duncan, no. Not now, not yet. You can't leave me so soon! For the love of the Goddess, why? Why couldn't I trust you with the truth?"

But I hadn't, and now he was dead. Because of me, he was dead. I'd never know his touch, his kiss again. Never look into his brown eyes. Never . . .

"Oh, why didn't I tell him! He'd not have died trying to save me if he'd known the truth of what I am!" I wailed my grief to the stars, ignoring the sloshing, splashing sounds Arianna made as she came out to where I was.

She stood waist-deep in the water, and gently she took my hand. "Come, love. Come away, now. You can do no more for Duncan here."

Shaking my head, I clung to him. "I can't," I whispered. "I can't leave him this way. Please . . ." The words were as broken as my heart, as my precious Duncan's body. *I* was broken. I felt I could never rise from that cluster of deadly rocks, never drag myself to the shore, never so much as lift my head again. The very life seemed to have fled me. And I thought then 'twould have been better if it truly had.

"The sea takes care of its own, Raven," Arianna said softly. "His body belongs to the sea now. But you know his soul does not. You know that. Let him go, Raven."

I shook my head and held him still closer, my face resting against his cool cheek. "I'll never see him again," I moaned. "Never again . . ."

"But you will." She kept stroking me, my hair, my back. "He'll live again, Raven, you know that, as well." She spoke louder now, perhaps hoping the strength and command of her tone would reach me.

But nothing could reach the dark place where I lived now. "What does it matter? He's lost to me."

Arianna drew my face toward her, staring intently into my eyes from where she stood with the ocean waves lapping at her waist. "He died trying to save your life, Raven. When he lives again . . . he'll be as we are. Immortal. His selfless act of love earned him the gift, don't you see?"

Opening my eyes, lifting my head, I released a breath. "'Tis true," I whispered. "And never was any man more deserving. But don't *you* see, Arianna? *I'll* never know him. Never find him again."

Arianna reached down to stroke Duncan's wet hair away from his face. "But you will. 'Tis the full moon, Raven, when our powers wax strongest. I . . . I couldn't save him. There was no time to cast a spell of enough magnitude to overwhelm so many bent on destruction. But I slipped away, to the woods. I did all I could, Raven. I did all I could."

And at last her pain made itself known to me. I'd been so immersed in my own . . . I covered her hand with mine, where it rested upon Duncan's face.

"I was actually growing to . . . to like the man," she whispered, tears welling in her eyes.

"I know you'd have saved him if you could, my friend."

She met my eyes, her own glistening. "More than your friend, Raven. Your sister. I am your sister."

Sniffling, I nodded. "Yes, you are as a sister to me, closer even than that—"

"No. No, you aren't hearing me. You truly are my sister, or were, a lifetime ago. And my sister you remain."

I frowned, shocked and surprised. And yet it was as if she were telling me something I already knew.

"I was the eldest," she said, "practicing the Craft behind

our mother's back, in secret, with a group of Witches from our village. You never even knew, then—''

"But—''

She pressed a finger to my lips. "No, just listen. 'Twas many years ago, you know. I've waited a long while to tell you these things. So let me speak.'' In silence I nodded, and Arianna went on. "I didn't know what I was then. We were but girls, you and I, you a year younger, but always stronger.''

"*I?* Stronger than you?''

She nodded. "The year was fifteen-ten. We lived in the village of Stonehaven, in the shadow of Castle Lachlan in the Highlands of Scotland.''

"Scotland . . .'' I closed my eyes, lowering my face to Duncan's once more. " 'Tis where Duncan comes from, you know.''

"Yes, I know.''

"I didn't think I'd ever been there.''

"You were born there. Once.''

Sniffling, swiping away fresh tears, I nodded at her to go on.

"We were forbidden, of course, to play in the forests and lochs, but we did so all the same. I went too far into the water one day. My stomach cramped inexplicably, and I couldn't get back to shore.'' She touched my face, smiling gently. "You came for me, though, held me afloat and fought to get me to shore. And then there were others, the sons of Laird Lachlan himself. They swam out to help. But by then you'd been struggling with me for more than an hour. You were exhausted. Of course, they didn't realize it. They were concerned only with me, for I seemed to be the one in trouble. You never told them otherwise.'' She swallowed hard, loudly. "And when they eased me from your arms and drew me safely toward the shore, I looked back . . . and you were gone. Just slipped beneath the blue waters of the loch, leaving them so still 'twas as if you'd never been there.''

Staring at her, I whispered, "I drowned.''

"You drowned trying to save my life. The life of an immortal High Witch who didn't even know she was one at the time." She sighed slowly, and a tear slid down her cheek. "The lads went back after you, of course. And I stood there on the shore, knowing you'd left me, praying 'twas not too late to perform an incantation, so that I might know you again, one day. I called on all the powers of the Universe, Raven, and cast a potent spell. That when you lived again, 'twould be within my lifetime, and that you would look the same, and your name would again be Raven."

I tilted my head to the side, touched beyond measure at her words. "You did that for me?" I whispered.

"For me," she replied. "That I would have the joy of finding you again someday." She shook her head slowly. "Of course I had no idea then how long my lifetime would be. But the spell worked, Raven. I did find you, and you do look the same—older, yes, but just as you'd have looked before, if you'd had the chance to reach womanhood. And your name is Raven, just as it was then. And . . . and I love you, my sister."

A great sob welled up in my throat, choking the words. "I thought I had no family left . . . but I do. I have my sister."

She put her arms around me, held me tenderly for just a moment. Then stood back and stared hard into my eyes.

"I performed the same incantation tonight."

I frowned, searching her face.

"For Duncan. Even as he plummeted from the rocks, I hid myself in the forest and conjured with everything in me."

Now I looked at her, truly looked at her, though she blurred through my tears. And then I lowered my gaze to stare at Duncan's lifeless face. God, how I ached for him already.

" 'Twas all I could think of to do," she whispered. "He will live again, Raven. He will look the same. And his name will again be Duncan. You'll find him again someday, I promise you."

Blinking in disbelief, I muttered, "When?"

"I've no way of knowing that. Nor is he likely to re-member you, Raven, just as you had no memory of me when we met on the Coast Road that day. I did all I could do. I only hope 'twas enough to ease the grief I see in your eyes.''

Closing my eyes, I clutched her chilled hand in one of mine, and clung to my lost love with the other. '' 'Twill be enough,'' I promised. ''It shall have to be. 'Tis all I have.'' Then I opened my eyes and met hers. ''You've given me hope where I had none before. How will I ever thank you for this?''

She shook her head. ''I only wish I could have done more.'' Then she cleared her throat, lifted her chin. ''Raven, we have to leave here. If you hope to live long enough to find this man of yours again, we have to go at once.''

I stroked Duncan's face. ''We should bury him.''

''Listen to me,'' she said, and the urgency in her voice cut through the haze of mourning in my mind at last. ''The Witch-hunter Elias Stanton sent for arrived only a short while ago. I overheard some of the men talking about it. Saying the man was furious that Elias had taken action, instead of waiting for his arrival as he'd instructed. Saying the man would be out here soon, that he insisted on seeing the spot from whence you were thrown.''

My eyes widened, but I calmed myself quickly. ''They can kill me as many times as they wish, Arianna. I've no fear of them.''

''You don't understand. The Witch-hunter is an impostor, Raven. His name is Nathanial Dearborne and—''

''Nathanial Dearborne?'' Now she had my attention. ''The same arrogant priest who hanged my mother! I hope he does come. I'll—''

''He's no priest,'' Arianna whispered. ''He's a High Witch. One of the Dark Ones, Raven. One of the oldest and most powerful I've encountered.''

''You know him?''

Grimly she nodded. '' 'Twas he who murdered the only man I ever loved, and used me to do it. I nearly killed him then, but he escaped me. But it isn't me he'll be challenging this time, Raven. It's you he's come for. You can't best him in a fight and I can't protect you every minute of the day and night. If you want to keep your heart intact, we'd best not be here when he arrives.''

Nathanial Dearborne, a dark High Witch. It made sense
now. My mother's note had told me that I'd know another
only when I touched them—and that tingling sensation, the
one I'd become used to since Arianna had come into my
life—was the same one I'd felt when that beast touched my
hand as I hung in the stocks. I simply hadn't made the connection before now.

"Duncan wouldn't want you risking your life to bury his
empty shell, love," Arianna whispered. "Leave him to the
sea, and come. He'd want you to stay alive, to await his
return. You know he would."

I looked down at Duncan, lowering my head as tears
rained from my face to his. "Yes. I suppose he would."
Bending low, I kissed his cheek. "I love you, Duncan Wallace. In this lifetime and the next, I will always love you. I
vow it on my heart."

And gently I eased his broken body from the rocks. Even
as I did, an unusually large wave broke over us and swept
him from my hands as it washed back out to sea. As if the
sea were claiming him.

"Goodbye, my love," I whispered, but my words were
only whispers, my pain so great I could speak no louder.
And yet, I thought he might hear me.

Arianna touched my shoulders, and together we turned
and made our way back to shore.

Nathanial Dearborne ran all the way to the base of the cliffs
where she was supposed to have been thrown, but there was
no sign of the dark-haired wench.

Nor of his beloved Duncan.

He clenched his hand into a fist and shook it at the heavens. Again! She'd eluded him *again*.

And this time she'd taken young Duncan Wallace into
death with her! A death from which she could return . . .
and he could not.

"Damn her," Nathanial whispered. And fury rose up to
engulf him. Oh, Duncan would be back. Yes, he'd return.
But when he did, he, too, would be a High Witch. One of
the Light Ones, and as such, Nathanial's sworn enemy.

And if he knew Raven St. James, she'd manage to find the lad again, even then.

Then he paused, narrowing his eyes. What if she did? And what if, *when* she did, she found *him* as well?

Yes. Oh, he'd likely take the selfish bitch's heart long before then. He'd never stop trying to exact his vengeance. But if all else failed, he could use what he knew . . .

He could use Duncan . . .

If he could find the lad before she did.

But he would. He had to. He'd find a way. And he wouldn't rest until he'd exacted vengeance upon Raven St. James, until he'd cut out her heart and held it beating and bloody in the palm of his hand.

11

Weak. Heavy. Languid. My body did not want to move, and I had no will to argue with it. Arianna gripped my forearm, tugging me along in her wake as we trekked into the woods. The village lay to the north, and the forest was but a thin strip of shelter between Sanctuary and the sea. And that might have been enough to protect us, if everyone in town truly believed me dead. They'd have no reason to suspect Arianna would have lingered in the vicinity for so long.

But there *was* someone who knew better. Nathanial Dearborne. And my gut told me he hadn't traveled all the way from England only to accept defeat so easily. No, he would be searching for us. I felt it in my bones.

And still, I felt no desire to move. I only managed to continue sloughing along, dropping one foot ahead of the other, for Arianna's sake. If I sank to the ground as I wished right to my soul to do, if I surrendered, she'd stay with me. I knew she would. And there would be yet another life lost because of me. More blood on my hands. Yet another one dead because of having loved me.

I would not let that happen. So I moved. But I felt numb, and dead inside. Truly, had it not been for Arianna, I'd have simply remained in the icy cold sea until Dearborne came for me. Not because of a desire to die, but because I had

no desire not to. No reason to cling to my life. No will to
fight for it.

I loved Duncan, and he'd been murdered, and my heart
bled so profusely it seemed I could feel my life force draining away, bit by bit. Every breath drawn without him
seemed to come a little harder. Every heartbeat cost more
effort. Even lifting my head became too much work, so that
I slogged through the forest without looking up. Head hanging, hair in my face, wet dress dragging through the brush.
My only link to life, that small, strong hand gripping my
arm. A lifeline. An undeniable force dragging me slowly
forward, and maybe, inch by inch, out of the black swamp
of deadly grief into which I had fallen. It sucked at me like
quicksand, that grief. Pulled me under, choked me. But Arianna never let go. She refused to let it win.

And eventually, I surfaced enough to blink in the darkness
and ask in a voice without life, "Where are we?"

She turned her head sharply, her steps ceasing all at once.
But she did not remark on my finally having spoken. "Deep
in the forest, heading south," she explained. "We got past
the settlement, and we're well into the mainland by now."

It seemed it took my brain a long moment to process her
words. They fell on my ears like meaningless noise and
gradually worked through the machinery of my mind and
made sense. "Already?" I asked her, not really caring, but
vaguely aware of how disoriented I was.

"We've been walking for hours," she said, her eyes intense, probing mine. "It's nearly dawn, Raven."

Nearly dawn? How strange . . . how very . . . *wrong* that
the sun would rise again now that Duncan was gone. It made
no sense, somehow.

"Dearborne's following. We must keep moving." And
she started forward again, tugging me into motion.

My legs hurt, and I glanced down to see that my dress
was ripped to ribbons now. I could see bloodstains here and
there. Obviously I'd walked like a blind person, through
brush and brambles, never moving them aside, scratching
my flesh and never feeling the sting. I felt it now. It began
slowly, as my brain registered what my eyes were seeing,
and told me that my legs should hurt. Then grew sharper,

hotter. I lifted my hand to my cheek when that, too, began to pulse, and I discovered a long scratch there.

'Twould heal soon enough. That was part of the powers we both possessed, the rapid regeneration of any wounds we might suffer. Already, even the faintest bruise caused by my fall from the cliffs would have vanished. These new injuries would, as well. 'Twas one of the things we all had in common.

Our other powers were not so easily identified. For they were different from Witch to Witch, even in ordinary mortal ones. Some were gifted at divination, some at reading the stars. Some were psychic, some in touch with the spirit realm. Some could manipulate the weather, while others could communicate with animals. In immortal High Witches the area of power became magnified, and, Arianna had explained, other magickal gifts began to appear, and to grow. She'd told me that some of the very old ones had even mastered shape-shifting, though I doubted the validity of that tall tale.

My own powers were those of healing, always had been. But the longer I remained in this new form, this stronger, more sensitive, immortal form, the more I realized that my healing magick was only one very small part of my abilities.

There were more. Many more. Some, I'd discovered aboard the *Sea Witch* during my crossing. The acute hearing, the enhanced eyesight, and night vision. The ability to scent things, and people. And every spell I had cast since coming here had been incredibly potent, bringing immediate, incredible results. The fertility ritual I'd done for Aunt Eleanor's old cow had produce a successful mating the very next day, and twin calves, big and healthy. When I'd worked a charm to increase our flock of laying hens, the results had required a larger shed be built for them all! When I wanted a sunny day for Aunt Eleanor, or rain for our vegetable patch, it happened almost as soon as the thought appeared in my mind. And a prickling sense in the back of my neck usually warned me when danger was near.

'Twas there now.

"He's close," I said.

Arianna stopped walking, turned to scan the woods. "I

know. I feel him, too. But I don't think he'll make a move when I'm with you, Raven. He knows I—''

An explosion ripped through the forest, and Arianna stopped speaking and jerked. Her jaw gaped, worked soundlessly, and I cried out as I saw the gaping wound in my beloved sister's chest. The blackened edges of the hole in the shirt she wore.

I reached for her, but Arianna's eyes rolled and she slumped to the ground. Whirling, I scanned the trees, and then I saw him. Nathanial Dearborne, there among the pines. In his hands he clutched a musket, which stank of sulphur and spewed black smoke from its dark, deadly eye.

''You bastard,'' I whispered. ''I'll not let you take her heart. I will not!'' In a heartbeat my dagger was in my fist, and the numbness was fleeing from my body. I may have had no reason to live a moment ago. Now, though, I had found one. Vengeance. ''You killed my mother in the name of God, when you're nothing but purest evil. And I lost my love to the same vile lie. I'll not let you kill my sister as well!''

''Sister, is it?'' He stepped forward, dropping the now useless weapon to the ground, knowing, perhaps, that should he try to load it again, I'd attack before he could finish the job. He pulled his own dagger from his hip, saluted me with it mockingly. ''For now, Raven St. James, 'tis your heart I want, not hers.''

''Then try to take it!'' I shouted.

''Oh, I will. And long before your . . : *sister* revives to come to your rescue. It's almost too good. Not only do I get my vengeance on you . . . but on her, as well. Can you imagine her grief when she wakes to find your lifeless body lying at her feet?''

''The only corpse to litter this ground will be yours!'' I cried, and crept closer, my blade before me, though my hand trembled.

He came a step closer to me as well, then another. ''I've killed hundreds, over the centuries,'' he told me, his voice strong, sure. ''How many have you taken, Raven?''

I blinked. He was trying to frighten me, to shake me. And

he succeeded. I'd never killed. And despite all of Arianna's training, I doubted my skills now.

"I could kill you so very easily, so quickly," he said, coming still closer, then standing near enough so I could feel the heat rising from his body and see the fog of his breath appear and vanish again on the deadly blade he held. "So very quickly, you'd never know what happened." Then he smiled. "But I'm not going to."

I lunged forward, swinging my blade, and nicking his belly before he could jump back. He hooked a leg behind mine as I drew back from him in anticipation of his return thrust. Then he shoved me with his hand, so that I toppled backward to the ground.

He was upon me in an instant, straddling my chest and pressing me down into the earth so forcefully that I could scarcely draw a breath. Clutching both my wrists in one of his large hands, he pinned them to the ground above my head. He smiled down at me, a frightening grimace of a smile. "It's going to be slow, Raven," he said. "We have time."

"Why?" I whispered. "Why do you hate me so much?"

"You figure it out," he told me, and with his free hand, he sliced open the front of my dress, from my waist to my neck. Using the blade again, he parted it, baring my chest, my breasts. Then, the knife still in his hand, he touched me, the backs of his knuckles pressing to the center of my chest. "Right there," he said. "Beating so fast . . . so hard. It's strong, your heart. You'll stay conscious as I begin to cut it from you, you know. I know how to do it."

"Please," I whispered, a tremor working through me from head to toe. Suddenly I didn't want to die at all. Not at all, and most certainly not like this. "Please, I'm so young. What good can my heart possibly be to you?"

"You're so clueless, my dear," he whispered. "So very young, and naive." He traced a path on my breastbone with the cold tip of his dagger. "You have immense power in you. Wasted on one with no idea what to do with it."

"I . . . I . . ."

"And then there's vengeance," he went on. "Always a strong motivator." He traced the same path again, this time cutting me, but not deeply. Just breaking the skin and leaving a bloody outline of the pattern he drew.

I whimpered. He smiled wider.

"What have I ever done to you?" I cried.

"You took my s . . . you took Duncan. You turned him against me, and now you've cost him his life."

"B-but he'll return—"

"As my sworn enemy! All because of you! Damn you, Raven St. James!" Eyes blazing, he lifted the dagger high above me, blade pointing down.

I opened my mouth to scream, but the sound never emerged. There was, instead, a soft hissing sound, and then the thud of an arrow driving into Nathanial's chest. He looked surprised for just an instant, then fell over backward.

I scrambled to my feet, pulling my torn dress around me and searching the forest.

The silver-haired red man . . . the one who'd given me the fish for breakfast a full two years ago . . . he stood in the distance, his bow in one hand, his black eyes holding mine. My hands went to my face as relief swamped me and tears sprang to my eyes. And my dress fell open again. The man's eyes lowered, affixed upon my bared breasts, I thought at first. And then I realized that wasn't it at all. He looked at the place where Nathanial had cut me, and his eyes widened as the skin there drew itself together, and mended. I quickly covered myself, but too late. He'd seen.

And even if he hadn't, our secret would have been out. For when I turned, 'twas to see two other shirtless, dark-skinned men in buckskins, leaning over Arianna, then backing away as she sucked in her first new breath with a loud, desperate gasp. Her back arched off the ground, even as the hole in her chest closed in on itself and the younger men's eyes widened.

I lunged forward, uncertain what they would do to her. But the silver-haired man touched my arm, and when I turned, implored me with his eyes. Narrowing my gaze, I searched his face. And finally, seeing no ill intent there, I nodded once.

He in turn raised a hand to the other two, and they picked Arianna up even as she was blinking her eyes open and looking around her. Silver-Hair took my arm, his grip gentle, and the five of us marched away, through the forest. I tugged free once, turning back, realizing Dearborne would revive, that there was only one way I could ensure that he stay dead.

But the old red man met my eyes, shook his head once, and took my arm again.

"Another time, then," I whispered. "Another time."

His name, in English, was Trees Speaking. In his own tongue, 'twas impossible for me to pronounce, and my constant attempts only made the other members of his tribe laugh at me as we all sat around a central fire that night, in their village. Long, narrow buildings all covered in pale bark served as their homes, and it seemed many generations of a given family resided in each one. But the gathering place, which seemed to serve as many purposes as the meeting hall in Sanctuary, was the area around this central fire.

'Twas there we were taken, and urged to sit. The old one spoke in a tongue that was like something ancient and sacred to my ears, and people spilled from their homes and stopped whatever they were doing, to stare at us, with wide, shining dark eyes. In a moment they broke away, running in a dozen directions. A dark, beautiful woman brought cloaks of whisper-soft doe hide to drape gently over our shoulders, while another, a plump young woman with an infant strapped to her back in some ingenious contraption, brought bowls filled with something like stew. Another draped a dress across my lap, and another dropped beads atop it. And one by one every member of this clan gathered round the fire, all seeming to vie for the spots nearest Arianna and me. We kept exchanging glances and shrugging. Neither of us knowing what to expect, much less what to say as they spoke to us in words we could not understand.

Finally a young girl, perhaps twelve or even younger, began to speak to me in halting English.

"I know some . . . white man tongue," she said slowly. "My name Laughing River."

I was surprised at her knowledge of English. And yet should not have been. The settlers were all around these people. They'd be wise to learn their language, and obviously they were that.

"My name is Raven," I told the beautiful, sloe-eyed child.

"Raven?" And when I nodded, she turned to repeat the word to the rest in their tongue. Then turned to Arianna.

"I am Arianna."

Laughing River tilted her head. "Ahhhrrrr . . ."

"Arianna," my sister repeated.

"Ahhrranna." Laughing River nodded hard and said it again, with authority this time. Many in the circle tried to pronounce the name, but it only resulted in more laughter.

Laughing River pointed to the silver-haired elder. "Trees Speaking."

"Trees Speaking," I repeated. " 'Tis beautiful."

"When Trees Speaking is born," she told me, and waved a hand toward the towering pines around us, "wind in trees tell all he is Shaman."

I tilted my head. "Shaman? What is a Shaman?"

Laughing River frowned hard. "Trees Speaking tell us you are Shaman, like he. He say you . . ." She moved her hands trying to express her words, and Trees Speaking spoke softly to her. She nodded hard, and translated. "He say you like him. You walk with spirits. You make powerful . . . medicine."

I blinked, and glanced at Arianna. She lifted her brows and looked at the girl. "Magick?"

"Yes! Magick!" Laughing River said, nodding hard.

"Is that what a Shaman does?"

"Yes."

She looked again at Trees Speaking, as I did. And then at those around him. They looked at him with respect, listened when he spoke, seemed to love the man.

"Then, I guess we are . . . Shamans . . . of a sort," Arianna finally said. I heard the relief in her voice, for it seemed obvious a person of magick would be treated far differently here than among the whites.

"White man fear Shaman," Laughing River said. And her eyes went sad. "Trees Speaking say white man try kill all who make magick."

I nodded. "Trees Speaking is telling you the truth, I fear. They don't understand us."

The girl translated, and the old man nodded. Then he spoke again, and the girl smiled. "Trees Speaking say no one hurt you here. Magick sacred, even white woman's magick. He say you stay."

I glanced at Arianna. She swallowed hard. "I don't know," she whispered. "I hate to drag them into this. Suppose Dearborne hurts them because of us?"

Laughing River quickly translated what was not meant to be shared, and to my surprise, the men around the fire burst into laughter. Our eyes must have registered our surprise, because the girl quickly explained. "They laugh because they know one white man no threat to them. They warriors, Crow-Woman."

Crow-Woman? I supposed it might be close to "Raven" from her point of view, but . . .

"No white man harm you here. Our warriors fierce. Strong." There was pride in her voice.

Trees Speaking rose from his cross-legged position on the ground and smiled down at us. "Show me," he said, very slowly, eyes narrow as he struggled to put the words together properly in his deep, raspy voice, a voice like the wind he was named for. "Show me . . . your ways . . . your . . . *magick*." Then he touched his chest, patted it three times. "I show you my ways . . . my magic."

I looked at Arianna and blinked. A sparkle appeared in her eyes. "There are many, many kinds of Witches, Raven," she whispered, "and not all of us use that particular word for what we are. Some call themselves Druids, some monks, some holy men." She glanced at Trees Speaking. "Some Shaman. He could teach us a great deal, I think."

Looking back at him, I recalled the way he'd watched me—perhaps, watched *over me*?—when I'd spent that lonely night in the woods so long ago. "Why not?" I replied. "We have nothing to lose."

A flash of sadness clouded her eyes, but she turned to Trees Speaking and nodded. "Yes. We'll stay."

Trees Speaking smiled broadly. And so we stayed.

We spent well over a fortnight at that Iroquois village, sharing knowledge and esoteric wisdom with Trees Speaking. And I realized that Arianna had been right. There were many kinds of Witches. He was practicing virtually the same belief system we did ourselves. We only called it by different names. Trees Speaking told us of the sacred importance of the circle, and how he worked within one when doing magick. And we told him we did the same. He spoke of calling upon the Divine spirit residing in things like the wind, and the water, and the earth itself, and we marveled at that, for we had, as well. He told us how the basis of his power was his belief that all life is truly linked together through a common source, and again, we were awestruck.

But there was more Trees Speaking taught us. Things we hadn't seen or practiced before. He taught us to hear what animals might be telling us by watching their movements and picking out signs and omens. He taught us the medicinal uses of many plants and herbs native to this land and growing wild within its forests. And perhaps, most amazingly of all, he taught us the secrets of invisibility.

I thought the man insane when he brought this up with us, but he only smiled, and, through Laughing River, explained. One doesn't truly vanish. One simply becomes so attuned to his surroundings that he blends into them, and onlookers don't see him there. He demonstrated this by hiding and asking us to search for him. When we did, we couldn't find him anywhere. But then he spoke, and we turned and saw him clearly, standing with his back pressed to a tree trunk. He insisted he'd been there all along. So we listened and practiced and learned, and tested our newfound knowledge by games of hide-and-seek with the villagers.

Each night Trees Speaking would whisper some of his beautiful words to me before I retired to a place of honor in his family's longhouse. He would move his hands over me and chant. And he told me he was working to mend my broken heart, for he could see it clearly in my eyes. Truly, my time there helped me far more than anything else could have done. By immersing myself in learning about these people and their ways and their magick, I was able to go on living. But the pain of losing Duncan remained fresh and strong in me. I thought it likely always would.

Finally we had to move on. 'Twas not planned, nor even thought through. But we knew 'twas time to leave when one of the young men returned from a journey bearing meat and furs aplenty, and bringing news that shook me to the marrow. He spoke it to Laughing River, and her face paled, eyes widened. She turned to me, and I saw moisture spring into her shining eyes.

"Crow-Woman," she said. "Bear Killer say white women . . . die. Many, many killed."

I frowned. "I . . . don't understand. What white women? How were they killed, and why?"

She lowered her head. "White man say they . . . like you. Shaman. Witches."

My stomach convulsed, and my lips pressed tight as if to stop it.

Arianna's face went stony. "Where?" she asked.

"If you go they kill you, too!" Laughing River cried.

"Where, Laughing River?"

She closed her eyes. "Place called . . . Sa-lem Village."

"Salem Village." Arianna shook her head, closed her eyes. "I doubt there's a genuine Witch in the bunch."

"Does it make a difference?" I asked her.

"Of course not. They're executing innocents either way. Innocent Witches, or innocent women who know nothing of magick, wrongly accused."

I tipped my head back, searching the sky. "We have to go," I said softly. "We're stronger, more powerful, harder to kill—"

"*Much* harder to kill," she said.

"We have an obligation, then."

"We do," she agreed.

We stared at each other, both of us wondering what turn life would bring to us next. Both of us afraid, and yet a bit excited. My losing Duncan had done one thing for me besides cause me unspeakable pain. It had made me lose my fear of dying.

For the next six months Arianna and I were shadows in the night. We'd slip into Salem by darkness, freeing women from the stocks, and from the locked rooms where they were imprisoned. Often with their children, even babies, locked up with them. Filthy, malnourished, and thirsting, no blankets. Many had been tortured. And none of them seemed to have a working knowledge of the Craft of the Wise. Perhaps some genuine Witches had been hanged or burned when the madness had first run wild in Salem. Perhaps . . . but not now. Now anyone with a grudge could cry accusations against her enemy, and see that enemy tried, her very life in the balance.

'Twas the purest form of evil I'd seen since the day I set eyes on Nathanial Dearborne. And 'twas only much later that I learned that Dark Witch himself had been in Salem Village only a short while before the madness began. No doubt the bastard had been instrumental in starting this fire that swept through the place, destroying everything it touched.

We rescued dozens, Arianna and I. Women and children whose fates had been sealed. We took them deep into the forests and hid them there. Some had families still alive and not yet accused. So we located those loved ones and brought them out as well. Our band of outcasts and refugees numbered fifty and more by the time the fury in Salem ran its course. And at last we led them all southward, into Pennsylvania Colony and a Quaker settlement there.

The journey took nearly two months. Alone, they'd have perished. But Arianna and I were able to find food, to fish the streams, and gather roots and greens thanks to all Trees Speaking and his people had taught us, and they survived.

In their new village, they used false names, just in case. But they'd be safe in this place. I sensed it, and felt good about something for the first time since I'd lost Duncan.

And yet those we hadn't been able to save . . . how they haunted me. I knew their names, every one of them. Sarah Osborne. Bridget Bishop. Sarah Good and her tiny baby. Elizabeth How. Susannah Martin. Rebecca Nurse. Sarah Wildes. Martha Carrier. George Jacobs. John Proctor. John Willard. Ann Foster. Giles and Martha Corey. Mary Esty. Alice Parker. Mary Parker. Ann Pudeator. Wilmot Reed. Margaret Scott. Samuel Wardwell. Sarah Dastin. I knew not whether they had been of my own faith . . . nor did I care.

They'd been living, breathing sisters of the human race. My sisters. And brothers. And children. My dear mother's face seemed to appear in my mind as I tried to imagine the faces of the women who'd died.

And Duncan's face hovered in my mind's eye when I thought of the Reverend George Burroughs, a minister who'd suffered the same fate as my beloved Duncan. Not being pitched from the cliffs, no. Reverend Burroughs was hanged. Choked to death by a rope, and I knew that feeling all too well. But just like Duncan, the man had died at the hands of his own flock. Had I been a Puritan in Salem then, I'd have renounced my faith out of sheer shame for what had been done in its name.

I wept for all of them nightly for a long, long time after that. Sometimes, when it's quiet and I'm alone, I still do. I cry for them . . . I cry for Duncan . . . I cry for myself, having lost him.

And my grief, it seems, is as immortal as my body, for it lives on still. Every bit as powerful, every bit as painful, as it was before . . . though three full centuries have come and gone.

Part Two

12

Three hundred years later, on the anniversary of Duncan's death, I stood on the cliffs of Sanctuary, facing the sea. There was a lighthouse standing offshore now. It reached skyward from the tiny, lonely island where before there had been only seabirds and the occasional treasure hunter. Built a century ago, it had been used for a time, and then forgotten. Then it had been abandoned for the better part of five decades, its rounded glass looking like a lifeless, sightless eye. A sad reminder of the way time moved on all around me. The way the world grew and changed and evolved.

I did not.

There had been movement at the lighthouse a month or so ago. For a moment I'd felt an absurd hope spring up in my heart, a foolish joy the place seemed to be about to come back to life.

But I had not.

I was in limbo, living, but incomplete, waiting, always waiting for the return of my soulmate. My lover. I'd been many places in the endless years of my life. But wherever I roamed, I had but one purpose—to search for him. I scanned every sea of strange faces in search of the one I hoped to see.

In three hundred years that search had left me with nothing but disappointment.

I stood with my feet apart, arms spread wide, head tilted back. The sea wind whipped my hair behind me, and a soft glow painted my face as the full moon rose over the ocean. I knew, had always known, of the power in the moon. A physical tug, a pull. The waves felt it; the tides changed because of it. Animals felt it. Coyotes and wolves bayed in response. Lunatics felt it, stirring the sickness in their minds.

Witches felt it.

The surge of power within growing stronger and peaking with the moon. At the full moon I felt I could do anything. I was invulnerable, invincible, and as powerful as the Goddess herself. And I had only one focus for the immense power the full moon gave to me.

Duncan.

But something was different tonight. Perhaps it was only the endless longing in my heart—heaven knew it had been often enough before—but I felt more hopeful than usual. I felt as if . . . as if perhaps he were near.

And yet I couldn't trust my own feelings where Duncan was concerned, for "wishful thinking" was real and powerful and sometimes too potent to distinguish from true intuition.

Standing at the eastern edge of the circle I had cast, I spread my arms and felt the wind on my face. "Mighty Energies of the East, Sacred Ones of Air, I call on you to attend this circle and empower these rites." Immediately the wind in my face sharpened.

To my right, facing South, Arianna stood in the same position I had, arms spread outward and upward. She'd kept her blond hair short, and it ruffled in the breeze like the feathers of a golden bird preparing to take flight. Softly she intoned, "Ancient Energies of the South, Blessed Ones of Fire, I call on you to attend this circle and empower these rites."

As I watched her, Arianna's face glowed, just for a moment, as if someone held a candle before her, but no candle was there. Only the balefire we'd built, but that was behind her, in the circle's center. Her huge brown eyes flicked open, and she tilted her head as if she'd felt that warmth on her face.

Solemnly, I crossed to the opposite side, the west. "Healing Energies of the West, Ancient Ones of Water, I call on you to attend this circle and empower these rites."

Dampness . . . dotting my face, my forearms. I blinked at the mist that rose from the ground to leave its kiss of moisture on my skin. Truly some powerful magic would be worked here tonight.

Arianna had moved to the North now, and in a strong voice she called, "Powerful Energies of the North, Eternal Mother Earth, I call on you to attend this circle and empower these rites."

And then I started, because I felt the earth herself rumble beneath me. A deep-throated vibration welled up from the ground, trembling against my feet and shaking my body so slightly I might have imagined it. When my wide-eyed gaze shot to Arianna's, she met it, and nodded once. She'd felt it, too.

I moved to the center of the circle, then, to invoke the fifth element, that of spirit. And then together we said the words that would bring the presence of Divinity to our circle this night. When we finished it seemed that the circle pulsed more powerfully with unseen energies than it had ever done before.

Meeting Arianna's eyes, I saw that she knew what I did. Something had changed. Something was happening. I'd planned to recite an incantation, to cast and to conjure this night, just as I had on every Esbat night for the past three hundred years. I used every power I possessed to ensure that when Duncan returned, as I knew he would one day, he would come here. To Sanctuary. To me. Over and over I'd willed the elements and every force of the astral plane to bring Duncan back here, to the place where I'd lost him. I could not hasten his return; it would have been wrong of me to try. His soul would incarnate again only when it was ready, when the time was right. But my greatest fear was that when he did live again, I'd never find him. The world was a big place, after all.

And though I sought him everywhere I went, I always returned here, where I waited. Endlessly waited, for his return.

But tonight was not the same as all those other nights when I'd worked my magick. As I stood in the center of my circle this night, with the large flat stone before me and the tools of my craft spread out upon it—cauldron and blade, wand and pentacle, censers and candles—I felt something different.

The winds of the four directions seemed to spin and whirl about the two of us as Arianna and I knelt before the altar, and she looked up into my eyes.

"No conjuring tonight, Raven," she whispered. "Something's not right here. I *feel* it."

Blinking, I lowered my head. "Perhaps the Universe is angry with me. . . . Plotting to make Duncan come here even if it's against his wishes is not exactly ethical."

She shook her head. "I've never seen the elements react this way to a tiny bit of arguably manipulative magick before." She moved closer to me as the whirlwind swept around us, around the balefire and the altar stone at the circle's center. The swirling action of the wind on the flames was something to see, for they narrowed and lengthened as if the fire reached toward the heavens. A loud cry made me look up fast, gripping Arianna's hand as I did, only to see a large raven land upon the stone altar. It looked at me, tilted its shiny black head, and looked at me again. The balefire's flames leaped with a snap and a hiss, and I gasped as in the brighter light of the fire, I saw more clearly.

"Look! He's injured!"

Arianna squinted, leaning closer, and saw the tiny droplet of blood that clung, quivering, to the bird's gleaming breast. It trembled as if in time with the tiny rapid heartbeat. I reached out very slowly. "Come, namesake. Let me tend that for you."

But the bird only squawked once more and, lifting its great wings, pumped them mightily and flew away.

Still staring at the spot where the bird had been, I whispered, "What does it mean?"

Arianna squeezed my hand. "The Druids said Ravens brought warnings. I don't know, Raven, it was as if he were trying to tell you something."

"But what?" I saw the blankness in her eyes, and rubbed my hands over my chilled arms. She wouldn't speak it, but I knew what she was thinking. A raven—with a wound over his heart. It could well portend my death. Even now there might be a Dark One lurking, waiting to . . .

"You've survived their attempts before, Raven," Arianna whispered, as if reading my thoughts. "You're as good with your blade as I am now. You can defend yourself."

I nodded, but the chill of fear still danced barefoot over my spine. "Let's close the circle, Arianna. Something feels . . . wrong."

"All right." Quietly then, we performed the closing rites, and then gathered up our tools and turned our backs to the sea, facing the giant of a house.

It had begun as a simple home built on the site of my dear aunt Eleanor's cabin. But it had . . . grown. We had money enough. Two talented Witches with several centuries to accumulate wealth would always have money enough to do whatever they wanted. Adding on to the house had become a bit of a hobby. A tradition. Almost an inside joke. The rambling structure was so utterly outrageous now it would no doubt have drawn curious sightseers from town in droves . . . under normal circumstances.

But we were *Witches*. We cast spells over the place, and wove astral shields to protect it. It wasn't invisible, of course. But it blended in with the woods if one viewed it from the east, with the sea if one viewed it from the west, the sky if one looked at it from below. There were ways to avoid notice. There was magick.

Of course, we came and went often . . . and sometimes were forced to let years pass between visits, just to make sure the locals never became suspicious.

It was easier now, though. Sanctuary boasted few actual residents. Oh, there were the lobster men on the north shore, and the shop owners on the south. Innkeepers scattered

hither and yon, and a handful of restauranteurs. But most of
the people who came here today were vacationers in search
of a coastal getaway and some autumn foliage. That log
village with its mud tracks that I'd ridden into so long ago
was long forgotten now. A tourist-trap had emerged in its
place. It was no longer even part of Massachusetts, but of
Maine, which itself had been a part of Massachusetts Bay
Colony three hundred years ago.

As we approached the sprawling home we'd created, I
felt Arianna nudge my ribs. "Shall we add a new wing this
visit? Georgian this time?"

She was attempting to cheer me, I knew. "We did that
in thirty-seven, love," I said, pointing to the stately brick
section that housed our overflowing library, our favorite sitting room, and a small alcove for . . . for whatever purpose
we could think of. I'd thought as we'd built it how Duncan
would love it. How we could sit there together, in that alcove, and reminisce, and . . .

Tears welled up in my eyes. I rarely spent a day when
they didn't.

"Oh," Arianna said. "Well, Victorian, then? Or Gothic?
Gothic would be so poetic for a pair of Witches, don't you
think?"

"You're forgetting the west wing, Arianna. With the gar-
goyles we imported from France in eighteen-ninety-nine lining the roof."

"Right, that slipped my mind." She pouted. "Do we
have a colonial wing?"

"Complete with a cobblestone hearth," I said, smiling,
letting my friend draw me out of my contemplative state.
"Face it, Arianna, we have everything except a log cabin
sprouting from this house of ours."

"A log cabin . . ." Arianna said, clasping her chin and
tilting her head as she studied the many roofs, some steep,
some shallow, some flat, some slate, some steel, some shin-
gled, all sporting chimneys—cobblestone, brick, block, and
steel. "No," Arianna said thoughtfully. "Logs would simply clash."

The laughter burst from me just as she'd intended it to.
And she smiled at my reaction as she reached for the back

door. "It's good to see you laugh, Raven," she said softly, pulling our door open, smiling back at me. "It's so seldom that you do." Then her smile died as she stared past me, out toward the sea, and a curious frown creased her brow. "Oh, look."

"What is it?" I turned to follow her gaze and saw that the old lighthouse standing dark and lonely on its tiny island was coming alive again. A light came on in one of the lower windows. Why it should thrill me so, I had no idea. Seeing a light in formerly dead eyes . . . perhaps somewhere inside it reminded me of my long wait, and my hope that my dead lover would be restored to me one day soon. Another light came on, followed by another. And for just an instant I felt a shiver as an icy finger trailed a path up my spine.

"Just what we need," I muttered. "A new neighbor—and so close." A reaction that made far more sense than the one I truly felt.

"Raven," Arianna whispered. "Raven, look . . ."

She pointed to a dark shape moving in the sky, and as I squinted and it moved into the moonlight, I realized it wasn't one shape but several; a dozen or more ravens, flying toward the lighthouse. One by one they landed atop it, or around it. And then in chorus they began to shout.

Drawn by invisible hands, I walked toward them, until Arianna clasped my shoulders, drawing me to a halt.

"Come inside, Raven."

"I should go there," I whispered. "They're telling me something, don't you see?"

"Yes. And what if what they're telling you is 'Stay away from here, Raven St. James!' What then, hmm?"

I blinked, shaking my head. "I don't think—"

"The Celts used to say that when evil preachers died, they were transformed into ravens," she blurted.

And I blinked, my stomach clenching. The only evil preacher I knew—had ever known—was Nathanial Dearborne. The bastard who'd killed my mother and hunted me all my days. How many times had I barely escaped his blade? How many more would there be before one of us paid the ultimate price?

Perhaps it was he the birds warned me of. Perhaps he'd

caught up to me again after all these years. He was long overdue for another attempt. And maybe he'd finally found our haven, the place we'd kept so secret we'd hoped no other immortal would ever know we came here.

"Why is that bastard so determined to have my heart?" I whispered.

"You know why, Raven."

I closed my eyes. "Because of Duncan."

"Yes. Because of Duncan. And because of your magickal power—you've always known how special it is, Raven. You have a healing gift like no other, and you're able to draw luck and good fortune to you like no Witch I've known."

I closed my eyes. "I've lived three hundred years without the man I love. You call that luck or good fortune?"

"You know what I mean. The wealth, Raven. The way you and your aunt prospered back then, and the way we do now."

"Any Witch could do that."

"I lived two hundred years before I found you again, Raven. And I never managed it."

"You got by."

"Getting by is irrelevant. Have you looked at our bank statements lately?"

I sighed. Making good financial decisions had always come as naturally to me as breathing. It wasn't something I was overly proud of, but I doubted I could help it if I tried. If I bought a stock, it skyrocketed. If I opened a bank account, the interest rate went up. If I bought so much as a lottery ticket . . .

"And now there's your age, as well," Arianna went on. "Nathanial would get a lot of life force from a heart three centuries strong. Besides all of that, the more times you thwart him, the more angry and determined he becomes. You know that, as well."

Lowering my head very slowly, I said, "I'm going to have to kill him, aren't I?"

Arianna nodded. "I'm afraid it's the only way you'll ever find peace." She searched my face. "You've killed before, Raven. He wouldn't be your first."

"Yes," I admitted, "but only in battle, when it was

forced on me. Only when I had no choice. It takes something from me when I take a life, Arianna. I die a little each time."

"The bastard needs killing," Arianna told me.

"But not by me. Not unless he forces me to." I bit my lower lip. "We'll leave here for a while. Tomorrow. I'd rather avoid confrontation if I can."

Tipping her head skyward, Arianna rolled her eyes. "Raven! Why must you be such a pacifist? After three centuries of living as a being who must kill or be killed, how can you cling to that mortal idea of morality? I swear, if I get the chance, I'll cut out that black heart of his myself." I looked at her harshly. "I *will*!" she vowed. "I've owed that bastard for a long time. But he's as slippery as a snake where I'm concerned."

"He does avoid you," I said, contemplating. "It's as if he's always out there, watching us, waiting. Every time he's attacked me since Duncan, it has been when you and I were apart. In Virginia, when I stayed behind to care for that ailing woman, while you went off to find her husband. In California, when I sat on the beach thinking of Duncan while you slept soundly in the beach house. In New York when we got separated in that crowd at the theater . . ."

"Because he knows I can take him."

"I suspect you're right," I told her. "And that's why he never gives you the chance. It's me he comes after. Always me . . . and those I love."

"So you'll run from him again," Arianna went on. "And what if Duncan returns here while you're hiding from Dearborne? What if you miss your chance to find him again?"

I only shook my head. "That won't happen. We can keep watch from a safe distance."

"He won't come after you if I'm here, Raven."

"You can't watch over me twenty-four hours a day, Arianna."

"But we're not even sure Dearborne is here yet!" she wailed.

I turned to stare out at the night sky, at the full moon, and even as I did, a dark cloud eclipsed its golden face.

"He's here," I whispered. "I feel it. He's here."

• • •

Duncan stood near the curving glass windows of the lighthouse for a long time. Alone, as utterly alone as he'd always
been.

She'd been out there again tonight.

The same woman, he was sure of that. The same one he'd
glimpsed that first night he'd come here, a month ago. When
this had been just another job, and not one he particularly
wanted at that. Not that restoring a century-old lighthouse
wasn't exactly the kind of thing he loved best . . . just that
it meant spending months surrounded by water. And he
hadn't been over the fear of water all that long. Heights
barely gave him a second thought anymore, but the water . . .

Still, he'd agreed to come out here, take a look at the
place. And he still wasn't exactly sure why he'd done that
when he'd been certain this was one restoration job he'd be
turning down. He only knew that a strange sort of pit-of-
the-stomach feeling had started gnawing at him from the
moment he'd set foot in this tourist mecca town. And when
he and the owner left shore in a small motorboat the first
time to head out to the lighthouse, the physical reactions,
the cold sweat and rapid heartbeat he'd been expecting,
hadn't come. They'd been overpowered by different reactions, unexpected ones as he stared back at the peninsula,
and the cliffs at its tip. A clenching sensation in his stomach.
An empty well opening in the vicinity of his heart. A tight-
ening in his throat that made it hard to swallow.

All of that only got worse once he was inside the lighthouse, discussing the renovations with the owner, who
wanted to fix it up and sell it. Already, he'd been reconsid-
ering his earlier decision not to take on the job.

Then he'd glimpsed her. Through these very windows.
She stood like some kind of sea goddess, on those cliffs,
with the wind lifting her satin hair like a flag. Her face
turned up to the rising moon as if she were drinking in every
moonbeam. And he'd lost track of what the owner was saying, of what he was supposed to be doing here as he'd
watched her, mesmerized. Someone said, "So how much

do you want for this place?'' and he realized later it had been him.

And now he owned it. *Him.* The guy who'd had a crippling, inexplicable fear of water ever since he'd been a toddler had bought himself an old abandoned lighthouse surrounded by the stuff. And he wasn't even sure why.

But he was pretty sure it had something to do with *her.*

She'd been out there again tonight, soft breeze fingering her long, dark hair, yellow moonlight bathing her face. There had been another one with her, a tiny blond, but he'd barely noticed. The two had gone inside now . . . back into that twisted-up mishmash of a house that towered up there.

Odd, that house. He'd commented on it to lighthouse's former owner, and the guy claimed he'd never even noticed the place.

How could anyone not notice *that*?

He shook his head and looked at the place atop the cliffs once more. The bonfire burned low, and by and by the blond one came back outside with a pail of water to pour over it. But of the dark one, he saw no more.

The cell phone bleated, and Duncan reached for it, still watching for a glimpse of the woman on the cliffs as if he were some sort of stalker. God, what was wrong with him? He jerked his gaze away deliberately and answered the call. Just before he brought the phone to his ear, he thought of his father, and almost laughed at himself. He often got an inkling of who was on the other end when the phone rang.

Then his jaw dropped when he heard his father's voice on the other end. ''Is that you, Duncan? There's so much static . . .''

''Father?''

''Ah, then it *is* you. Good.''

Duncan licked his dry lips. His father wouldn't be calling unless . . . ''Is something wrong?''

''No, no. I heard you'd bought a lighthouse . . . on an island of all things! Couldn't believe it.''

Frowning, Duncan shook his head. ''It's true. To be honest, Father, I can't imagine you'd be all that interested.''

His father cleared his throat. "I know we haven't been . . . close . . . since you left home."

"Since I left home?" If he sounded sarcastic, he ought to. His father had ignored him most of his life . . . and Duncan often wondered why the man had bothered adopting him in the first place. As a newborn, no less. He couldn't imagine a less paternal man. There had been nannies, an entire staff to care for him, until he'd been old enough to ship off to boarding school, followed by summer camp, followed by an expensive, private college. He'd barely known his father.

But he'd always wanted to. A relationship with the cold, distant man was something he'd craved in secret all his life. Sometimes he thought that might be the answer to that emptiness, that ache in his heart that he'd never been able to explain.

"I'm in Sanctuary, son."

Duncan's thoughts ground to a halt. "You're . . . where?"

"In town. I arrived on Monday."

Blinking, Duncan gave his head a shake to clear it. "You've been in Sanctuary for three days? And you didn't even call me? No, no, that's not the surprise, the surprise is that you'd bother calling me now. What do you want, Father?"

There was a long pause. "I want . . . to *be* your father, Duncan."

The breath seemed to have been stolen from Duncan's lungs. He couldn't inhale, and couldn't speak until he did. How long had he imagined his father saying those words? How many nights had he dreamed them, wished for them, as a child? And why, why had his father waited so long? Why couldn't he have started this conversation years ago, when a little boy had needed it so badly? Why now?

Swallowing, Duncan said, "I'm a grown man with my own business and my own life. I don't *need* a father now."

"I know. Duncan, I know, believe me. My mistakes . . . well, they're too numerous to mention, but I'm well aware of every last one of them. I want to start over, to try to . . . to make up for the past. Please, give me that chance."

Duncan had to close his eyes, because they burned. When

he spoke, his voice was gravelly, coarse. "Do you mean it?"

"I do, son. I swear to you, I do."

But Duncan was almost afraid to let himself believe it. He'd wanted this too badly for too long to trust that it could be real.

"You aren't convinced," his father said. "But you will be. I sold my house, Duncan. And today I bought a new place, the old courthouse right here in Sanctuary."

Frowning, Duncan took the phone away from his ear, stared at it for a moment, as if he could read his father's expression through it somehow. Then he brought it back.

"That's how serious I am about this. I want to be close to you, close enough so that we can work on . . . on building a relationship, Duncan. I want to start over with you. Will you let me try?"

Blinking the moisture from his eyes, Duncan nodded. "Sure, Dad. Sure, we can both try."

His father sighed in relief, and Duncan could almost imagine the stern face cracking in a rare smile. "Meet me for breakfast tomorrow?" his father asked. "Here in town, at the Coast Road Café?"

With a quick swipe at his eyes, Duncan said, "Okay. Around eight?"

"Perfect," his father said. And then he hung up without another word.

Duncan set the phone down after a long moment. He told himself not to hope for too much, not to invest any emotions in this apparent softening of his father's hard heart. It would only lead to disappointment. But he'd had plenty of that over the years. He should be used to it by now.

Kneeling, he resumed the unpacking he'd been in the midst of when he'd become distracted by the dark woman on the distant cliffs. It was the first box. He traveled a lot. Always searching, it seemed, though he could never quite figure out what for. But wherever he went, this was always the first box he unpacked. His collection, the one he'd been accumulating ever since the fourth grade, when he'd bought the first piece at a five and dime with his allowance money. He thought the fascination might have begun when he'd read that poem by Edgar Allan Poe . . . or maybe the love of the birds had already been there, and that was why the poem had affected him so deeply. Why, that haunting refrain ''Nevermore'' could still bring tears to his eyes.

Either way, he liked them. Had over a hundred now. And the tiny sills along the insides of all these curving windows would be the perfect shelves for them.

He opened the box, removing the protective paper that cushioned them, and began removing his collection of ravens, one by one, placing them carefully, just so. And as he did, he whispered the words of the poem he sometimes heard in his sleep.

''Take thy beak from out my heart, and take thy form
    from off my door!
Quoth the Raven, 'Nevermore.' ''

13

Duncan was early. His father wasn't at any of the round, lion-footed stone tables or their matching rock-hard benches outside the Coast Road Café. And the inside of the place was all but deserted. Too nice a day for anyone to want breakfast inside, he figured. The foliage-seekers filled almost every available spot outside—uncomfortable stone benches notwithstanding. The tourists wore cardigans and sunglasses. The locals wore flannel and baseball caps with the names of their favorite products on them. John Deere. Mack. GMC. His father fit into neither group, but Duncan would spot him easily enough. He'd show up in his traditional funereal suit with his thin ribbon of a tie dangling.

Duncan glanced at his watch. Twenty minutes. Daddy dearest wouldn't be a minute early, either. Well, he'd walk, then. He was too nervous to stand still, or grab a table and wait. Besides, it was high time he got to know this town a bit, if he was going to live here.

The sun blazed so brightly from the clear blue sky that the hillsides nearby seemed fluorescent. The air had a bite to it, but it was invigorating rather than chilling. Made a man want to taste it.

Something had lifted his spirits this morning. He had a good feeling, and he hoped he was intelligent enough that

it wasn't because of his father's apparent change of heart.
That would be a foolish mistake. It didn't seem as if it was,
however. Something else lingered in the air. Expectation. A
sense that something big was going to happen. A feeling
that he ought to be holding his breath.

He often got . . . feelings . . . intuitions about things. But
he'd never had one like this before.

Strange.

He walked a full block, then stopped dead in his tracks
and stared. Across the street a woman stepped out of a small
shop. She carried boxes, empty boxes, stacked inside one
another. They towered so tall in her arms that they hid her
face. But it didn't matter. He knew her.

He knew her.

Sure he knew her. She was the woman who stood on the
cliffs in the middle of the night. The woman he was compelled to watch. That was all.

*It doesn't feel like that's all, though. It feels like some-
thing more.*

When she turned and that long ebony hair swung around
her shoulders, his heart did a crazy leap in his chest. He
couldn't make his legs work, could barely make his *mind*
work. He could only stand there, staring at her, wondering
why the hell she got to him this way. Cars passed back and
forth between them, traffic increasing as the morning aged,
but they didn't disturb his intense study of her. He couldn't
have looked away even if he'd wanted to.

She shifted the boxes to one side, balancing them on her
hip. She wore black. Leather, he thought. A snug leather
dress with a zipper that traced a path up the front of her,
cool metal, he imagined, pressing to her center and running
right between her breasts. The hemline hugged her thighs.
Below that her legs were encased in black stockings that
ended at short, laced-up boots with pointy toes.

His gaze rose once more. Her head turned toward him,
slowly. Very slowly. As if she sensed him there, looking at
her. Her dark, dark eyes met his, locked on them, held them.
Then widened, and the boxes fell from her hands. The
smaller ones spilled out of the larger ones when the stack
tumbled in the stiff autumn wind. Her hair danced with the

breeze, moving in apparent slow motion. Her lips parted, seemed to form his name.

She stepped off the sidewalk and into the street. Into the traffic. Eyes glued to his, blinking rapidly now, but never glancing to one side or the other, she came closer.

He did manage to look away—but only when the shadow loomed and the horn blared. The traffic—she was stepping right into the traffic, and there was a truck, and—

He opened his mouth to shout a warning. Before he made a sound, the dark enchantress lifted a hand toward the rumbling vehicle—like a traffic cop signaling "stop"—and abruptly the truck skidded to the left as if something had shoved it. Something *big*. It came to rest neatly against the curb. She never even looked at it, never took her eyes from his, just kept coming. The wind blew harder, and her hair writhed and twisted like Medusa's.

And suddenly Duncan felt an icicle of fear slide up his spine. Why?

She stepped up onto the sidewalk. Came closer. Tears, he could see them now. Welling deep in her eyes, glimmering, spilling over. Wet black lashes shining, dampening her cheeks. Longing so intense he could *feel* it, flowing from her eyes with the pain and the tears. Closer. And she was so close now she was nearly touching him. God, was he dreaming this? Her body brushed his and he felt a snapping, crackling electricity spark between them as she tipped her head back, searched his face. A trembling hand rose to touch his cheek, brush at his hair, and he felt it again. Delicate brows drew together. She tilted her head slightly to one side, and she whispered, "Duncan?"

"Yes," he said, amazed he could speak at all with the force of these unnamed, and utterly illogical, emotions swamping him. He felt absurdly like pulling her into his arms, like kissing her endlessly. It was an effort to keep his arms at his sides, and the muscles flexed and his fists clenched as he reminded himself to do just that. "How did you know my—"

"Duncan?" she asked again, both hands running over his face now, as if she couldn't believe he were real. Her breaths came faster, and the tears flowed like rivers. "Oh, Duncan . . ." There was more, but the words were garbled and choked out on sobs so he only got bits and pieces. "Waiting" and "centuries" and "living without you." Not that it mattered what she said. Not to him, because it was what she *did* that had his full attention.

She pressed herself against him, twisted her arms around his neck, and she kissed him. Even with the sobs making her hiccup and gasp, she parted her lips over his, so that he tasted the salt of her tears. She clung to him as if she'd never let go. And something happened to him. He didn't know what. Something. It was as if he were someone else, someone who knew this woman and returned her wrenching emotions fully. He wrapped his arms around her slender waist and it felt . . . familiar. The shape, the size of her, the way her body rubbed against his. And he bent over her—just the right amount to compensate for the differences in their heights. He returned her kiss. But it was more than a kiss. It was like . . . coming home when he touched his mouth to hers.

His mind seemed to shut down. It no longer mattered who he was, or who she was, or how insane this entire encounter was. All that mattered was the taste of her mouth, and its warmth. The texture of those lips moving against his, that tongue as soft and rough as velvet when he stroked it with his own. The feel of her waist clasped in his hands, or of her hair when he touched it, plowed his fingers into it, rubbed it against his cheek. Sweet. God, she was sweet. And small and pliant in his arms. And he wanted her. He wanted her with a power and a passion that exploded inside his mind. His hips arched against her belly. She didn't even pull away.

He fed from her mouth, and his head spun. His heart pounded, and it felt as if something stabbed into it, but he ignored the sudden pain as his lips slid around to her jaw, and lower, to suckle the skin of her neck. No matter where he put his mouth he found sweetness, salt, softness, heat. And wanted more.

Panting, he lifted his head to stare down into her eyes. Still wet with tears, but wide and deep and incredible, they gazed back at him. He couldn't speak above a whisper, felt dizzy, weak, and entirely disoriented.

"Who are you?" he managed to ask her. And next he'd ask who *he* was, he thought vaguely. Because for a few minutes there it was as if he'd lost his own identity. This shock, this dizziness, must be the aftermath of that temporary lapse.

She blinked up at him, and Duncan saw the fire in her eyes flicker and, slowly, begin to fade.

"Not that it matters," he went on, very quickly. To hell with the fear of losing himself, losing his identity or even his soul to her . . .

Odd thought, isn't it?

His only fear now was that she wouldn't let him kiss her again. "I mean, it doesn't matter," he blurted. "Not at all. I just—"

"Oh, Duncan." The words were a sigh. Unspeakably sad, then riding away on a stray breeze. Closing her eyes, she untwisted her arms from his neck, took a step backward. "Oh, sweet Duncan, I didn't mean to do it this way." She shook her head slowly. "What must you be thinking right now? You don't even know me, do you?"

He swallowed hard, reaching up with one hand, stroking her cheek, and absorbing a tear into his fingertips. "Oh, yeah," he whispered. "I know you. I've seen you on the cliffs . . . I've watched you . . . from the lighthouse."

"*You* live in the lighthouse?"

He nodded, watching her face, wishing he could kiss her again. But even now the confused yearning of that moment was fading, and he was beginning to realize how weird all this was, and to feel self-conscious about losing his head with a total stranger. Practically making love to her in the street.

Still wanting to.

"How did you know my name?" he asked, maybe because it was all he could think of to say—to distract himself from thinking of her taste, and wanting more. To ground himself in something solid and logical and practical. To grab hold of the first rational thought to come into his mind in several minutes, and cling to it for dear life.

"I know a lot of things about you, Duncan." She closed her eyes, lowered her head again. "But I'm messing this up. Badly." And she looked up at him again. Like the sun emerging from behind the clouds. "I meant to take it slowly. To give you time to get to know me again and—"

"Again?"

She nodded. "Yes. But don't worry about that now. Don't worry about anything now. I'll explain it all, Duncan, and this time I'll tell you everything. I won't keep anything from you this time, I swear it."

Frowning, he studied her and wondered for the first time if this beautiful young woman were, perhaps, slightly insane.

Good, Duncan. Better that than wondering what happened to your own sanity just now, isn't it?

"This time?" he said, pretending not to hear his own mocking thoughts. God, how her black eyes gleamed. She reminded him of something . . . some . . . one.

"All that matters now, Duncan, is that you're here. You're here." Her beautiful lips curved into a smile so enticing he found he really didn't care if she were sane or not. "You're really here."

He found himself smiling back at her, a reflex beyond control. "Yes, I certainly am."

She shook her head from side to side. "You don't sound the same."

"The same as what?"

She shook her head again. "You've lost the lilt of the Highlands. But beyond that . . ." She stroked his hair once more, tugged a strand away from his head and ran it between her fingers. "Beyond that, you're the same. Lord, but I've missed you so much. And to think I thought it was *him*. And I left poor Arianna home packing, convinced we had to go away and—"

"Go away?" She sounded crazier all the time, but for some reason the idea of her leaving here shook him. His hands were on her shoulders now, and he battled a rising tide of panic that usually only crept up on him this way when he tried swimming or looked down from some substantial height. "But you can't. Not now, not when—"

"Oh, but we're not going away. No, Duncan, not now, I promise you that. I'm not about to leave you when I've only just found you."

He sighed his relief. "I'm glad."

"Are you?"

He nodded. "We . . . we know each other, don't we?" he said, a little uncertain.

A cloud covered the light in her eyes. "We did . . . once. I'd hoped you might remember, but Arianna told me you wouldn't. It's all right, Duncan."

He licked his lips, swallowed hard. "I can't imagine meeting you and not remembering," he said.

She shrugged, averting her eyes. "It was a long time ago."

He tilted his head, studying her face. "You do seem . . . familiar to me. Maybe that's why I've been . . ." He let his words die. Maybe that was why he'd been so drawn to her, so compelled to watch her from the lighthouse. Maybe he *had* known her once.

"Well, if I'm a bit familiar to you, then that's something, isn't it?"

"I'm half afraid you're mistaking me for someone else."

"There could never be someone else, Duncan. Not ever." Lowering her head slowly, she whispered, "There's so much we need to talk about. So much I have to tell you."

"Apparently so."

She drew a breath. "This must seem so strange to you."

"It's . . . yeah. It's strange." She bit her lip, and he rushed on. "Strange in a very nice way," he added, and he caught her chin, lifted it so he could look into those mesmerizing eyes of hers. "Tears," he said. "They've got no business filling eyes like these."

She sniffed, and the tears welled deeper and spilled out onto her cheeks. "Will you hold me, Duncan? I know it makes no sense to you now, but I need to feel your arms around me more than I need to draw another breath right now."

She didn't have to ask twice. He pulled her close, and she nestled in his arms. She fit herself against him as if she were custom-made for him to hold. Her arms around his waist, her cheek resting on his chest. Her hair just below his face so its scent wafted up to entice. Something stirred a memory when he smelled that scent. Lavender and honeysuckle. He'd smelled it before, he knew he had.

For a very long time he stood there and just held her. It felt . . . potent. Emotions more powerful than any he'd ever known roiled around inside him, and he couldn't even figure out why. But he didn't want to let her go. Hell, he'd hold her like this forever if he had time.

Time.

Damn, the *time*.

He glanced at his watch, realized he was late now for his meeting with his father. Almost decided to let the old man sit alone all morning. But his conscience gave a twist. No, he'd wanted this chance with his father for too long to blow it when it finally came. He had to at least try.

"I'm sorry," he told her as he stroked her hair and gently lifted her head from his chest. The regret he heard in his voice was genuine. He didn't want to leave her. It made his knees weak, made his head ache to entertain the idea! Clenching his jaw, he forced the words to come. "I have to meet someone. I swear, if it wasn't so important, I'd—"

"No, it's all right. I . . . I should go, talk to Arianna before she has the entire house packed up." She shook her head. "Besides, I need to . . . put my head on straight. Seeing you . . . it made me forget everything I'd planned, everything I wanted to say."

A lump came into his throat. "I . . . will I see you again?"

Her smile was soft, edged with sadness and joy all at once. "I'll come to you, Duncan. Tonight, I'll come to the lighthouse. We'll talk then. I promise you, all of this will make sense then."

He nodded slowly, doubting anything she had to say could make any of this make sense. But he didn't care. All that mattered was that she would come to him. She'd be with him. Tonight, and that was only hours away, and if she hadn't made that promise, he didn't think he'd be able to walk away from her right now. "I'll be waiting," he told her.

Leaning forward and up, she pressed a gentle kiss to his lips. Then, stepping away, she turned to go.

"Wait," he said, and she stopped, glanced back at him. "I don't even know your name."

She blinked, as if to cover something in her eyes. "No, you don't, do you? It's St. James. Raven St. James." Then she turned again and hurried away.

Duncan stood staring after her until she was out of sight. Raven.

Raven?

My God, what the hell was going on here?

"Duncan?"

Blinking out of his stupor, he half turned toward the voice that called his name. His father stood three feet away, on the sidewalk, hands thrust into the deep pockets of the long black coat that made him look like a mobster's grandfather.

"Hello, Father."

His father frowned, and the additional lines lost themselves with all the others on his face. It was a stern face, narrow and pale. Steel-gray hair, too long for a man his age, surrounded it. He looked like winter, Duncan thought. He'd always looked that way. Never seemed to change.

"I waited a good fifteen minutes at the café," he said, his voice a monotone.

"I was on my way there." He met the old man's eyes, wondered if there would be a confrontation, accusations and defenses now. No, he wouldn't defend himself to his father. He wouldn't apologize. He was an adult.

His father's gaze wavered first, and the man sighed. "No matter. I was just on my way back to the old courthouse building. Walk with me, Duncan?"

Duncan nodded, turning around and falling into step beside his father. Awkwardly trying to think of some light conversation, some casual words to break the ice. "So how have you been?"

"Same as always. And you?"

Duncan shrugged. His father spoke without making eye contact. It was a trait Duncan had never really become used to. "The business is going well," he told his father at length.

"Yes, well, it should. There will never be a shortage of old buildings in need of restoration."

"I hope not."

"You bought that lighthouse." He made a clicking sound with his tongue, gave his head a shake, but other than that didn't break his stride or raise his head. "I found that surprising."

"So did I."

The old man did look up then. Sharply, quickly, scanning Duncan's face in one sweep of his pale eyes and then facing the sidewalk again.

"I bought it on impulse," Duncan explained. "I'm not sure why. As soon as I saw it, I knew I had to stay there."

"Mmm." Their shoes tapped in sync over the sidewalk. Passing traffic. Dry leaves rustling against bare limbs in the breeze. Silence.

"You regret it yet?" his father asked.

Duncan sent the man a sideways glance. "No. No, I don't."

"So you'll be staying around here for a while."

He thought of the woman. Raven. Tonight. "Yeah, I think so."

"Then I have a proposition for you." The old man paused and waved a hand. Duncan followed it to the square flat-topped building, made of deep gray stone blocks. Broad stone steps, with pillars top and bottom, led the way to the entry, which was by itself impressive with big, dark double doors attached with brass bells. "This is it."

It took Duncan a minute to process the announcement. "The old courthouse? The one you bought?"

Nodding, his father mounted the steps. "Come, I want you to see inside. My apartments are above, on the second floor, but it's the ground story you'll be interested in, Duncan. I've already acquired some of the most—" He broke off there, turning his key in the lock and swinging the doors wide, and Duncan joined him. "Here, see for yourself."

Duncan stepped inside. His father reached for a light switch, and then stood back and waited while Duncan's gaze skimmed the crates, the boxes, the odd items stacked hither and yon, the large wooden items standing in one corner of the room. Were those . . . were those *stocks*?

Finally his gaze fell on a sign. The Gothic letters printed in red on a black background read: YE OLDE WITCH MUSEUM.

He blinked. "What *is* all this?"

"Just what it looks like," his father said. "A tourist trap, but a moneymaker, Duncan, I guarantee it."

"A *Witch* Museum?"

Nodding, his father moved around, touching first one box and crate and then another. "Torture devices, antique stocks, handwritten confessions—"

"And you don't think it's slightly morbid?"

"Ah, Duncan, don't be foolish. It's all in fun."

Gee, do you suppose it was fun *to the women who saw this stuff firsthand?*

"Besides," his father went on, "what do people come to this part of the country for, if not this? Why is Salem doing such a booming business, eh? This will succeed, Duncan, I'm sure of it." He slapped Duncan's shoulder—the most physical contact he'd made with his son in a dozen years. And as always, a shock of something like static electricity sparked where they made contact. Duncan stiffened, and pulled away instinctively. Oddly, it reminded him of the static he'd felt when the strange beauty touched him . . . and yet it had been different with her. Pleasant and exciting, rather than slightly repulsive the way it always was with the old man. Duncan had never understood it, and assumed he simply tended to conduct static more than most people.

His father's lips thinned for a moment. Then he acted as if nothing had happened. And nothing had. Nothing new, anyway. "I hoped we could work on it together. Partners. You and I."

Duncan lifted his head slowly to meet his father's eyes. "You . . . you want me as your partner?"

His father nodded. "Yes, son, I do. It will give us a chance to . . . well, to make up for the past. Time to get to know each other, the way we should have done long ago."

Duncan couldn't believe it. A lump came into his throat,

but he swallowed it down. "I . . . I don't know what to say."

"I'm an old man, Duncan. When a man gets to be my age, he starts to think . . . starts to wish he'd done certain things in his life a little differently . . . starts to understand what's really important."

Nodding, Duncan had to look away. "I've waited a long time for a chance like this."

"Then take it, Duncan." His father's hand returned to his shoulder. Jolted him, then tightened there. "What do you say? Partners?"

Duncan faced his father and said nothing. How many times had his father made false starts like this? How many times had he seemed to want to get closer, only to pull away again, without explanation? And, God, even if he were sincere this time . . . something about the idea of putting these relics on display seemed crude. Repugnant, even.

"Duncan?"

"I . . . I don't know." *Say no*, some inner voice told him. And yet he wanted so much to be close to this cold man. Had wanted it for so long. "I . . . I'll think about it."

"That's good enough."

Good enough. When nothing Duncan had ever done had *ever* been good enough.

God Almighty, Duncan thought. Could this day *get* any stranger?

14

"Raven."

I turned around, holding my hair to the back of my head in a temporary bundle and craning my neck to glimpse the effect in the mirror behind me. Then I frowned. "Maybe I should just leave it down."

"Raven—"

"What do you think, Arianna?" Letting my hair fall, finger combing it slightly, I arranged it over my shoulders. "Yes, I'll leave it down." With a firm nod I faced the four-poster bed and the clothing draped over every inch of the mattress and hanging from the foot. "I just wish I knew what to wear."

"Raven, will you stop for one minute and *listen* to me?"

Smiling—I hadn't been able to stop smiling since that morning—I faced Arianna. "This is all because of you, you know. If it hadn't been for your spell . . ." I closed my eyes, tipped my head back, and mentally saw my beloved Duncan again. "He looks just the same. It's as if . . . as if he never left me."

"No, Raven. It is *not* like that at all." Arianna stood close, gripped my shoulders, and the warm, familiar tingle passed from her body into mine as she stared hard into my eyes. "He *did* leave you. For you, everything seems the same, but it's not, love. Not for him."

I sighed softly. Poor Arianna, trying so hard to protect me from my own hopes and dreams. She just didn't understand. "I know he may not remember me now, but he will. And he'll love me again, and—"

"And how do you know it will happen that way?" she asked me.

I blinked. A finger of doubt crept into my brain, but I banished it. Ignored it. Pretended it didn't exist just as I'd been pretending all day.

Just as I'd been pretending for three hundred years.

I'd spent all this time waiting for his return—none of it pondering how things might have changed between us.

"It has to happen that way," I told her.

"Yes, that's just the way I was thinking, Raven, when I set out to find my little sister more than three centuries ago. But your reaction was quite different. Do you remember?"

I did remember. And the doubt in my heart grew larger. "But—"

"You thought I'd come to kill you. You drew your blade, Raven. You'd have fought me—perhaps to the death. To you I was a stranger. Nothing more."

My heart contracted at her words. Slowly I lowered my head. "You're right." Drawing a deep breath, I met her eyes. "But we're sisters again now, Arianna. Closer, even, than that."

"But our past together is just as gone. The life you led before is lost to you. You remember none of it. Not our father, a lowly saddle maker, nor our mother, nor our poor cottage in Stonehaven. Not the loch where we played . . ." She closed her eyes. "Our closeness now is based on this lifetime . . . we've built it together over centuries, Raven. It's strong, and it's real, but it's not the same. It can *never* be the same."

Turning slowly, eyes downcast, I felt tears well up and burn my eyes. "I . . . I hadn't thought . . ."

"I know. That's why I'm trying to *make* you think. Raven, Duncan may look the same, bear the same name,

but he is *not* the same. To him, you're a beautiful stranger
who kissed him on the street one day.''

My head came up sharply. ''*He* kissed *me*, too!''

''Of course he did. But, Raven, you could fling yourself
into the arms of any red-blooded, heterosexual male and he
would do the same. You're a beautiful woman. Duncan is
a man.''

''No,'' I said. Biting my lip, I paced to the bed, snatching
up a dress, eyeing it through my tears. ''There was something there, something between us, Arianna. I *felt* it.''

''Yes. *You* felt it. But did *he*?''

The fabric of the dress crumpled in my fists, I slowly
lifted my head, faced her, bit back a sob. ''He . . . he doesn't
love me?''

''He doesn't *know* you.'' Arianna came closer, took the
dress gently from my hands, and laid it on the bed. Then
she cupped my face and wiped my tears away with her
thumbs. ''I only want you to be aware . . . to be careful,
darling. He'll fall in love with you again, I don't doubt it
for a moment. But, Raven, he's going to need time. And so
are you. Time to get to know him again. He might be very
different from the man you remember. You might decide
you don't even want—''

''I will never decide *that*!'' I sniffed, brushing at my wet
eyes. ''I love him, Arianna. I will always love him.''

''I know,'' she said softly. Turning, she fingered the
clothes on the bed, pausing on a sheer, soft dress of ivory
silk. ''This one, I think.'' She gathered the dress up, draped
it gently over my arm. ''It won't be easy for him, you know.
He's going to have a lot to deal with, when you tell him.
He's immortal now, Raven. A High Witch like us, with
maybe no clue that he has some fledgling powers coming
to life inside him. You must remember what a shock learning of your own nature was to you, how difficult it was to
accept, to understand.''

''I remember.'' I let the robe I wore fall from my shoulders to the floor, then pulled the dress over my head. But
the bubbling excitement I'd felt all day ebbed now. I was
suddenly unsure, afraid. What if Duncan . . . what if he
never loved me again?

"Be gentle when you tell him. Go slowly, love. Slowly."
She guided me to the mirror, lifted a brush to my hair, and
smoothed it with long, soothing strokes. "And don't expect
too much all at once."

I nodded, staring at Arianna's reflection beside mine in
the mirror. We stood in sharp contrast to each other, she so
fair with her sunshine hair, cropped short around her face.
With her pixielike features and huge brown eyes. Me, so
dark, long ebony curls, jet-black eyes and lashes and brows.

"It must have hurt you, all those years ago," I said. "To
find me and realize I had no memory of you."

She nodded. "I don't know what I was expecting. An
emotional reunion, I suppose. If I'd given it any thought I'd
have realized that wasn't going to happen."

I turned toward her. "But it *did*. You *are* my sister, Arianna. You're the sister of my soul. And while my mind
may not remember our past together . . . my heart has never
forgotten. The feelings live on there."

She dipped her head, shielding her eyes from me.
"Truly?"

"Oh, yes. Truly."

Lifting her head, smiling and misty-eyed, she hugged me
tight. "I do love you, little sister."

"And I you," I told her.

Finally she stepped away, looking me up and down.
"Well, put your shoes on and go, then. This man of yours
has kept you waiting quite long enough, don't you think?"

I nodded emphatically. "More than long enough," I told
her.

Duncan paced. He wore jeans. Jeans should be okay, right?
They were the all-purpose, fit-for-any-occasion uniform of
the twentieth century, after all. He hoped jeans were all
right.

He hoped she'd come. She said she would, but any
woman crazy enough to kiss a man she didn't even know
in broad daylight on a busy street might not be too good at
keeping her word. Or even remembering she'd given it.

No. She'd come. And who was he kidding, anyway?
There was more going on here—with him, with her, with

them—than just an impulsive kiss on a busy street.

It *had* been a busy street. Too busy.

And that was part of it, the way she held up her hand and that truck skidded to the side like it had been pushed there. That was . . . that was . . .

That was nothing. The driver must have locked up his brakes and jerked the wheel. That was all. It was nothing.

But she knew his name. She knew his name, and then there was *her* name. Raven. And he'd been collecting ravens all his life, been fascinated by them. Had books on them, paintings of them, and miniatures everywhere. Wooden ravens, stone ravens, cheap plastic dime-store models, and some made of glass. The large one, carved of pure black onyx, that was his favorite. Three hundred bucks he'd paid for that bird, even while asking himself why the hell any sane man would plunk down that kind of cash for a hunk of rock. He looked at it now, perched on a pedestal table all its own like a queen holding court. His fingers stroked its cool hard feathers.

But that was beside the point. Her *name* was *Raven*. And *that* was . . . weird. Not to mention that since he'd come here there had been real ravens stalking him. Okay, not stalking him, but he'd sure as hell seen more of the big black birds perched around this lighthouse than he'd ever seen in one place in his whole life.

Oh, but there was more. There was *her*. The obsession he'd had with her since that first time he'd laid eyes on her, over there on the cliffs, doing whatever it was she did on full-moon nights.

And she knew his name.

He felt nervous and jittery, and not like himself at all. He kept fighting smiles and warm, fuzzy emotions and even a tear or two, and he didn't know why. He felt as if he'd stepped out of reality and into the Twilight Zone.

The soft hum of a motor jerked him back to himself, and he braced his hands on the sill to stare out the window. Then he tensed. The small johnboat came closer, and he peered, squinted. She sat in the stern, one hand on the outboard motor's rudder. She wore white, or off-white. Something soft and flowing. It rippled with the breeze as the boat came closer. And then she steered toward shore and cut the motor. Tipped it up, so its prop rose from the water, dripping beads of the sea back into itself. The boat moved forward of its own momentum for another second or two, stopping only when its nose scraped along the shore. And then she was stepping out.

So graceful, he thought. She didn't even get her feet wet.

She bent at the bow and gave the boat a tug to pull it more securely onto dry land. Then, turning, she faced the lighthouse. He should have gone out to help her. Some gentleman he was, standing here gawking at her while she manhandled the boat on her own. Not that it had seemed to give her any problem. She must be stronger than she looked.

His throat was dry. His stomach, queasy. She started forward, and he turned, went to the door, opened it, and stood there wondering what was happening to his stable, boring life. His solitary, predictable, lonely life.

And then she was standing there, facing him, looking uncertain, a little afraid, utterly beautiful, and he knew that old life was gone forever. Nothing would ever be the same again. Why he knew it, or how, didn't matter. It was real, gut deep, and true. Telling himself it made no sense didn't negate that certainty in the least.

"Hello again," she said.

Was that a slight waver he detected in her voice?

"I'm . . . glad you came." Or was he? Yeah. He was. "Come in." He stepped aside to let her pass, holding the door for her. She moved past him. The front door led directly to the main room, which he'd made into a living room for himself. A curved sofa fit perfectly to one concave wall. Above it the windows looked out on the sea, on the cliffs and her home beyond them. No curtains. He hadn't wanted anything blocking his view.

But she wasn't looking at the view, or even at the paint cans and tarps, or the stepladder in the corner. She was looking at the birds. Staring at them, one by one, blinking, and then turning to him with a question in her eyes.

"Yes," he said, wondering just how much of himself he wanted to reveal to her. Wondering if he even had a choice about that. "They're ravens. I've been collecting them since I was a kid."

Her lower lip trembled. She caught it in her teeth.

"Quite a coincidence, isn't it?"

Meeting his eyes, holding them with some kind of magnetic force he couldn't resist and didn't want to, she shook her head, first to one side, then the other. "I don't believe in coincidence."

He shivered. "What, then?"

Licking her lips, she lowered her head, freeing him at last to look away. But he found he didn't want to. "I don't want to frighten you, Duncan," she said very slowly, and it seemed she chose each word with great care. "But there *are* things you need to know. Things I have to tell you."

He nodded. "Like . . . how you knew my name, for example."

"Yes."

"It all sounds very mystical."

"Some might call it that."

"I think you should know I'm pretty much a skeptic where anything . . . you know . . . *flaky* is concerned."

A tiny frown knit her brow as she tilted her head. A look so startlingly familiar it hit him like a blow to the solar plexus and took his breath away.

"Flaky?"

"Paranormal." He waggled his fingers in front of him. "Supernatural."

"Oh. Well, that's all right. It's all quite . . . *natural*, Duncan. It's just that most people don't know . . . or understand it."

"But you do?"

She nodded.

They were still standing in the middle of the room, facing each other. He didn't know what to do with his hands, so he stuck them in his pockets. "Why don't you sit down. You want some coffee or a beer or—"

"No, thank you." She sat. On the sofa. And now he had to go and sit beside her. There was a tension between them, something that made his skin tingle and his nerves jump. Something that made him want to touch her, pull her closer.

If he sat down next to her, it would be hard not to.

"Well, *I* want a beer," he said. And he fled into the kitchenette. Not much of a kitchenette so far, actually. Just a mini-fridge, a card table with a hot plate on top, two folding chairs, and a couple of boxes full of supplies. And tools. There were tools everywhere. He took a beer out of the fridge, popped the top, and went back in to join her.

She'd turned sideways on the couch, one leg folded beneath her, arm resting on the back as she stared out the window. She didn't turn to face him when he came in. "What made you buy this place?" she asked.

"The view." He blurted it before he thought better of it.

Turning, she smiled gently, a tremulous little smile that he suspected contained a wealth of emotions, though he couldn't guess what they might be. "You're fond of the sea, then?"

"Actually, I've always pretty much detested it." Safe subject. His personal neuroses never failed to cool things down with women, whether he intended them to or not. He usually kept them to himself. This time, though, he needed things to cool down a little. Maybe if she thought he was nuts . . . hell, they'd be pretty much even then, wouldn't they?

He sat down, took a long pull from his can. "I've had a fear of water since I was a kid. Even baths were a major trauma when I was real young."

She didn't look as if she thought he was nuts. Instead she nodded. "Yes, I can see why."

"Funny. I never could." He lifted the can to his lips.

"Heights, too, I'll bet?"

His hand froze with the can in midair. He blinked slowly, said nothing, and then took a larger gulp of the cool brew than he'd intended.

Licking her lips, she went on. "But you moved into a lighthouse, on an island, despite your dislike of water. And all because of the view?"

He lowered his head. "Sounds pretty crazy, doesn't it?"

"No. There's a reason for it. For all of it."

He took another sip of beer before facing her again. "And you know what it is?"

She nodded.

"Well? Don't keep me in suspense, Raven. I'm dying to hear your theory."

Drawing a deep breath, she lifted her chin. "You've lived before."

Ahhh, so that was it. She was some kind of a psychic, or considered herself one. Well, it was interesting, if not exactly earth-shattering.

"You were born over three hundred years ago, in Scotland. Later you lived in England, where you were studying for the priesthood. And then—"

He choked on his beer, set the can down, and swiped his mouth. "The priesthood," he repeated. "Me."

"Yes. But you gave it up and came here. You lived right here in Sanctuary. And when you died . . ." She closed her eyes. "You died right there," she whispered, pointing. "On the rocks below those cliffs you can see so clearly from this window. And that's probably why you came into this lifetime with a fear of the water, and of heights, and part of the reason why the view from these windows affects you so deeply."

Her words made his stomach cramp and turn, and his spine tingle, and his jaw clench. But they were utterly ridiculous, and there was no reason in the world he should feel any reaction at all.

"Next you'll tell me that we knew each other in this . . . past life."

She got to her feet. The ivory dress slid down her legs, brushing her calves. The light was behind her, and he could see her silhouette through the soft fabric. And that feeling, that craving he had no business feeling, stirred to life in him all over again. Then he realized she was crying. Not noisily. She wasn't a noisy crier, he suspected. It was just one silent tear, glimmering on her cheek.

He rose, too, and touched that tear, absorbed it into his fingertip. "I wasn't making fun," he told her.

"But you don't believe me."

"I told you I was a skeptic." When she would have turned away, he touched her shoulders, gently keeping her there, facing him. "Why does any of it have to matter,

Raven? I like you. I'd . . . like to get to know you. Can't we forget about all this hocus-pocus stuff and just be two people who just met? Two people who . . . maybe . . . could feel something for each other, given time? Hmm?''

She seemed to search his face. "It would be easier, maybe, if we could. But there's more, Duncan. So much more. And it does matter . . . especially to you."

He shook his head. "It really doesn't matter in the least to me. But it does to you, doesn't it?"

"It does. To both of us." She cleared her throat. "We . . . were . . . you and I were . . ."

Frowning, he probed those black eyes of hers. "Lovers?" he asked her.

"Oh, Duncan, it was so much more than that. So very much more. When you held me, touched me, it was a kind of magick beyond anything I'd ever felt. And it was the same for you, I know it was. . . ." She bit her lip as if to stop the words.

Too late, though. That irrational desire for her was sizzling through him now, and no amount of reasoning would vanquish it. "I suppose that would explain," he whispered, and he let his hands slide from her shoulders, down her arms, and to her waist, "why I want you so badly right now."

He leaned down, and he kissed her. Tentatively, lightly, so that she could object if she wanted to. The power of his attraction to her . . . was that what made such a jolting awareness between them? Was it something chemical? Something physical?

She didn't object. Her lips formed his name against his, and then she melted into his arms. Her mouth parted, her arms twisted around his neck, and she kissed him back.

Warm, she was so warm, and soft, and her taste was like a drug that he couldn't quite get enough of. He bent over her, deepening the kiss, hands at the small of her back holding her close, then burying themselves in her hair, and then slipping lower again while his tongue dove into her mouth. He gathered the dress up until he could touch her bare thighs, run his palms over them. Heat met his hands. Her skin seemed to be burning him. Fevered . . . for him. And when he explored the soft mound of her buttocks and found it bare, he knew this was what she'd come here for. He cupped her there, squeezed her and pulled her hips tight to his. The soft sound she made was like a plea.

So he turned her, and scooped her into his arms. He kept marauding her succulent mouth as he carried her up the curving stairs to the bedroom above. Glass all around . . . the old light in the center, and the mattress on the floor. It was all he had here . . . all he'd needed. Until now. Now he needed something more, and it was a need more powerful than any he'd felt in his life.

He laid her on the mattress, knelt beside her, and peeled the dress away.

And then he looked at her.

There was no shyness in her, none of the first-time nervousness other women had displayed. She lay still, proud and naked and utterly beautiful. He stripped off his shirt and tossed it aside.

Her soft small breasts rose and fell with every breath, quivered with every heartbeat. Their centers like sweetmeats, dark, dusky rose, their peaks hard, elongated, expectant. He bent over her slowly, saw her close her eyes, arch her back. And when his mouth hovered a hairsbreadth from her, she clasped his head and pulled him down, until he took her nipple in his mouth and suckled, and nipped, and tugged at it. Then he moved away, stretching his body out alongside hers, twisting his arms around her slender waist, pulling her against him. Her breasts against his naked chest, her body tight to his, her longing as intense as his was as he kissed her again.

Rocking his hips against her, he muttered, "God, lass, it's been so long," and was barely aware of his own words as he reached for the button of his jeans.

A buzz made him pause. He closed his eyes, sighed in agony as the sound grew louder. Another boat. Dammit, who the hell could be coming out here now?

He met her eyes as the sound grew louder and then died. Someone was here. No question. And his own little launch sat outside, so they'd know he must be home. Suddenly protective of her, he reached for a blanket, drew it to cover her even as he got to his feet.

"I'm sorry," he whispered. "God, you have no idea *how* sorry. But I'll get rid of them. I'll be back."

I knew it would be a mistake to let him make love to me. But how could I resist him? How could I resist my own burning need to hold him inside me again, after all this time? I craved him just as I had before . . . no, even more so. I loved him. I loved him, and none of the things Arianna said made a difference in that.

He trotted down the stairs, pulling on his shirt. I heard his steps cross the floor, and the creak of those hinges as the door swung open. And then I heard him say, "What in the world are you doing out here?"

Curious, and suddenly sure he wouldn't be returning as quickly as he'd promised, I pulled my dress on, and found my shoes, which I'd kicked off at some point. One lay in one direction, one in another. I slipped them on, then crept to the stairs. Then down them. I was quiet, not wanting to interrupt Duncan and his guest, just eager to glimpse the visitor.

At the bottom of the stairs I paused. I could see through the main room to the door at the far end from here, and so far, I remained unnoticed.

But as Duncan spoke, the other man's head came up. He met my eyes, finding me there unerringly, as if he'd known exactly where I was. And my blood rushed to my feet. Dizziness swamped me, and I nearly lost my balance. Because the man I hated above all others, the man who had tried to kill me more times than I could count over the centuries, *Nathanial Dearborne*, was staring back at me, and the message in his eyes was clear. He meant to have my heart this time.

And just when I thought my shock and surprise had reached the precipice of a dozen lifetimes, I heard the words that chilled me to the bone.

Duncan said, "Come in, Father."

15

I stepped off the bottom step and darted to the side, out of their sight. Pushing open the first window I came to, I rapidly clambered outside. What was wrong with me? Was I a fool? I hadn't even brought my dagger tonight! It was at home, tucked away in a drawer in my bedroom, and I was helpless. A sheep awaiting the slaughter. How many times had Arianna told me I must carry it with me always? *Always!*

I ran to my small boat, shoved it away, and then leaped inside. Taking the oars from the floor, I dipped them, and stroked with all my strength. The craft shot away.

And then I paused, looking back. What about Duncan? What if it were him Nathanial was after?

But no. Duncan had called the man Father.

Father.

I shuddered again, sick to my soul. But how, why? And was Duncan safe?

I closed my eyes, searched my mind, sought the wisdom of the ancient Witches whose blood flowed in my veins. If Nathanial meant to have Duncan's heart, he'd have had it by now. Duncan never would have lived to reach adulthood. It was obviously something else the bastard was after.

Me. It was me. He must have known that if he remained

close to Duncan, he'd find me, eventually. And suddenly I knew with great clarity exactly what Dearborne intended. I knew it as surely as I'd known Duncan when I'd seen him again standing on the sidewalk in town. He would use Duncan . . . to get to me. But once he took my heart, his need of his *son* would be as dead as my lifeless corpse would be. He might very well intend to kill Duncan, too. But only after he'd cut the living heart from *my* chest.

There was only one thing for me to do. Kill him. Kill him before he could hurt Duncan.

I would not again be the cause of my lover's death. Not again.

"It's really not a good time, Father."

"No? And why not?" His father stepped inside, pulling the door closed behind him and idly stroking the antique dagger he insisted on carrying. He'd had that thing belted to his hip for as long as Duncan could remember. But then, his father had always been fascinated with antiques. His collection of obscure books on the occult was probably the largest around. Nathanial loved things salvaged from the past. Duncan figured the dagger must be his favorite piece. That he likely treasured it the way Duncan treasured his own onyx raven.

Raven.

He glanced uneasily toward the stairs. But the sound of a motor drew his head back around. He ran to the window, to look out, only to see Raven's small boat churning steadily away from the island, heading toward the rocky shore. "Damn."

His father looked over his shoulder. "Who . . . ?"

"A girl. A strange, beautiful girl. I can't believe she left like that."

"I should apologize. I didn't know you had . . . company."

Duncan eyed his father then, immediately doubting the man. Her boat had been right outside, after all, and . . . No. He'd never build a relationship with his father if he kept doubting every word the man said.

"It's all right. I'm sure I'll see her again." With a longing

glance through the windows, he sighed and told himself to
focus on the *other* stranger in his life. His father. "You want
a beer?"

"Only if you have no wine."

"I detest wine." He headed into the kitchen, bit his lip,
then turned to look back into the living room and forced a
smile. "I'll make a point to buy some, though." It felt fake,
this jovial attitude. This farce of friendship. And it hurt to
realize just how strained things between him and the old
man had become. God, could this ever work? Or was it too
late?

Maybe, Duncan thought, it was too late a long time ago.

His throat tightened on that thought. He grated his teeth
and resolved to give it a chance. Again. One last time.

When he joined his father with a beer—in a glass, in
deference to Nathanial's sensibilities—he found the old man
holding one of the miniature ravens in his hands. The tip of
his thumb kept running across the bird's wooden breast. It
gave Duncan a chill, though he couldn't say why. He had
to resist the urge to snatch his treasure away and replace it
lovingly in its spot. But his hands itched to do just that.

Instead he held out the beer.

Clutching the bird too tightly in one hand, his father took
the glass with the other. "So tell me about this mysterious
beauty. Are you . . . involved with her?"

"I just met her."

"Really? You'll have to introduce me sometime."

No way in hell.

And just where did *that* thought come from?

"Maybe. Sometime," he said. "But right now, I'd rather
talk about why you're here."

Nathanial shrugged. "Can't a father visit his son without
a reason?" He set the bird down carelessly, and it tipped
onto its side with a clunk that set Duncan's teeth on edge.

Instinctively he reached for it, set it upright in the spot
where it belonged. As he did, he stroked its back, almost as
if he were soothing it. As if it were real. Man, he *was* losing
it.

"I'd like you to come to the courthouse—er, that is, the
museum tomorrow."

"Oh?"

Nathanial nodded, his pale blue eyes skimming the furniture, the floor, lighting, everywhere but on Duncan. "I've already taken care of most of the paperwork involved. Acquired the proper permits, and so on. There's still the advertising to be done, but that won't be a problem. Still, Duncan, there are physical aspects to this project that a man of . . . of my age—"

"Oh." Was this his father? The cold, brutally independent, utterly secretive man he knew, asking for his help? "Look, I'm not real comfortable with this Witch Museum idea," Duncan began.

"I know, you made that clear this morning. Still, there are all those crates to unpack, you know. The sign to hang. Shelves to be assembled and placed. All of that."

And maybe *that* was why he'd asked Duncan to be his partner. He could handle the business end himself, and money was no problem. So all he wanted was a strong body for the grunt work.

Duncan frowned, looking away. He was jumping to conclusions. Judging Nathanial according to the pattern he'd set in the past. If this "one more try" routine were going to have any chance of working, he'd have to try to curb that tendency. But hell, old habits died hard.

"Besides," Nathanial went on, "if you do decide to be my partner, I'll want your input on things." He looked at Duncan's face, very briefly. Not his eyes, just his face. "I do hope it doesn't upset you that I've done so much of the early work already."

"No, of course not." So maybe it *wasn't* just a set of strong arms the old man wanted. A spark of hope flared in Duncan's chest. A tiny kernel of belief in the man he'd always *wanted* to believe in.

"We need a gimmick," his father said. "A hook to draw in the tourists for the grand opening."

Duncan lowered his head. Part of him was ready to agree, while the other part grimaced in distaste. And still another part warned him not to hope for too much where his father was concerned.

Slowly he said, "I suppose if I *were* going to get involved in this—and I'm not saying I am—but if I were, I might suggest Halloween for the grand opening."

Nathanial slapped his knee, sloshing beer from his glass onto the couch cushion. "There, you see! That's the kind of brilliant idea I'd hoped you'd generate. It's perfect. The holiday most sacred to Witches, as the grand opening of the Witch Museum."

Duncan felt the blood leave his face. "I didn't realize . . ."

"It's perfect," Nathanial said again.

"No, Dad, it's not. Look, it was a bad idea. I spoke without thinking it through. Given the origins of the holiday . . . hell, it would be offensive."

"Nonsense. It's the perfect date, I tell you."

"You don't think it's like opening a Nazi war crimes museum during Passover?"

"Not at all!" Nathanial rubbed his chin. "I hope we can be ready, though. It's only a couple of weeks away."

His father's face seemed more animated to Duncan than it ever had as he talked about his plans—talked about *their* plans. It didn't *feel* right, this idea of a museum devoted to relics of the Witch trials. Not that he knew much about the subject. But it sent an odd feeling up his spine to think about it.

Yet, his father was speaking to him as if he gave a damn—for the first time in Duncan's memory. Besides, he hadn't even seen the items to be put on display yet. Maybe it wouldn't be as bad as he thought.

He . . . hoped not.

Who was he kidding? He'd seen enough. Those stocks.

"I can't be your partner, Father. It doesn't mean we can't try to work on things, but—"

"Does it mean you can't help an old man unpack a few crates?"

Sighing, Duncan shook his head. "No, it doesn't mean that, either. I'll help with the heavy work, all right?"

"Wonderful. Wonderful. As I said, there are the shelves and the sign, and . . ."

Duncan turned, barely hearing the animated buzz of his father's voice now, as he gazed across the water to the main-

land. It was too dark to see the cove far to the west of the
cliffs, where Raven kept the small boat. There must be a
path from there up to the house atop the cliffs. Perhaps he'd
walk it one day soon.

He had to see her again. He knew that much. Crazy or
not, he couldn't seem to shake the woman's image from his
mind. And even if it turned out she was a raving lunatic, he
had a feeling it would always be this way.

When I slammed the front door, Arianna leaped off the sofa,
as startled as if a gunshot had gone off beside her ear. One
hand pressed to her chest, she drew a deep breath and stared
wide-eyed at me. "What in the name of the Gods are you
trying to do, *scare* the heart out of me?"

I met her brown eyes, and she stared into mine. And then
her face changed. She came forward, one hand going to my
shoulder. "What is it? What's wrong?"

Lifting my chin, I swallowed hard. "Nathanial Dearborne," I told her.

The roses drained from her cheeks. "You've *seen* him?"

I closed my eyes. "Oh, Arianna, what am I going to do?
I didn't expect this! Even *he* couldn't be this clever, this
low, as to set himself up as . . . as . . . Sweet Goddess, I can't
even say it."

Gripping my shoulders, she steered me backward to the
velvet settee in the Edwardian parlor. I went easily, my
bones like water.

"Go on," she whispered. "Tell me what he's done."

I met her eyes, but they swam in my tear-hazy vision. "I
don't even know. I only know I was with Duncan, at the
lighthouse, when Dearborne came to the door. And when he
opened it . . ." I bit my lip, shook my head in reborn disbelief. "Duncan called him *father,* Arianna."

"What?"

I nodded, reaffirming what I'd said. "I don't know how,
but that beast has managed to set himself up as Duncan's
father. And Arianna, I think . . . I think he was planning all
along to use Duncan to get to me."

"That's impossible. Raven, listen to what you're saying.
No Witch, neither Light nor Dark, could manage a spell so

powerful. To chose the soul who would incarnate as his own child . . . It can't be done.''

I met her gaze, my own narrow. "So you believe it's coincidence?''

Arianna lowered her head, shook it. "Of course not. It can't be that, but there's simply no way Nathanial could have . . ." And then her head came up again, slowly. "Unless . . ."

"Unless?''

"Do you suppose Duncan is Dearborne's *adopted* son?''

I blinked. "That's it. It has to be.''

"And if that's true, then you're right. It has all been a part of Dearborne's plan to get to you. Otherwise he'd have killed Duncan by now. He has to know the man is immortal.''

"Oh, he knows." I got to my feet, too upset to sit still when every nerve in my body seemed to be squirming. "He knew Duncan would find his way to me again, one day. Somehow, he knew.''

Pushing both hands through her hair, Arianna paced away from me. "This is not good.''

"And *that's* an understatement.''

"What are you going to do, Raven?''

I faced her. "What choice do I have, Arianna? I'm going to kill Nathanial Dearborne.''

She gripped my shoulders. "Oh, no. Not so fast, my friend. In the first place, if you murder the man Duncan thinks of as his father, he is going to hate you.''

"That's just a chance I'll have to take. Dearborne is out for my heart, Arianna, and you must realize that once he has it, Duncan's could easily be next.''

"I know, I know, but—''

"Then what would you suggest I do? Wait for him to attack? Let *him* decide when and where and how it will be? No. My best advantage will be to surprise him. He won't be expecting me to make the first move.''

"That's because he thinks you have half a brain, Raven.'' I scowled at her. "You can't beat him.'' She stated it flatly, dropped it as if it were a proven fact, with no room for doubt. "You know it, *I* certainly know it, having faced the man in battle myself . . . and Nathanial Dearborne knows it. You won't stand a chance.''

"You told me I was as good as you now."

"I lied."

I blew a sigh and turned away.

"Let me do it, Raven," she said.

I stiffened and stopped in my tracks. "You didn't lie," I said very slowly. "I am as good as you. You're trying to protect me."

"Duncan can't blame you if I'm the one who does it."

I went to her, took her hands in mine firmly, and made my gaze as penetrating as I could. "I won't let you fight him for me, Arianna. You beat him once, yes, but that was centuries ago. There's no way to be certain you could do it again. He's had time to improve."

"So have I," she said.

"And so have I. The difference is, this is my battle, not yours, Arianna."

She averted her eyes, but they slid back to mine. She understood, I knew she did. Didn't want to accept it, but she would. I knew her well enough to know that.

"If you insist on fighting him yourself, Raven, then please, please wait. Put it off, just for a little while."

"Why?" My suspicion had to come through in my voice.

"Not to give me a chance to do it for you, love. But . . . because there might still be a way out of it. If there is, you should take it, because if you fight him, you'll die."

"He's going to force me to face him sooner or later, Arianna."

"If you die . . . Duncan might be next. You said it yourself."

I couldn't reply to that. She was right, and there was nothing else for me to say. "So I put it off, if I can. But what if there *is* no way out of this? How is delaying it going to help matters then?"

"The delay will give us time, Raven. Time to find out exactly what his plans are, maybe what his strengths and weaknesses are, as well. And knowledge is power."

I nodded, hesitantly, but even so I couldn't deny the relief

I felt in knowing I wouldn't have to face Nathanial right away. Unless he attacked me.

"You'll have to avoid him. And in the meantime, you can work on making Duncan see him for what he really is. So if you do manage to survive the battle, he won't hold it against you."

"Do you really think that's possible?"

"Anything's possible. Including your winning this thing. If we work very hard between now and then. Are you willing?"

"Work is something I'm entirely willing to do—if it will help me rid the world of that bastard."

"No time like the present," Arianna said. There was a familiar hiss as she drew her blade and faced me, dropping into a ready crouch. "Let's get to it."

Sighing softly, I felt my lips pull into a reluctant smile. "Damn," I whispered. "You can make me smile no matter how bad things get, you know that?"

"Don't smile," she said, though she was disobeying her own order even as she said it. "Fight."

So we fought.

Arianna and I walked side by side along the route that led through the center of Sanctuary the next day. All but invisible, or we tried to be. We'd honed our talent for blending in with our surroundings, drawing so little notice we might as well have been invisible—one of the skills we'd learned from Trees Speaking long ago. Invisibility, he'd taught us, was not a physical state, but a mental one. It came in handy when one needed anonymity. And an immortal Witch living in a mortal world always needed that.

"Did you learn anything at the café?" I asked softly, leaning close to her.

"My waitress—Shelly, the redhead—said she didn't recognize the name, but that *someone* had recently moved into the old courthouse building on Main."

I nodded. "Jeremy at the herb store heard that someone was converting the courthouse building into some kind of museum."

Arianna frowned. "That makes no sense. Why would Dearborne want a museum?"

I shrugged. "One way to find out."

She nodded in agreement and we turned at the corner, walked to the old courthouse building, a truly lovely structure. I remembered when it had been built just over a century ago, all the hoopla of the brass band playing as the mayor cut a ribbon and the townsfolk applauded. Women in layered skirts and bonnets. Whiskered men in bowler hats. Children in knickers, pushing hoops with sticks.

Arianna's arm came across my middle to stop me, so I bumped into it with my next step, then paused to look at her. "Look," she said, pointing.

I did. And saw the two of them, Nathanial smiling in that frozen way he had, so that it didn't look like a smile at all, but an icy grimace suitable for a Halloween mask. And Duncan, looking slightly confused, a bit uncertain, but so hopeful.

Of what, I wondered?

My heart felt as if it were in the grip of a large, contracting fist, just for a moment. It did every time I looked at Duncan. I could still barely believe I'd finally found him again. After all this time.

My narrow gaze returned to Dearborne. The man who would try to tear us apart all over again.

"We'll wait," Arianna said, drawing me with her toward the park, just across the little circle that made up the center of Sanctuary. There was a fountain in the center of the circle, pavement all around it. This was the point of the teardrop-shaped Coast Road. From here, the road ran out along the northern edge of the peninsula, broadening, circling around near our home on the very tip, and then running along the southern coast all the way back to this very spot. From here one could also head northwest, back into the mainland.

We sat down on a bench near the fountain—a piece I'd always found vaguely distasteful. A scene of a group of Puritans gathered round their preacher, a mean-looking fellow, book in one hand, the other one pointing skyward. It was sculpted in bronze. The water flowed up through its base and cascaded down several levels to pool at the bottom.

"What, exactly, are we waiting for?" I asked, staring back toward the courthouse.

"For them to leave," she said. "We'll take a look inside when they do."

"They'll lock it up."

"Not if we make them forget to." Arianna turned halfway to study the fountain. "Does this guy remind you of anyone?" She tipped her head toward the bronze preacher.

"Arianna, that's manipulative magick and you know it."

"Ah, but with harm to none," she told me. "And you didn't answer my question."

I glanced at the sculpture. "Certainly not Duncan," I told her. "He never looked like that. So haughty and threatening. When he wore the robes of clergy, they seemed more like blankets than bronze. Inviting, warm. Safe."

She sighed, lowering her head. "You really do still love him, don't you?"

"You know I do."

I met her eyes, and Arianna pitched a penny into the well, making a wish in silence. "I wasn't talking about Duncan, anyway," she said softly. "Look at the eyes, the belly. No doubt the artist underplayed its true girth. Look at the jowls, Raven."

I did, and then my own eyes widened. "My goodness, you're right. He resembles Elias Stanton!"

Laughing, Arianna got to her feet, turning to face the sculpture. "Hello, Elias, you filthy old pig. Did some Witch get angry enough to turn you to bronze, I wonder?"

"Oh, what a thought," I said. But on looking, even I wondered if it could be true, though I'd certainly never heard of a Witch, even an immortal High Witch, with that kind of power. Still, the resemblance was uncanny. And in a moment I was laughing, too.

And then the courthouse doors swung open, and Duncan emerged, his father behind him.

We sat down at once, as if on cue, and I focused my attention on the color and texture of the bench. Sun-bleached granite, hard and cool, slightly rough. Focus, focus, until

my body seemed to soften, and to blend in with the bench
on which I sat.

Arianna's gaze remained on the two men while I did this,
and I knew she was willing them to leave the door unlocked.
Sending her thoughts, though gently. If she were too obvious, too agressive, Nathanial might well sense her thoughts.
If she were too gentle, on the other hand, he would be un-
affected. If she were perfect, "thinking" at him with just
the right amount of force, he'd simply forget to lock the
door.

Seconds later Nathanial and Duncan came down the steps
and toward us. Arianna put her back to the fountain, and
she, too, went still and quiet and granitelike. Sinking into
the granite, my body melding, it seemed, with the stuff, I
watched as Duncan and his father approached us and kept
on walking, passing within five yards of where we sat and
never even noticing we were there.

When they were out of sight, I pulled myself from the
heavy, slumberous pose of stone as if waking from a short
nap. I drew a breath, wondered if I'd breathed during that
time. Granite benches didn't, so I might have forgotten to
myself.

"All right," Arianna said. "Let's go."

"I don't like this."

"Oh, for heaven's sake, do we want to know what's going on in there or not?"

"Well, yes, but—"

"Then come on!" She took my hand, and together we
crossed the curved portion of street and headed up the courthouse steps. Arianna gripped the ornate doorknob, gave it a
twist. "Unlocked. Lord and Lady, I *am* good." She pushed
the door open, and the next thing I knew, we were standing
inside.

It was a large room, the entry hall. Towering vaulted ceil-
ing and gleamingly finished cherry woodwork everywhere.
On the floor were boxes and crates in various shapes and
sizes. Standing hither and yon were small stands and
shelves, some assembled, some still in pieces.

And in one corner a large, old object that made me gasp
and look again. Old, rough wood, rusted hinges. Stocks.

My stomach convulsed a little, and I gripped Arianna's hand, squeezed it, and inclined my head so she'd see them as well.

"That vile bastard," she whispered. "Look, Raven." And as I met her gaze, *she* nodded toward something. So I turned.

The huge sign, elaborately painted in elegant Gothic letters of black on a shining red background, stood upright, propped against a pair of crates. It read: YE OLDE WITCH MUSEUM.

But it got worse. Underneath in smaller block letters it went on: GENUINE RELICS FROM WITCH TRIALS AROUND THE WORLD.

Bile rose in my throat. For a moment I neither moved nor breathed.

Arianna had no such reaction. She bent over the nearest box, tearing the cover off and pushing aside the protective paper. "Candleholders," she said. "A pentacle, a staff . . . my Goddess, they have some Witch's *staff*. And there's more. Shackles, fire irons . . . Raven, these are instruments of *torture*."

Shaking my head from side to side, I, too, opened a box. "Diaries," I said, gently opening the cover of one such book, so old and fragile its pages were like butterfly wings. "Oh, no, it's a *grimoire*. And there's an athame, and . . . and a cauldron." I closed my hands around the small, stout iron pot, with its three squatty legs, lifted it, and saw the rose painstakingly painted by hand on the front. "No," I whispered. "No, not this." Tears burned in my eyes, and anger rose to overwhelm the sickness all of this brought upon me, as I stared for the first time in well over three centuries at my mother's own sacred cauldron. It had been taken with every other possession when the villagers—or *someone*—had ransacked our home in England.

My fury, my outrage, became a deep buzz in my ears, and a red haze formed before my eyes, so that I didn't even hear the sounds of Duncan and his father opening the front door.

Not until Nathanial Dearborne said, "Oh, good. Trespassers."

16

Duncan stood in the huge arching doorway, not sure what to think, much less what to say. Raven St. James stood facing him, one of his father's antiques in her hands. A pot of some kind. Stout black iron, encircled by slender, pale fingers that moved restlessly over its surface. Red nails, glossy red, and smooth, and he thought of fire. Wondered if it showed when his blood heated, and quickly lifted his gaze.

She wasn't looking at him, though, and that surprised him. Instead, she stared at his father, and the hatred in her eyes was second only to the horror he saw there. Potent emotions that shook him. Then they worried him.

Beside her was her blond pixie of a friend, who didn't look any more amused than Raven did. Unlike Raven, though, *she* hadn't lost the power of speech.

"I didn't see any signs," she said softly. "Last I knew, the courthouse was public property. Besides, the door was unlocked."

"It's not public property anymore," Nathanial said, and he spoke softly, his voice odd. Challenging. A dangerous edge to it and a frisson of something he couldn't hide. Something that sounded a lot like fear.

Duncan felt the tension in the room, thick enough to slice through, but he didn't know why.

"It's privately owned now," Nathanial went on. "And you know that."

"Ease up, Father," Duncan said sharply. He didn't know what the hell Raven and her friend were doing in here, but he didn't like the edge to Nathanial's voice. "They said they didn't know."

"They knew," Nathanial said.

"Oh? And are you a mind reader?" the blonde asked, glancing down at the wooden sign on the floor. "What's the meaning of this?"

"I think it's fairly self-explanatory. It's a museum. We're going to open it on Halloween—or, um, should I say, *Samhain*?"

The blonde gasped. Raven's eyes went wider and her lips parted. Her words were spoken so softly it was as if they emerged without a single breath pushing them. "Even *you* couldn't be this vile, Nathanial Dearborne."

"Wait a minute," Duncan said in confusion. "You two *know* each other?"

Nathanial didn't look at him. Neither did Raven. The blonde only glanced his way briefly, then focused on the other two again, her gaze nervous, darting. Her stance poised, knees very slightly bent, as if she were ready to spring into action. What was she expecting here? An actual *fight*?

Raven lifted the cauldron. "This . . . it was my mother's. But you already knew that, didn't you?"

Duncan stepped forward, touched Raven's shoulder, putting himself between her and his father in the process. His hand on her was gentle, and he squeezed slightly, instinctively wanting to calm and comfort her, even though it looked very much as if she'd come here to pick a fight with his old man.

Maybe because that was an emotion he could understand.

"Raven, look again. Come on, that pot must be a hundred years old."

"Three hundred," his father said from behind him, but Raven blurted the same words at the same moment. And Duncan only blinked and told himself this was all some kind of twisted dream.

"Regardless of who it belonged to, it's mine now," Nathanial said. "And it will be put on display with the other items confiscated from executed Witches."

"No, Father. It won't." Duncan's tone was hard, firm. He didn't know why, but the idea obviously made Raven sick inside. And the paleness of her skin, the wideness of her eyes, was all it took to tell him which side he had to take here. Right or wrong.

"You're a murdering thief, Nathanial Dearborne," Raven stated passionately.

And it surprised him. His father might be an insensitive, argumentative, unfeeling bastard, but he'd done nothing to deserve that.

"Raven . . ." Her friend's voice held a warning. But Duncan didn't let her finish.

"My father's political correctness might be in question here, Raven," he said, still standing between them, both hands on her shoulders now when she moved to step around him. "But I don't think he's a murderer or a thief."

Finally she looked at him. He'd been waiting, expecting, hoping she would. But when she did, he wished she hadn't, because there was such intense pain in her eyes. Round, wounded eyes, searching his for something he didn't think she'd find. The woman was traumatized, that was clear now. By him, by his father, or by the things she saw here, he didn't know. Nor did he know why it stabbed at his heart to see her hurting like this—but it did.

"You're involved in this obscenity as well," she whispered.

Unsure how to answer, he hesitated. And then it was too late. She tried to speak, swallowed hard as if she couldn't, as if something were blocking her throat, and then tried again. "So this is what he's made of you, is it, Duncan? How could you be involved in something like this? How *could* you?"

"Like father, like son," Nathanial almost sang.

Whirling, not even aware he was about to move, he snatched his father's lapels in fisted hands and glared at the man. "Not another word, dammit."

But Raven's hand was gentle on his shoulder, easing him

aside. He didn't have to move, but he did. He looked down at his hands, trembling as he clutched the front of his father's jacket, and he wondered what the hell he was doing. She touched him, and he let go—shocked, angry, but unsure where to direct that anger.

Shaking his head slowly, he stepped aside. "Someone tell me what the *hell* is going on here."

He shouldn't have moved. It left Raven facing his father, and whatever was between them, it was potent and it was ugly.

"It ends here," she whispered.

His father tensed, Duncan frowned, and Raven's hand shot to her waist, disappearing beneath her draping, dark blouse. Duncan got the sickening sensation that she'd pull a gun in a moment. Instinct took over. He swept his father behind him with one arm and gripped her wrist with the other, stopping it where it was.

She met his eyes, and hers were hurting. And there was a message in her eyes, or he thought there was. *Him or me, Duncan. Him or me.*

Her friend lunged forward, clasping Raven's hand in hers and dragging her away from Duncan, both from his touch and his sight, blocking her with a small, slender body. But he could still see Raven's hand, and just beneath the hem of her blouse a small jeweled hilt clutched in her fingers. My God, a knife?

"No, Raven," the blonde whispered. "Not here. Not now."

For one tense moment Raven's white-knuckled grip remained tight, half hidden in the folds of the blouse. But then it relaxed and the blood flowed back into her small hands as she lowered them to her sides.

"I think you'd both better leave," Duncan said. His hands were shaking, his vision blotchy with the shock of knowing she'd just come very close to attacking his father with a knife. And here he was wondering just what the bastard had done to her to make her want to gut him.

Some chance he had of building a relationship with the man, he thought grimly, when he trusted him so little. Or maybe it was just that he knew him so well.

No, it was neither of those things. It was Raven. He'd defend her against the Devil himself or God Almighty without giving it a second thought.

The women hadn't moved.

"Go on. We'll talk later, Raven."

"You don't understand what he's doing," Raven said, very softly. "I know that. But even so, you ought to know how wrong this is." Her friend released her and stepped aside. Raven lifted her head, dark eyes wet, probing. "These were the most cherished possessions of real women. Wives, mothers, daughters, sisters. Grandmothers, Duncan. Some were Witches, but most didn't even know what a Witch truly was. And regardless of that, they were people. Human beings, Duncan. And here you have the plunder, the booty taken from them after they were brutally tortured and murdered." Her voice grew louder with every sentence. "You have the weapons that hurt and killed them. The hot irons that seared their flesh until they broke or until they died. The stocks that held them like cattle in the streets. You have objects they considered sacred. And you plan to put them on display on Samhain, of all times!"

He lowered his head. "No," he said. "I don't."

"And just why does this bother you so much, anyway?" Nathanial boomed, reaching for the cauldron Raven held, only to have her pull it away, holding it protectively at her side. "Anyone would think you considered *yourself* a Witch the way you're taking on."

Duncan blinked. Instantly the image of Raven standing on the cliffs in the light of a full moon, head back, arms extended skyward, wind blowing the dark gown she wore . . .

"You do," Duncan said softly, without judgment. "You do consider yourself a Witch, don't you Raven?"

She swallowed, faced him, a new fear lighting her eyes.

"Oh, do tell him," Nathanial urged with a smirk. "He won't hang you for it, after all."

"Shut up, Father." He searched Raven's face. "You don't have to answer that if you don't want to."

At those words her eyes welled with tears. "I won't lie to you again, Duncan. I don't *consider* myself a Witch, I *am* a Witch. I live by Witches Creed, which tells us to do harm to no one. But there are those who don't. There are those who harm who they will without a hint of remorse. Some who even *enjoy* the harm they bring." And she shot a poisonous glance at his father.

Duncan felt his eyes widen. "I'm not even certain I believe there are such things as Witches."

"How can you doubt it when there are four of them in the room right now, Duncan?"

He looked at the blonde, then at his father. But that was only three. "Oh, *come on* now—"

"You've no idea what you were born into this time around, Duncan. You're a High Witch, like Arianna and me, a Witch of the Light. But your father isn't. He's one of the Dark Ones, and he means to kill me—"

Duncan threw up his hands. "That's enough."

"You know you have powers, Duncan," she rushed on. "Think about it. Haven't you ever known things before they happened, sensed things, heard someone's thoughts, wished for something and had it come about almost instantly? Haven't you ever—"

"That's enough."

She fell silent.

"I'm trying to understand you, Raven, but you're way over my head with this. I think the best thing would be for you and your friend—"

"Arianna," the blonde said.

"Arianna." Duncan glanced at her, saw recognition in her eyes, as if she knew him. But she couldn't. Then he returned his gaze to Raven. "It would be best if you went home. You're angry. My father's angry. Go home, Raven."

"Is that what you truly want?"

Those eyes of hers—God, they had something so powerful pouring out of them he could almost believe her nonsense. Right. She was a Witch and his father was a murderer. "You just tried to pull a knife on my father," he told her . . . or was he reminding himself? "If it were any one else, Raven, I'd be calling a cop."

"If you were any kind of a son, you'd have done just that!" his father yelled.

"I didn't let her kill you," he said softly. "Leave, Raven. I need to have a talk with my father."

"Dammit, Duncan, this man you call your *father* is nothing to you! He can't be! He conspired and plotted to get control of you from the moment you were born, but I tell you he's not your father. He's evil."

"Have it your way, Raven." Duncan reached for the phone. He had no intention of calling any cop on her, but she'd have no way of knowing that, and right now he just wanted her to leave so he could sort this out—and make his father tell him what the hell was going on between the two of them.

"He hanged my mother and me in a snowy square in England in the winter of sixteen eighty-nine, and you were there, trying to stop him!"

Duncan paused with the phone in midair. Because when she said those words an image passed through his mind—one so vivid it startled him. He saw two women, one unmistakably Raven, the other looking like an older version of her. They stood on a gallows with nooses draped round their necks. He saw his father wearing pastoral robes, eyes gleaming and cruel, and himself on the ground below, struggling against men who held him back. Raven and her mother faced the crowd, chins high, proud, unafraid, and then the floor fell away from beneath them and—

He closed his eyes fast and tight, lowered his head and pinched the bridge of his nose hard, as if to pinch away the disturbing image and the physical reaction it had evoked in him. Dizziness spun his brain wildly. He thought he might vomit.

"Duncan?"

He blinked, shook himself, met her eyes.

She stared back at him, and he kept doubting himself. Doubting she was the disturbed, confused beauty she appeared to be. Doubting everything he'd ever known or believed in. "I'm sorry," he said softly. "But you really do have to leave."

Tears brimmed, but she lifted her chin. Looking a lot like she did on that gallows in the vision or whatever the hell it had been. "All right," she whispered. "All right, if that's what you want."

She turned away from him, heading for the door.

"Leave the cauldron," Nathanial commanded.

"Father—"

"No. It's . . . it's all right." She looked at the pot she clutched, eyes tormented. But she set the cauldron down, stroked it lovingly, then pressed a kiss to her fingertips, and her fingertips to the rose painted on the front. That was when the tears spilled over. That was when Duncan's insides churned, and his throat tightened up.

Facing the door unblinkingly, she strode through it like a martyr to the flames.

Arianna shook her head hard. "You're going to pay, Dearborne," she stated. "This is one time you won't wreak your havoc and walk away unscathed. I'll see to that, I vow it."

"You're no part of this, Arianna," he said in a low voice.

"Oh, I'm a part of it. Make no mistake about that." Then she swung her gaze to Duncan's. "And you—I'm beginning to wonder if you're even worthy of her this time around."

Then she, too, sailed out the door.

Duncan shook himself, pressed his hands to his temples, closed his eyes, and tried to clear his head. "What the hell just happened here?"

When he looked up, he saw his father quickly wiping an expression of fear away from his face as he stared after the blonde woman who'd just left—watching so intently it was as if he were afraid she'd burst back in at any moment. But . . . Raven was the one who'd all but threatened him with a blade.

Nathanial covered the look quickly, and shrugged. "We were accosted by two admittedly attractive, but seriously disturbed women who think they're some kind of Witches, and who take offense at our establishment." He waved a hand. "That's all."

"No, Father, that's *not* all. Those two 'attractive but seriously disturbed women' acted as if they *knew* you."

"Yes," Nathanial said, rubbing his chin and moving to

a window to watch as the two moved away down the street. "That *was* rather strange, wasn't it?"

"Well, is it true? Do you know them?"

Nathanial faced Duncan, put one hand on his son's shoulder, as fatherly a gesture as he'd ever made. But he took that hand away again very quickly. Just as well. There was that static again. Duncan was always getting shocks from Nathanial on those rare occasions when the man deigned to touch him.

"I swear to you, son, I've never seen either of them before in my life. And you can believe that. I'd sooner cut the heart from your chest than lie to you."

Lowering his head, Duncan released all his breath at once. "I just wish I knew what the hell their problem is," he muttered. Then he glanced at the pot, and recalled the pain in Raven's eyes when she'd had to set it down and leave it behind.

Forget about her, he told himself. Unbalanced, crazy women who broke into houses and accused innocent men of murder while wielding blades did *not* make the best love interests.

If he could just convince himself of that, he'd be far better off.

He couldn't sleep. The events of the day kept replaying in his mind.

Nathanial had spent the rest of the afternoon showing Duncan around Sanctuary. The old man hadn't even been angry when Duncan told him he couldn't in good conscience have any part of his Witch Museum. He'd said he understood, and that he hoped the incident with the two women wouldn't derail things between Duncan and him. He said he respected Duncan for defending the woman, that he'd been far too angry to think rationally himself, and that he regretted having been so harsh with her. He said he hadn't been himself lately, and aplogized for it.

And the part of Duncan that was still a desperate, lonely son aching for a father . . . wanted to believe him.

Wary, burned too often not to know how foolish the still small gleam of hope was, he nonetheless gave the old man the benefit of the doubt. One more time. One more chance.

Jesus, when would it be enough?

There had been a strained banter between them that day. At lunchtime his father insisted on buying.

It was almost as if they were . . . real. A real father and son for the first time. It had never been this way before. Not because he was adopted, Duncan knew that had nothing to do with it. But because his father had never seemed to care.

Now he did . . . or . . . he was pretending to.

So why, just when things were going so well, did a mysterious beauty have to come along and throw a wrench into the works? Why did Raven have to show up now and make him doubt his father even more than he had before?

Why was this tiny voice whispering in his mind that he ought to be with her tonight? He ought to be with Raven.

Duncan closed his eyes, rolled over in his bed, told himself to forget about her. Sleep eluded him like some rare butterfly flitting away from a clumsily swung net. And as for forgetting about Raven . . . hell, he knew better, didn't he? Not why, not how . . . but he knew he couldn't forget her. It was as if she were already a part of him, even before he'd met her. As if she'd somehow wheedled her way into his soul and waited there like a spider in the center of a web. Waited for him to stumble into Sanctuary, into her sticky clutches. And now the more he struggled, the more entangled he became.

A Witch. He sighed, rolled again, punched his pillow. A *Witch* of all things. Hell, the way he was feeling, maybe she *was*.

I sat alone in a darkened room. Arianna was out. Making herself scarce, knowing I needed some time alone. Privacy to lick my wounds. She wouldn't have gone far, though. Not with that predator so close. She'd be watching over me like a tigress guarding a cub. My big sister. Three hundred— over four, since she'd lost me the first time—and she still played the part.

It made me feel warm inside. And it was a warmth I needed, because everything else suddenly seemed cold and dark and barren.

I'd been sitting there a long time, bathed in candleglow, smothered in a cloud of incense. A round table that had a pentagram painted on its surface sat in front of me, with a few tools laid out and ready. A slip of paper with Duncan's name on it stood in the center, to represent him, since I had no photo. Surrounding it was a ring of stones. Fluorite to bring past life memories. Bloodstone to remove the blocks in his mind that prevented those memories from coming. Around the stones were purple candles, for purple is the color of hidden knowledge. And in each candle I had engraved Duncan's name in sacred runes, along with the spiral of rebirth and the eye, representing the conscious mind. My herbs stood ready.

It was manipulative magick I was about to perform. The memories were his, but if his conscious mind were ready for them, he'd have regained them himself by now. And yet I knew he might be in danger from the very man he called his father. Unless he could remember, unless he could know the truth, he'd be defenseless.

This was the Temple-room. Sacred space, because Arianna and I had made it so. This place was used only for magick, on nights when we preferred to work indoors, whether it be due to the weather or for some other reason.

The reason tonight was privacy. I didn't want Duncan spying on me, because I would know he was there, in that lighthouse, staring out across the waves. I'd know his gaze was on me, burning over my skin. And knowing that tonight would only distract me from the work to be done.

I'd been still for a very long time, chanting, breathing, keeping my mind utterly blank until I had descended into an altered state. My body was limp, and I could barely feel it now. I was sinking into my soul, connecting to the utter essence of my spirit, because that is the where the power pulses strongest. That is where my connection to the Universe lives. Only when I felt that connection open, felt the power flow freely through me, did I move. Slowly, very slowly, I opened my eyes, focused on the candle flames, and then on the censer, where charcoal burned, heating the powdered incense I'd sprinkled atop it. Now I added other herbs.

I sprinkled rosemary and watched it turn cherry red, siz-

zling and popping and sending its scent to the heavens, as
I whispered, "Sleep."

A pinch of dried marigold petals went next, crackling,
blazing up briefly only to settle into a gentle smolder again
as I whispered, "Dream."

Then the holly, dropping from my fingertips in tiny green
bits, and burning with the rest as I whispered, "Remember."

Settling again into a comfortable position, legs crossed,
eyes falling half closed, I watched the smoke rise steadily
as the herbs burned, releasing their magick. And I continued
to chant those three words over and over. I only hoped it
would work. For without the memory, Duncan might never
believe me. And unless he did, he'd be putting his life in
grave danger. I wouldn't lose him again—especially not to
the likes of Nathanial Dearborn.

Funny, he thought he smelled something. A smoky, pleasant
scent that . . . Nah, he must have been imagining it. There
was nothing now.

Scent or no scent, his eyes were finally getting heavy.
Lids drooping as his body relaxed bit by bit. Better. Sleep
wasn't eluding him now, but coming closer. Timidly, but
steadily, and finally curling up beside him like a favorite
pet. He drifted away, relieved that he was finally able to.

And then he forgot all that, because his bed seemed to be
tilting back and forth . . . as if his island had become a boat,
rocking on the waves. His throat was dry and sore, his skin
burning hot. He was sick. Damn, when did he get sick,
anyway? He'd been fine just . . .

Wait, someone was there. Hands, cool and soft on his forehead. For just a moment he saw Raven's face in the glow of a
candle, saw her hair, tumbling freely over her shoulders.
" 'Tis you, lass," he whispered in a brogue not his own. And
then he realized that it couldn't be her, because Raven was
dead.

Dead. No, that wasn't right, but even as he thought that,
the images faded from his mind. He wasn't on a boat anymore, and her hands were not on his skin, nor was she
soothing away his fever. No. The hands on him now were

hard, strong, callused ones. And he struggled against them.

In front of him was a gallows, and upon it he saw Raven, with her mother beside her, and his own father standing with his gnarled hand on the lever. "Do you confess?" his father demanded.

"My soul is less stained than yours, Nathanial Dearborne. You're a murdering thief. You enjoy the harm you cause. You stole my mother's cauldron." Raven said those things, and Duncan sensed he was mixing her words together with more recent ones. But it didn't matter. His father's hand closed around the lever.

"Nay!" Duncan screamed. "I willna watch her die!" But he heard the horrible groan of the hinges, and the sudden slam of the trapdoor flinging open, slamming downward. He even heard the snap of delicate bones when the two women plummeted to their deaths.

And then he was standing there in the snow, gathering Raven's broken body into his arms, cutting the filthy rope away from her bonny neck, kissing her hair, her face. He couldn't believe the force of the pain that engulfed him. He felt empty inside, crippled, devastated. He'd lost her. *Lost her!*

"Dinna die," he whispered hoarsely. "You canna die, Raven, I love you."

Her body stirred, then, and he brushed the hot tears from his eyes to look down at hers, and saw them open. "Don't cry, my love," she whispered. "See? I'm not dead."

He felt his heart leap in fear. Sitting up in bed his eyes flew open wide, and he drew in fast, open-mouthed gasps in an effort to catch his breath. His skin beaded with cold sweat, and real tears burned paths on his face.

"Damn!" He flung back the covers, put his feet on the floor—not far away, since his bed was but a mattress—and then leaned over, elbows braced on his bent knees. "Damnation, lass, what're you doin' to me?" Then he clapped a hand over his mouth, for he'd shouted the words in some other man's voice. The accent . . . Scottish and archaic and . . .

"What's the matter with me?" he whispered in his own voice.

Her. That was what. It was all her. Raven St. James. What he could do about that, he didn't know. Was she really some kind of Witch? Could she possibly have powers he never would have believed in? Making him utterly obsessed with her? Making him think of her ahead of his own father, for God's sake? Subconsciously, at least.

Right, right. And making him dream crazy dreams and wake up speaking with an accent. It wasn't even possible.

But some small part of his mind didn't believe that.

All right, all right, enough. There was a library in town. First thing tomorrow he'd go there and read up on this nonsense. He'd find out once and for all if there *was* such a thing as magic, or Witchcraft, or whatever she called it. And then he'd confront her, armed with at least a small amount of knowledge, and he'd tell her to stay the hell out of his life. And out of his father's life.

And most of all, out of his *mind*.

17

"I need to see him. Alone. Without worrying about that bastard Nathanial bursting in on us at any moment." I paced, as I'd done most of the night, wringing my hands and wondering if anything I could say or do would ever make a difference, when I could see so clearly the feeling in Duncan's eyes for that bastard. He cared for Nathanial. Dearborne had *made* him care. Learning the truth was going to break Duncan's heart. And for that I hated Nathanial even more.

But Duncan had to know. He had to.

"I have to make him believe me," I told Arianna.

"He doesn't *want* to believe you."

She sat at the table in our small breakfast room. The octagon-shaped area was completely surrounded by windows, and the sun streamed in like a warm yellow waterfall, drenching us both. Arianna bit into her bagel and sipped orange juice. I was too ill with tension to eat a bite.

Chewing, she mumbled, "As for you seeing him alone, that won't be hard to arrange. I doubt it will help anything, though." She swallowed, sipped, set the glass down. "I don't remember Duncan being so dense last time."

"He didn't love the man last time, Arianna." My stomach

churned at the words, and in my mind I heard those I hadn't spoken. *Back then, it was me he loved.*

I closed my eyes, ignoring the self-pitying voice in my head, talking above it to drown it out. "In those days everyone believed in Witches and magick, though they barely knew the meaning of the words. Today no one does."

"Today no one believes in *anything*," Arianna said. "It's pathetic." I sighed my agreement, while she tilted her head in thought. "But there's nothing we can do about that. What I *can* do, though, is keep Nathanial out of your hair long enough for you to see Duncan alone. He probably isn't going to listen, but I suppose you have to try."

"Of course I have to try."

She nodded. Rising, she moved closer to the glass windows that surrounded us, shielding her eyes and facing the sea. "Duncan is still at the lighthouse. And I don't see any other boats there. Go on, pay him a visit before he decides to go into town to babysit the so-called father."

I blinked, stopped my pacing, and studied her stance, the tilt of her head, the shape of her brow. Everything. In three centuries you begin to know a person too well to miss anything. Even the slightest change in Arianna's breathing would have told me a tale.

"You won't confront him," I said, looking hard at her. "You won't even let him know you're there."

"Not unless it looks as if he's heading out to interrupt you. And then, I swear, I'll make it casual. Public, even."

"You won't challenge him?" I asked, suspicious.

"He wouldn't take me up on it even if I did, Raven. The man has an agenda, and I'm not on it. Not yet, anyway."

I believed her, and nodded at last. "All right. Now is as good a time as any, I suppose." I glanced down at my clothes. Unremarkable. Jeans, a snug black T-shirt with a flannel shirt pulled over it in deference to the autumnal chill in the air.

"Don't even think about changing. He might leave while you primp. He already left the island once this morning. Thank goodness he came back in short order. You might not be so lucky next time."

I sighed, shaking my head.

"Go, will you?"

I knew she was right. I was only putting it off . . . out of fear, really. His reactions . . . well, so far they'd fallen short of what I'd hoped for. I didn't expect they were going to improve now that I'd accused his father of murder and not only claimed to be a Witch, but informed Duncan he was one, too. He probably thought I was a lunatic. And goodness only knew what kinds of lies his father had told him after I'd left that horrible place yesterday.

Arianna looked at me, making her eyes big and impatient.

"All right." I sighed. "I'm going."

My big sister smiled, touched a hand to her blade, and then got to her feet.

We parted at the door, Arianna heading into the small garage where we kept our car—an old Volkswagen Bug we'd both grown too fond of to replace—while I walked toward the cliffs. We rarely used the Bug while we were in residence out here. Walking to and from the village was so much more pleasant, and less damaging to the earth and the air. But I supposed in this case Arianna felt she might need the advantage of speed on her side. She could beat Nathanial back here and signal me if anything went wrong.

I hoped nothing would.

The path began at the top of the cliffs, wandered at angles down them, zigging this way and that way and finding the shallowest route. As I started my descent I heard the VW's deep, froggy-voiced motor come to life, growl a few times, then fade as it moved away toward town.

The path was old. It had been here longer than I, and, Aunt Eleanor had confided, longer than she, as well. I often wondered whose feet had first trodden here, and if they'd been feet at all, or perhaps paws or hooves.

Sand-covered stone lay beneath my feet, slippery and gritty all at once. A chill breeze blew salty moisture onto my face, dampening the flannel shirt I wore with its misty droplets. I could smell the sea, taste the salt when I licked my lips, and feel it leaving wet sloppy kisses on my hair.

At the bottom my johnboat sat on the narrow strip of sand, dry and safe. I pushed it into the water and hopped aboard, then, crouching in the stern, tugged the rip cord and started the motor. All that remained then was to steer the little craft as the propeller whirled and pushed me forward. I sat down, felt the dampness of the sea creeping through the denim of my jeans, wished I'd brought something dry to sit on.

And then the shore was fading behind me and Duncan's island grew larger, closer. I bit my lower lip as I stared ahead, wind blowing my hair back and chilling my face until my nose went numb and my cheeks burned with cold.

He heard my approach. I knew it a moment later when he stepped out onto the front step and stood there, hands deep in his pockets as he watched me all the way in. His face, so beautiful, just as it always had been to me. Those deep brown eyes, and dark, thick brows. His full lips and strong jawline.

But that beloved face was expressionless this morning. It told me nothing of how he felt at seeing my approach. And I wondered if perhaps he might not *know* how he was feeling about that.

When I killed the motor and stepped out, he came down to the beach. Bending beside me, gripping the squared-off nose of my vessel, he tugged it up, out of the water. Then he stood facing me, and I straightened and turned to face him in return.

"I decided last night to tell you to leave me alone," he said. No greeting. No welcome. Just that.

"Did you?"

He nodded, his eyes roaming my face like a touch. "I can't do it, though. I've been rehearsing the words from the moment I saw you start down that path, to the boat, and the whole time you were crossing. But it didn't help."

"I'm glad of that."

He sighed, lowered his head, no longer looking at me. "Raven, I got some books on this . . . this Witchcraft thing. This morning. Now I haven't had time to read a lot, but—" He broke off, perhaps because I was smiling at him, slightly, but smiling all the same. "What?"

"Why?" I asked him. "Why did you go to get the books, Duncan?"

He took his time about answering, licking his lips, looking skyward as if for help. "Because I thought you were crazy, and I didn't want to think that, so I thought if I understood what you were talking about, I might see that . . . that it made some kind of sense."

I nodded. "And not because you were curious about your own . . . abilities," I said softly.

"I don't *have* any abilities."

"Oh."

He looked down at his feet, quiet for a long moment, while I stood, waiting, knowing.

"Sometimes . . . I know who's calling when the phone rings." He shrugged, looking up again. "Sometimes I reach for it before it rings without even realizing it. And then it does." He shook his head as if to negate everything he said. "But that's nothing."

"Of course."

"I mean, everyone does that. It's like when you hum a song and then flick on the radio and it's playing. Or when you wish the guy ahead of you on the highway would change lanes just before he does. . . ."

"Or when you mentally tell the red light to turn green and it happens," I added with a nod.

"Exactly."

"Exactly," I repeated.

"That stuff happens to everyone."

I didn't speak. He looked at me, as if awaiting my confirmation, my agreement. I met his eyes and shook my head. "No, Duncan. It doesn't."

He looked away, hands plunging into his pockets. "Yeah, it does," he said. "It has to."

I was trying to go carefully, gently. He didn't seem ready for any of this, and I was pushing it on him. But I didn't have a choice. "It's my fault you're having trouble accepting all of this, Duncan. I didn't explain things as well as I could have."

He shook his head. "Maybe not, but it's all right now. I think I understand. There's nothing supernatural going on here. And as for Witchcraft, according to the books, it's pretty much just a belief system based on—"

"No."

He looked at me, brows knit in frustration.

"For some, that's all it is—those things you've found in the books. A religion, a belief system one can study and learn and adopt. But those things are not what it is to us, Duncan. We're different. We were born different. Witches, yes, but not like all those others practicing the Craft. Most of them don't even know we exist, for it's a secret we guard of necessity. We're born with something extra, senses beyond the five. Weak, unpracticed, raw, but real."

I was losing him. I could see the skepticism in his eyes even now, but like a fool I rushed on, because it had to be said. "We . . . we're *immortal*, Duncan."

"Immortal." He closed his eyes and bent his head. "Dammit, dammit, *dammit*," he whispered. His voice was harsh, raspy, emotional. Then he looked up again, his hands gripping my shoulders gently as he probed my eyes, and his were worried, filled with some kind of concerned sympathy that was all wrong. "It doesn't matter," he said. "I told myself it did, that I should stay the hell away from you, but I can't do that, Raven, no matter how . . ." He stopped himself, closed his eyes briefly, then went on. "Listen to me. I have a wonderful therapist in Boston. He helped me beat my fear of heights, and the water thing, helped me deal with all the baggage my father has dumped on me over the years and—hell, he even helped me get rid of the dreams . . ." He stopped there, his voice trailing off as he frowned hard.

"Dreams?" I swallowed the hurt I'd felt at his insinuation that I was mentally unstable, and focused instead on Duncan. On *his* pain, *his* confusion.

"Damn, I'd forgot all about the dreams."

I sighed at the way his face paled, just slightly, and closed my hand around his, turning him, beginning to walk beside him along the shore. "Tell me about the dreams."

He shook his head quickly, jerkily. "It was a long time ago. I was only a little boy. They . . . they don't mean anything."

I squeezed his hand. "Please," I said softly. "I'd like to know about them."

He lowered his head, and his head clutched mine tighter,

reflexively, I thought. I could feel the tremor of pain move through him. He was quiet for so long I didn't think he was going to tell me. And then he began to speak in a soft, halting voice.

"I used to dream of a woman." He shivered. "Holding me, crying . . ." His voice grew even softer. "She kept whispering my name and . . . saying she didn't want to let me go."

He looked at my face. I hoped my tears didn't show. "The doc said it was a memory of my birth mother, embedded in my subconscious."

I caught my lower lip in my teeth to remind myself to think before speaking. To go gently. Lifting my gaze, I looked out across the water, toward the shore a short distance from my home. To the place high on the cliffs, beside the Coast Road, where I'd lost him three hundred years ago. I felt that crushing pain again, that crippling grief. My heart contracted at the memory of his beloved broken body lying lifeless on those rocks, and suddenly, going gently seemed like the least important thing in the world.

"Do you see those jagged rocks thrusting up out of the water, just offshore?" I asked, pointing. I didn't wait for a response. "That's where I found your body, Duncan. That's where I found you, and I thought it would kill me. I went to you, slogged through the waves out to where you were, and gathered you close, and held you against me and cried. I cried your name, and told you I couldn't let you go, and that I refused to go on alone, without you."

The old tears welled up in my eyes again. I didn't look at Duncan, but out there at those rocks, reliving the nightmare as I spoke. I half expected him to interrupt, but he didn't. So I went on.

"Arianna had cast and conjured even as your body plummeted from the cliffs, Duncan. She willed that when you lived again you'd look the same, and that your name would be the same so that I'd be able to find you and know you, and love you again."

I faced him, so that the sight of him alive, and whole, and here beside me could chase my most heartbreaking memory from my mind. Hands trembling, I reached up to stroke his face. "And that's exactly what happened."

I could see his skepticism. But I could also see the man I loved, alive and well behind his eyes, yearning to escape— to love me again.

"If I'm immortal, then how did I die?" he asked slowly.

"You weren't immortal then, Duncan. I was, though. They pitched me from those cliffs for Witchery. You tried to save me. You're immortal now because in that other lifetime, you died trying to save the life of a Witch. That's how the gift is earned."

Shaking his head, sighing heavily, confused and frustrated and torn between his instinctive knowledge that I spoke the truth and his absolute certainty that all I said was impossible. He turned away. I drew my dagger. "Look at this," I told him.

Slowly he turned. I did something then I was taught never, ever to do. I handed my blade over to another being. I gave Duncan my only means of defense. And he frowned as he turned it over and examined it.

"The man you call your father has one just like it, doesn't he? One he carries with him everywhere he goes."

Slowly Duncan's dark gaze rose from the blade, to my eyes. "Yes. He does. But that doesn't mean—"

"I know it isn't enough, alone. But there is more, Duncan. More that I can show you . . ." I stepped closer to him, my hands, trembling, going to the button of the jeans I wore. Duncan went utterly still, his gaze riveted to my fingers as he dropped my blade to the sand.

"You have a birthmark, Duncan. When we were together in the lighthouse, you only took off your shirt. So I couldn't have seen it. But I know about that mark all the same. It's in the shape of the crescent moon, and it's on your right hip."

Blinking, he said nothing. But I saw the amazement in his eyes. And then they darkened as I tugged my zipper down, and pushed the jeans down over my hips. They tripped my feet, making me clumsy, so I stepped out of them, right there on the shore in the biting October wind. I lifted the T-shirt slightly, moved the panties I wore so my right hip was revealed to him, and whispered, "Look."

He did. And then the color drained from his face.

"We're all born with the crescent, Duncan. That's how I knew you had it."

"That . . . that can't be real. You . . . you put it there." I could hear the desperation in his voice.

"Do you really think so?"

His knees bent. I never knew whether he knelt deliberately or simply lost the ability to stand, but the result was the same. Duncan on his knees in the sand, his face very close to my hip. I felt his warm breath on me there, and closed my eyes. This was no time to let carnal desires overwhelm me. But then his fingers came to me, running over the crescent, tracing its shape, making me shiver more even than the cold wind was doing.

"Madness," he whispered, so close I could almost feel the movements of his lips. "This is utter madness. . . ." And then his mouth touched my hip. His lips moved over it, pressed to it, parted as if to taste my skin, leaving it damp and vulnerable to the wind. I drew in a jerky, noisy gasp when his tongue ran along the mark, hot and wet. Hungry.

Shuddering, I sank into the sand in much the same way he had done, until I knelt before him, facing him, seeing the desire burning in his eyes just the way it used to do. "Duncan," I whispered.

He kissed me—pushing me backward into the sand, pressing me down with his body, he kissed me. And it was as if he felt the frustration of the three hundred years of waiting as desperately as I did. Or maybe it was a different frustration. That of wanting so badly to remember and not being able to. I didn't know. I only knew he wanted me as much as I wanted him, for I could see it in his eyes and feel it in his touch. He wasn't gentle. I didn't want him to be.

Already atop me, he ate at my mouth with unrestrained greed, then lapped a path over my throat. One hand gripped and squeezed my breast while the other battled my flannel shirt, and the T-shirt underneath, relentlessly striving to bare my body. As if he couldn't wait, his mouth closed on that breast, despite the T-shirt barrier. The shirt grew wet from his nursing, my nipple felt sore, deliciously hurting when he bit and tugged at it. And at last he shoved the clothes away, tearing them over my head, shoving my panties down now as his hands closed on my buttocks, fingers parting, exploring the dark, damp places of me. His mouth found my breast without defenses now, exposed, and returned to applying exquisite torture.

One hand moved around to the front of me, cupped me, and then two fingers pushed my folds apart, wide apart, while another stabbed up into me. I arched against him, whispered in his ear, "Don't make me wait, my love. I've waited so long already."

His breath shuddered out of him, but he complied, loosening his own jeans, pushing them down, and then pressing his erection against me. A second later he filled me, and the sigh that initial thrust drove from my lungs seemed to contain all the longing of the past three centuries—for it all melted away with that first joining. It was as if I'd come home.

I held him, kissed him, moved with him there in the sand, told him I loved him over and over. My hands on his back, his shoulders, feeling him, knowing him so well. And then I forgot everything as Duncan drove me higher—to points beyond those where conscious thought existed. To a place where only feeling lived. My body writhed with pleasure as I cried his name aloud and clutched him tight with every part of me, and he cried mine, when he emptied his passion into me.

Then he was still, braced up on his elbows, staring down into my face with something—wonder? Awe—sparkling in his eyes. His fingers tangled in my hair, and he bent to kiss me.

"You're going to be all right, Raven. I promise you that. I'm going to make you all right."

Blinking away the haze of pleasure, slowly understanding that he still didn't believe me, I felt all my joy fall to the ground like the dying spark of a falling star.

"You still don't believe me."

He stroked my forehead, pushing my hair away. "There's something to what you're saying, I realize that. The birthmarks . . . that's too much to be coincidence, I know. And whatever it is, it's feeding this . . . this . . ."

"Fantasy? Delusion?"

He smoothed my hair again, kissed it. "Don't worry about that now, Raven. All that matters is that you get past it. I want you well, because I . . . I feel something for you. Something I can't explain."

"I've *already* explained it."

He kissed me again, my forehead this time. "I'm going to call my doctor and force my father to go along with us on this. Arianna, too, if she's involved. Then I'll take you there myself, and we'll get to the bottom of this, one way or—"

"Your so-called father has the mark as well, Duncan."

He stopped talking, went silent, looked down at me with such sweet sympathy and genuine worry in his eyes that I almost laughed at him.

"I know you think I'm insane, but before you drag me off in a straitjacket, at least do me the honor of checking. Nathanial Dearborne bears the same mark we do, but his is on the left flank, just as it is with all the Dark Ones."

"Raven, you have to let this go—"

"He adopted you, didn't he?"

Rolling off me, slowly righting his clothes, Duncan nodded. "But that has nothing to do with any of this."

"No? Then why do you both have the mark? Not heredity, Duncan. Look at the man. Find a way and you'll see I'm right. He wants me dead, Duncan, and that's why he adopted you."

"No," he said.

"He used you, Duncan. He knew you'd find me again one day, and when you did, he would as well. Because he wants me dead."

"Stop it, Raven. He wouldn't—"

"My Goddess, I wouldn't be surprised if he were even instrumental in getting your natural parents to give you up. Perhaps he even harmed them once he realized who you were! All just to—"

"That's enough!" Duncan sprang to his feet, glaring down at me. "God, I must be as crazy as you are to have let this happen."

I gasped, cut to the quick. But slowly I sat up, gathering my clothes, retrieving my dagger from where it lay in the sand. "I'm sorry it hurts you, Duncan, but it's true. All of it, and you have to know."

"It's impossible, that's what it is. You're spinning yarns too farfetched to even be called a fairy tale, and expecting me to turn against my own father based on them. God, Raven, do you know what a vile thing that is to say? That he had something to do with my birth parents dying in that accident?"

I lifted my head, met his eyes. "Then they *are* dead." I lowered my eyes. "That bastard."

He fell silent and lowered his head.

"Duncan . . ."

"He's my *father*," he whispered.

I'd gone too far. I knew it then. "I'm sorry, Duncan. . . ."

"Get back in your boat and go home, Raven. I . . . I thought I couldn't say it, but it turns out I can after all. Stay the hell out of my life. Stop playing with my head. Leave me alone, and more important, leave *my father* alone. If you go anywhere near him, I'll have you tossed in jail. Understand?"

Blinking, I nodded. "I understand. But you should understand something, too, Duncan. That man murdered my mother, and probably yours as well. He's tried to kill me more times than I care to remember, and brought nothing but grief to me all my life. But none of that matters to me. *You* are what matters to me, Duncan. And if it takes my very life, I'm not going to let him hurt you. You won't die because of me. Not this time."

He closed his eyes. I got to my feet, pulled on my jeans.

"I love you Duncan. You loved me, too, once, so much you gave your life trying to protect me. So don't feel badly if I return the favor this time around, okay? It'll only be karma evening things up."

He whirled on me. "What the hell are you saying? Are we making some kind of suicide pact now?"

"No. If I die it will be at Nathanial's hand. And if it happens, Duncan, no matter what you believe now, I want you to leave here. Get away from him as fast as you can, because you'll be next."

I turned to leave, striding toward my boat.

"Dammit, Raven, wait!"

I stopped. Duncan ran up behind me, catching my shoulders and spinning me to face him. Then he kissed me, hard and long and deep. And when he stopped, I saw moisture in his eyes.

"Do you have any idea what I feel for you? No matter what kinds of ridiculous tales you spew, I . . . Raven, it's powerful, this feeling. It could be so much, if you'd just let it be. I think about you all the time, dream of you at night, *ache* for you, for Christ's sake. It's going to kill me to lose you, and I know that sounds like bull, because this is so new, between us. But that's what it feels like."

He searched my eyes, shaking his head, and the wind lifted his hair as it was lifting my own.

"Please, just let all this nonsense go. Stop harassing my father, stop spinning these fantasies. And just . . . just be with me. Just be with me, Raven."

Tears blurred my vision, but I blinked them back. "I tried it that way last time." I sniffed. "Then you used to beg me to trust you with the truth, the entire truth, the parts you sensed I was keeping from you. I didn't . . . and you died because of it. So this time I'm telling you all my secrets, Duncan. But you don't believe them, don't even want to hear them. You want me to pretend they don't exist, like I did before. And just be with you. The way I did then. But I can't. No matter how wonderful the memory is of all those nights in your arms, I can't do it to you again, Duncan. Because the memory of the way it ended is pure agony." I touched his cheek. "It would kill me this time, I swear it would."

He frowned so hard his brows touched.

"Know this much," I whispered. "I love you. With every breath I take, I love you Duncan Wallace, just as I have for three hundred years while I wandered this earth in search of you, mourning you, aching for you. Utterly alone, I waited all this time to find you again. And now that I have, you won't have me." I lowered my head. "Your father and I have to settle things, Duncan, and when it's over, one of us will be dead. If it's me, don't mourn. Just get away from him.''

He shook his head. ''You won't be hurting my father, Raven, and he won't be hurting you. I'm going to protect you from each other. And you . . . from yourself.''

I nodded. ''And if it comes to a choice between him and me?''

''Jesus, Raven, he's my *father*.''

It was as if he drove a blade straight into my heart. But I said nothing. Just walked to my boat.

Duncan watched her go, a tear rolling down his cheek. Why did it have to be this way? What kind of madness was inside her that she had it in for his father the way she did? God, would she really try something? And why? Why did he fall in love for the first time in his life with a woman who had so many problems?

And why was this insistent feeling in his gut telling him she was perfectly sane, and that everything she'd said made some kind of sense?

He wanted to make it all go away. To love her so much she'd forget about all of this. To hold her and cherish her and exorcize whatever demons must be tormenting her.

But he also wanted to continue building a relationship with his father. A real one, a genuine one. The one he'd been hoping for and dreaming about since he was old enough to dream.

Hell. He couldn't risk that Raven might actually try to harm Nathanial. She wouldn't, though. She wouldn't *really*.

As for the rest of it—his dreams, his memories, the fact that she'd called him Duncan Wallace—a name he'd never heard before, but that sounded perfectly familiar when he said it—the dagger, the birthmarks—all of those things, he refused to think about. For now.

Or thought he did.

But they were there, niggling at his mind, eating away at his disbelief. Making him wonder.

Two hours later he arrived at the courthouse in town, determined to be his father's shadow until he knew for sure just how much of a threat Raven was to him. Until he knew for certain she was imagining things when she said his father wanted her dead.

When he got there, Nathanial did something so out of character that Duncan *knew* he was sincerely changing.

He handed Duncan the small black iron pot that Raven had tried to steal the other day.

"What's this about?" Duncan asked, confused.

"I want you to give it to that girl. Raven . . . what's-her-name. You know who I mean."

Duncan could only stare at his father in surprise.

Nathanial shrugged. "Hell, son, it seems to mean something to her. I suppose in her poor twisted-up mind she must think all that she was saying was true. I have no reason to fight with her. So I thought, as a gesture of friendship, I'd let her have the damned pot." He shrugged. "Call it a peace offering."

Taking the pot from his father's hands, Duncan shook his head slowly. "That's really kind of you," he said. "It must be worth—"

"It's only money." Nathanial waved a hand in dismissal. But his eyes seemed to be watching Duncan's face very closely. As if he were doing this for a specific reason, and that reason had to do with Duncan's reaction. As if it were a part of this whole act he'd been perpetuating. This whole "I-want-to-be-your-father" game the old man had been playing for reasons Duncan didn't understand.

And now I'm just letting Raven's madness poison my mind against my own father. Just what I don't want to do.

But he'd been suspicious of his father's motives long before Raven had come onto the scene. Hell, he'd been suspicious of his father for most of his life, particularly whenever the coldest man he'd ever known started making fatherly overtures toward him.

He just wasn't sure anymore how much of that feeling was his own gut instinct, and how much was the power of suggestion Raven St. James wielded.

"Frankly, son," Nathanial went on, "part of me wanted to call the police, swear out a complaint, something like that. But I realize she . . . well, she means something to you."

"You do?"

"She does, doesn't she?"

Blinking, wondering just when his father had become sensitive enough to pick up on something like that, he nodded. "Yeah. She does."

"That's why I decided it would be better to make peace than to wage war. For your sake."

"For my sake."

"I don't want her coming between us," he said, very softly.

And a tear shimmered in Nathanial's pale, cold eye. A real tear? Duncan didn't know. He'd never seen his father shed one before.

Jesus, between the two of them, they were ripping his heart to shreds.

Swallowing hard, feeling a softness he hated toward the hard man who was his father, he reminded himself not to believe too strongly, not to hope for too much. And he made a decision. One way or another, he was going to get a look at Nathanial's left hip. Tonight.

18

"Why don't I pay the girl a visit tonight?"

Duncan paused in his constant, sickening perusal of the place—his father had been busy today—and felt a new chill lift the hairs on the back of his neck. "What girl?" But he didn't really need to ask.

"You know," Nathanial said. He stood in the center of the room, hands on his hips, looking around just as Duncan had been doing since he'd arrived here. Duncan had refused to take part in things, until his father had hurt his back trying to set up shelves, and Duncan had somehow ended up jumping in to help. He'd been here ever since. Shelves stood everywhere, all of them filled with "artifacts." It made Duncan sick to look at them.

"The self-proclaimed Witch," Nathanial went on. "I can deliver the cauldron along with an invitation to our grand opening. Maybe smooth those pretty ruffled feathers of hers, hmm?"

Straightening, Duncan sent his father a look of disbelief. He didn't like being here. Didn't like *himself* right now, for giving the old man the benefit of the doubt. Wasn't he surrounded by proof of the man's true nature? Wasn't all of this just a little too cruel to be the result of ignorance or even narrow-minded bigotry?

"I don't think visiting Raven St. James is a very good idea, Father."

"And why not? It's the least I can do! After all, you were making inroads with her before I stepped on her delicate toes with this museum. I'm well aware I messed things up for you."

"No, you didn't." He lowered his head, shook it, couldn't quite bring himself to tell his father that he thought Raven might be a bit . . . confused. Maybe because when he said it aloud he realized that he didn't believe it. Not really.

"Still, I fear I got off on the wrong foot with the woman. And she *is* a local. I'd rather not have the locals turning against me before I even begin. Maybe I can make her see reason."

"She doesn't seem to know what reason is," Duncan muttered. Then again, neither did he just now. "Besides, she'd never agree to see you."

"I've thought of that. Still, I want to gift her with the pot, personally, an overture of friendship. You'll just have to arrange it *for* her."

Duncan turned from surveying yet another shelf and faced his father slowly. "What do you mean?"

"Set us up. She'll never agree to meet with me, but she *would* if she thought she were meeting you. So ask her to meet you somewhere. Someplace . . . private. I . . . wouldn't want to embarrass her, after all. And then I'll meet her instead, gift her with the cauldron, and become her friend."

His father's eyes were as still as glass. His lips smiled, but the rest of his face seemed frozen, expectant.

"I don't think I can do that," Duncan said.

"Nonsense! Of course you can. It's the only way it will work. I can see you care for the girl, son. This way she and I will mend our fences and she'll see I'm not the monster she thought. That ought to smooth things over substantially between the two of you. Don't you think?"

Swallowing the dryness in his throat, Duncan nodded. "It might." No way. No way in hell. And what was he reacting to? His own gut instinct? The cold look in his father's calculating eyes? Or maybe Raven's crazy stories were making him feel this icy foreboding in the pit of his stomach.

"Well then?"

Duncan shook his head firmly. "It would be too cruel, Father. She thinks you're some kind of murderer. Can you imagine how frightened she'd be to show up somewhere and find you there, waiting?"

"Yes," Nathanial said. "I can."

Duncan blinked. He'd never seen his father's eyes look so dead. What the hell was happening here? Wasn't it obvious? Nathanial was trying to manipulate him into setting Raven up. The question was why?

He wants me dead, Duncan.

No. Not that, it wasn't that. Nathanial might be a cold, mean SOB, but he was no killer.

"What do you say we grab a late dinner, hmm?" Anything to change the subject. He didn't like discussing Raven with his father. It seemed like some kind of blasphemy.

He wanted her. Maybe even needed her. Probably loved her. My God, he probably loved her.

But he needed her sane, dammit, with all these delusions blown out of her mind.

Unless of course, they *weren't* delusions.

And now who's crazy?

"Dinner?" Nathanial said. He glanced at his watch. "Damn, boy, dinner was hours ago! You should have said something. I got so caught up in this project I lost track of the time."

"I've been doing that lately myself."

"It's late to go out." His father frowned in thought.

"We could order in," Duncan suggested. "If you'll tolerate pizza, I'll tolerate wine."

"Ahh, we'll dine in that quaint style . . . early redneck. Perhaps even put one of those . . . videos into the machine and stare mindlessly at it."

Was he being hatefully sarcastic, or joking around? Tough to tell. He'd never *heard* his father joke around before. "You don't have a VCR," he reminded the old man. "But I'm sure we can find something on TV. It's Monday night. Should be a football game on."

"Ahh, yes, the sport of champions. Well, I'm willing if you are."

"Great. What do you like on your pizza?" Duncan picked up the phone, punched buttons.

His father shrugged, not even looking at Duncan. "I can't imagine it much matters." Then he sighed. "Perhaps we could invite your friend here. Not that blonde she had with her. I . . . I didn't like that one. Still, your Raven could join us in this modern-day ritual. It would give me a chance to get to know her."

Duncan's hand tightened on the phone and he knew without a doubt he didn't want his father anywhere near Raven. "You're like a dog with a bone about this, aren't you? She wouldn't accept. Just give her some time and space, and maybe she'll come around."

"And if she doesn't?"

"Then she doesn't." Duncan shrugged. "It doesn't matter."

"Oh, but I'm afraid it does, Duncan, my boy."

Before he could ask what his father meant by that, the pizza guy answered the phone to take Duncan's order. And by the time he hung up, his father was off on another subject. As if he'd forgotten all about Raven.

But Duncan had a feeling that might be an illusion.

So far, neither Raven nor Nathanial was proving to be what either seemed.

I paced outside the courthouse, a safe distance away, but close enough to watch the door. Duncan was inside, and he hadn't left yet. There had been a delivery boy, a pizza box, and the mouth-watering aromas had reached me. Spices, tomato sauce, cheeses, and fresh crust. My stomach rumbled. I'd been too tense and worried and . . . yes, heartbroken, to eat today, and now I regretted it. But I didn't regret being out here. I glimpsed Duncan in the doorway, just briefly. Dark, and beautiful, forbidden to me just as he'd always been. By choice this time, rather than by vows. But just as forbidden. Just as unreachable. His dark hair played with a stray breeze as he handed the delivery boy some bills. And when the boy left, Duncan stood there a moment longer, head cocked to one side, eyes scanning the benches and the fountain and the park beyond. Scenting the air like a wolf,

I thought. He knew I was there. Sensed my nearness somehow. He probably didn't even realize it, but he did.

And yet it seemed he'd deny the connection between us
with his dying breath. Why must he be so stubborn?

Sighing as he moved inside and the door closed again, I
sank onto the stone bench beside the fountain, elbows on
my knees, head in my hands.

"Raven . . ." The harsh, familiar whisper brought my
head up fast. Arianna came skulking from the shadows like
a Halloween spirit. "What are you *doing* out here?"

"You must have radar," I told her. "It's barely been an
hour since I slipped away."

"I don't need radar and you know it." She came closer
but didn't sit. Instead she stood over me, feeling taller than
me for a change, I thought. Her short hair riffled like dove
feathers as she looked down at me from those huge brown
eyes. Her Peter Pan stance, I called it, when she stood like
this. Legs shoulder-width apart, hands planted on her hips,
elbows pointing to either side of her. Give her a hat and a
feather, and she'd probably fly. The leggings she wore, and
the green velvet tunic that reached to midthigh enhanced the
image considerably. I almost smiled.

"Are you going to tell me what you're up to, or sit there
inspecting my wardrobe?"

I shrugged. "Peter wore less jewelry, of course," I muttered. She frowned harder. "Then again, so do most of the
royals."

"Are you mocking me? After I came all the way out here
worried half to death about you and—"

"Hush, Arianna. I love you, you know that."

"Then talk to me." Her hands lowered to her sides, and
she paced. "It's to be tonight, isn't it? You'll go after him
tonight."

"Yes." I drew my dagger, ran my thumb across its edge
to test its readiness. A nervous habit I'd repeated a dozen
times today. "It's time."

"You're not ready."

"And I'll not become any *more* ready by putting it off."

"He'll kill you."

"Duncan is in danger!"

She rolled her eyes. "Duncan should have listened to you in the first place." Then she paused, glaring at the courthouse as if trying to send it up in flames with the sheer force of her gaze. "I'm beginning to hate them both."

"Not Duncan," I protested. "You're my sister. You can't hate the man I love, Arianna."

"I can if his foolishness gets you killed."

I closed my eyes. I didn't want that to happen. And I knew it was possible. I just wished she wouldn't remind me quite so often.

"So what are you waiting for? Having second thoughts?"

I shook my head. "Duncan's inside. I'm afraid he's going to spend the night. He thinks he needs to protect his . . . *father* from me."

Arianna lifted one brow. "His *father* could probably roll a bus onto its side without breaking a sweat, as old as he is."

I wasn't being fair, I knew that. Duncan had said he meant to protect both of us, from each other. But it still felt like betrayal to me.

Arianna eyed me. "What if he's weakening?" she asked suddenly. "Maybe that's why Nathanial is so determined to have you this time, Raven. Maybe he needs a heart soon. You . . . um, you didn't tell Duncan about that part of it, did you?"

"There are a lot of things I didn't get around to telling him," I whispered, averting my eyes.

"So what *did* you do all that time you were with him this morning? Or need I ask?"

My chin dipped lower. "It doesn't matter."

"I beg to differ! It certainly *does* matter. If he made love to you, Raven, then he must care. And if he cares, he'll believe you over Nathanial." I looked at her, my doubt in my eyes. "He *will*!" she insisted.

"He thinks I need mental help." I heaved a deep sigh, leaned over, and trailed my hand in the icy-cold water that rippled in the fountain. Soft blue lights lit it from below, so my hand seemed to glow in the choppy water. Pink lights illuminated the flow that spilled from above, tumbling down the stairlike layers of the statue's base, and losing itself in the pool.

"He'll believe you if you just give him time."

"There *is* no time. I can't let him go on being so close and so damned vulnerable to a man who could kill him at any moment. And I can't just wait for Nathanial to come for me. The waiting is going to drive me insane. I can't eat or sleep, and that will all work to the old man's advantage. You know that."

"What I *know* is that your lack of appetite and restful nights has nothing to do with Nathanial, and everything to do with Duncan."

I shook my head. "It doesn't matter." My gaze returned to the courthouse. My vigil began anew. The lights still blazed from the windows.

"You can't go through with this," Arianna said, apparently reading my eyes as easily as I could read hers. "Not tonight, not with Duncan right there."

"I didn't think I could kill Nathanial in front of Duncan," I told her. "But it doesn't look as if I have a choice. Besides, when he sees his father wield that blade with every intention of doing me in, when he sees the old man's skill—his *well-practiced* skill—then perhaps he'll know I told the truth all along." A light flicked off on the lower level. But seconds later one came on upstairs. "Still," I said, sheathing my blade, getting to my feet, "I'll spare Duncan seeing it if I can."

"How?"

I shrugged. "He has to sleep sometime." I started forward, crossing the cobbled street so reminiscent of old England. But Arianna's hand on my shoulder stopped me, and I turned. "This will be a fair fight," I told her before she could speak. "I won't have murder on my conscience. I won't attack Nathanial with the odds stacked in my favor. You'll stay out of it, no matter what. I want your promise on that."

Lifting her chin, my sister swallowed hard. "I don't want to lose you again, Raven."

It was not often I'd seen tears in Arianna's eyes, but I

did now. All her harshness and brass melted into twin pools
that shimmered in her eyes.

"I know." I hugged her gently. Stroked her short hair,
kissed her face. "If I'm meant to triumph over him, I will."

She nodded, sniffled, and straightened away from me.

"If I fall . . ." I began.

"If you fall, I'll kill the bastard myself," she told me.

I met her eyes and knew there would be no talking her
out of it.

His father had seemed averse to the idea of Duncan staying
over. That reaction offended Duncan slightly, hurt him a
little, and prodded his suspicious mind a lot. Still, he'd
talked the old man into it. No way was he leaving Nathanial
alone tonight. He was half afraid the old man would head
out after Raven the minute he was alone—and half afraid
she'd come after him instead.

There was a guest room overlooking the circle, the park,
and the fountain. His father's room was on the opposite end
of the hall, overlooking the road that led back to the mainland. There appeared to be several bedrooms in between,
but the doors were all closed, and Duncan didn't want to let
his father know how little he trusted him by peering inside
those other rooms as they passed. Still, he thought there was
likely no reason he couldn't have used any of the in-between
rooms. And then he wondered why his father would want
to keep him at a distance.

It didn't matter though. This one was fine. He'd sensed
something, got that little shiver up the back of his neck
earlier when he'd looked out on the town circle. That same
prickly awareness he got when *she* was near. Not Witchcraft. Just intuition. Normal intuition. He hadn't seen anyone
outside, but it was dark. And he doubted a nightbird like
Raven would be seen if she meant not to be.

Going to the window, he stared down at the circle again.
And again, saw no one. So he paced, and he waited, and he
battled the growing feeling that something was going to happen tonight. To distract himself from it, he tried to figure
out how he could check his father for the birthmark, and
wondered if his intention to do just that made him as crazy

as Raven was. Probably. He couldn't understand why he *wanted* to believe the woman so much when he *knew* that everything she said was just part of some grand delusion. And it wasn't that he wanted her to be right about his father. Just that he wanted her to be sane. No, it wasn't that, either. It was something else. Something deep inside him, so deep he couldn't reach it. Couldn't examine or explore it. But it was there. Knowledge. Truth. Buried, but present, and whispering every once in a while. Words that he couldn't quite hear. Reality that he couldn't quite grasp.

Closing his eyes, lowering his head, he wondered what his shrink would think about this latest crisis. That he'd fallen head over heels in love with this particular woman from the second he'd set eyes on her. And why, for heaven's sake? What was it about her?

Her eyes. Dark, as black as midnight, and full of mystery and onyx fire.

Her hair. Tangled silk. As twisting and writhing as Medusa's, but gleaming and glossy and soft. Tempting his fingers and his lips to touch it. Threatening to bind him up and never let him go.

Her skin, like moonlight. Warm, when he touched it. Responsive against his lips. Sweet and salty and as addictive as a drug.

Her laugh, though she laughed very little. And her voice, deep and rich, slightly coarse. Whiskey and roses, that was what her voice was like. If whiskey and roses could sing in harmony, they'd sound like Raven St. James. It seemed he'd known her voice before he'd ever heard her speak. It seemed he'd known exactly the way she would sound.

But there's more. Her courage. The way she faced that crowd from the gallows, shamed them all, she did, an' never once cried out as she plummeted to her death! Aye, an' the way she refused to confess to anythin' when she'd done nothin' wrong. An' her strength. When the bastard Elias Stanton attacked her, tried to rape her, she laid him out cold. Damn near killed him. The way I wanted to do when I saw her later—her dress torn, her satin skin bruised, scrubbin' herself raw in the crystalline cold o' the stream.

I didna think I'd ever seen anythin' so pain-filled as her eyes that day. An' . . .

Duncan went very still. Utterly still. "What the *hell* was all that? Where . . ." He looked around the room, as if he expected to see someone else there. But the someone else wasn't in the room—the other man was inside him, inside his head, spewing memories that did *not* belong there!

None of those things had happened!

And yet they kept flashing. Bits and pieces. He was kissing her bruised skin as she cried, and trembled. He was whispering, "No one will every hurt you again, lass. I swear it on my life." He was facing his father, only they both wore robes, and he was demanding to know where Raven's body was being taken. And then he was there, searching a horrible place filled with the stench of death and decay, livid because he couldn't find her there.

"Stop!" he moaned, pressing his hands to the sides of his head and turning in a slow circle. "Stop, dammit!"

Nay, Duncan, I willna stop. I canna. You must remember.

The lights had gone out at last, and I had slipped inside by means of a small window in the back. Silently I crept up the stairs, my dagger in my hand, at the ready, lest Nathanial be aware of my intent, and be lying in wait around some dark corner.

The stairs creaked as I mounted them, and I went still. But only for a moment. Testing the next step with care, I moved to the top, and there I paused, looking up the hall and down. Unsure which way to go. And finally turning left, and tiptoeing down the hall.

Just outside the door at the end, I heard Duncan's anguished, "Stop, dammit!"

My heart leaped into my throat, and I kicked the door open, springing inside and landing in a ready crouch, dagger high, eyes darting.

He stood by the window. His back to the pane, staring at me. His face seemed tormented, unsurprised, too caught up in whatever was eating at him to feel startled at my rather dramatic entrance. But I saw that he was alone in the room, and slowly sheathed my blade. "I . . . I heard your voice. I thought . . ."

"Thought what? That my father was in here trying to murder me?"

I didn't nod. It seemed the wrong time to speak ill of his father. "Where is he?" I asked.

"You think I'm going to direct you to his room so you can attack him in his sleep?"

I lowered my head. Turning, I glanced back down the hall to calm the rising goose bumps on the back of my neck. I saw no one, and then I closed the door. Moving forward slowly, I reached up, touched Duncan's face.

"What's wrong?"

His eyes moved over my face as if he couldn't look at me enough to suit him. And then he closed them. "What *isn't* wrong would be a better question."

"Okay, what isn't wrong?"

He met my eyes, smiling a sad, sarcastic smile. "Nothing."

"That's very good."

"The woman I think I'm falling in love with has just broken into my father's house, kicked in my bedroom door, and jumped in wielding a knife. And I ought to be calling the cops and having her hauled off to a rubber room somewhere. And instead I'm standing here wishing I could . . ." He let his voice trail off.

"You love me?" I whispered.

One hand rose to delicately cup my chin, and then he lowered his head, holding my eyes with his until mine fell closed, and his lips pressed to mine.

So tenderly he kissed me. As if he thought I might break. And when he straightened away, I stared at him in wonder. "Does this mean . . . does this mean you . . . believe me?"

He shook his head sadly, walked to the bed, sat on its edge. "I don't believe anything. Not even my own feelings right now."

"Oh."

"Will you tell me something?"

I put my back to the window, half sitting on its sill, so I

was facing Duncan, and the door beyond him. "I'll tell you *anything*," I promised.

He drew a deep breath, blew it out. "Was there ever a time when you were . . . attacked?"

I nodded. "Many have tried to kill me."

"Now, that's something I don't understand," he said quickly. "You keep saying how my father has tried to kill you, but then you claim to be immortal."

"There is only one way to kill an immortal, Duncan. And that's to cut the still-beating heart from his breast."

"God," he said, turning his head away in disgust. Then he closed his eyes, cleared his throat. "But I got off the subject. The attack I asked you about . . . this man wasn't trying to kill you, he was trying . . ." He looked away, and it seemed he couldn't finish.

Finally I understood. "To rape me?"

Duncan nodded. "Did it ever happen?"

"Once. It was Elias Stanton, the pig. Claimed I'd bewitched him into feeling desire for me, and so it was his right to act on it—teach me a lesson."

Duncan closed his eyes. "When did it happen?"

"Sixteen ninety-two. I remember it well, Duncan. It was later that night I lost you."

Lifting his head slowly, meeting my eyes, he said, "Tell me more."

I searched his face. "Are you sure you want to hear this?"

"I think . . . I have to hear it."

I nodded, licked my lips. "I was walking home from town, when he approached me. I resisted, he pursued. I wound up with my back to a tree, while he groped at me. In the end, he was on the ground with a heavy limb atop him, and I was racing back to my aunt's home in his wagon." I closed my eyes. "I told Arianna, but not Aunt Eleanor. It would have killed her had she known. I couldn't even face her. I felt . . . contaminated. So I went to the stream, stripped off my torn clothes, and plunged myself into that icy water, and I scrubbed and scrubbed. But it did no good. I could no more rid myself of the memory of his vile touch than I could wash away the bruises." I shuddered at the memory. But then I opened my eyes and faced Duncan again. "Then you came. And it was all right."

Duncan bit his lip. His jaw was taut, as if he were bearing a great weight and straining to support it. "Why would my father want to kill you?"

I blinked. He jumped from one subject to another so fast it made my head spin. "I told you that you died trying to save my life, and that was how you earned the gift of immortality."

"Something I still think is impossible."

"Yes, I know." I sighed. "So pretend it's fiction, a story I'm telling to entertain you."

"That's exactly what it is." But he said it as if trying to convince himself. His gaze held mine for a long moment. But it was Duncan who finally looked away.

"There is another way one can gain immortality, and that's the way the Dark Ones, the evil ones, go about it. They gain it, Duncan, by stealing it. When they take the heart of another immortal, and keep that still-beating heart captive in a small box far away from the ever-young body of their victim, they hold that victim's power as well. The first kill gives them immortality. But they need more. The ones that come later increase their strength and powers, and replenish their life force when it weakens and dims. They use the hearts like . . . like a child's toy uses batteries. Drain them all but dry, then toss them aside for another."

"And you think my father is one of these . . . these *Dark Ones*?"

I nodded. "I'm a powerful Witch, Duncan. He wants that power for his own, and each time I've thwarted him he's become more determined to have it." I lowered my head. "But it's not just the power. He hates me because he blames me for coming between you and him three hundred years ago. And here I am, doing it all over again."

He shook his head. "It's so far-fetched."

"But you're starting to wonder, aren't you?"

He looked at me, saying nothing. "I called a lawyer this morning, after we talked. Asked him to find out any details he could about the car accident that killed my birth parents."

I nodded, trying not to show him how deeply those words

touched me, moved me. He was trying to believe me . . . or maybe trying to prove me wrong, but at least giving me the benefit of the doubt. "Thank you for that."

He nodded, drew a breath, lifted his eyes to mine. "Don't go after my father, Raven. Please, for my sake. Not yet. Give me some time to find out what . . . what the hell this is about. Time to understand."

I lowered my head. Was he giving me the benefit of the doubt after all? Or just trying to distract me, to protect his father?

"Please. I don't believe he's this evil being you think he is. Raven, if you knew what he told me tonight, how he wants to make peace with you, you'd—"

The bedroom door flung open, and the old man stood there, dagger clenched in his fist, black satin robe held around his rail-thin, beanpole of a body with a sash. In a half crouch, just as I had been, he lunged into the room.

I flew forward to meet him, quickly putting myself between Nathanial and Duncan. And though we faced each other, blades at the ready light and nimble in our hands, the old man still tried to feign innocence.

"What is *she* doing here?" he asked. "Did she try to hurt you, Duncan?"

"You know I'd sooner die than hurt him," I answered before Duncan could.

"If you insist," he rasped, and he lunged at me, swinging the blade in a deadly arc.

"Stop!"

Duncan's cry pierced my mind, but I didn't straighten or take my eyes from his father. I knew better than to glance away, even for an instant, from a cold-blooded snake poised to strike.

"Dad, come on, this is insane. Raven, Christ, if you ever cared for me . . ."

Nathanial lunged again, but I dodged his blade with easy grace.

"Father, tell her about the pot. Give her the damn pot. You said you wanted to mend fences with her. Go on, go get the pot and—"

"That cauldron is worth nine hundred dollars," he muttered.

"But you said—"

"He lied, Duncan," I whispered. "He's been lying to you all along."

"Shut up and fight me, wench," Nathanial snarled.

"No, Raven," Duncan said softly. "If you love me, please, Raven, don't. He's an old man, please. . . ."

"He's an old man, all right. Centuries old, how many, even I don't know." I lunged, feinted, dodged. "You killed my mother, you son of a bitch, and now you've stolen Duncan from me. You *will* pay. But not tonight."

Again, my blade flashed out, easily slicing the sash that held his robe together. I leaped past the man, dodging his returning slash, hooking the robe with my blade and tugging it back. Far enough. "There, Duncan!" I cried, knowing full well that crescent was in full view, if only for a moment. And then I landed in the hall. One hand on the rail, I vaulted over, landing on the floor of the foyer below, and then I spun around even as Nathanial's footsteps pounded into the hall after me.

There. My mother's cauldron sat on a shelf. Looking up, I saw Nathanial leaning over the rail, hatred blazing from his eyes. I gathered the cauldron in one arm. "Thanks for the token of friendship, Dearborne!" I cried. "Unfortunately, it was never yours to give."

And as he raced for the stairs, I left the building by the front door and vanished into the shadows where I knew Arianna would be waiting.

19

It was there. The mark Raven had told him about was there, just as she'd said it would be. Dark, bloodred, on his father's left hip.

But that didn't mean . . .

Jesus, how long was he going to keep denying it? Everything she'd shown him, everything she'd said—the flashes and dreams that kept haunting him. This feeling that he knew her, that he loved her . . . there had to be some reason for all of it.

God, just not the reason she said.

He raced into the hall, down the stairs, catching his father at the door, and gripping the man's arms from behind. "Stop! I'm not going to let you go after her!"

The ease with which Nathanial broke Duncan's grip was shocking. He was old. He had no business being so strong. But he didn't run off in pursuit of Raven. Instead he turned, eyes as cold as ice.

"I suppose you'd rather I wait for her to sneak back in here. To kill me in my sleep. Is that what you want?"

"Of course not!" Duncan pushed both hands through his hair, sighing. "Look, she didn't hurt you, didn't even try. Because I asked her not to." And he knew that much, at least, was true. "She's not going to come back here to-night."

Nathanial's eyes narrowed. "She stole my blasted pot. I should call the police—"

"You were going to give it to her anyway."

"Mmmph." It was a growl, not an affirmation. "I changed my mind when I saw her in your room with her blade."

"Yes." Duncan moved past his father, closed the door, then turned to face the old man again. "It's just like yours, her blade."

Nathanial's head came up slowly. "It's similar."

"And so is the mark on your hip."

"Seen that much of her, have you?"

Duncan looked away. He wasn't going to answer that. "She knows you, knew you before you came here. You lied to me when you denied that."

Nathanial thrust his small blade into the sheath at his hip, turned away, muttering under his breath.

"God, you even wear that thing to bed?"

"I wear it everywhere," his father replied without facing him.

"It's time for you to tell me what this is all about. I want to know. And I mean *everything*."

His back still to Duncan, his father kept walking. "No, you don't." Then he paused. "And even if you do, it's not your business, Duncan. This is between her and me, and will remain that way."

"For how long? Until one of you is dead?"

A long sigh emerged from his father's lips. A raspy one. But he said nothing. And a moment later he kept walking, up the stairs, to his room. He closed the door firmly.

Duncan sank to the floor, holding his head in his hands. He didn't know what to think, what to do, who to believe. It was obvious there was a fierce enmity between Nathanial and Raven. They had a past, those two. A violent one. Raven was all too willing to tell him all about it . . . but the things she told him surpassed belief and even the most distant realms of possibility. His father, on the other hand, would tell him nothing. And Raven's version of things was looking more and more like the truth.

He knew one thing. There would be no killing, no dagger wielding, no bloodletting tonight. Not tonight. He'd make sure of it.

He couldn't sleep anyway, so he played the part of sentry. And long after dawn, while his father still slept, he called the lawyer he'd contacted the day before. He called the man at home—woke him up, judging by the thickness of Jack Cohen's voice.

"What did you find out?" Duncan asked without preamble.

It took a moment for Jack to identify him, another for him to figure out what it was Duncan wanted. They were acquaintances, not friends. Jack had done some work for Duncan's restoration business, helped out with contracts periodically over the last several years, and Duncan had his home number. For emergencies only, Jack had told him when he'd scrawled it on the back of a business card.

Hell, if this wasn't an emergency, Duncan didn't know what was.

"I have office hours, you know," Jack finally said.

"This is too important to wait. What did you find out about the accident that killed my birth parents?"

Jack sighed, hesitated. "It . . . was easier than I expected to check into it. You had their names and everything, so—"

"What did you find out?" Duncan asked again.

Jack cleared his throat. "This isn't the kind of thing I like to tell someone over the phone," he said. "But, uh . . . there *was* no car accident. Your parents were murdered, Duncan."

His throat closed off. He closed his eyes, drew a breath. "How?"

"A mugging. Wallet stolen. The cops figured they must have resisted, tried to fight back."

Opening his eyes, Duncan whispered, "Shot?" *Please, please, please say yes.*

"No. No, it was, uh . . . it was a knife."

A knife. Or maybe an antique dagger with a jeweled handle.

"Did they get the guy?"

Another sigh. "The case is still unsolved. I'm sorry, Duncan, I wish the news had been better."

"So do I," Duncan said. "So do I." He put the phone down and turned to see his father coming down the stairs.

Nathanial paused, frowning. "You're up early!"

"Couldn't sleep." Duncan reached for his coat, hanging on an antique tree near the door.

"You're leaving? But what about breakfast? We really do need to talk, Duncan."

"We can talk later." Duncan pulled the coat on, then eyed the old man. "When you're ready to tell me the truth. Right now there's . . . something I have to do."

Lowering his brows, Nathanial said, "You're going to see *her*, aren't you?"

"Yes. So don't bother charging out there to confront her, because I'll be there to prevent it."

He disliked the harsh, condemning tone of his own voice, and the way his father flinched and paled slightly at every word. Even though things looked bad, he had to remember his father might not be guilty of a damn thing. All of this could be . . .

His chin fell. Could be what? Coincidence? Some elaborate con? Bullshit. It was none of those things and he knew it.

Still, his tone gentled, almost as if there was still some part of him, some fatherless child inside, who *wanted* to believe the old man innocent. "I'll be back later on."

"She's crazy, you know. She'll try to turn you against me, Duncan. Don't let her."

"Look, all I want to do is fix this, make it all right, get at the truth. And I *will*."

His father shook his head slowly. "I only wish you could. Make it all right, I mean. But you can't, Duncan. You're dealing with things you don't understand. The way things are . . . is the way they've always been. It can't be changed."

"Anything can be changed."

His father lowered his head tiredly. "I wish that were true. I'm . . . I'm *tired*. You've no idea how tired."

Narrowing his eyes, searching his father's face, Duncan took a step closer. "Tired of what?"

When Nathanial looked up again, his skin seemed pale, and dark circles seemed to have appeared beneath his eyes overnight. "Death. Life. All of it. I'm an old man, Duncan, and I ought to know it. I ought to just let go, but I can't. I can't. Maybe she'll be the one to end it. Maybe it's time someone did."

"Father, what the hell are you talking about?"

Nathanial shook his head. "Nothing. I sound as crazy as she does, now, don't I?" He smiled softly. "Go on, go to her. Do what you have to do, Duncan. We never know how much time we have left. We ought to spend it doing what we want."

"You'll be all right?"

"Fine. I promise. Go on, go."

Sighing, suddenly uncertain his father should be left alone just now—but even more certain than before that he had to see Raven, he finally nodded, and left. He walked the two miles to Raven's house. A pleasant walk, or it would have been if there hadn't been so many unanswered questions swamping his brain. He walked along the Coast Road with the sea crashing to the shore below, giving him slight goose bumps and making him walk as far to the left of the road as possible. Raven's story about him having been tossed from these very cliffs kept creeping into his mind, but he pushed it away. Still, it was sunny. The air held a brisk chill that invigorated, but no real wind. And the sound of the waves was pleasing, even if looking down on them did make him dizzy.

He paused once, near those very cliffs she'd pointed out to him—the place where she claimed he had died. Swallowing a lump of foreboding, he stepped closer to the edge, stared down at the froth and rocks below, expecting the slight dizziness that still hit him from time to time when he looked down from on high.

It didn't come. Instead, there was a flash. Darkness, moonlight. Dancing red-orange torches and men all around him. Holding him. Holding . . . *her.*

"Disavow her, Duncan. Save yourself."

"Never!"

"Do as he asks, Duncan. Please, trust me! Do as he asks."

Tears glittering on her cheeks in the moonlight.

A soft rending of his heart as he looked into those dark eyes. "Not on pain of death, lass. Nay, not if it meant my own soul would I speak against you."

They carried her to the edge. Duncan broke free of those who held him, ran forward, reached for her.

"They cannot take my life!" she cried. "Save yourself, Duncan, I beg you!"

They pitched her over the side, and he lunged for her, and then fell with her into the abyss.

Duncan pressed a hand to his head and staggered backward, away from the edge. God, what *was* that? A memory? A hallucination? Real or imaginary?

The image, the dream, was gone. But the feelings . . . the emotions . . . remained. Pressing out from somewhere inside his chest. Expanding, making it hard to breathe.

"God, what is happening to me?"

When he arrived at Raven's driveway, he heard voices, and the rhythmic chink of metal clashing against metal. Was his father here before him, then? Were Nathanial and Raven fighting to the death, even now? A beat of panic pulsed in his throat, and he rushed forward, following the noise around to the rear of the house, and stopped in his tracks when he saw Raven and her blond friend wielding their deadly little daggers as if they meant to kill each other.

He lunged forward, then stopped. They were . . . laughing. Swinging those double-edged blades and ducking, rolling and springing to their feet again, and *laughing*.

My God, they *were* insane.

But graceful. So skilled in their movements that it started to resemble a dance the way they circled and lunged and dodged. Then Arianna let loose with a spinning kick that looked like some kind of martial arts move, and Raven's dagger sailed from her hand to land point down, in the dirt, its jeweled hilt quivering.

Arianna leaped forward, her blade to Raven's throat. "I

have you now!'' she shouted, a beautiful smile on her face.

"No, don't!''

The shout was wrenched out of him, a knee-jerk reaction he hadn't planned. The two women stilled, turning toward him. Raven looked surprised, but not the least bit afraid. Arianna, on the other hand, straightened, sheathed her blade, and rolled her eyes.

"Isn't *this* familiar?'' she said, her tone sarcastic.

And it was. He had a dizzying sense of déjà vu all of a sudden. It was as if he'd done this all before. He had to close his eyes to regain his balance.

But then Raven was coming to him, stroking his hair with those loving fingers. "Are you all right?''

"More to the point,'' Arianna said, "are you *alone*?''

He drew a steadying breath. "Nathanial is back at the courthouse. I wouldna . . . *wouldn't* . . . bring him here.'' Then he gazed at Raven to see if she'd noticed his slip— God, for an instant it felt as if that stranger inside had leaped to the surface and taken over.

Raven's hair was tousled, and his fingers ached to smooth it. Her cheeks gleamed pink with exertion and her eyes sparkled.

"It's all right,'' she said. "We were only practicing. We do it all the time.'' She didn't mention his slip, but she'd noticed. He knew she had.

"I don't even want to ask why,'' he said.

"To stay sharp . . . you'll pardon the pun.'' Arianna smiled at her own joke. "So when people like Nathanial come for us—and they do, Duncan—we're ready.''

"So you believe this nonsense, too? About immortal High Witches and beating hearts in little boxes . . . ?'' He shook his head, not wanting to think about it anymore.

"I see Raven *did* get around to telling you a few things,'' Arianna said. "Well, Duncan, old friend, you might as well come inside. If you won't believe your lover, then perhaps you'll believe me. I'm far older than she is anyway. Just over five hundred, actually.''

"You'll have to give me the name of your plastic surgeon.''

She lifted her golden brows. "You can still joke about it.

I think that's a good sign. Do you drink coffee, Duncan, or is it still strong English tea you prefer?''

Strong English tea was exactly what he preferred. But how did *she* know that? "To be honest, I think I could use a beer about now," he told her.

"Used to go straight to your head," she replied with a smile. "I think you need all your wits right now. So tea it is." She turned and led the way inside.

Raven gripped his hand and followed. "I was so afraid to leave you with Nathanial last night. Was there any trouble after I left?"

"He's my father, Raven."

"As if *that* means anything."

They walked into a pretty room, with a fireplace flickering from one wall, and claw-footed furniture of deep cherry wood all around.

"You two sit. Talk. I'll get that tea." Arianna left them there.

Raven took a spot on the love seat, and Duncan sat beside her. He took her hands in his, stared into her eyes. "I want you to end this feud with my father," he said. "It doesn't matter whether all of this other stuff is true or not. Nothing matters right now except that it has to end."

She closed her eyes. "Do you think I *want* to fight him? Duncan, believe me, I don't. I'd end this if I could."

"You can. I can help. I don't think he wants this any more than you do, Raven."

"He has no choice, Duncan."

Duncan closed his eyes. What now? Would she tell him more far-fetched tales?

"Didn't you understand what I told you last night, Duncan? The Dark Ones take hearts, and keep them, and eventually, they use up the power. The hearts weaken, perhaps even die if they're tapped long enough in this vile way. I don't know. But I do know they weaken, and as they do, so does the Dark Witch who holds them. They need to take more, to kill again and again, in order to continue living."

He swallowed hard. "You can't truly believe this," he said, but in a hoarse whisper, because somewhere inside him, he knew it was true. It *couldn't be*. But it had to be.

"It's why he wants me," she went on. "He could have taken your heart, Duncan, but you're young, and you've never even wielded the power of nature. Your heart might sustain him for a few decades at most. Mine would give him centuries."

He only stared at her, wrestling with what she'd said. Arianna came in with the tea. She set the tray down and stood there looking from one of them to the other. "He's never going to believe you until you show him, Raven."

"I know."

"So?"

Sighing heavily, Raven got to her feet. She bent to a drawer in an end table and pulled it open. And then she pulled out a small-caliber weapon. It looked like a derringer. Duncan's blood rushed to his feet.

"What the hell are you—"

Raven handed the weapon to Arianna, then stood facing her friend. "Go on, do it. Let's get this out of the way."

Arianna pointed the gun squarely at Raven's chest, from a distance of no more than two feet.

"My God, no!" Duncan lunged between them just as Arianna pulled the trigger.

Fire tore through his chest even as the explosion rang in his ears. Warmth oozed and he drew a hand upward, pressed his palm hard against his sternum, and felt the blood pulsing from beneath it. "Jesus Christ," he said, but the words were slurred, and he sank to the floor. "Jesus Christ, you shot me. You freaking *shot* me."

Raven snatched a towel from somewhere and pressed it to the wound. But she seemed more interested in keeping his blood from staining her carpet than in halting its flow. "I'm sorry, Duncan," she whispered. Sitting down, she cradled his head in her lap. "You'll be all right. In a moment."

Her words were fading. Why wasn't someone calling 911? My God, were they just going to sit there and watch him . . . ? "I'm *dying*. . . ." he rasped.

"Only for a moment," Arianna said. "You'll be a believer very soon, Duncan. I swear, I don't know why Raven didn't just shoot you in the first place. Would have saved

so much time.'' Then she grimaced at his chest. ''It is
messy, though.''

''The phone . . . Someone call . . . an amb—''

''Oh, you're well beyond that, Duncan. No ambulance
would do you any good now.'' Arianna tipped her head back
and laughed, and Duncan tried to call her a bitch, but he
wasn't sure the word was audible.

Raven bent closer, pressed her lips to his. And everything
went black.

It felt as if he'd grabbed a bare wire with about 220 volts
going through it. The jolt split him, surging up his breastbone, and for an instant he figured he must be in some
operating room somewhere, with a surgeon opening his
chest.

He arched up, tipped his head back, and dragged in a
ragged gasp, starved, it seemed, for oxygen. And then his
body relaxed and the power surge faded. He opened his
eyes.

He was still in Raven's house. On the sofa now, stretched
out, shirtless. His head felt achy, light, still buzzing with the
remnants of whatever current had zapped through him.

''For the love of Christ,'' he muttered. ''You still haven't
called an ambulance?''

''No need, Duncan.'' Raven sat beside him, brushed his
hair off his face. ''Come on, sit up.''

''Yeah, right.''

''Sit up, Duncan.'' Her hands slid under his shoulders,
and she eased him into an upright position. Arianna sat
nearby. A basin of blood-tinted water at her side, with a
pink-stained washcloth floating in it looking like a donor
organ. His heartbeat quickened at the sight, and he instinctively pressed a hand to his wounded chest to keep himself
from bleeding to death.

And then he frowned, because there was no pulsing
warmth oozing now. No sticky residue on his skin. His fingers probed, and then he bowed his head, staring at his bared
chest. His *clean* bared chest.

No blood. No wound. He blinked, pressing both hands to
his chest now, moving them, pressing again, searching for

the bullet hole. It had seemed gaping before. Maybe it was just smaller than it seemed, and . . .

"There's nothing there, Duncan," Arianna said. "You died. Right there on the floor. We cleaned you up, and put you on the couch. In less than an hour the wound healed and you revivified. You're alive now, and there's no hole in your chest because you're immortal."

He gaped at her, then stared up at Raven.

"I know it's shocking the first time," she whispered. "I know how difficult this is for you to believe. But, Duncan, we didn't mean to. Arianna was aiming at me—"

"Oh, but this is so much better. Really drives the point home."

"Arianna, *please*!"

Arianna shrugged, making a lip-zipping motion with one hand. Raven turned to him again. "From now on, you won't age. You're going to start noticing other changes, as well. You'll get stronger. Your other senses will sharpen. And your ability to manipulate nature, to do what we call magick, will be far stronger than it was before. Although, since you've never *been* a practicing Witch, I don't suppose you'll notice that."

Again, he looked at his chest. "I can't believe this."

"Get him a mirror, for heaven's sake," Arianna said in exasperation.

"You have to believe it, Duncan. It's true."

"It's true," he whispered. "It can't be . . . but it's true."

"Yes." He searched her eyes, and she repeated the word. "Yes, Duncan."

His head was whirling. Unreal. It was all so unreal.

"I want you to read this," Raven said. And she pressed a very old book into his hands. So old its pages were curled and yellow, and the leather cover cracked in places. "This is three hundred years old. It was what my mother left for me."

"Your mother?"

She nodded. "You see, I didn't know, either. Not until Nathanial Dearborne hanged my mother and me in a snowy square as you looked on, fighting to prevent it, but unable to. That was the first time we met, Duncan, on the gallows just before I was to die. And something happened between us there, some connection was made. But it was over before it even began, or so I thought. We were hanged. Our bodies were pitched into a heap of the dead, where criminals and victims of the plague were dumped. That's where I awoke. But my mother didn't. Nathanial came for me there, intent on taking my heart before I could revive. And he must have been desperate then, because as young as I was, it wouldn't have sustained him long. I *was* a powerful Witch, though, even then. And perhaps it was my magickal skill he sought. Or perhaps it was because you'd turned against him that day. You'd taken my side over his, and when he killed me, you hated him for it. You went to the place of the dead, too, looking for my body. You intended to give me a decent burial. But I awakened before either of you arrived, and I carried my mother into the woods and buried her there. And then I went home to find this book. Our cottage was ruined, had been plundered. My mother's sacred cauldron, with the rose painted on the front, was gone. But the book she'd left for me, hidden behind a loose stone in the hearth, remained.''

Duncan opened the book reverently, scanned the first page—and knew, though it seemed impossible, that these really were her mother's words . . . and really had been written some three centuries ago. So sad, his eyes grew damp as he read them, and then he met Raven's again. ''But I found you again after that, didn't I, Raven?''

She nodded. ''I booked passage on a ship to the New World. You boarded the same ship. And later came to this very town, as its new minister, and met me again. But even then I didn't tell you the truth. I didn't trust you enough, Duncan. So when they pitched me from the cliffs for the crime of Witchery, you lunged after me, trying to save me.''

Yes. Because it had seemed better to die trying to save her than to go on living without her.

How did he know that?

''If you'd known that I couldn't die . . . you wouldn't have fallen from those cliffs. You died because I didn't trust you with the truth. And that's why I've been so determined to tell you everything this time.''

He stilled as the one memory that had remained intact came rushing back to him. The dream he'd had as a child, the one he'd thought had to be of his birth mother, came back to him now. Clearer than before.

"You found my body on the rocks," he said. "You were crying. God, it hurt me to see you crying. I wanted to touch you, to tell you it was all right, but I couldn't. I was . . . hovering above, somehow. You held me. You wouldn't let me go."

"Yes," she breathed, tears springing into her eyes. "Yes, Duncan, that's exactly the way it happened."

"And . . . *you* were there," he said, turning to Arianna. "You protected her, told her they were coming for her, made her let me go, and took her away from the danger."

Arianna nodded.

"The last thing I remember is watching the waves sweep my body away, swallow it up." He closed his eyes as a chill rushed through him. It was a terrifying memory. But real. And there. He recalled the clothes she wore, and those he'd been wearing. He remembered the differences in her speech as she held him and spoke to him. Old, arcane.

"My God, it's true, isn't it?"

Raven nodded. "Yes, Duncan. It's true."

"And my father . . . ?"

"Is one of the Dark Ones. He wants my heart, and likely yours, too."

Duncan shook his head slowly. He knew it was all true, all of it. And still . . .

He blinked his burning eyes dry. "People can change," he whispered, and he knew he was grabbing at straws. "If it's been as many years as you say it has, Raven, then how do you know he hasn't changed?"

She closed her eyes. "Oh, Duncan, I know you want that to be true, but he can't change. If he stops taking hearts, he'll weaken and die."

"But save his own soul."

"He sold his soul long ago."

"But there's a chance, Raven. There's a chance you're wrong about him. I've *seen* the changes in him since he came here. He's been kinder, more *real* than before."

Arianna got to her feet. "Why would the old man change after all this time? What motive could he possibly have to suddenly value his soul at all?"

Duncan looked at her squarely. "He has a son now."

The sorrowful looks the two women exchanged let him know they didn't believe him for a minute. He wasn't sure he believed it himself. But he wanted to. God, how he wanted to.

"I have to give him a chance," he said, turning to Raven. "I *have to*. He's the only father I've ever known, Raven. I . . . I care for him."

"Even though he might have killed your birth parents to get his hands on you, Duncan?"

"I don't know that," he insisted. "I . . . don't *want* to believe that."

Raven's eyes went round and soft, and she nodded. "All right. I . . . I understand."

"You're giving him a second chance," Arianna snapped. "A second chance that's liable to cost Raven her life, do you realize that?"

"Let him be, Arianna."

But something cracked in Duncan's heart. Was Arianna right? Was he making a huge mistake? He stared into Raven's eyes and hoped to God he wasn't. "I won't let him hurt you," he promised. "I swear it, Raven."

"I know you'll try," she whispered. Then she lowered her head. "Go on, go to your father, Duncan. Do what you feel you must."

20

Duncan supposed he must have walked back into town. The evidence was there. He stood on the cobbled circle, the fountain on his right splashing as if the entire world hadn't just tilted off its axis. The courthouse loomed in front of him like some big, shadowy giant. No curtains yet on the lower floors. Nathanial had never been fond of frills or fluff. So the windows stood empty . . . just like the old man's eyes.

So he was here, and he hadn't brought the car in the first place, so he must have walked. He didn't remember the trip. Only the haze that had been descending over his brain—or was it a haze burning away, revealing a light too bright to look upon?—ever since he'd finally understood that Raven St. James was *not* delusional. But immortal. And so was he. Immortal.

My God. It was so immense a concept his brain couldn't seem to grasp it. He kept thinking it must have been a dream, that it couldn't really have happened. No one had shot him. He hadn't bled. He hadn't died only to come back to life again on Raven St. James's sofa. But he knew that was bull. It *had* happened. And he needed to swallow it before it choked him. Swallow it, get over it, and figure out what the hell to do next.

Stop this ridiculous urge that kept surfacing . . . to test it. Jump off a roof or step in front of a bus just to see what would happen. Stupid. If a bullet in the chest wouldn't kill him, what the hell would?

He closed his eyes and swallowed. Damn, it was as if he had to think about every step. Go to the door, open it up, step inside, speak to his father. His mind was so busy turning this over and over, examining it from every angle, he kept forgetting to pay attention to what he was doing. Forgetting to *breathe*, for God's sake.

"Duncan?"

He looked up, drew himself out of his mind, and met his father's darting gaze. An old man. A weathered, careworn face, a little paler than it was a couple of weeks ago. He was no killer. And he certainly had aged, hadn't he? Didn't Raven say immortals stop aging? So why hadn't Nathanial?

Who are you kidding, Duncan? Can you remember him ever looking any different? He's always *looked like a man in his sixties.* Always.

He shook his head as if to clear it. "Father," was his greeting.

"Did you see her?"

Duncan nodded.

"Well? What did she say? Did she fill your head with lies and fantasies again? Did she—"

"She said she'd like peace as much as you would, Father," Duncan interrupted. Tired—he sounded tired. *Felt* it, too. "She said if you'd be willing to drop this ridiculous feud, so would she." It wasn't *precisely* what she'd said, but he was confident he spoke nothing but the truth. And she *did* say she wasn't pursuing this battle because she *wanted* to.

His father's brows bent, eyes narrowed, but instantly all of that stopped. His face went as still as stone, and slowly he averted his eyes. "Good," he said, and then he let his shoulders slump a little. "You can't imagine my relief."

Duncan studied the old man with a practiced eye, but he couldn't judge a thing, couldn't be objective, was all too aware that he wasn't in control of the situation. He never had been.

"Relief?" he asked Nathanial. "Is that what you're feeling?"

Slowly his father's head came up. "You think *I'm* the one who started this with her? She's the one who came in here screaming accusations and trying to come between us!"

"Come between us? You could park a semi between us, Father, and that's been true all my life. Long before she came into our lives."

"She's *always* been in our lives." Nathanial's head lowered. "I've been trying to change that, son."

"Why?"

The brows crooked, the face puckered. "Why do you keep asking that?"

"Because I want to know. Was this a change of heart, *Dad*? Or is that just where it's leading?"

He held his father's pale eyes for once, willing the man to look at him, face him. And slowly he saw the knowledge dawn there. The realization that Duncan knew the truth.

"I was shot tonight, Father. Right in the chest." He touched the spot with one hand. "Point-blank."

His father seemed to go even whiter. "That's . . . that's ridiculous. Look at you, you're . . . you're fine."

"Yes, I know. Because I'm immortal." Nathanial's eyes fell closed. "And so are you," Duncan added.

There was a long taut strand of silence hanging in the air between them. Until it was broken by his father's ragged sigh, and this time when the old man's shoulders slumped, Duncan believed it was for real.

Duncan bent his head, knowing by his father's reaction that it was true. His father was immortal. And if he'd kept that truth to himself all this time, how could Duncan expect him to be honest now?

Sighing deeply, Nathanial said, "I can't talk to you about this now."

"No, not now," Duncan agreed tightly. "Not for the past thirty-five years, and not now."

"Duncan, you don't understand—"

"Or maybe I just don't want to."

Nathanial faced him. "I'm no immortal, Duncan," he

said, and suddenly Duncan saw the shadows underneath his eyes. "Far from it, in fact. I'm sick, Duncan. I'm . . . I'm dying."

Duncan actually reeled backward at those words. "But—"

"That's why I came here, bought this place. To be close to you. To make up for all that time . . . to be your father just once . . . before it was too late." Shoulders shaking, the old man sank into a chair. And the sounds he made were as close to heartbreak as anything Duncan had ever heard.

Slowly, questions swirling still, he stepped closer. A hand went to his father's shoulder, and then he knelt and stared up into the old face. "That can't be."

"It is. I . . . I don't know what fantasies that pretty young thing has been weaving, Duncan. She's . . . she's disturbed. And tricky. I've dealt with her before, it's true. I don't know how she made you think you'd been shot, and convinced you of all this nonsense. Starter pistol, blanks, blood capsules . . . perhaps even some kind of hallucinogen. She does claim to be a Witch, you know. Maybe it was a spell of some sort. I don't know. I don't care. It doesn't really matter in the scheme of things."

Duncan swallowed hard. He tried to fit what his father said with what had happened this morning at Raven's, knew intellectually that it didn't fit, didn't make sense, but set it aside for now. He'd hear what his father had to say. He'd listen to the lies. One last time. And it *would be* the last time.

"Every day I get weaker, son. I don't have much time left. I don't want to spend it arguing over some girl."

Just as Raven said . . . They weaken in time, and have to kill again. . . .

Nathanial lifted his head, eyes imploring, looking suddenly very much like the eyes of a dying old man.

"I should have told you sooner. I'm sorry for that."

Duncan knew better, he *knew* better. Hadn't he just been wondering about his father's unusual strength? Hadn't he just been noticing how the man had never changed?

"This confrontation has taken a lot out of me, I'm afraid."

"Rest, then," Duncan said. Because he needed time, time to think, to figure out what Nathanial could have to gain with this latest ruse. "I'll, uh . . . I'll make us some dinner."

"I've no appetite," his father said, and he got slowly to his feet. "I'd like to go to bed."

"But there's so much more to talk about." He faced his father, made his voice firm. "I want the truth, and I'll have it before this night is over."

"And what does it matter now? I told you, Duncan, I'm *dying*."

"So you'll take the truth to your grave with you?" He felt mean. Cruel. Hell, he was being heartless, but he'd had it with the lies. "I know damn well it was no parlor trick Raven pulled on me this morning. I *felt* the heat of that bullet that plowed through my chest, Father, and I had a hole the size of a golfball to show for it. It was my blood all over me, not some trick capsule."

His father closed his eyes, shook his head, and turned toward the stairs. "You won't let up on me, will you? Even now?"

"I'm sorry. I need to hear the truth, and I'd like to hear it from you."

"All right, then." Nathanial mounted the bottom step, moved up one, then another. "You'll hear it. But not now. Come back in an hour, Duncan. Come back in an hour and I'll tell you everything. *Everything*. I promise."

Duncan breathed deeply, trying to clear his head. His father was dying. It would have been easier to believe than anything else he'd heard today. But he didn't believe it. Oh, he might be weak, maybe feeling poorly. Raven said the hearts wore out in time.

He swallowed the bile that rose in his throat, marveled that he was referring back to conversations he'd considered nothing more than symptoms of mental illness only a few hours ago. He was exhausted, drained.

"All right. Rest. But I'm not going anywhere. I'll be here waiting. And we *will* talk."

Without looking back, his father climbed the stairs, seeming old. Weak. Sick.

Duncan sank to the floor, glanced at the empty crates all around him. Crates that had held the most cherished possessions of murdered women. It was wrong, what his father was doing. Just wrong. He'd known it from the beginning.

And he knew other things, too. Raven wasn't lying to him.

She wouldn't. The things she said about Nathanial were absolutely true. If she said he'd killed, then he had. If she said he wanted her heart, then he did. He'd hoped his father could be capable of change, but he doubted that now.

As for his father . . . he would lie to Duncan without batting an eye. Duncan sighed. He'd give the old man some time, let him rest or get his story straight or whatever he was doing up there. And then he'd get the answers he needed. He'd insist on that. An hour. Two at the most, and then he'd make Nathanial tell the truth, for the first time.

I picked up the phone when it jangled.

Nathanial Dearborne's voice rasped at me. "I need a heart. I wanted yours, but I'm out of time, Raven. Duncan's will have to do."

My throat went dry. I swallowed, tried to speak. "No," was all I managed.

"You or him, darling. You or him. I won't wait long."

Lowering my eyes to shield them from Arianna's probing ones, I said, "Where are you?"

I tried to keep my face expressionless as the man who'd been hunting me for most of my life told me where to meet him.

Slowly I replaced the receiver, keeping my eyes carefully turned away from Arianna's curious, probing brown ones.

"Who was that?" she asked.

The lie stuck in my throat. I loved her—lying to her made me physically ill. But I forced the words anyway. "Duncan. He . . . wants to see me. To . . . talk."

"Does he?"

"Yes. I, um, said I'd meet him."

"Where?"

I looked up quickly, knowing I'd stumbled, and forced a smile that felt as weak as it probably looked. "Someplace private. Perhaps he's beginning to remember after all.''

"Why are you lying to me, Raven?"

I looked away fast. "I'm not. Is it so hard to believe he might want some time alone with me?"

"It is when I combine it with the look on your face. You look shaken.'' She gripped my chin, tilted my head to the side and stared down at me as if she were a sergeant inspecting some soldier's rifle. "No, Raven, this isn't the face of a girl rushing off to meet her lover.''

"I'm no girl.'' I pulled myself free of her grasp, tried to act huffy when all I felt was guilt for lying to the best friend I'd ever known. My sister. "I'm over three hundred, for heaven's sake. And you know how important this is to me. Can you blame me for being nervous?''

She only kept looking at me.

"I'd better get ready.''

"Yes. Don't keep him waiting.''

I swallowed hard and headed from the room into one of our countless corridors and up one of the many sets of stairs. Arianna didn't follow. My room was my refuge, and I needed it right now. I think she sensed that.

The small, oval portrait I'd labored over for months stood on the night table beside my bed, bearing little physical resemblance to Duncan, but holding his essence all the same. The face I'd blurred, but his dark gleaming eyes shone from their deep wells, and his tumbling satin hair tempted my fingers just as it always had. His shadowed jawline spoke of feelings, immense feelings, all bubbling inside him in search of escape. It captured him, my experiment in painting.

I paused a moment, to run my fingertip over the image of Duncan's face. "For you,'' I whispered. "I do this for you.''

A tear burned at the back of my eye. Sadness welling up, not because I might be about to die, or worse. I hated to think of what that sort of death was truly like. For it wasn't death, really, but a kind of limbo. The body alive, but inanimate. The heart beating, but captive, providing life force to a foreign body. And yet that wasn't why I cried.

I cried for the love Duncan and I had once shared. The

love I'd spent so many lifetimes searching for, only to realize, at long last, that it wasn't coming back to me. A once-
in-a-lifetime kind of love like ours had been was just that.
Once in a lifetime. I'd never find it again. All these years
I'd naively believed that Duncan would feel just the way he
had before when I finally found him again. But he didn't.
Perhaps he couldn't. Oh, he was attracted to me, drawn to
me—even claimed to love me. But it was only a faint echo
of what we'd had before. And that was all it would ever be.
I supposed it was time I accept that.

Yes. Difficult though it was, it was time.

And this was not the moment to let the knowledge
weaken me. I needed to acknowledge, accept, and move
beyond it. Tonight I would fight for my life, as I'd done so
many times before. My opponent was the most powerful foe
I'd ever be likely to face. He could kill me very easily. I'd
need to be sharp, to be quick. I'd need to be smart and
I'd need to be ruthless.

Or I'd die.

Sniffling, I drew my hands away from the portrait on the
stand and opened the table's drawer. From inside I took a
velvet pouch and, pulling it open, removed the agate pendant. No stone was more protective than agate, and this one
had been charged with a spell to make it even more so. I
fastened the chain around my neck, then turned to the door.

Nathanial had given me thirty minutes. No more time for
dawdling. I left my haven, my bedroom, grabbing a cloak
on the way. The dark blue velvet one that hung by the door,
because it reminded me of that one I'd worn long ago. The
one left to me by my mother. I pulled it snug around me as
I tapped down the stairs. Swathed in those soft, warm folds,
I felt protected. Safe.

But I wasn't. I was far from safe. And there wasn't much
I could do about it.

I left on foot, by the Coast Road, and I knew Arianna
must be watching me. She knew me too well to have believed my lie. But it didn't matter. All that mattered was
that she not follow me. Or that I lose her if she did. I
wouldn't have her jumping between Nathanial's blade and
mine, and dying in my place.

I walked quickly and with purpose, but not so quickly that I didn't take time to *feel*. The sea wind in my face, tugging at my hair. The tiring sun, already relaxing on the western horizon, warm on my skin, bright in my eyes.

When I'd gone around a bend in the road, I turned sharply left, cutting down the steep cliff's face. There was one instant when Arianna could have seen me change direction, but only an instant. And I hoped the road's curve hid me from her sharp eyes for long enough.

Pebbles clattered away beneath my feet, and I slipped, gripped a sharp rock, scraped the skin of my palm, but held on. Digging in with fingers and the toes of my shoes, I managed to keep from falling, and slowly inched my way to where this steep face melded with the path I'd taken so many times. Here, the going eased. When I reached my boat, I took it, hoping Arianna would never think to check. And then, keeping close to shore, I paddled back the way I'd come. Avoiding rocks, bounding on waves as they tumbled toward shore, but unable to go out further, for fear Arianna would spot me from above. I moved past the point where our house stood high above, and in the other direction, until the cliff's sheer face eased again, shallowed, melted. There I rowed toward shore.

My feet got wet when I stepped out, and a wave rolled in at the same time, but I barely noticed. Too busy looking for a place to hide my craft. I dragged it into some brush, laid some loose branches and weeds over it, and brushed off my hands, satisfied that at least it didn't leap out and shout my presence to anyone who happened to pass this way. A trained eye would still spot it, but not unless they happened to be looking. And if I'd done everything right, Arianna would have no reason to be looking for me here.

That done, I stood still, ocean at my right, and the woods to my left. The woods where I would meet Nathanial. My hand touched the hilt of my blade, closed around it, and remained there. I glanced out at the whispering trees. They glowed with soft green-yellow auras as the sun sank behind them. Like magick, a brief, luminous magick, that faded away, and the light with it.

And I felt its loss. No light now. Nothing. Just me, and

the woods, and the darkness, and out there somewhere, Nathanial Dearborne, and his bloodstained blade.

He didn't intend to fall asleep. And when he woke, head
thick and eyes foggy, he had the oddest sensation that it
hadn't been sleep. Not really. It had been something else.
Something foreign, and malignant. Its remnants made him
shudder as if something slimy had slipped over his spine.
He felt soiled.

He got up, didn't even remember sitting down, but he
apparently had. And then he remembered his conversation
with his father, and the reason he hadn't left when Nathanial
had gone upstairs to nap.

He didn't trust him.

But now, there was more.

There was an old man on a gallows, the rising sun painting his bony face, a light of malicious glee in his pale eyes
as his hand caressed the lever. There was a girl more afraid
than any he'd ever seen before, and yet so brave she shamed
everyone else there. There was a warmth, an intense, magnetic *warmth* that seemed to melt from her eyes into his
when she looked up at him.

"Believe me, mistress, I'd help you if I could."

"They'd only kill you as well, did you try."

He felt it. Felt *her*. All of her. Her innocence, her power,
her allure. Her beauty, not just the way she looked but the
beauty inside her. He felt it flowing through him like warm
honey, cleansing everything ugly from his soul. Filling
every empty spot there was in him.

"I willna forget you."

*"If there is memory in death, Duncan, I shall remember
you always."*

He remembered that moment. He'd been wearing loose
black robes, and Nathanial had, too. He'd fallen in love with
her, with Raven, right then. With that look, that intense moment of feeling, all of it magnified a thousand times by the
imminent presence of the Reaper.

And then he heard it again. That sound. The creaking, the
slam, the horrible snap of a slender neck when it reached
the end of a rope. It sickened Duncan, and his face contorted

in remembered anguish as the memory played out in his mind. And then he was there, beneath the gallows. Holding her, his tears wetting her hair. Her body so soft, so small in his arms. Innocence. Utter innocence snuffed out without a thought. And Nathanial . . .

In his mind he looked up at the man. Nathanial looked back. Smiling.

"God, no . . ." The words were a rasp, a whisper, as Duncan shook the memories away, blinked the past from his eyes and turned to face the stairs the way Raven had faced those of the gallows. Fists clenched at his sides, he strode up them.

"It's time, Nathanial," he muttered as he moved upward. Somehow he couldn't bring himself to call the man "Father." Not now. "And you'll tell me the truth. For once in your life, you'll tell me the truth."

At the top he turned toward Nathanial's room, stepped up to its closed door, and gripped the knob, not bothering to knock.

But when he twisted, he felt resistance. "Unlock this door and let me in. We need to talk. *Now*."

There was not so much as a breath in answer. Duncan's stomach clenched. "Nathanial?"

Nothing.

His heart tripped, and he thought of Raven, and for once, he wasn't worrying about her hurting his black-hearted *father*. He was worried about Nathanial hurting her. Stepping backward, he slammed his shoulder into the door, then stumbled through when it split and fell beneath the force of the blow.

"You'll grow stronger than you were before." Raven's voice whispered through his mind. He managed to keep his footing, barely, but the splintered wood on the floor shocked him. He *was* stronger.

He turned, then, toward the bed. It was perfectly made, not a rumple, not a wrinkle. Beyond it the window stood open, its curtains billowing inward like ghosts.

"My God, he's gone after Raven. . . ."

Duncan raced to the window. Hands braced on its sill, he looked out, but his father was nowhere in sight. Not only that, but the sheer drop, and the distance to the ground loomed huge. No way out but to jump. "Quite a feat for a weak, dying old man, isn't it?" he asked himself, and then his shoulders sagged. He'd done it, hadn't he? Given Nathanial the benefit of the doubt in spite of what Raven had said. And now Arianna's warning rang over and over again in his mind. *It could cost Raven her life.*

God, he'd been a fool.

He remembered the gallows. Then the cliffs. He couldn't lose her again. He *wouldn't.*

"Duncan! Duncan, are you here?"

He spun around at the sound of Arianna's voice and called back to her. "Here. I'm coming." Then he ran down the stairs to greet her.

"Where is he?" She didn't bother with preamble, and he could see she was breathless, wide-eyed, pale with worry.

"I don't know. He did something to me, made me sleep, and slipped away. I'm afraid he's gone after Raven."

"She had a call a half hour ago," Arianna said, turning in a slow circle, pushing one hand through her blond locks. "She told me it was you, that you wanted her to meet you somewhere."

He shook his head. "I didna call her."

She glanced at him sharply, even as he bit his tongue, but didn't remark on his speech.

"Nathanial, then," Arianna said after a moment. "I thought as much. She's gone to meet him." Closing her eyes, she tipped her head back. "But I don't know where. I tried to follow, but she gave me the slip. Damn her for being so protective of those she loves."

"Why would she go to fight him?" Duncan asked desperately. "I believed her, not him. And she promised she wouldn't."

"Oh, don't kid yourself, Duncan. Nathanial knows exactly how to get Raven to dance to whatever tune he plays. All he had to do was threaten one of us." She tilted her head. "Probably you, since I was safe at her side when the bastard called."

Duncan felt a crushing sensation in his chest. "She'd face him down to protect me?"

"She'd die for you, Duncan. Just as you would have for her . . . *did* for her . . . once."

He brushed past her, yanked the door wide. "We have to find her."

Her hand on his shoulder brought him up short, but he didn't turn. She spoke to his back. "I don't think she can beat him. Prepare yourself, Duncan. By the time we get to her . . . it may be too—"

"Don't even think it."

21

I waited, paced, and grew restless. When the sun had descended fully beyond the western horizon to sleep in some distant place far beyond the trees, I shivered. The air cooled all at once, and gooseflesh rose on my arms and the back of my neck.

An owl hooted three times, and I turned my head quickly toward the sound. The people of Old Sanctuary would have said it was an omen, a warning of death. Accurate. There *would* be a death tonight. The only question was, would it be mine? Or Nathanial's?

A chill worked up my spine, settling right between my shoulder blades, as if someone's eyes were on me. I looked behind me, but there was only the sea. Waves rolling gently over the stony beach, pausing there like a breath held in anticipation, and then receding in a slow-motion sigh.

Swallowing my fear, I turned to face the forest again. I stiffened my resolve, drew my blade, and walked forward. One step, then another, and another. I reached the edge of the woods and paused there, sensing the presence of my enemy. I couldn't see him, but I knew he was near, and likely had been ever since I'd arrived.

My fingers tightened on the hilt of my blade, and I stepped through the first line of trees and into the darker area beyond. "Where are you?" I called out.

"Waiting," he answered, and his hoarse voice had little substance. Like the voice of a ghost. He must be weakening. No, it wouldn't do to underestimate him. Perhaps that was only what he wanted me to think.

I moved forward a few more steps, which took me beyond the clusters of trees on this side and into a small clearing. Pines towered all around me, a circle made by nature. Standing in a half crouch on a carpet of grass, I moved my fingers on the hilt and scanned the shadows that loomed amid the trees.

I didn't see him. Didn't hear him. Instead, I *felt* him; the crushing impact of his aged body when he hurled himself at me from behind. The red-hot trail his blade left as it arched across my back.

I hit the ground hard, face first, but rolled fast and sprang to my feet again. He'd knocked the wind out of me, taken me by surprise, and sliced my flesh. I pulsed with pain, felt the blood dampening my blouse, soaking through it, to stain the cloak.

Facing him, I reached to the ties at my neck and pulled, then tossed the cloak aside. "You had the advantage, Nathanial," I told him, careful to keep the pain from my voice. "And wasted it."

"Too eager to see my enemy bleed, I suppose."

"No more than I am." I lunged and swept my dagger's tip across his soft belly, drawing away just as quickly and avoiding his return thrust. We battled, fought, nicked and cut each other, but neither scored a killing blow.

We circled each other, both of us breathless, then lunged again, slashing and stabbing in a tangle of blades and limbs and then drawing back again.

I was tiring, panting.

He danced forward, I danced back, into the thickest cluster of trees. Then I focused on the pines. Their scent, the stringy, sticky bark, the needles that whispered their secrets all around me with every breath of a breeze that passed through them. In effect, I vanished. Melded with the pine trees and, in silence, thought of Trees Speaking and all he'd taught me.

When Nathanial pursued me, he slowed, stilled. His eyes darting this way and that as he searched for me. Then narrowing as he understood.

"You're very good," he whispered. Then thrust his dagger into the trunk of the tree nearest him. "*Very* good. But you can't keep your focus long. I'll find you, Raven."

Not long, he was right. But long enough.

My feet are roots, sinking deep into the rich, black earth. I curled my toes. I wouldn't move. Not yet. To move would break the enchantment. I'd wait until he turned his back to me. It would give me the advantage I needed if I hoped to survive.

My body is still and strong, and my skin is like bark. The blood in my veins is pine sap, sticky and smelling of the very spirit of Earth herself.

Nathanial came closer, jabbed another tree.

My arms are limbs. Each nerve ending a fine needle, quivering, sighing on the breeze.

I could feel my heart pounding, hear it in my ears as Nathanial came still nearer, stabbing his blade into first one trunk and then another, until he reached the one right beside me. So loud, that beat in my chest. So strong with fear as I stood motionless, praying he wouldn't hear it. *It's the pulse of life through my trunk. It's the thrum of the spirit in me.* I told myself anything to keep the image alive, the image I projected, the only thing between Nathanial's blade and my heart right now.

He came closer, lifted his blade, tilted its tip up and spasmodically clenched his fist on the hilt.

Just as he thrust it at me, I let the image dissolve and dodged to the side. He missed me cleanly, but stood grinning at me all the same. "You can't outwit me, Raven," he said. "Never that. I'm too old, too clever to be fooled by your tricks."

I couldn't even argue it. "So I see. Then I suppose my only hope is to outfight you."

"We both know you cannot."

"We'll see." I lurched, swinging my blade, and when he dodged the blow, I leaped and kicked him hard in the belly. A loud grunt gusted from him as he doubled over. By the time he got his breath and straightened again, I was racing through the trees, taking an uphill course. If I could tire the old man, I might stand a chance of beating him. Maybe. If he were as desperate for a heart as he'd claimed, he should be weak. He should lack stamina.

He'd shown no signs of it so far, though. And if he'd lied . . .

I wouldn't think of that now.

He gave chase. I knew when I paused for a breath and heard him crashing through the pines, branches snapping, needles raining to the ground in his wake like minuscule raindrops, whispering down.

Higher, then. And I ran on.

And then the trees parted before me, opening all at once onto a sheer drop to the sea. Planting my feet, I nearly overbalanced. My arms whirled backward twice, then I went still, blinking at the vista spread out below my feet. Endless space, and below it, jagged rocks winking and blinking up at me as the waves covered and uncovered them. White froth.

"Oh, now, this *is* amusing."

I turned slowly, faced Nathanial. He stood in a powerful crouch, and if his face was flushed, it was with excitement, not exhaustion. His eyes gleamed. He wasn't tired. If anything he was thriving on this battle. "You made a grave mistake, didn't you, Raven?"

Grimly I knew Arianna had been right. I didn't have the skills to beat him. I'd never beaten him. And if I fought him now, he would kill me. And then perhaps he'd kill Duncan.

But if I didn't . . .

He'd promised he would go after Duncan anyway.

I couldn't die here. I had to survive, even if it meant running from this fight. At least that way I would be alive to warn Duncan, to protect him, or try to. Goddess, I should have listened to Arianna in the first place. She'd *told* me I couldn't beat him.

I looked to the left, to the right. In the distance I saw two forms coming toward me. Far below, they moved along a path leading up to these cliffs. And as I stared down at them, focused my vision, I saw the woman's soft blond hair riffling in the breeze, and then the dark locks of the man beside her. Arianna . . . and Duncan. As if sensing my eyes on them, they both looked up. Duncan pointed, and I saw his lips move. It was likely he called my name, though he was too far away for me to hear him. Then the two ran. They'd be here soon.

I met Nathanial's eyes again. Cold.

"Yes," he said, having seen my thoughts in my eyes. "But by the time they arrive, you'll be dead. And I'll be gone. And know this as you die, Raven. I will take Duncan's heart, too, once you're out of the way. Your friend can't protect him forever."

I narrowed my eyes on him. He was lying. I saw it there clearly. He wouldn't take Duncan's heart unless he had to. And he wouldn't even attempt it while Arianna was nearby. He feared her.

But there was no time to work this out in my mind any further, because he leaped at me. His blade drove directly at my midsection, and though I moved to block the thrust, I moved too late. Hot steel sank deep into my belly. Burning pain, terrible pain. I cried out, but all that emerged was a gurgling sound and a mouthful of blood.

He jerked the blade out again. Then he reached for me. And I knew he would hold me and carve into my chest, rip out my heart, end it all now. I took a single step backward as he reached for me. And there was nothing there. Air. I fell into its breath. In silence I plummeted. No sound at all. Not until the impact.

Duncan ran. His lungs worked in a way he'd never felt them work before. Efficiently. Powerfully. The beat of his heart seemed like an engine. Unstoppable, strong. His legs pushed his body to speeds greater than he could have reached before. But he didn't marvel at these changes. Only noted them and felt grateful, because it meant he could reach Raven faster.

He could still see her, facing his father—or the man he'd called his father—on the cliffs. Nathanial moved closer, until Raven seemed trapped.

"We're not going to make it in time," Duncan rasped.

"We have to." Arianna's voice was a monotone of utter determination.

Then Nathanial drove forward, and Raven went stiff. Duncan could see her eyes widen, see her lips move, and the scarlet that bubbled from them. She looked down, then toward him. And Nathanial jerked his blade from her belly.

"No!" Duncan screamed with a voice that rolled like thunder, like the words of the gods themselves; his command broke the silent pause on that cliff. "Dammit, Nathanial, leave her alone!"

But it was as if no one heard. Nathanial reached out. Raven stepped back and into oblivion. She didn't even cry out. Just fell. *Just fell.* He could hear her clothes snapping like flags in the wind, see her hair fluttering. He screamed her name in anguish. His head felt as if it were exploding, splitting, when her body hit the rocks below. A shock went through him. Pain, horror, devastation . . .

And memory. The clear, vivid memory of all of this happening before.

His heart filled with long-repressed emotions, unbearable emotions he realized had been there all along. Condensed, perhaps, and bottled up somewhere. But the bottle had shattered and the feelings swelled until he didn't think he could contain them. And then he was running, clambering, half climbing, half falling, sending a shower of rocks down the cliffs before him, hearing their plunking sounds as they hit the water. Sliding, skinning his hands and chin and every other part of him, tearing his clothes, he made his way to the bottom.

And then he paused on the shore and searched the unforgiving waves for her.

There.

She lay faceup, half submerged. Her head and one shoulder and arm were sprawled on a sloped rock. The rest of her body submerged, broken, as the waves tugged at it, so steadily and greedily that she'd be swept out to sea soon.

He moved as if entranced. Sloshing into the water, walking out deeper, deeper, then swimming. He'd kicked free of his shoes at some point. He wasn't certain when. But he reached that rock and pulled himself up onto its slick surface. And then he gathered her broken body into his arms.

Limp. So limp, so shattered. A porcelain doll smashed and tossed aside.

"No," he whispered. "No, not now. God, Raven, not now."

Her hair, long, dripping with seawater that streamed over her face and shoulders. He gently smoothed it, stroked her face with his hand as his tears came. Burning hot, like acid on his cheeks, they flowed. They fell, and mingled with the water on her lips.

He clung tighter, pulling her full against him, rocking her slowly and weeping without control, without shame. So tightly, he held her body pressed to his, her lifeless head heavy on his shoulder. The enormity of it crushed down on him all at once. To have loved her this much, this damn much, so much it was every part of him, every cell, every breath, his soul, his life . . . all his lives . . . How could he not have known? How could he not have *felt* this? And now, now when he finally *did* feel it, and know it and recognize it for what it was, and remember it . . . she was gone. She was gone. Oh, God, she was gone!

He kissed her face, her hair, as sobs rose up and tore at his chest, threatening to split him in two. Now he understood how she'd felt all those years ago, when she'd held his lifeless, broken body on these rocks. Now he understood what she'd faced . . . all those years alone. God, they stretched out before him like a desert, where every grain of sand was a shard of glass, and which he had to cross barefoot without a sip of water.

"I willna," he whispered. "I canna do it, Raven. I dinna know how you did, but I canna. I canna go on without you, lass."

She had, though. Her strength must be an awesome thing, to enable her to survive with this kind of pain. Three hundred years. Three centuries, she'd dealt with it.

"An' when you found me again, what did I do? God, Raven, what did I do to you? I trusted *him*, believed *him*." He let her head fall backward, staring down at her face, so pale and still and lovely. "How that must have hurt you. How could I hurt you like that? You . . . you, Raven, my soul, my heart. How many times will I lose you this way? How many times?''

Still. So still. So dead. He closed his eyes and held her, loving her with everything in him, and another memory came to him. He was standing there, holding her in his arms for the first time. Beneath a gallows as he sawed at the filthy rope with a pilfered blade. And held her, and cried for the woman he didn't even know.

But he had. He'd known her then, somehow. Some way. His soul had recognized hers. His heart had known hers, and he'd loved her. He'd loved her from the first moment he'd set eyes on her.

''I told you I wasna the man you remembered, Raven. But I am. I'm Duncan Wallace, an' I was born in 1675 in the land of the Scots, the land of my father an' his before him. I'm the man who loved you all those lifetimes ago, an' I love you still, Raven St. James. I love you still.''

He drew a breath, somehow got to his feet, and holding her cradled as carefully as if she were made of ice crystal, he drew her with him as he made his way to shore. He wouldn't leave her to the sea. He couldn't. Something was niggling at him through his anguish. A faint, desperate hope that wouldn't leave him alone. He didn't want to let the hope form fully, for fear 'twould only destroy him if it turned out to be a false one. But as he stepped out of the waves and carried her onto the shore, he couldn't suppress it any longer.

He laid her down, in the lush green grass, in a spot dotted with tiny blue forget-me-nots. And then he sat beside her, leaned over her, and gently spread her hair to dry in the grasses. ''That first time I held you, lass, that first time I wept for you . . . you were nay dead then. You survived that noose. You told me you were immortal. You told me you couldna die unless the bastard took your heart.'' He closed his eyes, recalling the thrust of Nathanial's blade, but he'd been so far away. He couldn't tell. . . .

''Tell me that bastard didna do that.''

Gently he touched the front of her torn, bloodstained blouse. Even the cool kiss of the ocean hadn't washed those stains away. Nothing would, and he hoped nothing would wash them from Nathanial's hands, either.

His heart in his throat, he prayed in silence. *Please . . . please, dinna let it be. . . .*

Opening her blouse, he stared down at her chest. Pale, beaded with droplets of seawater, but unmaimed. There was no gaping hole, no wound near her heart.

He spread the blouse further and saw the wound she *had* suffered, the deep cut of Nathanial's blade, high in her belly. But even as he looked, that wound began to heal. Its edges puckered and pulled in on themselves as if magnetized. One side met the other, pressed like a kiss, and seemed to meld before his eyes.

Stunned, he drew his gaze upward, focused on her face, afraid to believe, afraid to hope . . .

"Raven?"

And then she went rigid, back arching off the ground, hands clenching fistfuls of grass at her sides, heels pressing the earth. Her neck arched as well, chin pointing skyward, and she sucked in a harsh, greedy breath. It made him think of electrocution, that brief seizure. Her eyes went wide, too wide, for just an instant. And then her body relaxed again, and she lay limp on the ground, blinking slowly, staring at him from unfocused eyes.

"Raven," he whispered. "Raven, Raven, Raven." He slipped his arms around her, beneath her, lifting her gently against him, holding her close, but not close enough. It would never be close enough. She hugged his neck, so pliable in his arms, melting there. His hands burying themselves in her hair, he drew her head back slightly, and then he pressed his lips to hers, kissing her more deeply, more urgently than he had in this lifetime. Kissing her the way he had before, in that other time, when he'd known what she was to him. Because he knew it now. He finally knew it now.

She blinked in confusion when he lifted his head away. Her slender, perfect fingers touched his cheeks, touched the tears there as she frowned. He couldn't speak, couldn't put the overwhelming things he was feeling into words. Not yet, not yet. He felt as if he'd been lost . . . wandering and lost,

and searching . . . and now he'd found her. He'd found himself. He'd come home.

He bent and kissed her again, and this time he didn't stop.
His hands pushed her blouse away, caressed her breasts, felt
them warming, felt her entire body warming to his touch.
He kissed her neck, her shoulders, her belly, where that
wound had been. He kissed the place where her heart beat
in her chest and willed that it would always remain there,
strong and alive and full of love for him. He kissed her hips
as he undressed her. Her thighs. Her center, where he lingered. How he loved her. *How he'd always loved her.*

She whispered his name with her heart in her breath and
her hands in his hair, and he tasted more of her, wanted to
devour her, make her truly a part of him, take her inside
him somehow and keep her there, cherished and safe. Always safe.

When she cried out, he moved up over her body once
more. He ran his hands over her flesh. Living and warm.
Over limbs, alive and responsive now, no longer limp and
broken. Did she know what she was to him? Could she
know? My God, was it even possible that he was that much
to her, as well?

Yes. It shone from her eyes and danced on the tiny, tremulous smile on her lips as she opened to him, held him,
drew him down, took him inside her. She held his gaze as
he moved, and she moved with him. Rocked him, loved
him. He stared right into her eyes, into her soul, it seemed,
as he made love to her. And the pounding of her heart and
the pounding of his own blended with the pounding of the
waves against the shore until it was all one. All one . . . and
he felt as if he and she were one. A single soul that had
been split for a time, united again at long last. She never
blinked, nor did he. And when her lips parted and her
breaths came in short little gasps, and he rode her faster and
harder and deeper, their gazes remained locked. He felt their
souls connect and touch, through their eyes.

She cried out his name, those black eyes widening. He
felt the pressure build inside him, and then the explosion as
he spilled into her, his entire body quivering with the force
of his release. And in that moment, he saw himself in her

eyes. As if he truly *had* merged with her, as if his soul really did live inside her.

And only then did those eyes fall closed.

He relaxed atop her, sliding slightly to the side, to ease the burden of his weight. "I have so much to tell you," he whispered.

She nodded. Kissed his head. "And I you. I'd been thinking, Duncan, that our chance had passed. That we could never be as we were before." Her hand stroked his hair. "But I know now that I can't go on without you, Duncan. So whatever you can give me, it will be enough. I'll *make* it be enough."

He lifted his head, stared down into her eyes. "You dinna ken what this was, do you, lass?"

She smiled slightly. "You sound like the Highland lad you were so long ago. Are you lapsing into a brogue you don't even recall, Duncan?"

"Am I? I dinna care if I am. It doesna matter. Nothing does right now, except . . ." He licked his lips, swallowed hard. "When I saw you on the cliffs . . . when I saw you fall—"

She sat up straight, eyes flying wide. "Nathanial! The bastard nearly had me! Duncan, we have to . . ." She paused, looking past him. "Oh, no," she whispered, and her face went pale.

"What is it?"

She snatched her clothes, wet and tattered, throwing them on haphazardly. "Arianna! She was with you. Where did she go, Duncan, where—"

He gave his head a shake. He'd completely forgotten about Raven's friend. "We . . . we were together when you went over the edge. I dinna ken where she went then, Raven. I was only thinkin' of you, trying to get to you. When I did . . . she wasna with me."

Her face crumpled, and her fingers went to her lips. Openmouthed, she sucked in a breath and got to her feet, righting her clothes as best she could. "She's gone after Nathanial." Closing her eyes, she shook her head. "He's better than either of us knew, Duncan. He'll kill her."

"We'll stop him." He helped her to her feet, and when

she stumbled, held her tight to his side. "Are you sure you're all right?"

Raven nodded. Always so strong, so determined. "I love her, Duncan."

"I know. I can see it."

"He probably ran back to his lair—that obscenity he calls a museum. He doesn't want to face Arianna. He fears her. . . . She fought him once . . . nearly beat him, I think."

"That's where we'll go. It'll be all right, Raven, I promise. He's never goin' to hurt you, nor anyone you care about, ever again. I swear it."

She stared up at him, and he saw the questions in her eyes. Maybe because he'd spoken with such passion just now, maybe because she sensed he meant every word.

"Later," he promised, bending to plant a quick, tender kiss on her mouth. "I'll tell you everythin' later."

He took her hand, closed his eyes briefly in ecstasy as he realized how good it was to hold that hand in his again . . . and together, they ran.

22

Damn!

She'd done it, Nathanial thought viciously. Raven St. James had come between him and Duncan all over again. And she'd gotten away with it!

He'd had the woman! Had her right in his hands, impaled on his dagger, and *still* she managed to escape him! He should have held on to her, should have . . . but what use were *should haves* now? She'd escaped him. Fallen from those cliffs, to send his soft-hearted son scurrying after her. Once again Duncan had chosen Raven over Nathanial, even now, when they were supposed to be father and son. Even now.

But not her fair-haired companion. No, Arianna hadn't been distracted for a moment. She'd headed *up* the cliffs, not down. And Nathanial had known then that she was coming for him.

He should have left this town, this state, perhaps this country, right then. Should have fled Arianna's wrath without hesitation. He could seek out some weaker immortal once he was safely away, take the first heart he found and get stronger. But to leave without the hearts he'd already taken—those he kept captive in small wooden boxes— would be to leave whatever vitality remained. So he'd returned to the old courthouse, to the small room at the top where he kept them, locked away from prying eyes inside their tiny wooden prisons. Some beat so weakly now they could barely be heard. He suspected they'd stop one day. But they hadn't. Most were no longer strong enough to support life, yet they kept beating on. One beat an hour, one beat a day. Were they truly immortal? Would they beat eternally? Somewhere, perhaps, in the dusty tomes he'd collected over the centuries, he might find an answer to that puzzle. An explanation. But he hadn't yet.

If *she* arrived in time, he never would. And there would be no time to take his books or his journals with him.

Quickly he opened a large case and set it in the middle of the floor. And then he snatched the most recent kills, the strongest hearts, from the shelf, carefully setting those boxes inside.

Speed was of the essence here. He couldn't face *her*, not now. She'd nearly beaten him once long ago, when he'd mistaken her for easy prey in Scotland. She'd been younger then. Weaker. He'd been at his best.

And she'd nearly killed him.

He would never forget the power of emotion again. Even as he'd battled, losing ground with every thrust, he'd wondered at her strength, her power. And reading his mind, it seemed, she'd uttered her curse. "You took the man I loved," she'd all but growled. "And I'll kill you for it."

She nearly had. He'd run. Fled for his life, from a mere infant of a High Witch. And a woman, at that.

Thrusting the memory away, he closed his case, hefted it and turned toward the doorway. Never again would he underestimate the power of hatred.

"It wasn't the power of hatred, Nathanial."

Her voice brought him up short. She stepped into view, into the doorway, blocking his escape. Arianna, a tiny mite of a woman standing with her legs wide, hands planted on her hips.

"So you truly *do* read my thoughts?"

"I hear thoughts sometimes. Yours are like poison. I'll be glad to end them forever. But in the meantime, Nathanial, know this. Hatred *has* no power. The power that nearly killed you then was the power of love. My love for one of the many you murdered. And it's that same power that will destroy you now.''

He took a step backward, setting the case on the floor to free his hands. "Which one was he, this victim of mine? It's been so long . . . I can scarcely remember them all. Was he the barbaric Celtic warlord? The Mayan Shaman?" He shrugged. "Not that it matters. They all died on their knees, begging for mercy."

"I can hardly wait to see how you do," she said, and drew her dagger, held it lightly, tossed it from one hand to the other. "But to remind you, his name was Nicodimus, and he died with the blade of a coward in his back."

She'd kill him. Nathanial knew it beyond a doubt. *If* he played by the rules.

He swallowed hard. "Will you kill me unarmed, Arianna, or give me a chance to draw my blade?" His hand inched toward the leather pocket at his side. He'd known she might get here before he could escape. He wasn't a fool. He'd prepared for this.

She narrowed her eyes. "I'll kill you in a fair fight or not at all," she told him. "Go on." And she nodded.

He drew the weapon from its sheath. Not his dagger. But a crude and inelegant handgun, the killing machine of the modern age. She sucked in a breath, but he simply leveled the barrel and pulled the trigger.

The impact sent her backward into the hall. She hit the stairs and tumbled, head over feet. Her body crashed down upon the first landing, bounced off the wall, and continued its brutal descent to the ground floor. Finally she came to rest at the bottom in a twisted, broken tangle.

Nathanial descended slowly, smiling to himself, and making certain she could hear his footsteps. He replaced the handgun, and drew out the blade as he approached her prone, battered form. She couldn't move. Dying, she was dying. He'd make sure it was permanent.

"It's a shame you prefer a fair fight," he said, and he crouched over her, gripped her blouse in one fist, and tore it open. Sliced the center of her silken bra so that her breasts spilled free. "I prefer a sure win, myself."

"Raven . . . will kill you for this. . . ."

"Oh, I'm sure she will try." He positioned the tip of his blade just to the left of the center of her chest. "Do you ever wonder about the bodies, Arianna?" he asked, pressing a little, drawing a droplet of blood, and hearing her suck air through her teeth. "They die, but don't really. They remain ever new, ever young. Do you suppose their minds are still alive, as well? Do you suppose they *know* that they've been buried alive?"

He smiled slowly at the terror in her brown eyes, and then he drove the blade in to the hilt.

Raven went still, eyes bulging, and screamed out loud. Her hands pressed to her chest, and she dropped to her knees.

Duncan was beside her in a heartbeat. They'd just stopped his car, got out, and had been running toward the courthouse when she'd suddenly . . . suddenly *what*?

"What's wrong? Raven, what—"

She didn't answer, just lifted her wounded, watering eyes toward the courthouse, and screamed, "Arianna! *Arianna!* Noooooo!"

He didn't know what to do. Didn't want to leave her, but he had to go inside, and sensed what he would find once he got there. He scooped her into his arms, and headed for the car, intending to lock her in where she'd be safe while he went to see to Nathanial.

Halfway there she squirmed free and hit the ground running. He saw her pull that dagger from her hip as she went. Could barely keep up with her speed. Damn, he didn't want her going in there if what he thought was true.

She burst through the front door, cried out, and raced ahead. Duncan entered on her heels, only to find her on the floor, holding Arianna's blood-soaked body in her arms, sobbing hysterically. Arianna was a slick, scarlet shimmer. Raven was rapidly becoming one, too. He saw the gaping, jagged hole in Arianna's chest, and then he looked away, unable to bear the sight.

It only took a footstep from above, and a glimpse of Raven's eyes to set him into motion. Nathanial would pay. He'd pay for this.

"Kill him," Raven whispered through gritted teeth, her voice raw.

Duncan nodded once and took the blade Arianna had given him from its place at his side. Carefully he stepped over the body at the foot of the stairs and headed up. And then he paused, because he swore he heard a whisper.

"Take mine, too."

He turned quickly. But Raven only knelt, crying, and Arianna couldn't have spoken a word. Still, he knelt and took Arianna's blade from where it lay on the floor beside her, blessedly away from the spreading crimson pool. He tucked it into the back of his jeans, and continued up the stairs.

The sound came from the room at the top. It lay up a second flight, and through a door.

Duncan stepped into the room to see his self-proclaimed father opening the window, a suitcase at his side. His hands were coated in Arianna's blood, his sleeves stained with it. Atop the suitcase sat a small wooden box, fresh blood dripping down its sides, a soft beat coming steadily from within. Arianna's heart.

"Damn you to hell for this," Duncan said softly.

Nathanial turned. He met Duncan's eyes, closed his own. "Not you, Duncan," he whispered. "I'll face any of them, but not you."

Duncan stepped forward. "Maybe I havena been immortal long enough yet to understand. You're willin' to fight with women, but not with a man?"

"Not with my son."

"I'm not your son," he said very softly. "The only father I knew was Angus Wallace, and he's been dead over three hundred years. I suppose I had another, this time around. But 'twasna you, Nathanial Dearborne. 'Twas never you."

Nathanial lowered his eyes. "So you remember."

"Aye. I remember the man you were. A killer in the guise of a priest. Makin' a mockery of the faith you pretended to serve."

"It's all true. But you don't understand, Duncan."

"I understand that you had my birth parents murdered just to get your hands on me. Raised me without a hint of love, all so I'd lead you to Raven one day."

Again, Nathanial nodded, confirming what Duncan had still hoped, in some tiny corner of his mind, he would deny. "It began that way, Duncan. But the truth is . . . I've come to care for you, boy. Just as I did before."

"I can see how you care for me. 'Twas clear in the way you tried to murder the woman I love."

"I might have died without another heart."

"You think that makes it all right? You kill others just to prolong your own life, an' you think that makes it all right?"

Nathanial shook his head slowly. "It's the way things are for us, Duncan. The way it's always been. . . ."

"Not for you," Duncan uttered quietly. "Not anymore."

Nathanial closed his eyes. "I don't want to kill you, Duncan, but I will if you make me."

"I rather thought you would. An' that says it all. Dinna you think . . . *Father*?"

Duncan lunged forward, still seeing Arianna's blood, Raven's pain, in his mind's eye. Nathanial dodged, and then drew his own blade, attacking, stabbing, fighting as fiercely as an animal, a rabid animal.

"You've no chance against me, Duncan. I've seven hundred years of practice!"

Duncan tried again, but this time Nathanial kicked and the blade went sailing out of Duncan's hand.

He heard Raven, her footsteps rushing up the stairs, through the door.

"Don't, Duncan! Don't fight him! I didn't mean—I wasn't thinking!"

Nathanial lifted his blade and came at him. Raven ran into the room behind him and cried out. And Duncan stood where he was. One hand flashed behind him, to close around Arianna's blade. He brought it forward just as Nathanial lunged at him. And the blade sank into the old man's chest, deeply and brutally, though Duncan hadn't even thrust it. 'Twas Nathanial's own forward motion, his attack, his own hatred, that killed him.

Blood welled, warm and thick, spilling over Duncan's hands, and he took them away, disgusted. Sickened.

For a moment he stood, looking down at the man he'd

called father, the man who lay dying. "I wanted your love,"
he said. "I wanted it more than you know."

Blinking slowly, his eyes already glazing over, Nathanial
whispered, "You had it, son. I *did* love you . . . in my
way. . . ." His eyes fell closed, briefly. But then they opened
again. His hand snatched the front of Duncan's shirt with
surprising strength, and he pulled him close. "I'll prove it
to you now," he managed, and then he whispered something
in Duncan's ear. A second later his breaths stopped, his hand
went slack, and Duncan straightened away from him.

Duncan's throat closed off and he turned away, eyes burning. Raven enfolded him in her arms. Held him tight to her,
where he belonged. Nathanial hadn't loved him. That wasn't
love. Even with that one final gesture, it wasn't love. Guilt,
maybe. *This* was love, this thing he felt right here, this
woman he held, who was healing him even now. This was
love, and 'twas all he needed. All he had ever needed, or
ever would.

"Don't mourn him, Duncan. The world's better off without him. He was evil."

"I know." He looked down at her, kissed her lips, finding
some soothing elixir in her taste that eased his heartache.
"But he's still evil. He'll . . . he'll revive . . . ?"

"I'll do what has to be done."

He stepped away from her, searched her face. "Nay, lass.
I canna ask you to do that—"

"I'll do it, Duncan. . . . I'll do it because I love you."
She touched his shoulders, kissed his face. "If you knew,
my darling, if you knew what you were to me . . . What you
still are to me, you'd understand. Let me do this for you."

"What I . . . still am?" he asked her. Lowering his head,
he shook it slowly. "I doubted you. I called you crazy and
gave my father more chances than a saint deserves, while
refusing you so much as the benefit of the doubt. I nearly
got you killed, Raven—"

"No." She shook her head hard. "No, Duncan, it was
your father who nearly killed me. You had no part in that."

"An' Arianna? Will you tell me now that *her* blood
doesna stain my hands?"

Raven took his hands in hers, holding them tightly. "This

is the way we live, Duncan. The Dark Ones pursue us, and when we meet them, we fight. Sometimes . . .'' Her eyes filled, though she blinked against the tears. ''Sometimes we die. Arianna knew that as I do, and she'd never have blamed you. She cared for you, Duncan. And I love you now, as I always have.''

''Do you, lass?''

She nodded. ''I always will,'' she told him.

Sighing, he nodded. He'd tell her the truth—that he *did* remember, that he *was* the man she'd been searching for all this time . . . that he loved her. By the Gods, *he loved her*! But first he wanted to give her something. A gift. A gift he knew how to give . . . because of an evil man's dying words. And they might have been lies for all he knew. But he had to try.

''I'll take care of Arianna,'' he whispered, saw her close her eyes in stark pain. Then he picked up the small box, felt the chilling thrum of its beat from within, and carried it down with him.

I took Nathanial Dearborne's heart. Not because I could grow strong by draining its power, but because it was the only way he would remain dead. The only way I could be sure. I would burn it, and his body, when this gruesome task ended. I would free his soul, and perhaps on some other plane, he'd learn what this long lifetime had been about. Perhaps he'd live again one day, a decent, loving man. A father, perhaps, who would learn the meaning of the word.

Gently, I placed Nathanial's heart in an empty box on the shelf, but as I did so, I couldn't help but notice all the other boxes, and the weak, slow beats emanating from them. His victims. All his victims. I'd burn this place. I'd destroy the hearts that lived on here, beating endlessly while the bodies that had once owned them lay in some nightmarish state between life and death. I'd burn them all and, in so doing, set their captive souls free.

Sighing, I felt my heart breaking for all of them, but mostly for my sister, my Arianna, my beloved best friend and kindred spirit. I felt empty, lost without her. As lost as I had been all those years without Duncan.

Had I ever told her, I wondered, how very much she meant to me?

Crying, I washed my hands in a basin of water, and then I went down the stairs.

Arianna's body was no longer there, tangled and bloody. Duncan had moved her to an antique chaise fit for a goddess. He'd draped a sheet over her as she reclined there. And for that, I was grateful.

Duncan awaited me at the foot of the stairs. His dark hair tousled, his eyes swirling cauldrons of emotion. I saw so much there as his intense gaze locked with mine; pain, grief, shock. And something more. He took me into his arms when I reached him. I thought he needed to hold me as much as I did him, just then. To feed from my strength, to bolster me with his. Together we were so much more than either of us was alone. But that couldn't be what he was feeling. Maybe three centuries ago, but not now.

"I have to tell you some things, Raven. An' I hope you'll do me the honor of listenin' before you interrupt."

Smiling just a little, tears still spilling from my eyes, I stepped back and looked up at him. "Your Highland lilt is back, Duncan. I . . . it was upstairs, but I was too . . ." I frowned hard, searching his face. "What does this mean?"

"I thought you liked my lilt."

"I do. I just don't understand why it keeps slipping into your speech."

" 'Tis more than the accent that's come back to me, Raven."

I blinked . . . then blinked again and searched his eyes. "Duncan?"

"I love you, lass," he said very softly. "I've been fallin' in love with you all over again, ever since I found you, Raven, but 'tis more than that now. It has come back to me. All of it, all you were to me, an' all I was to you. All we still are to each other." He closed his eyes, searching for words as his strong hands kneaded my shoulders in time with the beat of my heart.

I tried to speak and couldn't.

He opened his eyes, and they were wet. "When I saw you fall . . . 'twas like a doorway into the past opened up wide. An' God, my sweet bonny lass, when I held your poor broken body in my arms on those rocks, I knew. . . ." He cradled my face in his hands, his eyes poring over me. "You're everythin' to me, Raven. *Everythin'*. You always were. My mind might have forgotten for a little while, but my heart remembered you, lass, from the moment I set eyes on you again. I love you, Raven."

I touched his face, searched his eyes, and saw him there. Duncan Wallace, the man I'd loved so long ago, alive again, fully alive at last. "Duncan . . ." I collapsed in his arms, wanting to weep for joy. "Oh, Duncan, hold me. Hold me forever."

"We'll never be apart again, love. Never again, I vow it to you." He kissed me with such passion and love, and held me cradled against his chest, wrapped warmly in his arms.

"You truly remember everything?"

"Aye," he said softly. "The night I watched you through the cabin windows, bathin', singin' like a siren, an' drawin' me near. The first time we made love on the cliffs with the sea crashing below us . . . all of it."

I could barely breathe, so tight was my chest. I closed my eyes. "And how you died . . . just because I didn't trust in you enough to tell you the truth?" I asked him.

He stepped back slightly so he could see my face. "I'd die a thousand times for you, Raven St. James. An' even that wouldna show you the limits of my love. I canna . . . I canna find the words . . . there *are* no words. 'Tis beyond somethin' as mundane as language. 'Tis beyond anythin' physical . . . 'Tis pure, Raven. Spiritual. Holy. You . . . are a part of me. Even death couldna change that."

"No. Not even death," I told him.

"I need you the way I need air," he whispered, and my heart soared. He held me tight and kissed me, so tenderly, so deeply, that I knew he truly meant every word. "An' I believe all that happened to us was just as 'twas meant to happen. Had it been different, I'd be long dead by now, an' you with no hope of seein' me again."

I closed my eyes. "I can't even imagine living with that kind of pain."

"I want to take your pain away, my love," Duncan whispered. ''All your pain. An' I think I can. I think so long as I'm with you, you'll never hurt again. Not if I can prevent it.''

I lifted my head and glanced toward the sheet-draped body of the other person I'd come to love beyond reason. And my joy dimmed beneath a fresh onslaught of sorrow. The sister of my soul lay dead and beyond my reach.

''No one can ease this pain,'' I said very softly. ''Not even you, Duncan, though I love you with everything in me. I'm so glad you've come back to me. Truly come back, at last. So long, I've waited. And maybe . . . maybe someday Arianna will find her way back to me as well.''

Duncan looked toward where Arianna lay, and his eyes widened for just an instant. Then he smiled, a tentative, wary smile. ''Maybe sooner than you think,'' he said. He took my hands in his, staring down into my eyes. ''Nathanial . . . he said somethin' to me as he lay dyin'.''

I tilted my head, frowned up at him. ''I don't under—''

''He said, 'The heart beats on. The body only rests. Put it back.' An' then he repeated, it. 'Put it back,' he kept sayin'. '*Put it back.*' ''

I shook my head, and my breath caught in my throat. ''P-put it back?''

Duncan nodded. ''Aye. So . . . I did.''

''But . . .'' I looked toward the chaise. Blinked my eyes as the sheet seemed to move. And then it moved again. ''It can't be. . . . Arianna?''

The body beneath the sheet went stiff, the arms rigid, the sheet flinging aside as a desperate gasping sound filled the room. The sheet fluttered to the floor, revealing Arianna's body, arching and taut . . . then relaxing back to the chaise. Still, unmoving, eyes closed.

I took a step forward. ''Arianna?'' I whispered, almost afraid to hope. . . .

Her eyes opened. Arianna blinked, looked around, and then sat up fast, wide-eyed with fear. ''What—Where—'' Her hands clawed at her chest in search of the remembered wound.

I ran to her. ''Arianna . . . Arianna, it's all right. It's okay, I'm right here.''

She stared at me, shocked and disoriented. Slowly she tugged at the remnants of her torn blouse and stared down at her chest. Even now, I could see the lines of the jagged cut, barely visible in her flesh, fading fast.

"How . . . how did you . . . what . . ."

I stroked her hair. "It's over, Arianna. You're all right." My smile was watery and my chest nearly bursting with emotion. I hugged her close. "You're really all right."

"B-but . . ." She hugged me back, but she was trembling. "He took my heart," she whispered.

"I know, I know, darling. But now I've taken his. And yours . . . yours beats still, back inside you, where it belongs."

"But—"

" 'Twas Nathanial," Duncan said from behind me. His hands clasped my shoulders. Then he reached down and stroked Arianna's hair as she lifted her head to stare up at him. "He seemed to want to clear his conscience," Duncan explained. "So he told me how to bring you back."

Sitting back away from me, Arianna gazed up at him. "But how could he know that? *I* didn't even know that . . . and . . . and . . ." Her eyes widened and her voice became a soft croak, barely audible. "He has other hearts here. . . ."

"Well, yes, weak ones. Nearly lifeless, some of them. But—"

"Don't you see?" She grasped my shoulders, shook me gently. "My Goddess, Raven, *don't* you *see*?"

I met her eyes, and slowly shook my head.

She swallowed hard and seemed to gather herself. "Never mind. Never mind, I . . . this isn't the time. We have to get out of here. Cover this up. My God, if they find this place, the blood, his body up there like that . . ."

"You're right," I said.

She got to her feet, holding the sheet around her and moving slowly forward, until she stood toe to toe with Duncan. "You . . . you did all right for a newborn."

He lifted a brow. "Aye, I suppose so. Better than you, at least." And I saw a teasing gleam in Duncan's eyes.

"He'd never have taken me without cheating," Arianna

said, looking a bit more like herself, I thought. Slightly mischievous, cocky, arrogant.

"I have no doubt," Duncan returned.

She smiled, tilted her head. "You saved my life . . . returned my life, more precisely."

He nodded. "You did the same for me, that night when I died, with your castin' and conjurin'." He stared at me then, but continued speaking to Arianna. "You gave me back my life."

"Ah, so you finally got your head straight, did you?"

"I got my heart back, just like you," he said. "An' I'll never let her get away from me again."

"And I'll never let mine slip away, either," I promised him.

Arianna put one hand on Duncan's, one on mine, and drew the two together. "A love like yours is so precious," she said, and her voice got a little gruff, drawing my gaze to the tear that shimmered in her eye. "And a second chance is a gift beyond measure. Not everyone gets that. Cherish it."

The tear spilled, glistening on her cheek, rolling slowly downward.

"Arianna?" I whispered, instantly concerned.

"No. No, we have work to do tonight. And when it's done, we celebrate. This is no time for tears. Tears make their own time. Tears . . . belong in private. Come." And she drew us out, out of that house of death, and into the night.

Hand in hand, Duncan and I walked away from sadness and loneliness and grief. And for the first time I could remember, the future looked bright . . . and it would be. As long as we were together.

Epilogue

Hours later we stood far away from the courthouse as its red-orange flame licked up into the night sky. Duncan and I stood arm in arm, watching the fire. And I felt like a Phoenix. I'd survived the flames, I'd risen from the ashes, and now, at last, I would live again.

Duncan's arm was around me, strong and firm, just as I remembered it. *He* was just as I remembered him. Just as I loved him, and I loved him still.

Apart from us a little, Arianna knelt. She'd gathered all the small boxes with their weakening, barely beating hearts, and they sat around her in a circle. In her hands she held the other box, the one that held the heart of Nathanial Dearborne. She'd taken all of these, along with all of Nathanial's books, from the house before we'd set it alight. I suspected she wanted to work a special ritual over them before putting them to the torch and freeing their captive souls once and for all.

Staring at the flames that even now devoured Nathanial Dearborne's body, Arianna lifted the box that held his heart high above her. In silence Duncan and I closed our eyes and aided in empowering her spell by joining our will with hers as Arianna spoke in a low but powerful voice.

"Thy spirit is free, and separate from thee. Thy body's no more, thy spirit can soar! I release thee, Nathanial Dearborne, and commend thy spirit to the light."

Then she lifted the box higher, for the heart beat on.

"The life in this heart, this heart does not own. Return to thine own hearts, return to thy home!"

I caught my breath as at last I realized her intent. "Arianna, no. You mustn't—"

"As I will it," she cried, her voice ringing with sheer force, "so mote it be!"

The sound of the beating from within that box grew suddenly louder, suddenly deafening, and then all at once, the box burst into flames. I caught my breath as the blazing thing tumbled from Arianna's hands to the ground, snapping and crackling as if soaked in some propellant. In seconds it flickered and died, leaving only ashes. Arianna sighed and relaxed. Nathanial's heartbeat was silenced now. Utterly, completely silenced.

She sank to the ground, lowered her head. And one by one the soft, weak thrum of the dying hearts in the boxes around her grew stronger, louder, until they all pumped with the steady rhythm of life.

I lowered my head into my hands. "Oh, Arianna," I whispered. "What have you done?"

"The hearts live on, the bodies only rest," she told me. "That's what Nathanial said, isn't it?"

"Yes. But these were nearly gone. You should have helped them pass, Arianna, helped them find release, and peace. Now who knows how long they'll go on beating from those prisons?"

Slowly she shook her head. "No. We don't know that they'd ever have stopped beating entirely, do we?"

"Well, no, but we could have cremated them—"

"It would have been too much like murder," she declared.

"Those hearts were not strong enough to sustain life, Arianna."

"And now they are," she shot back. "Now they're as strong and as healthy as they were when he stole them."

"But I don't understand."

Duncan's hand closed around mine. "I do," he said. He met Arianna's eyes. "You're goin' to put them back."

She smiled gently, and nodded. "If I can find the bodies they belong to. Nathanial kept journals and diaries among all those books of his. There might be clues there. If it worked for me . . . Well, there's a chance."

I stiffened, and stepped forward. "You . . . you're *leaving* me?"

"Yes, my darling." She cupped my cheek with her palm, leaned forward, and kissed me very gently, very briefly. "It's time. This is your time, yours and Duncan's."

"No!" I cried. "No, you don't have to leave. We *want* you with us. Tell her, Duncan!"

"She knows," he said softly. "But I think this is her time, too. *Her* second chance . . . maybe."

Arianna's lips pulled tight, and her eyes welled with tears. "One of these hearts . . . means more to me than my own," she said, then she bit her lip, but her tears fell anyway. "If there's a chance in a million that I can find him . . . that I can restore him . . . I have to try."

I blinked, searching her face. "You . . . you loved him."

She said nothing, but I could see the truth in her eyes. So I hugged her close, held her a long time. "I will never be more than a wish away," I promised her. "And you'll come back to me. Promise me you will."

"You know I will, little sister."

Sniffling, I released her. Arianna gathered the small boxes, the six hearts of Nathanial's victims, and gently packed them in a satchel. Then she zipped it tight and gathered it up. "I love you, you know," she told me. Then she glanced at Duncan. "*Both* of you."

"If you need us—" Duncan began.

"Ha! Me? Need help? You do make me laugh, Duncan." But she said it with a wink and a smile. Then her smile died. "Take care of each other," she whispered, just before she turned and walked away, disappearing into the night.

But not from my life. She'd return to tell me all about her adventures, and this mysterious man she sought. I knew she would. We were sisters, and always would be. Nothing could change that.

Just as nothing could change the love Duncan and I shared. A love beyond mortality. Beyond life, or death, or the forces of evil.

"Well, we should get started, too," he said.

"Get started?" I turned toward him, and he gently brushed the tears from my eyes.

"I guess you didna believe me, did you lass? When I said I'd see to it you never hurt again."

"Of course I did, but—"

"Then we'd best get started. I've lots of time to make up for, you know. Three hundred years of lovin' to give to you. Three hundred years of sweet nothin's to whisper into your ears, an' of gifts, an' of kisses an' pamperin'."

I nodded. "And I suppose I have three hundred years of magick and of fighting to teach you."

"Aye. But first, we travel."

I tilted my head.

Duncan smiled and kissed my nose. "We dinna want that stubborn sister of yours to get too far ahead of us, do we?"

"We're . . . going with her?"

"Aye, we're goin' with her."

"But why?"

He stared down at me, his dark eyes growing darker, even as the light of that distant fire danced its reflection in their depths. "If you could see the joy in your eyes right now, love, I'd point to it, an' I'd tell you, 'That's why.' I love you, Raven St. James. What makes you happy, makes me happy. I love you. *I love you, lass.*"

I closed my eyes when he kissed me again, and I knew it was true. The darkest night of my soul had ended, though it had been three centuries long. Dawn had finally broken, and my heart was whole again.

Turn the page for a preview of the next book
by Maggie Shayne . . .

INFINITY

Available in paperback from Jove Books!

I rode my faithful Black. He stepped high, as though he knew the man he bore to be of an utterly different breed than those others who surrounded us. Beside me, an old friend . . . a mortal, Chieftain of his clan, and Laird as well. Joseph Lachlan welcomed my visit, and asked no questions about why I might need to lay low for a time.

And that was just as well, for I couldn't have told him the answers had he done so. The truth was, resting from the constant battle was only part of the reason I'd come. I had another.

"Ye never age, Nicky. Ye look to be the same fair lad I last saw five years ago."

I only sent a cocky grin his way. "And you've grown wrinkles about your eyes, Joseph! Soon I'll mistake you for my father."

"No hope of that, boy," Joseph said. "Your father was twice the man I'll ever be." He lowered his head. "I do miss him. But havin' you here on occasion is almost like havin' my dear friend back with me again."

I had to avert my eyes. Joseph had never known my father. He had known only me. But when he'd seen me die

at his side on a field of battle, I'd had no choice but to stay
away for a long time. And when I returned—as I had to
do—I simply claimed to be my own son. And he'd believed
me.

"My father often spoke similarly of you, Joseph," I said
then. And I nudged Black's sides with my heels. The stallion
trotted forward, along the narrow, twisting paths of the village, scattering chickens in his wake. A fat man rolled a
barrel of ale from a rickety wagon into the hovel that passed
as the village pub, while across the way a woman hurled
wash water from a window hole where no glass had ever
stood.

I'd seen London and Rome, great cities all around the
world. And yet marveled at how this tiny village had grown.
When I had lived here, it had borne no name, and my home
had been a thatched hut. My wife had cooked the meat I
killed over a central fire while my boys helped me stretch
the furs to dry. Anya. Beautiful Anya. I could see her if I
closed my eyes. Auburn hair and eyes like flaming emeralds,
her belly swelling with our third child, her lips smiling as
she watched over the other two. Jaymes, growing taller by
the day and too skinny to stand up to a windstorm, though
he ate more than his brother and I together. He had his
mother's coloring, Jaymes did. And Will, a head shorter but
strong, was already looking more like a man than a boy.
Hunting at my side, and outdoing me now and then. Begging to fight beside me as well.

Dead. All of them well over seven centuries dead. Rotted
to dust, and the dust blown away. As was my heart with
them.

"The village hasna changed since you were here," Joseph
said, pulling me out of my thoughts.

I looked ahead of me, to where the crofters' cottages
leaned crookedly this way and that, their thatched roofs old
and in need of replacing. I scanned the faces of the villagers
passing by, and realized I sought the child as I did on each
visit. But I did not see her there. And it occurred to me then
that I might not even recognize her at first glance, despite
her unusual coloring. Those dark brown eyes gleaming
against her ivory skin, in blatant contrast to her pale yellow

hair. It had been five years since last I'd checked on the
strange girl. She'd be ... seventeen now. Quite possibly
wed—though people here married much later than they used
to. I'd made Anya my wife when I'd been but fourteen. But
things changed. And married or not, the girl, Arianna, was
most likely still utterly unaware of what she truly was.

"Is that saddlemaker still in the village, Joseph? Sinclair,
wasn't it?"

"Aye. Is your saddle in need of repair?" Joseph eyed it,
likely seeing it was perfectly all right. Likely thinking that
I never paid him a visit but that I needed repairs done to
my saddle.

"Only a bit of loose stitching at the girth," I told him.
"But I ought have it checked before I leave again."

Joseph nodded. " 'Twas a cursed bad year for poor Sinclair. Cursed bad."

My head swung around, and perhaps my eyes were too
eager. "Was it?"

"Aye." Joseph's lips thinned. "Lost a daughter, he did."

At those words, my heart seemed to ice over. I'd been
watching the girl all her life, planning for a time when I
would explain her own nature to her. Perhaps I'd waited too
long. I tried to speak, but couldn't. Joseph never seemed to
notice the blood draining from my face, nor the way I nearly
fell from my saddle. He was involved in the telling of his
tale.

"Nearly lost the both of his girls, he did, that sad day.
Over a year ago, 'twas. They'd been up to no good,
splashin' and playin' in the loch when their father had forbidden it. My sons pulled the one to safety, but the other
... She drowned in the blue-black depths of the water."

"Drowned?" I asked, nearly holding my breath.

"Aye. And young Arianna has ne'er been right since the
day the loch claimed her sister."

I lowered my head. So Arianna was alive ... not that she
could have died by drowning. She'd have revived ... but to
what?

Joseph nodded toward some distant point. "See for yourself, Nicodimus. She's there now, at the grave. 'Tis no place
for a girl of seventeen to be spending all her time. An' alone,

no less! She's forever walking about alone!"

I frowned at that, knowing exactly what Joseph implied. It was said that only a Witch walked about all alone. Only a Witch. And she was one. But she couldn't know that. Not yet.

"Perhaps if I were to have a word with her."

Joseph drew his mount to a halt, frowning at me. "Do you think it wise?"

"Why not? I've lost loved ones myself. I know a bit of what she's feeling." I knew, I realized, far too much of what she was feeling. It was a feeling she would have to get used to, for in time she'd lose everyone, and everything she knew. I sighed as I looked at her. She would have to learn to close herself off. She would have to learn to stop caring, as I had.

Sniffing, Joseph nodded. "Take care, my friend, not to spend too long with her. She's promised to the cobbler's son, but even he's beginning to shy away. There's been some talk . . ."

"What sort of talk?"

Joseph shrugged. "I pay it no mind, nor will I tolerate anyone persecuting the poor lass. We must make allowances, after all. Grief can twist a mind in all manner of—"

"*What sort of talk*, Joseph?"

Joseph cleared his throat. "Some claim she slips out alone in the dead of night. An' she's been seen speakin' to The Crones more than once. What people will make of it . . . Well, you can guess as well as I."

The Crones . . . the outcasts. The word *Witch* was never spoken aloud, but everyone in the village knew what the three old women were. And yet they were tolerated, their shacks outside the village at the edge of the forest left alone, and would be only so long as good fortune smiled down upon the flocks and the crops and the people here. As for the blue-blooded *Christians* of Stonehaven, they'd no more exchange a greeting with The Crones in public than eat from the trough of a pig. But they visited the old women every now and then, for a potion to cure the croup or a charm for good luck.

I turned again to stare at the girl off in the distance, kneel-

ing by the grave of her sister. Perhaps she knew more than
I'd thought she possibly could. But who was there to tell
her? I'd never met another High Witch, Dark nor Light, in
this part of Scotland. Never. And our secrets were seldom
shared with anyone else. The Crones knew nothing of our
existence. I'd ascertained that years ago.

"I'll speak with her," I said. "Before she lets the gossips
ruin her."

Joseph nodded. "Perhaps 'twill do some good at that.
Shall I wait at the alehouse then?"

"If the owner still brews that secret recipe of his."

"Heather Ale?" Joseph whispered. "That he does, Nicodimus. That he does." And Joseph turned his horse about,
heading for the pub.

I turned my attention toward the cemetery once more, and
nudged Black's sides until he leaped into a spirited trot.
Stopping him a short distance away, I tied him up to a scrag-
gly tree, then walked forward to where she knelt. And for
a moment, I only stood still and silent, and looked at her.

She'd changed. In five short years she'd grown from a
waif into a woman. Her golden hair draped about her shoulders like a shawl of spun sunlight, moving in the breeze
every now and again. Kneeling, she lifted a fist, and let some
herb or other spill from it atop her sister's grave, as she
muttered soft words under her breath.

A spell. For the love of the Gods, had the girl no sense?
In broad daylight?

"What is it you're doing?" I called. I expected her to
stiffen with surprise and perhaps fear at being caught. The
lesson would do her good.

She didn't start, didn't turn to face me. "Should anyone
else ask, I'm planting wild heather upon my sister's burial
site."

"And if *I* ask?"

"I think, Nicodimus, you know better than to ask."

I blinked in surprise at the words. Just how much *did* she
know? And the familiarity of her tone with me . . . As if she
knew me far better than she did. We'd only spoken a handful of words to one another in the past. Polite greetings at
most, though my interest in her had always been more than

that of a stranger. She was my kind. A rarity in itself. She was without a teacher, and that made her my responsibility.

The herbs gone, she pounded her fist on the ground three times, a time-honored method for releasing the energy raised in spellwork. Then she lowered her head for but an instant, grounding herself. Finally, she rose, brushing her hands on her skirts and facing me at last. Her eyes hadn't been so large before, nor so velvety brown . . . nor so haunted. "It has been a long while since your last visit here," she said.

"Long enough so I must wonder how you could have recognized my voice."

" 'Twas not your voice, Nicodimus. Although 'tis true you speak distinctly enough."

"Do I?"

"Aye," she said. "Carefully. And slow, without a hint of an accent, so a body could never guess where you truly come from."

"I come from right here," I told her.

She shrugged, and I wasn't sure whether she believed me or not. "Regardless of how you speak," she went on, "I knew you were there before you uttered a word."

Her words gave me a start. If that were true, her natural powers were incredibly advanced—particularly for one so young.

"How?" I asked her.

She shrugged. "I always know when you're near. Have since . . . why, since I was a wee bairn toddlin' along and clinging to my ma's skirts . . . an' you came ridin' into the village alongside Laird Lachlan. Do you recall?"

I did. It was the first time I'd set eyes on her, and I'd known, even before seeing the birthmark in the shape of the crescent moon emblazoned on her chubby right flank, that she was one of us. "I remember it well."

"I always wanted to ask you about it—that feelin' I get when you're near. But it seemed I should remember my place, and be neither impertinent nor disrespectful."

"But you've changed your mind about those things now?"

She glanced toward her sister's grave. "They seem less important to me now than the dust in the highland wind,

Nicodimas.'' Her eyes were round and brown and filled with
pain—and something else. Rebellion. A dangerous wildness
that flashed from somewhere deep within her, and seemed
to fit with the way her hair snapped whiplike with the wind,
while her skirts flew about her ankles and bare, dirty feet.

"Propriety has its place, Arianna."

"Propriety," she whispered. "Society. Lairds and Chief-
tains and crofters and slaves. What good is it, I ask you?
What does any of it truly mean? Who cares whether a
woman wears her hair unbound until she bears her first
child, and bound up tight thereafter? Or if she walks about
alone, or if she addresses a Laird by his title? What arrogant
fool made up all these ridiculous rules that have us all hop-
ping and scurrying to obey?''

"Arianna . . ."

" 'Tis meaningless, I tell you! Everything is meaningless!
Life itself—''

Her voice had grown louder with every word, until I
gripped her hands gently in my own, and felt the jolt of
awareness that occurs when one of our kind touches another.
She looked at me quickly, shocked by that jolt, wondering
at it, I knew, but I said only, "Keep your voice down."
And I inclined my head toward the village nearby, where
already several sets of curious eyes were turned our way.
Hands shielding careworn faces from the morning sun.
Squinting, searching gazes trying to see who dared raise her
voice in the cemetery, of all places.

Arianna followed my gaze and saw her curious neighbors.
She sent them a defiant glare with a toss of her head that
reminded me of Black when he is agitated and smelling a
battle; the way he shakes his mane almost in challenge. I
moved to take my hands from hers, but she clung to them.

I looked down at our joined hands, and for the first time
a tiny rush of alarm tingled through me. For this was no
child clinging to my hands. This was a woman, young and
beautiful and full of fire. And her hands were slender and
strong, and very warm.

I swallowed hard. "You *want* to make them gossip about
you. Is that it?" I asked her.

"Let them gossip. I don't care."

I took my hands firmly away. "Do you care what pain you cause others, Arianna?" I asked, in a second attempt to put her firmly in her place, to let her know that what she might have been thinking just now when our hands were locked together could never, never be. "You're promised to the cobbler's son."

"*I* never made any such promise. Nor do I intend to abide by it. And believe me, that clod has no tender feelings where I'm concerned."

"No? Why, then, do you suppose he's asked for your hand, Arianna?"

She smiled slowly. "You know as well as I. He wants a servant. Someone to cook and clean and mend for him. Someone to lift her skirts when he demands it. Someone to relieve his needs so he'll no longer have to hide in his father's woodshed and do it himself—"

"*Arianna—*"

"What? A tender young girl is not supposed to know about such things, I suppose! No, we're to blindly agree to be some man's slave and his whore in exchange for room and board. Well, it won't be me, Nicodimus. Not ever."

I had to bite back a smile. So bold, and outspoken, and so damned determined. "A wife should be none of those things, Arianna."

"Name one who isn't," she challenged me, leaning slightly forward, hands on her hips, legs shoulder-width apart in a cocky stance.

"Your mother," I said.

She blinked and lost a bit of that cockiness. " 'Tis different with my mother."

"Why?"

"Because my father loves her, I suppose."

"And are you so certain your cobbler's son doesn't love you?"

She lowered her chin, but peered up at me from mischievous eyes. "Not so much as he loves his hand on nights in his father's woodshed."

I had to look away. To laugh aloud would only encourage her. And she needed no encouragement.

For just a moment I thought about how seldom it was

that I found myself inclined toward laughter. Genuine laughter. And then I was shaken out of my thoughts, for she clutched my hands in hers, staring up and probing with her dark brown eyes.

"You're different, Nicodimus. I know you are, I've sensed it always. You thumb your nose at the world and its silly conventions just as I do."

I averted my eyes. "You speak nonsense, child."

"Do I? You're supposed to be Laird Lachlan's cousin, yet I've never see you wear the Lachlan plaide, Nicodimus. You bathe just as often as you like, without a care that the Church calls it vanity. And what's more, you dare to talk publicly and alone to the girl half the town thinks is crazy—"

"And the other half thinks is dabbling in Witchcraft." I blurted, hoping to shock her into silence. She saw too much, this girl. And she was looking far too closely, tampering with parts of me that no one had dared come near in a very long time.

"An' what if I am?" she shot back, undaunted.

I stared at her, all fire and life and utter defiance. " 'Tis no business of mine, Arianna," I told her. "An' no business of theirs, either. Do what you will, but keep it to yourself, for the love of heaven. If you can't conform, then *pretend* to conform. For your own sake, girl, take the advice of one older and wiser who'd like to see you live to grow into womanhood."

"I'm already a woman," she told me. "A woman like no other woman you've ever known, Nicodimus."

I staggered backward as her bold, enticing eyes flashed fire at me. I'd come to her to try to help her. And instead I felt as if I were under attack. Her forces battered my innermost tower, and I'd a feeling they'd bring it to rubble soon.

"An' since you've mentioned it," she went on, "just *how much* older and wiser are you, Nicodimus?"

I saw her meaning flash in her eyes then. Saw it clear, for she didn't seem the least bit inclined to hide it from me. It startled me, shook me to my bones. I'd never thought of her in that way . . . not until this very moment—or perhaps a moment ago, when I'd seen her again, a woman grown.

"Too old for what you have in mind. Go find your cob-bler's son now, and torment him in my stead."·

But even as I turned to leave her there, my mind spun with justifications. She'd be eighteen in a fortnight. Oh, yes, I knew the date of her birth. I knew more about her than she knew about herself. Eighteen . . . and barely that. I was more than seven centuries old . . . Yet at the time of my first death, I'd been twenty and eight. Physically, I still was.

"You're meant for me, Nicodimus," she called·as I walked away. "You know that, don't you?"

I froze where I stood. She came toward me, but didn't stop when she reached my side. Instead she kept walking, brushing past me, and dropping a kiss upon my cheek as she did. The touch of her lips sent fire through me all the way to my toes. "You'll be mine one day," she whispered. "And then, Nicodimus, I will know all the secrets you hide behind your sapphire eyes."

A shiver raced up my spine as I watched her walk away. Pale gold hair dancing in the wind. She walked proudly, chin jutting high, eyes sparking with defiance—as if daring anyone to chide her for going about alone. Or for kissing a guest of their Laird so boldly. Or for muttering incantations over her dead sister in broad daylight.

Daring them.

No one took the challenge.

She was right when she said she was a woman like no other. For there had never been another that touched my soul the way she did.

PENGUIN PUTNAM INC.
Online

Your Internet gateway to a virtual environment with hundreds of entertaining and enlightening books from Penguin Putnam Inc.

While you're there, get the latest buzz on the best authors and books around—

Tom Clancy, Patricia Cornwell, W.E.B. Griffin, Nora Roberts, William Gibson, Robin Cook, Brian Jacques, Catherine Coulter, Stephen King, Jacquelyn Mitchard, and many more!

Penguin Putnam Online is located at http://www.penguinputnam.com

PENGUIN PUTNAM NEWS

Every month you'll get an inside look at our upcoming books and new features on our site. This is an ongoing effort to provide you with the most up-to-date information about our books and authors.

Subscribe to Penguin Putnam News at http://www.penguinputnam.com/ClubPPI